I t is no secret that planet Earth is home to the notoriously greedy species known as humans. What remains a secret to these humans is the community of aliens who live hidden under invisible force fields across neighboring planets and moons. They eat fried butterflies for lunch, travel through interplanetary vortexes, and coexist with giant bees, solar dragons, and hairy one-hundred-legged spiders—peacefully, for the most part.

Eighteen-year-old Truman Howard is not like his classmates. While they roll around in their parents' riches and travel the globe, Truman takes care of himself, working part time as a ski instructor and thrifting his clothes. He has no family, no friends, and a roommate who gives donkeys a bad rep.

But everything changes the day Truman meets a mysterious woman who invites him to an unforgettable place that will make him and anyone who reads his story feel like they belong. For it is there, among the stars, where Truman embarks on a remarkable voyage filled with new friends, fantastic creatures, and a dangerous destiny that's been brewing for him for many, many moons!

Praise for Gagliastro's "Whimsical"* Novel

Mercury to the Moon

"A whimsical and heartwarming young adult fantasy that takes readers on an <u>unforgettable</u> interstellar journey. With charm, imagination, and sly wit, this adventure is both <u>a thrilling</u> <u>escape and a powerful reminder that belonging is not about</u> <u>where you come from, but where you choose to go</u>. [The] dialogue felt suitably odd and out of this world, but also really accessible and humorous."   *~ Readers' Favorite* *

"As whimsical as it is poignant. *Mercury to the Moon* is an exhilarating cosmic coming-of-age story that thrives on rich world-building and emotional honesty. J.Q. brings a fresh voice to YA fantasy by pairing magical realism with real-world issues. The novel's greatest achievement lies in its balance: poetic prose pairs seamlessly with interstellar action; laugh-out-loud moments are layered with deeply vulnerable revelations. <u>The heart of the story remains in the relationships</u> <u>formed between characters, particularly the reunion between</u> <u>Truman and his long-lost sister</u>. The emotional payoff is <u>tender, surprising, and earned</u>."   *~ Likely Story* *

"Life in Aether is anything but boring! *Mercury to the Moon* is <u>a</u> <u>refreshing novel in the fantasy genre</u>, a coming-of-age story with a cosmic twist. The book explored themes such as being

queer, navigating teenage friendships, and finding one's place."
~ *San Francisco Book Review*

"Gagliastro's *Mercury to the Moon* is a sprawling space-fantasy that fuses coming-of-age themes with alien mysticism, social critique, and radiant, otherworldly worldbuilding. It's equal parts whimsical and sobering. [The] grounded, emotionally resonant early chapters read like a literary contemporary YA novel until everything changes. The concept of "wills"—alien abilities tied to one's emotions or traumatic experiences—adds a layer of allegory, suggesting that our most painful moments often unlock our greatest potential."
~ *Los Angeles Book Review* *

"Gagliastro's sweeping worldbuilding will draw readers into this riveting series starter, one rich with imaginative superpowers and layered characters. An out-of-this-world adventure!"
~ *BookLife Prize*

J.Q. Gagliastro

First Edition, June 2025.

Published by Gaggy Press, an American imprint.
Trademark—J.Q. Gagliastro

Library of Congress Cataloging-in-Publication Data is available.

Visit the author's website at
www.jqgagliastro.com

Instagram **@gaggypress**

Paperback ISBN   979-8-9912959-2-5
Hardback ISBN   979-8-9912959-1-8
Technicolor ISBN   979-8-9912959-3-2
eBook is available.

Mercury to the Moon is a fantasy novel, *not* the idealization of other planets as the place to be.
We already have a planet—Earth.
We ought to focus our efforts on saving her, not terraforming other worlds. Again, *Mercury to the Moon* is a fantasy novel. Turn my pages when you wish to dream.

Donate to the World Wildlife Fund!

To my mother, Tracy Lee,
whose heart is the size of the
Moon.

- 8 -

from the creative mind and bestselling author,

J.Q. Gagliastro,

here is…

Mercury to the Moon

Truman's Space Odyssey, Book 1

Prologue

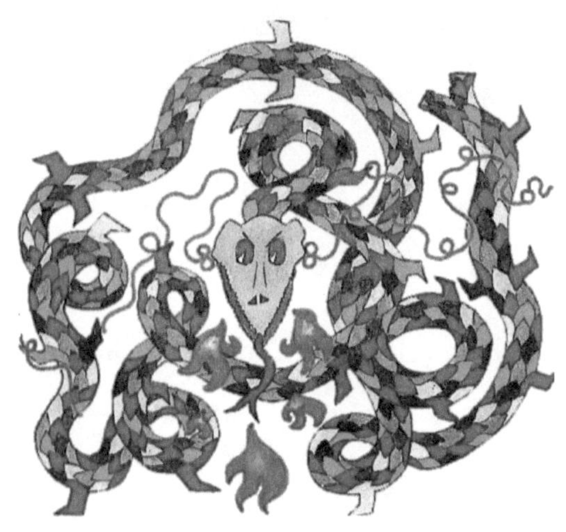

A Dragon Escapes the Sun

T he Sun was nailed to the sky, its dragons burning fiercely.

Krimmiel gazed out a dusty window overlooking the purple streets of the planet Mercury. His eyes brimmed with daydreams. Sunlight poured across his shoulders and illuminated his boyish good looks. He was an unrealistic beauty. Even his slicked-back blond hair and dark brown eyebrows seemed too good to be true.

Behind Krimmiel, in an armchair beneath a flickering lightbulb, sat an old human-sized bee. His name was Sin. Sin had seven limbs—six legs and one stinger—a furry thorax, and veiny wings. He was smoking a rainbow cigar. One puff was a deep crimson and another an icy blue. His body resembled a voluminous black-and-yellow striped evening gown. Honey drooped from his honeycomb hoop skirt. The amber liquid was hardened with age and smelled cloyingly sweet.

Krimmiel was used to the old bee's smell, but sometimes it gave him a headache.

The two friends sat in a musty hotel room, thick with the scent of honey, tobacco, and mothballs.

"I think I'll go for a stroll," Krimmiel said, coughing over the secondhand smoke. "Would you care to join me?"

"All's well, thank you," Sin replied, his voice deep and raspy. "But could you stop by the Dragon's Belly and pick up some fried butterflies and cherry blossom soup for dinner?" As he spoke, his eyes, sparkling like dull ruby gemstones, peered over the newspaper held in pollen-covered limbs. The headline read: *KRIMMIEL: A MENACE TO ALIENKIND!*

"Sure, no problem," replied Krimmiel. "Anything *enlightening* about me in the paper?"

"Just that you pose risk to all aliens and are a 'horrible citizen of Aether,'" Sin quoted dryly. "You really should stop warping wherever you want."

"Yeah, yeah," Krimmiel grinned. He threw on a crop top and headed into the blistering heat.

"Oh, and Krimmiel!" Sin hollered, fluttering up from the armchair and dragging his gown to the door.

"Yes?" Krimmiel turned, his chili pepper earring glistening in the city lights.

"Could you ask the hotel staff for another lightbulb? The one we have is dying, and I can barely read with my cataracts as it is! I don't know why you booked a room at the Heavenly Hotel…" grumbled Sin. "There's nothing heavenly about it!"

"Hey, I didn't ask you to come," Krimmiel shot back, still grinning. "You came of your own free will, remember?"

"Of course, I remember! I wasn't going to let you go to your hearing alone."

"Besides," Krimmiel pressed on, "we only need a place to sleep. We don't need to live it up in a five-star Venusian château, do we?"

"Well, it would be nice for a change!"

Krimmiel rolled his eyes. "I'll talk to the hotel staff."

The beautiful man strode into the street, bathed in the city lights.

The lampposts were tinted a shade of plum. The sidewalks were the color of wine. Buildings were painted entirely violet. And the parks were wild with lavender and wisteria.

The serpentine dragons of the Sun consumed most of the sky. They coiled and raged, smoldering ceaselessly. Krimmiel watched them, unfazed.

The heavy traffic halted. Krimmiel crossed, glancing from car to car. The alien cars were smaller than Earthling cars—a hybrid between a Martian rover and a Volkswagen Beetle. The solar panels on their roofs flared out like wings. Their logos varied from a blue crescent moon to a planet with rings.

He passed a boutique selling the latest Lunar boots and wandered down an alley. At its end was a sign that read: *Beyond This Point Is the Spider Cavity: TURN BACK NOW!* He veered down another alley and reached a second dead end. Another sign read, *BEWARE: Force Field Ahead.*

He doubled back to center city and passed two women gossiping.

"Is that the man who almost *exposed* our existence to an Earthling?!" one woman whispered with disdain.

The other woman nodded, alarmed and wide-eyed.

When Krimmiel met their gazes, they squealed and scurried into a nearby shop.

He ignored them and headed toward the vibrantly colored archway that read *The Dragon's Belly*. He hopped in line at a food truck shaped like a pink dragon. While waiting, he watched people in all sorts of odd outfits bustle around from vendor to vendor, buying Martian snacks, Neptunial seafood, and Earthling cuisine.

"Greetings, sir!" a man said, squinting down at Krimmiel. "How may I help you?"

"May I have two cups of blossom soup and a bag of fried butterflies, please? And can I make that the... *Heliconius charithonia* flavor?" Krimmiel stumbled over the butterfly's scientific name.

"Absolutely." As he put together the order, the man pushed his bifocals up his nose, paused, and gave Krimmiel a curious look. "You look familiar, son. Do I know you?"

"I don't believe so." Krimmiel took the food and handed the man an alien coin shaped like a golden star. "Keep the change!"

As he left, he noticed that several vendors were hastily closing shop. At the crosswalk, children played on the curb.

"KIDS, GET INSIDE!" shouted a woman from a window, her eyes stamped with fright. "There's a Leonian dragon loose in the city! HURRY UP!"

"That's not funny, Mom!" the little boy shouted, his voice trembling.

"It's not like a house could protect us anyway," replied the girl. "A fire dragon could burn down Violetteville in one breath!"

The boy blanched. "Stop it!" He cried and tripped over his feet as he bolted inside.

The girl chuckled but followed quickly.

As Krimmiel crossed the street, a car came swerving around him, honking wildly. It seemed to be speeding away from something. The driver slammed on the brakes. The car fishtailed and struck a pole, shattering its windows with a thunderous clap.

Krimmiel jumped backward onto the sidewalk, scalding himself with the soup. He yelped, but the sound was swallowed by a mighty *ROAR!* He jerked his head toward the end of the street. The searing pain washed from his mind as a fiery beast came barreling down the boulevard. Its face lacked flesh and resembled a bony carcass. Its feral red eyes narrowed. Its tongue was forked. Its scales shimmered like a king's regalia in red, amber, and gold. They were browning— a sign of the creature's old age.

In an instant, the laser-like ruby tendrils attached to its head whipped through the air, slashed down lampposts, and incinerated trees. Its body stretched for miles. The creature was so long that Krimmiel could not see the end of it. The dragon must have wrapped its tail around hundreds of city blocks, knotting itself like a tangled skein.

The beast scorched the sides of buildings. Pavement melted.

Krimmiel raced to help the driver out of their car. As the two ducked for cover, the dragon showered the street in flames, coalescing its roar with screams of terror.

Krimmiel covered his head and watched the dragon soar. Its scales morph into the faint image of a teenager, a boy, like a hieroglyphic in a torchlit cave. The boy's sharp features and caramel hair became an outline speckled with stars. Krimmiel felt time freeze.

When the dragon's tail finally caught up with the rest of its body, Krimmiel jumped to his feet. "Will you be alright?!"

The driver, still in shock, nodded.

Krimmiel shot after the dragon. As he turned the corner onto a massive square, a squad car zoomed past him, and a crew in red camo leapt out of the trunk. Ropes of ice and water unraveled from their palms.

At the center of the square, the dragon gathered itself like a spool of thread and shot columns of smoke into the sky. Embers waltzed with the wind.

The crew caged the animal with icy ropes. Its fiery scales sizzled.

The dragon roared again. But it wasn't a menacing growl like before. Instead, it was a howl. Its eyes turned a soft amber color—it was pleading.

A final lasso looped around its neck and tightened. The dragon slumped to the ground. The flames on its body were extinguished.

"STOP IT!" Krimmiel shouted at the dragon catchers. "YOU'RE HURTING HER!"

"GET BACK!" A man in camo pushed him down.

One crew member looked at Krimmiel and nodded. "Loosen the noose!" she commanded the man.

"But it's going to engulf us in flames!" the man shot back.

"Our orders were to return the dragon to the Sun *alive*," said the woman. "Loosen the noose so it can breathe, soldier!"

Grumbling to himself, the man flicked at the rope, and the dragon's flames returned.

"Don't worry," the woman said to Krimmiel. "I'll see to it that the dragon is safely returned. Now, please, vacate the square before you look like him!" She gestured to a man in a purple suit being lifted into an ambulance. Krimmiel did not catch the man's face but saw his burnt arms.

Stumbling to his feet, Krimmiel turned the corner and sprinted toward the Heavenly Hotel. When he burst through the door, he found Sin napping in his chair. Honeyed drool dripped down his mandibles.

"SIN!"

"What is it?!" Sin jolted awake.

"You'll never believe what just happened!" In one breath, Krimmiel told Sin all about the dragon attack.

When he finished, Sin looked at him disappointedly. "Ah man, you spilled my soup?!"

"Sin, forget the soup! Something else happened… I—I had another one of those visions!"

Sin's interest was piqued. The bee leaned forward, gravity washing over his face. "Which one? The one where Cherry dies or the one about—?"

"The boy," said Krimmiel. "He's about to embark on his journey." He wiped sweat from his brow. "I was right, Sin! I was right all along… He's an alien!"

Chapter 1

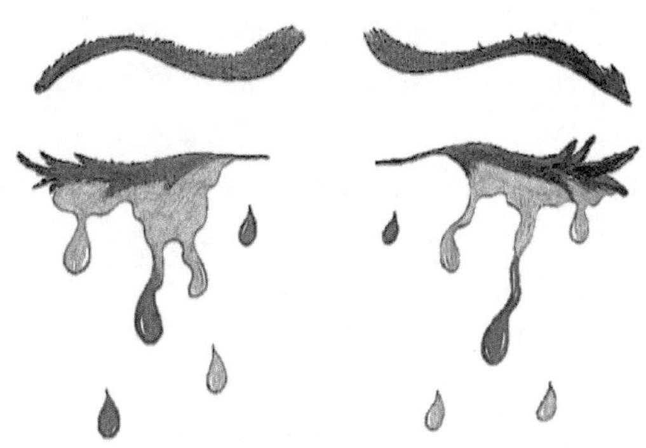

The Day the Snowcapped Mountain Spouted a River

About one hundred and twenty million miles away on planet Earth, Truman Howard stuffed his homework into a bag held together by safety pins.

A bell rang. He got up and left the classroom for his free period. He considered doing homework but found it impossible with all his peers talking loudly on their phones. They spoke in their native languages, but he knew they were begging their loving yet faraway parents for a visit soon and, of course, more money.

This was a daily activity for the students of Lonely's Academy, a world-renowned boarding school nestled in the Rocky Mountains on the border of British Columbia and Alberta, west of Calgary. The school, which included an elementary, middle, and high school, was a place where parents with busy schedules and deep pockets sent their children. Even with their children crying and pleading, their parents shipped them off anyway. To sleep at night, the parents reassured themselves that they were doing the right thing—giving their children the best education that money could buy.

But every time Truman witnessed a parent dropping their child off at the Academy, their tears and pleas would always chip away at his heart. After a while, he learned to avert his gaze and keep walking.

Despite the campus's massive size, Truman could not find a classroom devoid of whiny children. Resigned, he returned to the dormitories. As he walked, he overheard his classmates Josephine, Lidi, and Karleigh answering phone calls in their respective languages—German, Amharic, and Korean.

As one of the few Americans on campus, he, nevertheless, found it weird to call himself one. While his birth certificate listed Massachusetts, he arrived at the Academy when he was six. Canada was all he knew. *This campus* was all he knew.

Truman found the cross-cultural diversity of the school unique and valuable. In fact, it was what gave the school, especially the language department, its reputation. Truman had the opportunity to study English, French, Italian, American Sign Language, and Standard Mandarin. He found Mandarin the most difficult but enjoyable.

He reached for the doorknob to his room. Before his fingers touched the cold metal, the door flung open, and Ash swaggered out.

Ash Cole, Truman's roommate, was also an eighteen-year-old American boy.

The school thought that since Ash and Truman had "similar cultural upbringings," it would be best to pair them together.

They could not have been more wrong.

Ash was a small, straight, conservative boy who wore plain clothing, nothing too outlandish. His go-to was a stained white T-shirt and ill-fitting jeans. Truman, however, was a tall, queer, open-minded boy whose style was best defined as eccentric. Their biggest difference was that Ash was not a good person at all. He talked back to teachers, called people horrible names, and fought anyone who looked his way. Truman, on the other hand, found it pointless to be unkind.

"Move!" Ash barked, shoving Truman aside. "Oh, and by the way, I borrowed your book!" He guffawed, crumpling up a piece of paper and tossing it over his shoulder.

Inside, Truman found his mythology book torn apart, its pages weeping all over the floor.

As Truman knelt to salvage what he could, Josephine hung up her phone, entered the room, and crouched down to help.

"Thank you," he said.

She smiled and handed him the papers.

Josephine was a tall girl with long blonde hair and blue eyes. Despite these desirable traits, everyone, including Truman, found her a bit awkward. She wasn't well-versed in small talk and often asked overly personal questions. But she always meant well, which Truman appreciated. In fact, he quite liked her. He wasn't particularly close to her but did admire how unapologetically herself she was. That was something he could relate to.

Josephine looked around and noticed the stark contrast between Truman's and Ash's sides of the room.

"Where are all your photos?" she asked with a subtle German accent.

"Photos?"

"Yah, like, photos of your family? You don't have any up on your wall or on your desk."

"I—" He hesitated. "I just don't have any good ones."

He returned to shuffling the papers.

Josephine left abruptly without saying goodbye.

As Truman stapled what he could, loneliness crept into his skin. The feeling was all too familiar. He felt it every time he thought about his family. Since the day his parents dropped him off at the Academy, they had never visited. He was, for all intents and purposes, an orphan raised by Academy staff.

Truman grabbed his rusty umbrella. *Homework could wait*, he thought.

On his way out, his gaze fell on the pictures on Ash's desk. He saw Ash's family. Like Ash, his brothers were also bald.

Truman ran his hand through his full head of light brown hair and found himself thankful.

Next to the photo of his brothers was a photo of Ash and his townie friends hanging out of his red pickup truck. Like Truman, Ash struggled to make friends at the Academy. While Truman tried to treat everyone with kindness, Ash was cold and dismissive, particularly to the other international students and anyone else whom he considered "weird." That was why, instead of having friends on campus, Ash hung out with the people downtown, bonding over street racing and loud music.

Truman, on the other hand, hadn't found a group of friends on or off campus. While he liked many of the international students, he never felt like he belonged. He told himself he was too busy for a social life. But, deep down, he knew that he was out of his element at the Academy—at least, out of the average tax bracket.

As he stared at the photo of Ash and his friends, that familiar feeling stirred once more, this time with a dash of envy.

He stepped out into the fresh April rain and started down the mountain. While his classmates chose to stay indoors and sit on their phones during the free period, Truman headed toward Goodall, the thrift store just off school grounds.

Truman liked thrifting, at least, that's what he told himself anyway. The truth was he couldn't afford the clothes his classmates had. Though his parents left him with a pile of hand-me-downs, Truman had long since outgrown them. Getting a job was unheard of at the Academy, yet Truman had no choice if he wanted to afford even thrifted clothes.

He eventually learned to appreciate his secondhand wardrobe. He even developed a real knack for sifting through decades-old clothing and finding vintage yet inexpensive treasures like a Michael Jackson jacket, a pair of Apple Bottom jeans, and even a neon ski suit.

Some of his classmates complimented his bold fashion sense, but most stared judgmentally at him.

He checked his pocket watch. *Forty minutes 'til Greek Mythology.*

The store's musty scent and the front door's chime welcomed him.

He needed socks. His had holes in the soles. He went straight to the bin labeled *Socks*. To his disappointment, only baby pairs remained.

I suppose I could sew up the holes. He picked up a kit of needles and thread.

He then took a gander at the coats. The men's selection was uninspiring as usual. The women's was a bit better. Nothing was catching his eye until an older woman wearing a plain, floor-length dress pointed to a cowrie-shelled denim jacket and spat in a rural accent, "Who would ever wear such a *heinous* thing?!"

"I know someone who would," he said, grabbing it.

The woman gave him a look of disgust. Truman didn't care. He strode toward a mirror and slipped the coat on. He found that it paired well with his ripped jeans and muddy Converse.

The woman bustled over to her friends and pointed at Truman. They muttered words and snickered.

In the mirror, Truman saw his reflection return his gaze— his brown eyes dulled to a dispirited blue.

He made his way to checkout and handed the clerk the sewing kit and jacket. "Good afternoon, sir. What's the damage?"

"Six bucks."

That's the last of my month's pay. Truman took a second glance at the coat. *I don't need it. But I don't want those women to win.*

"Here you go." Truman handed the man the change. "Thank you!"

As he trudged up the hill back to the Academy, the rain stopped. Clouds still rolled overhead.

A red truck rumbled up the road, blaring a country song about tractors and beer. Truman didn't need to look to know that it was Ash and his entourage.

The truck slowed. Ash was in the front seat, chewing tobacco. "Whatcha doin'? Recycling cans, poor boy?!"

His entourage cackled.

"What's up, Ash?" Truman replied with an air of indifference. "Will I be seeing you in Greek Mythology today?"

"No!" Ash spat. "You think I care about Cronus?!"

"Well, at least you know his name."

"What's that supposed to mean?!" Ash scowled. "You calling me dumb?!"

"No, Ash." Truman kept walking. "We have a test on Friday. You'll show up for it, right? So you can pass the class and graduate?"

With a sullen look, Ash hocked a loogie at Truman's feet. He stomped on the gas pedal and sped up the hill, laughing.

Disgusted but unfazed, Truman wiped his shoe on the grass, glanced at his watch, and burst into a sprint toward the language wing.

He ran down a hallway past a boy ending a phone call in Farsi and bumped into a woman in a fur coat. He apologized without looking back and slipped into his final class, snagging a seat in the back.

Everyone craned their necks and stared at his noisy coat. He smiled back and took out his binder.

Halfway through the lesson, Truman—bored by the children of Cronus—glanced out a window. The Sun, stubborn and strong-willed, broke through thinning clouds. He squirmed in his seat, eager for the bell to ring so he could head to work.

☆ ☆ ☆ ☆ ☆ ☆

Unlike most people, Truman loved his job. He worked at the ski resort at the top of the mountain.

Before landing the job, he had never skied. He'd always enjoyed watching the tourists, though. Now, as an employee, the owner let him ski whenever he liked.

His boss hired him after he had begged her for a job. She noted that his clothes were two sizes too small and his shoes were ratty. She pitied the boy. At first, she paid him under the table and gave him little tasks like washing dishes in the cafeteria or fitting boots for children. Now, he was a certified youth ski instructor with benefits.

The bell rang.

Back in his room, Truman changed into his ski gear. The owner had lent him rentals. They weren't the best, but they got him to where he needed to be.

He headed for the ski lift along with his peers who were all part of an exclusive after-school program. Sometimes, Truman felt uneasy about working somewhere where they all went to have fun and socialize. It made the class divide between them painfully apparent.

The lift station was downhill from the Academy. Truman hopped onto a chair lift and ascended until the altitude was high enough for plenty of snow. His ears popped.

On weekdays, he usually worked from three until close. On Saturdays and Sundays, he worked ten-hour shifts. The weekends were always the busiest.

Learning to ski had been easier than Truman expected. Teaching, not so much. He coached children from ages six to twelve. The younger ones were surprisingly easier to teach. They were more unfamiliar and thus hesitant. The twelve-year-olds were the worst. They never listened. Most of them were more interested in impressing one another, not learning.

He taught them the basics—how to get on and off the lift, the mountain rules, and how to pizza and cut. Everyone started on the bunny hill, a gentle slope perfect for newbies. Parents often hovered nearby, wanting to witness their child conquer their first run.

If a kid showed promise, Truman moved them to the green trails. If they conquered the green and had a few days of practice under their belt, he'd then take them to a blue trail. He never brought them to a black diamond. Those were for experts and daredevils. Even Truman didn't always enjoy those, especially the double blacks.

He had witnessed a few accidents during his two years of working for the resort. Most accidents involved overly confident teenagers trampling other skiers or snowboarders who had the right of way. Once, a kid sped down a black diamond and completely flattened an elderly lady who was there with her grandchild. She was fine, but the resort got sued.

Truman couldn't blame newbies for crashing. His first time on a black diamond, he hit a mogul and flew into a tree. Ski patrol had to toboggan him down. His thighs stayed bruised for weeks.

Between sessions, Truman managed to get his homework done in the staff room, warmed by the fireplace. During peak season, though, he didn't have the time to squeeze in homework—this meant pulling all-nighters.

Today was a slow weekday. Apart from his peers, the slopes were mostly empty. He had one session scheduled. It was with a twelve-year-old rich kid named Jamal whose mother was in town for work.

"You're really good at this," Truman noted, as the kid pulled a shifty—a counter-rotation maneuver where the upper body spun opposite to the lower body. Then, he pulled a clean 180.

"I can't even do that! You don't need me."

"My mother doesn't want me to be alone," said the kid. "And I'm sure you could do it. Embrace the fear."

Truman understood. After his accident, he'd been terrified to ski through the alpines again. But once he pushed past the fear, the winding, scenic alpines had some of his favorite paths.

Together, Truman and Jamal explored all the greens and blues and some of the blacks. Truman led him through hidden trails only employees knew about.

Halfway down an alpine, the two paused to admire the view. The lake at the base of the mountain was a gorgeous blue set against an orange sprawling sunset. No matter how many times he'd seen them, sunsets at the summit always took Truman's breath away.

"The mountain's closing soon," said Truman. "We should head back."

As they came upon the final green trail, Truman spotted a commotion—some guy yelling at a girl who had fallen.

Truman gestured to Jamal to keep going and skidded to a stop. "Everything alright?" He lifted his goggles and recognized Ash and Josephine. Both were in the after-school program.

"She cut me off!" Ash shouted, red in the face.

"*I* was in front *you*!" Josephine shot back, scrambling to her feet. "I had the right of way!"

"Not true, sweetheart."

"Don't call me sweetheart!"

"I'll call you whatever I like, you worthless—"

Ash proceeded to call her what one should never call a German.

Josephine became rigid. Truman tensed up as well.

Tears filled their eyes.

Truman watched her sympathetically as she turned and skied off, sobbing.

Many of their peers had called her the slur behind her back but never to her face.

Ash smiled smugly.

Truman wanted to punch him.

Suddenly, the mountain rumbled. Their skis lost their grip and began to slide. The snow beneath Truman's skis looked like it was… melting?

"What the—"

A thunderous crash echoed from above.

Truman and Ash turned toward the peak and saw it—a wall of water, rushing straight at them.

Instincts kicked in. They turned on their skis and darted down the quickly melting trail toward the resort.

Behind them, the wall of water became a river and engulfed trees, chair lifts, and even the waffle house.

"MY WAFFLES!" screamed the old waffle maker.

Truman heard another scream—Ash. He had fallen, his skis and poles scattered in the slush. Truman thought about turning, but it was too late. Ash had been sucked into the river.

Truman kept skiing, but the water gained on him. His skis scraped across a patch of dirt with no snow. He toppled as the river engulfed him.

He braced himself for impact—a tree, a lift, a cabin? Instead, the water swirled around and carried him gently toward the resort.

Time slowed. While his ski suit was drenched, he didn't struggle to stay afloat. The current kept him buoyed, as if the water held him in its hands.

The Sun burned brighter. Golden rings dappled his vision. Something flickered across the Sun. Coiled?

Wisps of clouds danced around him and dissipated. He shivered.

The river sank into the earth, and Truman's back found solid ground. He inhaled a sigh of relief.

Then, he looked around and saw nothing but chaos. Trees had been uprooted. Waffles were bloated and scattered on the ground among skis, poles, and wood. The river had vanished seemingly evaporated, as well as all the snow along the lower trails.

Yet, the rest of the snowcapped mountain, well, it looked perfectly untouched.

☆ ☆ ☆ ☆ ☆ ☆

"B-but the r-river and th-the mountain! IT CAME OUT OF NOWHERE. Just WHOOSH and BAM! Gone! I was in! Sucked. I couldn't see. BLUE!" Ash sounded hysterical as the EMTs lifted him into the ambulance.

"Apart from the hysteria, he'll be fine," said an EMT. "Just a broken limb… Are you sure you're okay?" they asked Truman.

"Yes, just a twinge in my leg."

The EMTs left.

Truman's boss grumbled. "Another lawsuit. Great!"

He followed her inside, feeling annoyed on her behalf.

"It was a natural disaster," she mused. "Maybe we won't be held liable? Depends on how good his parents' lawyers are. Rich kid, right?"

"Yes. But ma'am, a natural disaster?"

"Rainstorms are a natural disaster, my dear boy. Shouldn't you know that? Isn't that school supposed to be the best in the world or something?"

"Rainstorm? What? That was no rainstorm…" He looked around incredulously. "That was a river!"

"A river?! What're you talking about, boy? You're starting to sound like that punk."

Truman knew better than to push it. A river appearing out of nowhere on a mountain sounded crazy. He saw how people looked at Ash. But he found it odd that no one else had seen the river. Even Jamal and the waffle maker had no idea what he was talking about.

"I spent all morning making that batter," grumbled the old waffle maker, picking up his ladle.

"You didn't see the river?" Truman asked him. "But you saw it consume your waffle house. I saw you screaming."

"It was just rainfall, my boy."

Truman frowned. That river was like a tsunami. It couldn't have been from mere rainfall. Something wasn't right.

"You really think a rainstorm destroyed your waffle house, melted all the snow on the Dreamweaver Trail, and tore up trees from frozen earth?"

"Rain and wind can be powerful," said the old man. "Never underestimate the power of Mother Nature."

Truman's boss told him to go home, but he was too baffled to leave just yet.

"I can help clean up," he offered, grabbing a bag and heading out to collect debris.

After filling a few bags with driftwood from the wreckage, Truman found himself alone on the green trail, overlooking the resort.

"Truman Howard?" said someone with a British accent.

He turned. A tall Black woman, likely in her mid-thirties, seemingly appeared from nowhere.

She strode down from atop the green trail where all the chair lifts had been turned off after the incident.

How'd she get up there? Truman thought. *And why isn't she wearing ski gear?*

Instead, she wore a jet-black blouse and high-waisted pants. Her Afro was voluminous and a striking shade of gray—not elderly gray, but a metallic silver. He had never seen hair that color before. She was beautiful, he thought.

"Yes?" he said, cautiously.

"It's a pleasure to make your acquaintance!"

"Who are you?"

"My name is Angenciel Mortimer. I'm here because I have answers."

"Answers?"

"To your questions, of course! I saw the river, too."

"You did?!"

"Yes, and I know where it came from." She paused. "It came from you."

He stared at her.

"Huh? What're you talking about?"

"You're what's called an *aquaura*," she said matter-of-factly. "An aquaura has the will to fashion water. A will is like a superpower. Essentially, you can freeze water, melt it, shape it, generate it, even pull it out of thin air, if you're skilled enough. You won't be able to do all those things until you learn to control your will.

What transpired here—" she gestured to the trail, "—was all *your* doing. *You* melted the snow, and *you* created the river. By accident, of course."

Truman burst out laughing. "HA! Yeah, sure! And I bet you can fly, can't you?!" He laughed some more, shaking his head and returning to pick up debris.

"I'm serious," she said, following him. "You're not just an aquaura, though. You're also an *empath*. An empath has the will to apprehend the emotional state of another being."

"I know what an empath is," he said with an air of annoyance. "And they don't exist. That's just what annoying people call themselves to garner sympathy and to humble-brag about what a good person they are. It's forced."

"Is that so?" She rolled up her sleeve and pinched her arm.

"Ow!" He felt a prick in his arm. "What'd you just do?"

"I told you—you're an empath. Empaths usually only *empathize* with people who are in their vicinity. The closer you are, the more you'll empathize. Strong emotions, like pain, anger, sorrow, grief, and happiness, you will sense those more. Weaker emotions, like annoyance, frustration, confusion, or boredom, you will sense less."

He sat on the ground. "Is… Is this… *What?*"

She plopped down beside him. "Your will triggered when your roommate bullied that girl. You *felt* her pain. I will say, that was rather unusual. Most wills trigger when something traumatic happens to oneself. But, since you're an empath, it makes sense.

"Unfortunately," she continued, "that means you have a weakness. While the will of an empath is valuable in certain situations, it also makes you more susceptible to manipulation. People may see you as easy prey."

Truman was too stunned to speak.

"But, you're also an aquaura," she said encouragingly. "That is a fierce will! Most empaths have only one will."

Truman squinted at a patch of mud left from the river.

"Are you trying to freeze it?"

"Just move it in general."

"Give yourself some time. With practice, you'll learn how to control your wills. Oh, speaking of which—these are for you!" She reached into her pocket and pulled out a plane ticket, an American passport, and a gold necklace with his name engraved on it.

"The necklace is made of a specific rock that, when worn, blocks others' emotions. If you don't wear it, you may become overwhelmed or nauseous, even mentally unwell. I recommend wearing it. However, know that it's good to remove it every now and then so you can practice controlling your empathic will. When you do remove it, stare at a focal point. It'll help regulate your breathing."

Truman fastened the necklace around his neck, flipped open the passport, and recognized his yearbook photo.

"We ordered your passport and plane ticket the moment your will triggered," she said.

"But… it's been barely an hour since then. How did you get a passport that quickly? And why? And how did you know my will was 'triggered?'"

"We have our ways."

"Who's 'we?'"

"You'll find out soon enough. The passport is necessary for international travel. The ticket is a one-way to Arizona.

"Arizona? For what?"

"For you to meet me and a few others like us in the Sonoran Desert. I won't be telling you too much now since the others will have a lot of the same questions. Anyway, the flight is for tomorrow—"

"Tomorrow?!"

"Yes. Is that an issue?"

"Uh, yeah! I'm still in school. I don't know what to pack. And I have no idea where you're sending me! Who even are you?!"

"The flight is to take you to Arizona, where you will meet others like you—"

"You've already said that."

"From Arizona, you'll travel a little ways away to a place where you... where you will belong. Regarding your schooling, your parents have—"

Truman's stomach dropped. "My parents?!"

"Yes. You'll reunite with them soon enough," she assured him.

"But—"

"Your parents called your headmistress and informed her you'll no longer be attending Lonely's Academy. Regarding what to pack, bring everything. You won't be coming back." She checked her watch. It was an odd contraption, Truman thought, with planets rather than numbers.

"My apologies, Truman, but I must leave you. There's another one of us in the area I must contact immediately. I also need to ensure that the bully's memory has been altered."

"You can do that?! Is that why no one saw the river? You altered what they saw?"

"Oh no, not I. I can't alter memories. But, like I said, we have our ways! And yes, that's why your boss, the waffle man, and the rich kid think this was all due to a rainstorm."

She chuckled to herself. "Humans will believe anything! Anyway—" She held out her hand, her eyes twinkling. That was when Truman noticed burn marks on her forearms.

"It was a pleasure to finally meet you, Truman," she said, shaking his hand. "I'll see you tomorrow!"

She walked back up the hill.

"Wait, where're you going? The street is that way!"

But in the split second it took for Truman to point down the hill and look back at her, she was gone.

Chapter 2

Rainbow Row & Cherry the Blossom Dragon

The first Monday in May was a beautiful day. It was a shame Truman had to spend it in an airport.

With only thrifted clothing to his name, Truman managed to fit his entire life into one suitcase—a parting gift from Josephine.

"Thank you for this," he said to her. "I've never needed one before."

It was true. The Academy offered plenty of school trips, but he could never afford them. While his peers explored the world, he always stayed back and worked at the mountain.

"No worries! I didn't even know I had it. My mother buys me a new one every quarter." She smiled abruptly. "I'll miss you! It'll be lonely here without my fellow misfit."

He smiled back. "I'll miss you too."

Truman had also quit his job. When he told his boss he'd been given the opportunity to travel, she frowned.

"Sois libre!" she told him. *"Be free!"*

Ash hadn't returned from the hospital in time to see Truman leave, but Truman was sure he'd be over the Moon to have the room to himself.

Though the Academy had been his home for the past twelve years, Truman was not particularly sad to leave. There was nothing tying him to the place—only memories, most of which he shared with no one else but himself.

That night, he lay awake, thoughts racing. *What will this adventure entail? What is my family like? Do they have powers? How will I control mine? What if I accidentally sink the plane?!*

The flight was early. He wore a monochromatic green outfit—army pants, a suede button-up, and cheap sunglasses. The school had kindly arranged for a shuttle to the airport.

At TSA, his necklace triggered the machine. They pulled out a hand scanner, but that, too, kept going off.

"Odd," said the agent. "Remove the necklace and place it in the bin."

The moment he did, a wall of nerves crashed over Truman. The nervous, frenetic energy of the security line overwhelmed him. His knees buckled. He struggled to focus.

Stare at a focal point. Angenciel had advised.

He locked onto the agent, gritted his teeth, and staggered through the body scanner, ignoring the many sideways glances thrown his way.

When his bin finally passed, he lunged at it. The moment the necklace touched his skin, the flood of emotions subsided, and he felt steady again.

At the gate, people were already boarding. The plane was packed.

Truman had a window seat, which made him happy. He could finally understand that Joni Mitchell song.

As passengers shuffled in, he saw a familiar face. It was Style Leone.

Style was a strapping twenty-one-year-old man with scruff and dark brown curls. He was American and of Italian descent. He had olive skin and a walk like June. He was born deaf and had never opted for a cochlear implant.

Back when Truman was a freshmen, Style had helped Professor Lincoln facilitate dialogues in his ASL courses. The girls in the class had worshiped the ground Style walked on. They would pretend to struggle with the signs just so he would tutor them.

Truman, too, had found him handsome and the look in his eyes dreamy. Whenever Style complimented his progress, Truman blushed.

After graduation, Style left for Gallaudet University in the States. It had been well over three years since they had last seen each other. His signing was much better now, but he was too nervous to say hello. Besides, the seatbelt sign was now on.

The flight was direct and reached its destination in the afternoon. Truman exited the plane, claimed his bag, and was standing, unsure of where to go, until someone hollered his name. The man was striking, dressed in a traditional shalwar kameez. His long tunic flowed over his billowing trousers.

"Mr. Howard!" the man said, shaking his hand. "It's a delight to meet you! My name is Humzah Lisan, and I work with Angenciel Mortimer."

"Nice to meet you, sir!"

"We're just waiting for—ah, there he is!" He waved to someone over Truman's shoulder.

Truman turned and saw Style. He wore a white tee, sneakers, and ripped jeans. It was a classic boyish look that showed off his muscles.

Humzah fingerspelled, *"S-t-y-l-e L-e-o-n-e! My name is H-u-m-z-a-h L-i-s-a-n."* He signed and spoke at the same time. *"But you may call me…"* He placed his fingers on his shoulders and pulled them into fists.

Truman recognized the sign for *brave.*

"I've been assigned as your interpreter for the next few months," Humzah continued. *"I'm what's called a polyglot. I know every language known to humankind—spoken, signed, even braille. I also know a bit of zoolingualism, though, some parts of the animal kingdom are more difficult to learn than others. Don't get me started on amphibians! Anyway, it's nice to meet you both. Style, this is Truman. Angenciel said you two may know each other?"*

Truman shifted awkwardly to Style and signed, *"Hey, stranger."*

Style smiled. *"Truman! Wow, you've grown up! It's been too long!"*

He had put his index finger to his lips and flicked it forward. Truman was touched. Style had remembered his sign name, *True.*

"*How are you?!*" Style asked. "*How's the Academy? Wait, do you have a will too?*"

"*Sorry to break up the convo,*" interrupted Humzah, "*but if we want to arrive on time, we should leave now. The ride shouldn't be long. Follow me!*" He led the boys out of the airport and toward a taxi.

"Where to?" the driver asked.

"I'll guide." Humzah sat in the front seat.

The boys sat next to each other in the back. The woman began driving, the blazing Arizonian canyons stretching across the horizon.

"*So, yesterday, I found out I'm a v-é-r-i-t-i-s-t,*" Style said to Truman.

Truman furrowed his brows. "A véritist?"

"*Yeah. Essentially, I know when people are lying. It's like mind-reading, but I only have the power to read people's truths by looking in their eyes.*"

"Hmm. *What do my eyes tell you?*"

Style blushed and looked out the window.

Truman tapped his shoulder. "*I'm an e-m-p-a-t-h and an a-q-u-a-u-r-a. I sense others' emotions and control water.*"

"*Wow, two wills! I'm jealous—except for the empath ability. That sounds exhausting.*"

"*It can be, but I have this.*" He showed him the necklace. "*It's made of some material that blocks others' emotions, according to A-n-g-e-n-c-i-e-l.*"

"*Angel,*" he shortened. "*She seems sweet.*"

Truman agreed, then turned to Humzah. "Where are we going?"

"Yeah, where are we going?" said the driver, seemingly irritated that she had to listen to Humzah rather than her GPS.

"Right here, actually!"

She stepped on the brakes. "Here?" She looked around questionably.

There was nothing around them but desert.

Truman's stomach flipped. *We're gonna be left here to die,* he thought, meeting Style's eyes. They were a frosty blue and held flurries of snowflakes. *Well, at least it's with Style.*

"What did we get ourselves into?" signed Style.

They unbuckled and retrieved their bags from the trunk.

Humzah paid the lady.

"Sir," she said, "the closest town is miles from here. Are you sure this is where you want to get out?"

"Yes. Don't worry. We'll be fine."

She cast the boys a worried look.

"Thank you for your service. Good day!" he said cheerily as he doubled tapped the hood of the car.

She hesitated before getting back in her car and driving off.

"This way," Humzah motioned.

They set off, dragging their bags through the desert.

"Almost there."

"Almost where?!" Truman exclaimed. "There's nothing—!"

Suddenly, Humzah, who was walking ahead of them, disappeared. Even his shadow had all but vanished.

Truman and Style stopped in their tracks.

"Where'd he go?!"

Humzah's head reappeared, but just his head. "I'm right here," he said. It was like he was wearing some sort of invisibility cloak from his neck down. His hand materialized, gesturing them forward.

Style and Truman exchanged curious looks before stepping forward.

Though they were still in the desert, a large pink beast now towered before them. It was a serpentine dragon with triceratops stumps along its vast body. Its head was the size of a blue whale, perhaps bigger. Its wingspan stretched a mile long, its body two. An effulgent forest of cherry blossoms crowned the iridescent scales of its boundless back. Butterflies fluttered from branch to branch.

Truman gaped at the dragon. *Am I dead? Is this real? What the—*

He noticed that the creature had three eyes shaped like a separated triquetra. They were an angelic white speckled with black pupils, like dragonfruit or the inverse of a starlit sky.

And still, the sight did not end there.

A rainbow spiraled above the beast. There seemed to be no end to it, like the dragon. The staircase of colors shimmered with every hue from a vibrant red to a rich violet. Truman felt yellow wind brush against his skin and yearned to fly into open blue. If it weren't for Style, who pulled him back to his frosty reality, Truman might have floated off into space.

"WOW! How did we not see that?!" signed Style. *"Must be some sort of invisibility charm."*

"This h-has to be a dream," Truman stammered.

"Welcome, newcomers!" hollered a woman. She stood before a group of seven teenagers. "Join us!"

It was Angenciel. As she spoke, Humzah interpreted for Style.

"We've been expecting you," Angenciel said, flanked by two colleagues. "I was just telling everyone about Ereus Eklöf here, our Neptunial *illusionist* from the Illusory Fleet."

She gestured to a tall Swedish man with wiry blond hair and a yellow bowtie. His face was long and chiseled, his nose aquiline, and his smile revealed an unsettling number of teeth.

"He's the one who hallucinated—or rather, constructed—the unseeable yet penetrable wall you had just walked through. The wall keeps Earthlings from seeing or hearing us."

Earthlings? Truman thought. *Aren't we all Earthlings? And what's an Illusory Fleet?*

"I also mentioned that Falsmira Ravendez here is our Plutonian *torcron*."

Angenciel gestured to a scowling Mexican woman with a razor-cut black bob. She wore opera-length gloves, velour boots, and a pocket watch around her waist. Her dark eyeliner, sharply arched eyebrows, and raven-colored robes gave her a cold and menacing appearance.

"Torcrons have the will to slow down time," Angenciel continued. She turned her gaze upward with admiration. "Let's talk about the elephant in the room, shall we? Ladies, gentlemen, anyone in between, both, or neither—say hello to Rainbow Row and Cherry the Blossom Dragon!"

As if on cue, the beautiful dragon lifted its head into the sky and let out a mighty roar.

Chapter 3

Common Tongues

nd this here, making quite the entrance," Angenciel said, nodding toward the dragon's wing, "is Reuel."

A thirty-year-old woman slid down a vine and landed gracefully in front of the group. She was fair-skinned with long brown hair. A worn Harley Davidson jacket clung to her frame. She paired it with leather pants and tall black platforms. A bracelet of ivy coiled around her wrist.

She dusted herself off. "Hi, everyone!"

A chorus of greetings—each in a different language—met her.

She and Truman caught each other's gaze. She smiled at him.

He noticed that she had his brown eyes, and his skin bristled. A vision popped into his mind. He was a child, stumbling around in heels, laughing.

"Alright everyone, all aboard Cherry!" Angenciel hollered. "Leave your luggage here. We'll bring them up once everyone's aboard."

"What do you mean 'aboard Cherry?'" asked a dark-haired boy. He trilled his *rs*, revealing his Italian accent. He had well-kept scruff like Style and darker skin. His face was lapped with curls. Though he was the same age as Truman, his voice dug deeper. He wore an emerald leather jacket that brought out the green in his eyes.

"I think we have to climb," Truman guessed.

"You can use her scales as footholds," said Angenciel. "Fun fact about Cherry: when she was a mere fledgling, she was discovered and cared for by the late, great Jupitarian wizard and prophet, Chiron. You'll study him in due time. Now, let's gather by the campsite!"

Jupitarian wizard? Prophet? Campsite on a dragon? Truman had many questions.

The small crowd lined up to scale the dragon.

Truman and Style found themselves separated. Style stood in the back with Humzah, while Truman shuffled behind the Italian.

"Ciao," greeted the boy. "Name's Vedrò. Vedrò Azzurro."

"Ciao! My name is Truman. Truman Howard. *Piacere!*" *Nice to meet you!*

Vedrò's face lit up. *"Parli italiano? Fantastico!"* he said, appreciative to hear his language after days of travel. "Nice to meet you too, Truman. You know Italian?!"

"I took classes in high school."

"*Americano?*"

"*Sì*, but I grew up in Canada."

"Well, I must admit, I don't know many Americans who speak Italian, let alone a second language."

Truman smiled awkwardly.

"So, what's your superpower?"

"I'm an empath and aquaura."

"What's an aqu-au-ror?"

"Aquaura. I have the will to manipulate water—freeze it, move it, melt it. I even melted a mountain."

Vedrò gave him an impressed look. "A mountain?"

"Yea. What about you? What's your will?"

Vedrò straightened. "I'm a *prophet*. Angenciel says I'm the first prophet since Chiron himself!"

"Oh, so you think you're somebody," Truman teased.

They laughed as the line inched forward.

"Wait, tell me about this mountain you melted!"

"Well, it's how my will was triggered. There was this bully—"

"Oh, I'm sorry."

"Don't be. I wasn't the one being bullied. It was this girl, Josephine. She's fine now. What about you? How did yours trigger?"

Vedrò hesitated, his gaze darkening. "It happened a week ago. I was home in Rome with my mamma and little sister, Vega. I was studying for my astronomy class when my papà came home drunk. And very angry. He screamed, broke glasses, and accused my mamma of cheating. Vega was hiding in my room, scared out of her mind. I was consoling her when I had the vision. I saw her shaking and sweating and… She was only eight years old." He turned away. "Before I could process what I saw—before I could calm her down—it was too late."

Truman laid a hand on his shoulder. "I'm so sorry, Vedrò." His heart broke for him.

A selfish thought then came to Truman: he was grateful for his necklace. He didn't want to know what it felt like to lose a sibling. Though he couldn't remember his own, it didn't sound like something he wanted to experience.

A girl scaling Cherry slipped. She nearly lost her footing and fell.

"You alright?" said Angenciel.

"All good!"

"Hold on," Angenciel said to the person next in line. "One at a time."

Truman gave Vedrò a weak smile. Vedrò wiped the shine from his cheeks and looked up at Cherry.

"Do you think everyone here has gone through something similar?" mused Vedrò. "We must have, right? Otherwise, our superpowers would not have been triggered."

"Our *wills* would not have *triggered*," said a girl behind them. They turned.

A tall girl, effortlessly striking, stood with her arms crossed. She had a charming French accent and wore high-waisted sailor pants. While she was also eighteen, she towered over the boys. Her thick silver hair framed her deep brown skin. Truman thought of a bright light across the sea or a star in the night sky. Her dark blue-grayish eyes resembled stormy seas.

"Huh?" chorused the boys.

"I corrected you. You said, 'our *superpowers* would not have *been triggered.*' I said, 'our *wills* would not have *triggered.*' In alien culture, we don't say *superpower.* We say *will.* Also, it's *to trigger,* not *to be triggered.* I read about it in *The Triggery of Magical Instincts: A Jupitarian Study.*"

The boys stared blankly at her.

"My name is Esmeralda. Esmeralda Mortimer."

"I'm Truman Howard, and this is—"

"*Enchanté, La Esmeralda. Je suis votre roi, Vedrò Azzurro. Vous êtes ravissante-uh!*" *Nice to meet you, the Esmeralda. I am your king, Vedrò Azzurro. You are ravishing!*

Vedrò bent over to kiss the back of Esmeralda's hand.

Esmeralda rolled her eyes. Inside, Truman did too. He found what Vedrò said to be a bit much.

"Yes, super." Esmeralda pulled back her hand. "You're holding up the line."

The boys shuffled forward, though Vedrò was still distracted by her beauty.

"*Tu dis que ton nom de famille est Mortimer comme Angenciel Mortimer?*" asked Truman. *You say your family name is Mortimer like Angenciel Mortimer?*

"Your accent is 'ideous, *mais oui.* But yes, I'm Angenciel's daughter. Her only daughter."

"I didn't realize Angenciel was French. I assumed she was British because of her accent. Oh, and for your information, it's 'my accent is *hideous,*' not '*ideous.* There's an h."

"So, what's your *will,* La Esmeralda?"

"I'm an enchantress. I can control minds."

"Prove it."

She stared at Vedrò and smirked. His finger rocketed to his nose. He picked it furiously, then licked his finger clean.

"Gross," said Truman.

"Hey! Not nice!" Vedrò protested.

"You asked," she said with a laugh. "Now, let's see your will. You're a prophet, no? Prove it."

"I, eh—I don't know how to control my will yet. My visions, they come randomly."

"Better get practicing then."

It was Vedrò's turn to climb. He wrapped his jacket around his waist and found a foothold. Truman and Esmeralda watched as his back muscles bulged beneath his shirt.

Truman let Esmeralda go next, then followed. As he passed Cherry's third eye, she batted her lashes at him warmly. Deep crow's feet tugged the corners of her gaze.

At the top, the magic of the dragon continued to unfurl. Cherry's wingspan and body stretched even wider than they had from below. A log cabin with red doors towered on her left wing. It was more of a mansion—a wooden mansion.

Cherry's back was overgrown with clusters of flowers. Truman saw a field of lavender and lotuses blooming on a lake, and smelled honeysuckle and jasmine. Trellises full of blooming red and white roses flanked the cabin. Hundreds of shimmering butterflies swarmed the roses, creating an illusion of red paint dripping onto white petals.

Bleeding hearts the size of cushions clung to the branches of a nearby redwood. A long, winding path unraveled around the lake. A sign by the path read: *The Dragon's Back Trail.* Truman did not know how far the trail went, but it seemed infinite.

The cherry blossoms were the most magical. They were in full bloom and covered the hills in pillows of pink petals.

Vedrò, Esmeralda, and Truman stood next to one another, mesmerized.

"Wow," they whispered in unison, accents converging into awe.

Chapter 4

The Assembly of Aether

U nless he looked over the ledge, Truman couldn't see an inch of the Arizonian desert—the dragon was that massive.

When he *did* look over the ledge, he guessed it was at least a hundred-foot drop.

Cherry's lofty sublimity enchanted everyone on board. No one even noticed that Angenciel, Reuel, Falsmira, and Ereus were already waiting by the cabin with their bags.

"Everyone!" Reuel clapped, as if to wake them from a dream. "I would like to begin by saying, welcome! I cannot wait to get to know you lot!"

She glanced directly at Truman. Like Angenciel, she had a British accent, though, hers leaned more Cockney.

"We are your fellow aliens! Ereus here is from planet Neptune and works for the Illusory Fleet. The Illusory Fleet allows us to travel and live across the Solar System without being seen, heard, or detected by Earthlings. The Fleet works in tandem with the Savvies Station. The Savvies Station are the ones who created an anti-drift, oxygen-preservative force field around all alien civilizations including Cherry. Speaking of…"

She nodded to Ereus, who reached into his pocket and pulled out a remote control. After fiddling with it, a wavy glimmer stretched above their heads.

Truman heard a faint buzz. *A force field? Aliens? Traveling through space?! I must be hallucinating.*

"Savvies are aliens who have the will to manipulate technology with their minds," Ereus said excitedly. "They've built many ingenious contraptions, which you'll learn all about on the journey!"

"Yes, indeed," Reuel went on. "Angenciel here is from planet Venus. As am I. When she's not with us, she works as a wellfarer—alien term for psychiatrist—at the Van Gogh Irisylum, a Venusian hospital.

"I, on the other hand, am an astrobiologist for Ivies and Oaks, researching extraterrestrial life," she said proudly. "All four of us also serve as mentors. We work with humans whose wills recently triggered, like you lot, and help them ease into living as aliens. Some years, we have only two or three voyagers. Other years, we mentor seventy. It varies.

"Regarding my will," she continued, "I'm what's called an *aster*. Humans who've encountered my kind have coined several names for us: Mother Nature, Gaea, even Poison Ivy.

Essentially, I have the will to manipulate plant life and make it do as I wish. Angenciel is a—"

"I'm an enchantress," Angenciel interjected, "like my daughter, Esmeralda here. We can charm people to do as we wish. But don't fret! I'm forbidden from using my will on any of you voyagers. Esmeralda, on the other hand, well, I can't speak for her." She winked playfully. "I'm kidding! No beginner is allowed to use their will on another alien. It could be dangerous."

Vedrò shot Esmeralda a glare.

"Falsmira, how about a history lesson then?" said Angenciel.

Falsmira nodded and said in a blasé voice, "As mentors, the four of us work for what's called the Assembly of Aether. 'Aether' is our name for the Solar System. The Assembly of Aether is our governing body.

"The Assembly was established during the Earthling Age of Enlightenment, which we call the Era of Chiron. The late, great Jupitarian wizard and prophet, Chiron, was an alien himself. A gifted polyglot—perhaps the only one in history able to speak with Cherry."

"Wh-what's a polyglot?" asked a shy Chinese girl with stringy bangs.

Falsmira gave her a withering look.

Esmeralda shot her hand in the air and blurted, "A polyglot is someone who can adapt their tongue for any language!"

Falsmira shifted her glare to Esmeralda. "Would *you* like to be the mentor, or shall I?"

Esmeralda wilted, lowering her hand.

"No? Good. Like Miss Arrogant said, a polyglot knows a myriad of languages. In fact, we have one with us now. He knows spoken languages, sign languages, brailles, and zoolingualism. Everyone, meet Mr. Humzah Lisan."

She gestured to Humzah, who was busy interpreting for Style. He paused and blushed as everyone's eyes turned to him.

"Good day, everyone!" Humzah said sweetly. *"Bonjour! Buongiorno! God dag! Guten tag! Buenos dias! Marhaba! Namaskara! Nǐ hǎo! Jambo! Ahoj—"*

"Yes, yes," Falsmira interrupted, annoyed. "There are around six thousand human languages and twice as many animal ones. We don't have the time! Conveniently—I mean, fortunately—you all know English. Most cohorts usually need multiple polyglots for the journey.

"Now where was I? Ah, yes—Cherry and Chiron. Over time, the pair became great friends. Chiron felt rejected by his family and confided in Cherry. She sympathized and sought out others like him—outcasts from across the globe—to help him feel like he belonged. Little did he know she was about to introduce him to the minds who'd eventually help him create the Assembly of Aether.

"You'll learn more about the Assembly's origins soon, but, for now, know this: it wasn't until the Era of Chiron that aliens began to terraform the planets in our Solar System."

"Speaking of our Solar System," Angenciel interrupted, "we, as a cohort, will travel from heavenly body to heavenly body so you understand how the Assembly functions and what Aether is like. You'll learn about the lifestyles of each world and discover marvels beyond your wildest dreams! From the Vivabees of the Venusian Hospitals to the Aristotelian dragons of the Sun, seas, and skies!

"Our wondrous journey through Aether begins today and will end before the Earthling New Year. That means we will be traveling for nearly nine months, Earth-time. Though faster methods of voyaging through space exist, they take time to learn. During the journey, you'll have classes."

A few voyagers groaned.

"If you're too dimwitted to guess," Falsmira snapped, "I'm teaching Aetherly History."

"And I, Astrobiology," said Reuel.

"Interplanetary Technologies!" Ereus chimed in.

"And I, Worlds Cultures," said Angenciel. "But don't worry, the learning will be mostly experiential.

"Our journey will be split into trimesters. Mercury to the Moon—as in, the Earth's Moon—will take three Earth months. Mars to Saturn, another three. And Uranus to the Kuiper Belt, three more. After every trimester, you'll return to Earth for a short break. When visiting family or friends, you'll be under standard alien provisions—more on that later. Oh, and after each trimester, you must take a test for every course!"

"Whyyy?!" Vedrò whined.

"Silence!" barked Falsmira. "As a citizen of Aether, it's your civic duty to take those tests. And after your journey, you'll be paired with a mentor to master your will. Once that's over, you'll discover which world—Mercury, Venus, the Moon, Mars, Jupiter, Saturn, Uranus, Neptune, or Pluto— you're best suited to live on for the rest of your pathetic life."

"Yes, well," Angenciel cut in gently, "the people around you will be your classmates. You'll share many experiences. You have already—otherwise, you wouldn't be here. So, respect one another. Learn from one another. Be nice."

Vedrò shot Esmeralda a sideways glance and scoffed.

"The nine of you will sleep in the log cabin here," said Angenciel. "You're all adults. You choose your roommates."

Vedrò and Truman looked at one another in agreement.

"The four of us mentors, along with Humzah, have a separate cabin at the end of the Dragon's Back Trail. In an emergency, simply pull a bleeding heart from the blood tree, break its heart, and lift it into the air. It'll float above the cherry blossoms, and we'll see it from afar."

As a demonstration, Angenciel grabbed a bleeding heart, snapped the shell of the flower, and lifted it into the air. The flower glowed as it found its way above the trees.

Truman stared in awe at the flower. He had seen a bleeding heart before, but not one this large, let alone sprouting off a tree, glowing, and floating.

"If that's clear," said Angenciel, "go ahead and move your things into your rooms. Meet back here in twenty. We'll be preparing for takeoff soon!"

Everyone grabbed their bags and headed up the spiral staircases.

"Hey, Truman!" called Reuel. "May I speak with you for a moment?"

"Sure."

"I'll save you a bed," Vedrò offered, and left.

Truman and Reuel stood alone.

Reuel cleared her throat. "I know this'll be a lot for you—but uh—"

"I think it's a lot for everyone. Wills and aliens and the Assembly of Aeth—"

"No, no, not that," she said, cutting him off. "I have… I have something to tell you. You may not believe me, but I'm—" Her warm brown eyes welled with tears.

"I'm your sister, Tru."

Chapter 5

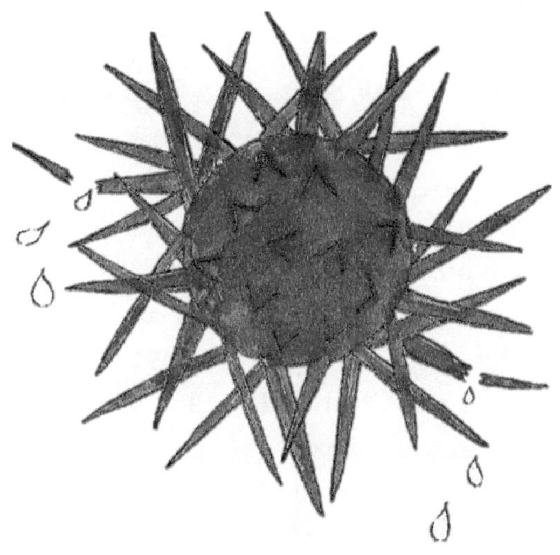

The Howard Bloodline

S ister?!" said Truman. "You can't be my sister. All my siblings are—"

"Where?" asked Reuel.

"I'm not sure. I… I can't quite remember."

"Exactly."

"What?"

"By order of the Assembly of Aether, your memory had to be modified. Let me ask you this: what *do* you remember about our family?"

"Our family? I—I know I'm one of six… That's about it. Why would the Assembly do that to me?"

"Not just to you. I went through it myself. It was awful. It had a terrible effect on Mum, though. Saying goodbye to her children like that… It nearly destroyed her. But she knew it had to be done because of PSA."

"PSA?"

"The Protection and Secrecy of Aliens. It's a law that forbids aliens from exposing the alien community to any Earthling under any circumstance.

"I'm the eldest," she pressed on. "After me is Coelho and Kahlil, our twin brothers. Coelho is a Neptunial, while Kahlil is a Martian. Then there's Saint. He's a Uranian. And then you."

"So, there's you, Coelho, Kahlil, Saint, and me." He counted on his fingers. "That's only five."

"Yes, Minli. She's not alien, though."

He froze, absorbing the information.

"Is she a human like me? Or, like I thought I was?" Truman asked, correcting himself. "Is she alive even?"

"Minli? Oh yes, she's as healthy as can be! She's in the U.K."

"I see." He paused to think. "So, say I understood the memory alterations and the legal separation between us and our… parents, why'd—" he faltered, "—why would Mom and Dad have six kids if they knew this was going to happen?" *Mom* and *Dad* fought clumsily to come off his tongue.

"Well, first of all, *don't* call him Dad, especially to his face," Reuel said with a serious look. "He *loathes* it! Finds it improper. He prefers 'Father.'"

"Okay…" He gave her a skeptical look but nodded.

"Secondly, Mum always wanted a large family. It's what she always said."

"But why couldn't we attend the same school, Minli and me? And why didn't you guys ever visit?"

"That's more difficult to answer. You see, memory modifications can be reversed. We call it *memory recall*. Basically, if we all went to the same school on Earth, we'd eventually remember something about Aether. We were all born here—"

"WHAT?!" spat Truman. "We were born in outer space?!"

"Yes. Each of us lived with Mum and Father for the first six years of our lives before our memories were wiped clean, and we were sent to Earth."

Truman gaped in disbelief. He looked around for something to ground him in reality, but the dragon didn't help. He lowered his gaze to Reuel's platforms.

"You and I, we used to play dress-up, didn't we?"

Reuel smiled. "Yes, you loved to wear Mum's heels. She used to say you walked better in them than she ever did."

"Wait!" A thought struck him. "How can Esmeralda Mortimer know about 'triggery of wills' and 'Jupitarian studies,' while we aren't allowed to remember our family? Wouldn't that be against this PSA?!"

"Her will triggered months ago. According to her mother, she's a voracious reader. She probably spent the past few months reading up on Aether. Angenciel must've given her books once her will triggered. Speaking of the Mortimers, like them, our family is a special one. I'm not boasting. What I mean is, there aren't many alien families like ours, Tru.

"Normally, when two aliens mate, their offspring still have a low probability of having a will. Being alien isn't necessarily genetic. It's very rare. That's what makes our family so unique, almost... suspicious. Some people admire that we, an alien family, can almost live like a typical Earthling family—together. It gives them hope that one day, they'll be reunited with their children. Others scowl at us, either out of jealousy or suspicion. They find the phenomenon 'too coincidental.'"

"Too coincidental? What does that mean?"

"I don't know. People think we're scammers."

"Scammers? How would we be scammers?"

She shrugged. "I think they're just jealous."

He looked around again, more thoughts zooming through his mind. "When will I get to meet everyone?" he asked.

"After Mercury and Venus, near the end of our Lunar visit."

"But that won't be for a while, right?"

"Yes. Unfortunately, everyone's busy with work. Not to mention, the journey has a strict schedule. On the upside, Mum's throwing you a congratulatory party. She's a Lunar. Father's a Saturnian. Everyone will be there, except Minli of course. Oh, and you'll have the opportunity to see everyone individually as we visit each of their ruling planets!"

She checked her watch. "I know you must have a million questions, but, right now, we must get going. Bring your stuff inside and come right back. You won't want to miss it!"

She gave him a hug. It was awkward but warm.

"Hurry up now!"

The other voyagers had already chosen their roommates and begun congregating outside.

As Truman entered the cabin, he dropped his bag in astonishment. Cherry blossoms grew inside the cabin. Vines curled up the interior walls. A fireplace crackled in front of water couches. Pink water and coral reefs filled the couches and a fish tank jutting out of a brick wall. Clownfish and seahorses swam freely between the tank and couches as if they were connected.

The ceiling was the most enchanting: a giant skylight made of stained glass depicting an African oasis. But this was no ordinary glass—the animals in the oasis were moving.

White light passed through the jagged panes, scattering a spectrum of colors across the glossy leaves of the cherry blossoms. Suspended from their patulous branches were three spherical treehouses swinging like a pendulum. Two of them alternated swinging outward as the third remained stationary in the middle. A sign in front read: *Newton's Cradle.*

Truman stumbled up a rope bridge that led to the treehouses. Vedrò hopped out of one of the moving ones.

"Truman, come look!" Vedrò said, hopping back into the spherical room. *"È magnifico, no?!"*

Truman followed. Though the treehouse swayed on the outside, Truman didn't feel it on the inside. The interior was also larger than he had expected. There were three wardrobes, three full-length mirrors, and three queen-sized beds. Like the couches, the beds were aquariums.

"I'm sleeping here," Vedrò said, pointing to a bed in which starfish were piled high, like an aquatic medieval tapestry.

The bathroom door flung open. It was Style. He was shirtless. His chest was muscular and hairy. Truman caught himself watching him put on a shirt.

"It's hot out there," Style signed, catching Truman's gaze.

Truman blushed. *"Are you bunking with us?"*

"Yes. I'm in this bed." He pointed to the one with blue sea dragons. *"That okay?"*

"Of course—yes, of course," Truman signed awkwardly, throwing his bag onto the third bed, which bore leafy sea

dragons. Their texture was unsettling to look at. He understood why the boys chose the other two beds.

Vedrò noticed Truman's natural blush but said nothing.

"Is this room taken?" A burly boy poked his head in. He wore a pair of Timberlands and spoke with a thick German accent. He looked from Truman to Style to Vedrò. "Never mind," he said, scurrying off with his luggage.

"That was weird."

"I'll see you outside," signed Style.

When he left, Vedrò nudged Truman. "You *so* have a crush!"

"Stai zitto!" Shut up! Truman shot back, embarrassed. "Come on, let's go."

They leapt out of the treehouse and found themselves trailing behind Esmeralda and the girl with bangs.

"I can't believe I got stuck with the waterbed full of goblin sharks," Esmeralda said with a grimace. "I'm going to have nightmares!"

"I like mine," said the girl. "I've never seen a narwhal before!"

They wound down the rope bridge and found the German boy talking to Reuel and Falsmira in the lobby.

"May I speak to you, Reuel… alone?" asked the boy.

"Whatever you need to say to me, Schmidt, you can say to Falsmira too. Now what's wrong?"

"I… I need my own room!" Schmidt demanded.

"And why is that?" Falsmira said, raising her brow.

"It's just… I can't share a room with those other boys!"

"And why is that?" Falsmira repeated impatiently.

"Well…" He glanced back at Truman and Vedrò. "I don't think I'd feel comfortable around them. They're… different."

"I see," Falsmira said, jaw clenched. "Schmidt Stein, is it?"

"*Ja.*"

"Well, Mr. Schmidt Stein, you should know that Aether is a place where people from all over Earth come to live in a community of their kind. You are now a part of that community. Do you understand?"

He nodded.

"Falsmira's right," said Reuel. "I suggest you talk to your peers, Schmidt. You may find yourself having more in common with them than you'd expect. You're aliens after all. Who knows, you might even make a friend or two!"

"I doubt it," muttered Schmidt.

"There's a third bed in Yari and Sweta's treehouse," said Reuel. "You can join them."

"But they're girls!"

"And?!" spat Falsmira. She was getting more annoyed by the minute. "You're nearly twenty years old. Grow up!"

Schmidt grumbled to himself and trudged toward the third treehouse.

Truman thought of his old roommate, Ash, and silently thanked the stars that he was sharing a room with Vedrò and Style.

☆ ☆ ☆ ☆ ☆ ☆

"Now that everyone is present," said Angenciel, "follow me to the orchard. It's time!"

Behind the cabin stretched a constellation of hedges spanning an acre.

They walked through rows of menacing trees flecked with apples. Truman went to pick one.

"I don't suggest eating the apples," said Angenciel. "They're not in season. The peaches and blessedbes are fair game, though."

"Blessedbes?" asked Vedrò.

"Yes, they're these purple ones." She plucked a strange fruit from a bush. It resembled a sea urchin. "They're perfect this time of year. To eat it, snap off the prickers and peel. Don't forget to suck the juice from each one—that's where the flavor is." She sucked at the end of a pricker like it was a crab leg.

"I find blessedbes taste like mint. The flavor varies from person to person, though. It adapts to whatever is most pleasing to your palate. Some say they taste lemon or basil. Reuel tastes escargot. Sounds gross for a fruit if you ask me. Go on. Try one! But don't scoff them all!"

Everyone reached for a blessedbe and pricked themselves on the long dark thorns.

Truman found the fruit peeled like a lychee.

"I taste red wine," Esmeralda said as she downed the juices from a pricker.

Vedrò eagerly snapped one from the bush and bit into a pricker with an audible crunch. "Ooh! Mine tastes like chili peppers," he said, his tongue sticking out like a dog.

"I taste... cinnamon," Truman said. A memory stirred inside him but did not come.

The voyagers gargled words of admiration as they popped more and more blessedbes into their mouths.

"Let's keep walking," said Angenciel.

As the group weaved through the orchard, they heard something rustling around the corner. At the heart of the orchard, Ereus sat in front of a marble piano. It was no ordinary piano. Instead of having only one row of eighty-eight keys, it was stacked with six rows. Each row was at a different angle, giving the piano a hexagonal shape.

When he saw them approaching, Ereus began playing a melody.

"*Nuvole bianche*," said Esmeralda, "Ludovico Einaudi, an Italian pianist and composer."

"Oh la la! You like your Italian men, no?" Vedrò said, smirking.

Angenciel shushed them.

"Cherry adores music," Ereus said over his shoulder. "We often use music to communicate to Cherry that it's time to go."

As notes filled the air, Cherry stood up and began to flap her great, wondrous wings. Truman felt not the slightest movement beneath his feet. Nevertheless, he clung to a tree.

"No need," Ereus said. "The force field retains our center of gravity."

And just like that, Cherry took off into the heavens, flying through the swirly Rainbow Row. Colors dispersed around the dragon in great ribbons.

The voyagers stood upright as if they weren't on the back of a flying dragon.

"This is the best seat in the house!" Ereus said, gesturing to the dip in Cherry's wing.

The voyagers peeked over the dip and saw the Earth begin to shrink. Baby blues faded into a refined sapphire. Desert sands stirred into white clouds. Waves of trees grew into continents. Truman felt terrified but also free in the bountiful sky that soon became the fabric of space.

Angenciel took an eager inhale and hollered, "Mercury, here we come!"

Chapter 6

The Dragon's Back Trail

T he Moon was barren, and Earth was now a dot on the horizon.

Rainbow Row unraveled before Cherry, guiding the dragon toward their first destination.

"Mercury is a measly one hundred and twenty-two million miles from Earth," Angenciel said nonchalantly. "We'll be there by nine in the morning. Tomorrow, you'll have three lectures: Worlds Cultures, Astrobiology, and Interplanetary Technologies. Be out of the cabin by 08:50, sharp."

"How will we know the time?" asked Schmidt. "Is there even time in space?"

"Of course, there's time in space!" exclaimed Ereus. "It's all relative. We keep track with these bad boys." He opened the piano bench and pulled out a box of black watches. "These are called Wylaways' Worldswide Wristwatches! Phew, what a tongue twister!" He passed them out.

Truman examined the watch curiously, flipping it over in his hands. The strap was normal, but the face was odd. Instead of hours and minutes, there were planets, moons, stars, and asteroids. Truman recognized Saturn by its rings. He spotted Earth and its cratered Moon. The Sun sat at the center of the watch's face. And next to every celestial body was a dainty knob.

"To know the time," Ereus said, holding up his wrist, "you press the button that corresponds to whichever world you're currently on. The watch will calculate your approximate location on that world and display the time over the drawing of the Sun. Because every world in our Solar System rotates at its own speed, some worlds have fewer hours in the day than Earth, while others have more. A couple of them even have much, *much* more! On Cherry, we'll be running on a twenty-four-hour clock, like Earth. At the top of the watch, there's a setting for Cherry."

Truman saw, beneath the topmost knob, a small, cramped drawing of Cherry. He pressed the button, and the watch flashed: *18:05.*

Dinner time, he thought.

"Since it's been a long day of traveling for most of you, let's end the day here and take the rest of the night easy," said Ereus. "I believe dinner is ready, no?"

"Yes," said Angenciel. "It was sent to us five minutes ago."

"Sent?" Vedrò said, raising a brow.

"Yes, *sent*. The Nutrition Unit and Transport, also known as the Nut, is responsible for sending us food throughout our journey. Fresh, nutritious, and homemade!"

Angenciel led the voyagers back to the cabin, where a table now sat, laden with curries, naan, and lassi. Though they had just eaten a bunch of fruit earlier, everyone's stomach growled at the sight.

"Looks like it's Indian tonight!" someone said with delight.

Before Angenciel could tell them to dig in, the nine voyagers sprinted toward the plates stacked at the end of the buffet, eagerly loading up whatever caught their eyes.

"Me first!" Vedrò called, jostling the others and passing Truman a dish.

Thanks to Lonely's Academy, a school where students from all over the world came to study, Truman had become acquainted with international cuisines. He fixed himself a plate of chicken vindaloo and garlic naan, snagged himself a mango lassi, and took a seat next to Vedrò.

They ate around a campfire Falsmira had kindled.

"If dinner is like this every night," Vedrò said, sputtering grains of rice, "I'm going to love it here!"

"Didn't your parents teach you to chew with your mouth closed?" Esmeralda said, wiping her shirt.

Vedrò stuck out his curried tongue and guffawed at her repulsion.

As they stuffed themselves, Truman learned the names and wills of all the other voyagers.

"My name is Yari Tajiri," a dark-haired Japanese girl said, bowing slightly. Her topknot and undercut, paired with ripped fishnets and scuffed Doc Martens, gave her a punk rock edge. "I'm an *immortal*." Calmly, she stabbed her fork into her thigh.

The others flinched, but Yari didn't even blink. They gawked, wide-eyed, as the four bloody holes in her leg gradually vanished.

"Wicked, I know," she said casually, returning to her tikka masala.

"I'm Letsatsi Khoza," said a tall South African girl with a pixie cut. She wore bright overalls that matched her easy smile. "I'm a *lightbearer*. I haven't learned how to control my wattage yet, so I'll only show you a bit. I wouldn't want to blind you."

She rolled up her pant leg, revealing her ankle, which shimmered like a diamond catching sunlight. A brilliant glow pulsed from her skin. Then, as quickly as it appeared, she covered it, exhaling like someone winded after a sprint.

"Even a little takes a lot out of me. Most of my light concentrates in my legs."

Esmeralda passed her a cup of water.

"Name's Schmidt," interjected the German boy. "I'm a *fleferro*, which means I have the will to manipulate metals solely with my mind." He held up his fork and narrowed his eyes at it. Nothing happened. After a minute, the utensil bent slightly forward. He wiped sweat from his brow. "I'm still learning."

Vedrò, Esmeralda, and Style shared their wills as well.

Truman tried conjuring a stream of water, but all he could muster was a droplet so small no one could see it.

"I'm Sweta Anand," said a short Nepali girl. She wore a thin ruby scarf and matching trousers. "I'm a *flutterby*, which means I can talk to plants."

"Really?" said Vedrò. "What are the cherry blossoms saying?!"

As Sweta listened to a breeze, the shy girl next to Esmeralda left for the bathroom.

"They find us curious," said Sweta. "They think our hair is foliage."

They all laughed and slumped onto the ground with satisfied bellies.

"Now that we've finished dinner," said Angenciel, "you're free to do as you wish. Since we have a big day tomorrow, I recommend resting as much as possible. Feel free to explore Cherry. She has a lot to offer. Breakfast is at eight o'clock Cherry-time. We arrive at nine! They'll be reminders on your watches."

"Also," hissed Falsmira, "we have some ground rules. Rule number one: curfew is midnight every night. Anyone out past that will receive detention! Rule number two: never leave Cherry without a chaperon. Understood? Good. Off you go."

Everyone dispersed.

They had several hours before curfew. Truman had to double-check his watch to be sure.

"I wanna explore Cherry!" he said to Vedrò. "Care to join me? I believe there's a trail over there."

Vedrò nodded and lethargically got to his feet.

The boys went around the lake, dodging unexpected geysers, and saw a herd of deer grazing in a field.

The light emanating from Rainbow Row began to dim as if the force field had an Earth sunrise-sunset feature.

While ambling around, Truman told Vedrò about PSA and the societal suspicion of his family.

"Is it going to be weird having your sister as a mentor?" asked Vedrò.

Truman shrugged.

"It is suspicious, though," Vedrò said. "I mean, I'm the only one in my family who is an alien. So, how can your entire family be alien?"

"Well, not everyone in my family is an alien. My little sister Minli isn't." He stopped to ponder. "Do you think I should ask Esmeralda what she thinks? She and Angenciel are both aliens. Maybe she knows something I don't."

"Maybe."

Truman's gaze fell to the edge of the pathway. He saw odd flowers dying in the shadow of a cherry blossom. They looked like shrunken skulls.

"What are those?" asked Vedrò.

"They're called *Antirrhinum majus*," said a voice behind a tree, "also known as dragon flowers."

It was the girl with bangs. Her hair was black and silky, and her face round and soft. She wore an oversized hoodie and tucked her hands in her sleeves.

"They're my favorite," she said. "They don't grow in Yunnan. My yéyé, or grandpa, used to travel a lot. One time, he brought home dragon flowers from the Americas for me. He knew I loved flowers. These are much bigger than the ones he gave me. I wish he could see them." She realized she was rambling and stopped.

She bent down and plucked a skull from a stem.

"I'm Halle Xióng by the way." She gave the boys a polite nod, avoiding their eyes. "I'm a *serena*. I can calm stressful situations. I know—it's a lame will."

"Doesn't sound lame at all," Truman said kindly. "Nice to meet you, Halle. I'm Truman, and this is Vedrò."

He watched her anxiously twiddle her bangs.

"So, how are you handling all these, uh, changes?" Truman asked.

She shrugged and pulled her sleeves down further.

"For a serena, you seem pretty nervous," Vedrò blurted.

Truman elbowed him.

"What?!"

Halle giggled.

"I mean, come on. It's ironic she's a serena and a bit… anxious." He met Halle's gaze. "I could be wrong!" he added quickly, hoping he hadn't offended her.

Halle laughed it off. "No, you're right. It *is* ironic. Sometimes, my anxiety makes it hard for me to channel my will."

"I get it," said Vedrò. "I mean, how can I predict the future, but I couldn't predict all of this?" He swept his arms around at Cherry. "So what if we can't control our wills right now? Not all of us are perfect little know-it-alls like that Esmeralda."

"Yes, I am a know-it-all," said a voice behind another tree. Esmeralda stepped forward. "But that's because I have to work harder than you two boys combined if I want to make it in this world—something you'll never understand."

She spun on her heel and walked away.

"That wasn't nice, Vedrò," Halle said with a frown, trailing after Esmeralda.

"I know name-calling is rude," Vedrò sighed, turning to Truman. "But it's true, is it not?"

Truman looked down at his feet. "Maybe. But just because we think something is true doesn't mean it needs to be said."

☆ ☆ ☆ ☆ ☆ ☆

When the force field dimmed to total darkness, the stars above shone crystal clear.

The boys stretched out on a bed of fallen petals. Somewhere in the distance, grasshoppers chirped.

"I think that's the Big Dipper there," Truman said, pointing upward. "Actually, I'm not sure. Everything looks different out here in space."

"That's the Little Dipper. Over there is the Big Dipper." Vedrò pointed to the correct constellation. "Astronomy was always my favorite subject in school."

"I used to stargaze back on the mountain all the time." He looked over at Vedrò and noticed a sad look on his face. "What're you thinking about?"

"My sister," he croaked. "Just wondering what happens once we die."

"What do you think happens?"

"Maybe she's up there, looking down on me." He gestured to the stars.

Their watches vibrated.

"Oh shoot, we're out past curfew," said Truman. "Our first night too!"

"It's not a far walk from here. If we run, we won't be caught."

They stumbled over roots and rocks and found their way back. As they headed up the cabin stairs, they heard footsteps.

Reuel stepped out from the darkness, a glowing bleeding heart floating beside her.

"Hey, Truman," she called. "Can we chat? It's okay, Vedrò. You go in."

Vedrò nodded and stepped inside.

"Am I in trouble?" asked Truman.

"No," she said, "but you're lucky I'm on curfew duty tonight. If it were Falsmira, you'd be in for a lecture. Besides, you're not the only ones past curfew. Halle and Esmeralda are still out. They're smart cookies from what I've seen and heard. I'm sure they'll be back any moment."

Truman glanced at the glowing bleeding heart. "How'd you keep the flower from floating too high? I thought they were for emergencies only."

"Oh, they are," Reuel replied. "But if you ever explore Cherry late at night, I recommend using one of these bad boys as a lantern. They're enchanted to follow you wherever you wish. When you lift it high into the air, that's when it floats above the trees. But if you wish for it to stay by your side, it will. It's a nifty trick I picked up during my first voyage on Cherry. Isn't Cherry just full of wonders?! Anyway, I just wanted to ask: how's my necklace working for you?"

"*Your* necklace?"

"Yeah, the one I made you." She nodded to the gold chain hanging from Truman's neck.

"*You* made this?!"

"Yes, I crafted it from pierre plants, also known as rock flowers! They're one of Aether's fathoms. You'll learn more about them tomorrow. I learned how to grow pierre plants during my apprenticeship. The gold is amberbush, which is a type of pierre plant. They're tricky to work with, but with time and care, the finished product can be rather beautiful. Do you like it?"

"I love it. Thank you so much, Reuel!" Truman hugged her.

"But it works, right? It blocks others' emotions?"

"Yes, it's perfect!"

"Good! But make sure you take it off every now and then. It's good to practice your will. Being an empath can be quite handy too. You'll always know where people stand with you."

"I never thought about it that way."

Reuel smiled and gave him another hug. "You go rest now. We have a big day tomorrow. Head inside with the girls."

Truman turned and saw Halle and Esmeralda walking toward the cabin. He followed, fingers brushing his necklace, and caught Esmeralda's eyes. They were puffy and red.

Chapter 7

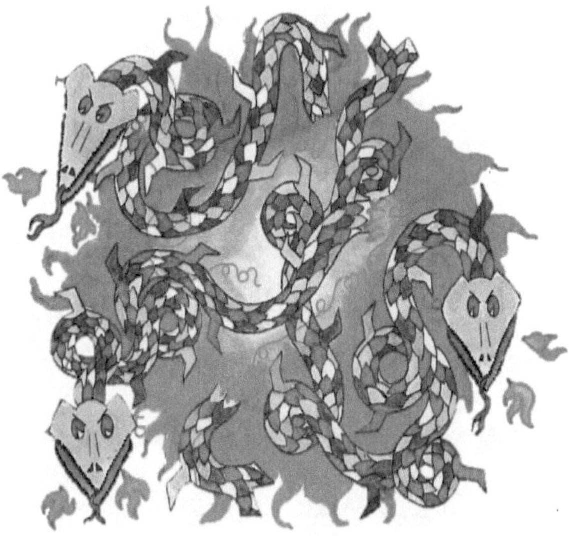

Wonders & Fathoms

Truman undressed and climbed into his waterbed.

In a dream, he found himself standing in Cherry's orchard, eyeing a plump Ambrosia apple. He took a bite and tasted raw honey. Juice trickled down his chin and hands, but the liquid felt too thick to be juice. The scent of iron assaulted his nostrils, and the taste turned tart and metallic. Something moved in his mouth. He looked down and saw blood and maggots oozing from the apple's core. His hands had lost their fairness and now bore Vedrò's golden undertones. Maggots crawled down his throat.

He jolted awake, heart pounding.

"Truman!" Vedrò wailed, jumping out of bed, his hair disheveled. "We're late!"

Their watches read five past nine.

Style's bed was already neatly made.

Truman quickly threw on his necklace and pants, then followed Vedrò down the rope bridge.

"Nice of you to show up," Falsmira hissed, thrusting notebooks and pens into their hands.

Esmeralda, who had extras of each, shot them a glare from the front of the pack.

"Now that we're all here, follow me!" Ereus hollered.

"Better grab a peach since you missed breakfast," Reuel whispered to the boys.

The two ate their peaches as they climbed off Cherry. It wasn't until his feet touched the rocky, barren crater that Truman remembered they were now on another world. Mercury. The crater stretched endlessly, merging into Cherry's lively tail. The juxtaposition was death and life in a tango.

As they walked beyond Cherry's force field, the planet's torrid temperature struck them like a wall.

Vedrò and Truman, both wearing pants and long sleeves, fanned themselves with their notebooks.

"Mercury," Angenciel started, "the planet of mind and knowledge, ruled by the versatile Gemini and meticulous Virgo. Our wondrous journey begins with the smallest and innermost of the four Rocky Realms." She led them to the rim of the crater. "Because Mercury is the closest to the Sun, the arid planet has little to no atmosphere to protect from the searing heat, as you can probably tell. It could be worse, much worse! Thanks to the Savvies Station, we have developed an ingenious force field that acts similarly to Earth's atmosphere, moderating the planet's temperature."

Truman and Vedrò exchanged glances, already sweating.

"But don't let the heat deceive you," Angenciel continued. "Right now, it's frigid on Mercury's other hemisphere. This is due to the planet's two seasons: shine and shadow! *Shine* occurs in the area where the Sun is shining upon Mercury, while *shadow* occurs where the Sun is not. To simplify, shine is the extreme version of Earth's summer, whereas shadow is the extreme version of Earth's winter."

The word *winter* teased Truman and Vedrò as sweat dripped from their noses.

"The reason there are only two seasons is because Mercury's axis is almost perfectly upright, and it rotates very slowly. A day on Mercury has 1,408 hours. That's about fifty-nine Earth days. But Mercury orbits the Sun faster than any other planet. A year here is only eighty-eight Earth days. In other words, while the time of day passes slowly here, you age much quicker."

"But how do you keep track of time?" asked Vedrò.

Esmeralda rolled her eyes from the front of the group.

"With our watches, of course!" said Ereus. "On the face of your watch, the worlds are in order from Mercury to the Kuiper Belt, with Cherry on top. Just remember the order of the worlds, and you'll know which button to press. I have a little song to help you remember. It goes: Mercury, Venus, Earth then Mars, Jupiter, Saturn, and Uranus, Neptune, Pluto all go around the Sun, WOOH-HOOH!"

Vedrò laughed under his breath.

Truman pressed the button next to the depiction of Mercury, and *1264:00* illuminated on the screen.

"It's going to be a *long* day," said Angenciel. "Let's keep moving!" She walked on, speaking with the confidence of a seasoned tour guide.

Truman felt like he was on a field trip. A very strange but wickedly cool field trip.

As Angenciel lectured on Worlds Cultures, Truman couldn't help but think ahead, eager to reach the Moon and meet his family.

But when he looked around, he noticed his peers were taking notes. He clicked his pen and began jotting things down, sweat dampening his notebook as they trudged up an incline.

"The most populated areas on Mercury are Violetteville, the Beethoven Basin, and the Carnegie Rupes," Angenciel continued. "Violetteville holds the Savvies Station and the Firm of Fleferros, and it spans the largest impact crater in our Solar System. That's where we're headed now."

Truman could hear Esmeralda scribbling away, her pen moving fast.

"After Violetteville, we'll head to the Beethoven Basin, home to musical omnihealers, aliens with the ability to heal various afflictions through music."

"Like an advanced form of music therapy?" asked Esmeralda.

"Precisely." Angenciel beamed. "We'll end our Mercurial visit at the Carnegie Rupes. That's our itinerary."

Reuel then chimed in. "Alright, you lot, only a quarter mile more, and we'll be in Violetteville! Just a warning: it's going to get very bright in a few minutes. Right now, we can't see the Sun because we're at the northern pole in a hollow basin.

Once we arrive at the top of this hill, though, we'll bask in all the Sun's glory!"

Truman scanned the sky for the Sun but saw nothing but far-away stars. He didn't see a moon either. If it hadn't been for the glow of Cherry and Rainbow Row, the group would've been in sheer darkness.

"Several years ago, during my apprenticeship," Reuel said aloud, "I came to Mercury as a prospective astrobiologist to study the planet's famous living lava that thrive within the northern volcanic plains. It was dangerous but thrilling."

"What's living lava?" asked Vedrò.

"Living lava *are*—plural—ever-moving, amorphous blobs of lava that are literally alive and breathing. They're one of Aether's *marvels*. Marvels are magical, extraterrestrial lifeforms that exist throughout Aether, and—"

"So does that make us marvels too?" Vedrò interrupted, looking up from the chicken scratches he called notes. "You know, since we call ourselves aliens and have magical powers and all."

"That is a good question, Vedrò. The answer is no. Marvels are creatures and plants, not *Homo sapiens*. Now, where was I? Ah yes, so there are two types of marvels. We call them *fathoms* and *wonders*. Living lava are fathoms, which depend on atmospheric pressure to survive. Wonders do not. Wonders can actually *wander* around outer space without dying. It's one of their many facets that makes them so... curious."

The sky brightened with every step.

"Most astrobiologists, including myself, have spent years studying these wonders and fathoms. As your mentor, I'll introduce you to the seven wonders and all the fathoms. You've already met one of the wonders." She turned and looked at Cherry, who was snug in the crater, resting. "Cherry is one of the *Aristotelian dragons.*"

Truman looked up from his notes. *There are more dragons?!*

"We refer to them as Aristotelian because there are dragons of all four classical elements: earth, water, air, and fire. Cherry is the only known earth dragon in existence. She is undoubtedly the largest and most powerful of all marvels. She has mystical powers that are beyond alien comprehension. Yet, that hasn't stopped aliens from trying to manipulate and extort her powers. People have attempted to use her blood to create an elixir of life, mind-control her, and even tried to kill her to prove their willpower!"

"Not Cherry!" Halle squeaked.

"Don't worry. She can handle her own," Reuel said confidently, moving onward. "Like how Cherry is the only earth dragon in existence, there is also only one water dragon. Her name is Rosavoir. She's the guardian of the Neptunial Seas—"

"Okay, now you're just rubbing it in," Vedrò muttered, wiping his face onto his already damp shirt.

Reuel laughed. "There are also air dragons," she continued. "They're hidden in our winds and can only be seen by a willing eye. Most of the winged creatures live in the Uranian Skies. Finally, the fire dragons. They're more commonly known as the *Leonian dragons.* They're the most infamous of the four because they're the hardest to conceal, the least understood, and the deadliest."

"Why-y is that?" Halle stammered.

"Take a look for yourself." Reuel smiled as she reached the peak of the crater and gestured to something ahead. Sunshine rained on her shoulders, and knots of fire reflected in her eyes.

Truman followed in her shadow and saw it. How could he not? The Sun took up the entire sky. Daylight seemed infinite. There was not a cloud in the sky to hide an inch of the heavenly body. If it weren't for the protective force field and its many features, the group would've been annihilated.

As his eyes somehow adjusted, Truman noticed sun flares and prominences contorting and pouring out from the heart of the Solar System. He then realized they were not flares and prominences at all. They were serpentine dragons with scales like armor decorated with rubies and gold. Tendrils dangled from their bony cheeks. Their wings were rudder-shaped. Their tongues were forked.

The dragons writhed around and tore their way through the star, like a skein of worms in an apple.

Chapter 8

A Hundred Hairy Legs

T he fiery dragons froze the voyagers in their spot.

"Down there, you'll find Violetteville," Angenciel said, interrupting their collective awe. "Earthlings refer to the area as the Caloris Basin."

The Leonian dragons mesmerized Truman so completely that he hardly noticed the metropolis ahead. Thousands of bridges stretched into the city. Skyscrapers curled out from the ground like wrought iron. The city's most striking quality was its color—every building was dipped in purple. Streets flowed like red wine, and houses were painted mauve.

On the city's outskirts, Truman spotted a hundred hollow troughs fanning out from a desolate pit. The formation resembled a grotesque spider.

The group crossed a bridge, where cars with solar-paneled roofs staggered through traffic.

"Nearly everything in Aether runs on solar energy," said Ereus. "Lights, cars, the force field—all solar powered! The force field, need I remind you, provides all worlds with a protective atmosphere comparable to Earth's. While the field deflects most of the Sun's dangerous UV rays and heat waves, it traps just enough warmth for a comfortable, livable temperature."

Truman and Vedrò exchanged annoyed looks. Their shirts were drenched in sweat.

"With the help of air filters, like Ivies and Oaks and the Uranian Skies, the force field also provides oxygen and other gases necessary for life. It even provides rainfall!"

The boys licked their lips at the mention of rain.

"When the savvies first created the force field, the Illusory Fleet worked alongside them to install an invisibility feature. The feature prevents Earthlings from seeing our civilizations whenever they send their silly little flybys to capture images of our worlds.

"Another feature of the force field is its artificial magnetic field. It protects us from powerful solar winds and prevents the alien-induced atmosphere from ever 'leaking out.' Isn't that neat?! Of course, the savvies couldn't have done it without Mercury's Firm of Fleferros. Fleferros, like Schmidt here, are aliens who have the will to manipulate metals and magnetic fields."

It became clear to Truman and the other voyagers that Ereus was a complete science geek.

"And remember yesterday, when I told you Cherry runs on a twenty-four-hour clock?" Ereus continued. "Well, savvies and torcrons have been trying to implement the twenty-four-hour feature across every force field, but with no success. Each planet's orbit is unique, so it's more complicated than you'd think. Since Cherry is flying us through Aether, it's easier to fabricate an artificial day on her back. But the savvies never stop trying to improve the force field. So, maybe one day."

He paused to give the voyagers time to write. Esmeralda—first to look up from her well-organized notes—cracked her knuckles and flipped to a blank page.

The group was now well into the city, engulfed in purple.

"Every world in Aether requires a custom force field tending to its terrestrial needs," said Ereus. "For example, Mercury's magnetic field is naturally much weaker than Earth's. To make Mercury livable, the savvies designed a force field that strengthens the planet's magnetosphere. Jupiter's field, on the other hand, is naturally much stronger. So, the savvies did the opposite and designed a force field that weakens its magnetosphere."

While Ereus droned on, Truman turned his attention to the people in the streets. They wore the most eclectic ensembles from all over Earth—traditional Indonesian and Swedish garments, French and Korean fashion, and Peruvian and Ethiopian patterns. Some dressed in animal prints—cheetah, zebra, and tiger. Others donned marvel prints—Cherry and Leonian.

Truman liked what he saw.

Out of the corner of his eye, near a dilapidated building called the Heavenly Hotel, he caught a sudden flash of light.

What was that? He looked around.

"Tru!" Reuel hollered. "Hurry up!"

Assuming the flash was merely a car, he jogged to catch up with the group.

"Arguably the two most famous savvies who ever lived were Heure and Ora Wylaway," Ereus continued. "Together, as husband and wife *and* partners in business, Heure and Ora developed the first edition of Wylaways' Worldswide Wristwatches! The Assembly mass-produced the clever invention to help interplanetary business and political discourse. Some aliens live on one planet but work on another, so having a universal way to keep time really helps. Plus, it ensures people don't miss the breakfast special at Lǐyú's on Neptune! I don't know why they ever stop serving breakfast—it's what they're known for!"

Angenciel coughed.

"Sorry, I digress," said Ereus. "Anyway, let me show you around the Savvies Station." He led the group into a massive building made of tinted purple glass.

☆ ☆ ☆ ☆ ☆ ☆

Throughout the tour, the voyagers learned about the inner workings of the force field and Wylaways' Worldswide Wristwatches. They were introduced to other odd contraptions under development, like a telescope that could see galaxies one trillion light-years away. They also glimpsed a starship and fireproof spacesuits being constructed for something called the *Martian Militia*.

For the rest of the day and the days that followed, the group bounced all over Violetteville.

One day, the mentors brought them to the shopping district. All the boutiques were promoting astronaut boots. Esmeralda bought more pens.

Another day, they meandered through the food district. A paifang at the entrance read *The Dragon's Belly*. The place bustled with food trucks, restaurants, and vendors in stained aprons. The aroma of sizzling meats and spices clouded the air. A café boasted about its "Aether-renowned espresso." The voyagers' mouths watered at the sight of all the foreign foods, especially the candy-like rainbow-colored pasta at a fancy Italian-Venusian restaurant.

From a food truck shaped like Cherry, an old man hollered, "Get Mercury's planetary dish here! Fried butterflies fresh from the fryer! Delicious when dipped in a cup of freshly brewed blossom soup!"

"Fried butterflies?" Vedrò said questionably. "Sounds… appetizing?"

Angenciel bought them all a bag. Some of the voyagers refused to try. Truman and Halle thought that the fried butterflies tasted like cheesy Doritos. Vedrò gobbled them up.

On another day, after leaving the Firm of Fleferros, the group wandered onto a street where volunteer citizens were re-erecting lampposts and clearing debris.

"What happened here?" asked Esmeralda.

The street was mutilated from end to end. Scorch marks climbed up the building walls. Tire tracks stretched across the street. Shards of glass from a car window dappled the purple pavement like a mosaic.

"A couple days ago," said Reuel, "a Leonian dragon escaped the Sun and came barreling down on Violetteville. Terrorized half the city, she did! But don't worry—she's been captured and safely returned home."

"They can do that?!" said Halle. "Escape the Sun?!"

"Yes, but it's a rare occurrence. The star *is* their natural habitat. From what I read, the dragon only escaped because the person on watch in the northern solar hemisphere provoked her with ice beams." She shook her head disapprovingly. "He was fired, of course."

☆ ☆ ☆ ☆ ☆ ☆

Ever since Reuel mentioned that Leonian dragons could escape the Sun, Halle had been worried. She couldn't sleep, eat, or focus on the lessons. She kept looking up at the sky, praying that today wouldn't be the day.

To ease Halle's worries, Reuel brought the voyagers to the peak of a hill and handed them all special binoculars that, without frying their eyeballs, allowed them to observe Leonian dragons up close.

Halle found most of them to be gentle. It was only their fiery exteriors that made them seem scary—a perfect case of don't judge a book by its cover.

"I mean, Reuel *did* say they're the deadliest of the Aristotelian dragons, and one *did* burn up half a city," Vedrò blurted without thinking.

Everyone shot him a glare. Truman elbowed him in the ribs.

"Ouch!" he uttered, holding his side and catching Halle's frightened gaze. "But, yeah, totally! They're obviously gentle creatures!"

Esmeralda rolled her eyes.

Halle inhaled.

With the binoculars, the voyagers could also see all the watch stations around the Sun. There were too many to count.

"See? You have nothing to worry about," said Reuel. "The dragon was only angry because she was provoked. That's something we could all relate to, I think. When treated poorly, one acts out."

Halle looked again through her binoculars and saw two Leonian dragons entwined, asleep and snuggling. She relaxed her shoulders and smiled to yourself.

☆ ☆ ☆ ☆ ☆ ☆

"If you recall from our first day of lessons," Angenciel said on their last night in Violetteville, "I told you lot that the Sun sets every fifty-nine Earth days on Mercury."

The voyagers were sprawled out in Cherry's lavender field, tired after Falsmira's lecture on Mercury's meteorite and terraformation history and Ereus' lecture on Einstein's theory of relativity.

"Today," continued Angenciel, "marks the fifty-ninth day on the Mercurial calendar… Ereus, can you please shut off Cherry's force field?"

"Already did!"

"Perfect."

The sky began to dim. And with the dimming came a bitter coldness.

The mentors craned their necks upward. The voyagers, confused, followed suit.

Then—it happened.

A dazzling light filled the sky in a dreamlike wave. Wave after wave rolled in until Cherry was cast in a halo of amber. The night sky, once blank, had become a watercolor painting of streaming yellows and oranges.

"This natural phenomenon is called the *Aurora Mercurialis*," Angenciel said. "Since Mercury is in close proximity to the Sun, it experiences heavy solar winds that buffet Mercury's magnetosphere, naturally giving off sodium atoms. When light passes through the sodium debris, the interaction releases photons, producing a yellow-orange glow." She turned to the voyagers. "Does anyone remember the names of Mercury's seasons?"

"Shine and shadow," said Esmeralda.

"Correct." Angenciel nodded approvingly at her daughter. "We've already experienced shine, which is characterized by the presence of the Sun and warmth. Shadow, on the other hand, is marked by the presence of the Aurora Mercurialis and coldness."

"But wait!" Esmeralda interjected, pulling out her notebook and swiftly flipping through the pages. When she found what she was looking for, she peered back up with a skeptical expression on her face. "A few days ago, Ereus said Mercury's force field has an artificial magnetic field that protects us from solar winds. Wouldn't that eliminate the Aurora Mercurialis?"

As if on cue, Ereus leapt to his feet and said, "That is some grade-A logic right there! Very smart, Esmeralda. Very smart indeed!"

She blushed.

"And you're right," he continued. "There would be no Aurora Mercurialis. In fact, that's exactly what happened when the savvies first installed Mercury's force field. Once they learned what they had done, they worked out the kinks and managed to bring back the Aurora and keep the artificial magnetic field. I'm sure Angenciel, mentor of Worlds Cultures, would agree: it's worth preserving each world's natural uniqueness as much as possible, while still creating a livable atmosphere."

Truman, enchanted by the orange sky, barely listened. He let his brown eyes glaze over and float upward into the long-lost world of familiar color.

Hours passed. Only Vedrò and Halle remained at his side.

Truman rubbed his arms for warmth. "Do you guys want to head back?"

They nodded, as if waking from a dream.

When they arrived at the cabin, they saw Humzah and Esmeralda around the firepit. The pair spoke in rapid French.

Humzah waved them over. "Would you guys like to hear a *spooky story*?" he asked in a hushed tone.

"What's it about?" Vedrò asked, settling near the crackling fire.

"The second wonder of Aether," he whispered.

"Is that the Aurora Mercurialis?"

"Really, Vedrò?" Esmeralda scoffed, rolling her eyes. "All the wonders of Aether are *creatures*. Not solar wind."

"Must you always be like that?" Vedrò muttered.

Esmeralda stood and stalked away.

"Does she not care to know what the second wonder is?"

"I *know* what the second wonder is!" Esmeralda bellowed from the stairs.

"I read about it in *The Wonders and Fathoms of Aether!*" She slammed the cabin doors behind her.

"So, uh… Humzah, what's the second wonder?" Truman asked awkwardly.

Humzah looked around and lowered his voice. "Well, it's right here on Mercury. But there's a reason the mentors don't mention it during this part of the journey. They're afraid that if we tell you guys about the demon while we're here, someone might try to find it."

"Demon?!" Halle gasped.

"Yes. A very dangerous one too!"

"What is it?!" Vedrò asked.

"It's a species that lived on Mercury long before us. They were the adversaries of the Assembly during the Webbed War of '44. Fearsome, thousand-pound, fifty-foot-tall spiders with a hundred hairy legs!"

Giant spiders? Truman thought. *How… derivative.*

"And their venom?" Humzah continued. "It causes intense psychotic delusions." He widened and crossed his eyes. "The name of the demons?" he paused for dramatic effect. *"The Arachnoids!"*

Halle squealed and trembled.

"Years ago, the part of the Caloris Basin where the species once thrived took a devastating blow. A giant meteorite struck near Violetteville, just southwest of the hill we hiked on our first day. The entire species nearly became extinct. Only one survived. It now inhabits the impact crater. The crater itself resembles—"

"A spider," Truman murmured, remembering the sight.

"Exactly," said Humzah. "A cruel, ironic Universe we live in, isn't it?"

"Why are you telling us this if we're not supposed to know yet?" Vedrò asked.

"Well, come on! Who in their right mind would ever go looking for such a thing? None of you are that stupid."

"Isn't it impossible anyhow?" Halle asked curiously. "I mean, this Spider Cavity doesn't have a force field around it, does it? Because if not, we'd die, right?"

"The Assembly installed one during the Webbed War so we could fight there. After the War, they shut it down. But recently, they turned it back on because astrobiologists have been trying to get snapshots of the last living Arachnoid in its natural habitat. But it hasn't been easy for them because the thing is just too quick. They say they're going to pay a pretty penny to whoever gets that snapshot first. I don't understand why they need the photograph, though. It's not like we don't have footage of the Arachnoids from the Webbed War! I suppose it's because this is the last living Arachnoid, making it unique. Anyway," he yawned, "it's time for bed, guys. Make sure you're in before midnight. Falsmira is on duty tonight, and she has eyes like a hawk!"

Humzah left for the Dragon's Back Trail.

Truman checked his watch and saw that it was only eleven.

As the three sat there around the dwindling fire, an idea came to Vedrò. "Guys, I bet we can find this spider!" He spoke in an excited whisper.

"Absolutely not!" Halle said hotly. "Are you mad?! We would die!"

"But think about the money we could get from one photo! With that kind of money, I could send Mamma more than she's ever dreamed of!"

"We don't have a camera, though," Truman pointed out.

"Yes, we do. I have a phone! I don't get service out here, but the camera works! If you bring your phone, we'd have double the chances!"

"I've never had a phone before," Truman admitted. "Never had the money for one."

"All the more reason to snap that photo!" Vedrò grinned, clapping him on the back.

"Guys," Halle said seriously, "don't be stupid! Is the risk of dying worth the money?"

Truman and Vedrò exchanged looks.

"We have powers," said Vedrò. "I should foresee the Arachnoid coming. And Truman should sense it. Worst comes to worst, he uses his aquaura will. Aquauric will?"

"Aquauric sounds nice!"

Halle, annoyed with the boys, leapt to her feet and stomped away.

"I'll get my phone," said Vedrò. "Be right back!"

Truman removed his necklace and put it in his pocket. He then grabbed a bleeding heart and snapped its petals. It floated beside him.

Vedrò returned with his phone. "Ready!"

Together, they dismounted Cherry, hearts pounding with a mix of fear and thrill.

Truman and Vedrò walked and walked until they reached the summit of the crater. They looked out over Violetteville in all its purple glory, then turned their eyes to the Spider Cavity. It was grim, a dark thorn in Violetteville's side.

They started down the hill. Fear crept in. Truman shivered twofold—once for himself and once for Vedrò. He itched to put his necklace back on.

They arrived at an opening to the Cavity. It stretched out before them, long and narrow like a trough.

"I-I can't believe you made me d-do this!" Vedrò stammered, his voice quivering.

"I didn't make you do this!"

"Well, I didn't t-think you'd actually agree to it!"

They stepped into the crater.

Vedrò felt the walls closing in on him and sank his nails into Truman's arm. Apart from the luminescence of the bleeding heart, only the Aurora Mercurialis and the stars above kept total darkness from consuming the boys.

They came to a fork in the path.

Vedrò gulped. "How much time do we have before curfew?"

Truman's watch read *13:00*.

"Hold on—the Cherry setting's not on." Truman pressed the button next to the figure of Cherry. The time adjusted to *11:30*. "We have time. Let's keep looking. Do you have your phone ready?"

Vedrò nodded and held up the Earthling device. "How much money do you think the photo will be worth?"

Truman didn't answer. He was sensing something odd. Familiar but odd. A wave of hopelessness washed over him. He felt lonelier than ever before. As if something—or someone—had left him. Abandoned him? It was a bleak feeling. Was this grief?

The loneliness was overwhelming. He leaned against the crater wall to steady himself.

Vedrò, on the other hand, froze. He was gripped by déjà-vu. But it was more than that—it felt like stepping back into a childhood nightmare. The passage ahead seemed to elongate. His knees wobbled.

"Everything in this Universe is precious yet evanescent," a shrill voice echoed. "Always hold what you cherish most close to your heart! You'll never know when your beloveds are slaughtered by the hands of imperialistic, bloodthirsty witches!"

The words reverberated off the trench walls, giving the impression that the speaker was omnipresent.

Truman tasted something bitter in his mouth and fought the urge to spit.

"You should not have come here," the voice clicked. "I LOATHE YOUR KIND!"

From behind the shadows of what looked like a wall, a grotesque, overgrown spider stomped forward on one hundred hairy legs. They were brown and arched over the boys like flying buttresses of a Gothic cathedral. The spider's eyes were dark and beady. Two were purple, six were black, all were fixed on the boys. Its fangs writhed and clicked, violet venom oozing from their tips and puddling on the crater floor.

It reeked of death.

Vedrò raised his camera. The flash went off just as he gagged at the stench. "Uh, it's disgusting!"

"IT?!" the Arachnoid spat. "I am a woman and have a name, thank you very much!" She lifted three of her massive legs and drove them straight through Vedrò's chest.

Chapter 9

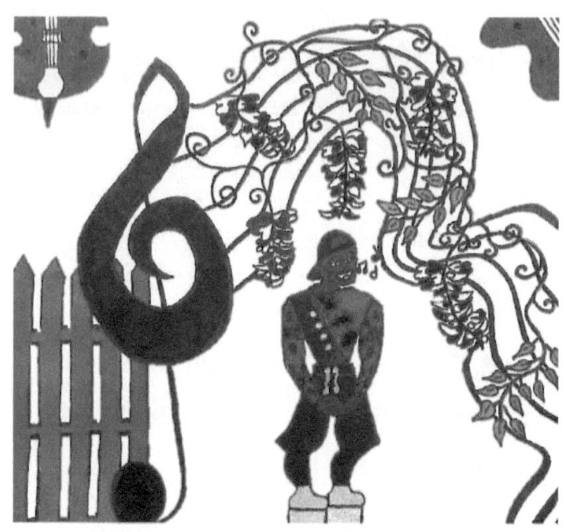

Warping & Omnihealing

V edrò blinked, déjà-vu heavy on his lids.

"RUN!" he screamed. If his prophetic will was correct, the second wonder of Aether was lurking behind the shadows, readying to kill.

Truman and Vedrò burst into a sprint, kicking up Mercurial pebbles.

The Arachnoid scurried after them.

Vedrò dropped his phone. Its flash went off. He didn't turn back.

A torrent of emotions consumed Truman—physical exertion, fear, heartache, vengeance, déjà-vu, and loneliness. It was too much. He tried to focus on something—anything— as he ran, but there was only crater.

They took a wrong turn and struck a wall, cornered.

"Thought you could outrun me in my own playing field, huh?" said the hundred-legged spider. Her voice was piercing. She steadied her scurry into a casual advance. Her fangs clicked.

"You know, everything in this Universe is precious yet evanescent. Always hold what you cherish most close to your heart! You'll never know when your beloveds are slaughtered by the hands of imperialistic, bloodthirsty—"

Suddenly, all of Truman's worries vanished. His racing heartbeat relaxed. A peaceful, auspicious silence filled the air. Vedrò felt it too. So did the spider.

The creature shuffled around in her spot, barely fitting between the trench walls. "Yummy," she growled. "More *witches* to munch on!"

"Halle!" said Truman and Vedrò.

Through the spider's dense, hairy legs, Truman caught sight of two figures on the other side. One was unmistakably Halle—he glimpsed her stringy bangs and knew the tranquility came from her serenial will.

The second figure glowed like a star. Silver hair whipped in the wind. Blue eyes, vacant. She hovered in midair, angelically demonic.

"Get out of here!" she screamed.

They recognized the French accent.

Her voice was strong and beguiling.

"I said, GET OUT!" Esmeralda screamed again, louder.

The Arachnoid's beady eyes glazed over. Her legs staggered. Without a word or a click, she crawled away in a daze.

"We did it!" Halle cried as Esmeralda collapsed to the ground.

Truman and Vedrò ran to her.

"We have to go!" said Vedrò. "If that thing returns, we're dead!"

They hoisted Esmeralda and carried her back to Cherry. With his free hand, Vedrò raised the bleeding heart into the air.

☆ ☆ ☆ ☆ ☆ ☆

Angenciel nestled Esmeralda into her goblin shark waterbed and kissed her forehead. Truman, Vedrò, and Halle babbled on about the Arachnoid, talking over each other, waking Letsatsi, who shared a treehouse with the girls.

"Apologies, Miss Khoza," said Reuel. "It's an emergency."

She turned to Truman. "Who told you about the Arachnoid? No one was supposed to find out until after Mercury!"

None of them spoke. They didn't want to rat out Humzah.

"I did," Esmeralda said groggily, eyes half-open.

Truman and Vedrò exchanged confused looks.

"I read about it in *The Wonders and Fathoms of Aether*," Esmeralda continued. "I wanted to see if it was real. Thought I could hold my own… I was wrong. Thank goodness the others came after me."

Truman and Vedrò gaped at her.

"*Mon bébé*," Angenciel said soothingly, "what were you thinking? You could've died!"

"Should we call the Hive?" Truman heard Ereus ask.

"No, she'll be fine. No major injuries," Angenciel replied.

"She's lucky," said Reuel.

"Lucky?!" Falsmira spat. "She's foolish! FOOLISH! All of them should be punished for staying out past curfew, stepping off Cherry without a mentor, *and* doing something as dense and reckless as searching for a killer Arachnoid!"

She glared at the four of them, then stormed out of the treehouse. Ereus followed.

"Come on, boys," Reuel said, showing them out.

"I'll stay here for the night," said Angenciel.

Reuel nodded.

Outside their treehouse, Reuel whispered, "So, what really happened out there?"

"What do you mean?" Vedrò asked, feigning ignorance.

"Based on your facial expressions, what Esmeralda said was a lie. So, spill it."

Neither of them answered.

"Well," she said, "if you're not going to tell me, I'll say just this: if Esmeralda took the blame back there, which I feel she did, I dare say you owe her."

☆ ☆ ☆ ☆ ☆ ☆

Truman and Vedrò slept restlessly, jerking awake the next morning from nightmares filled with thick webs and scurrying hairy legs. Vedrò shot upright screaming.

"Your sister was right, Truman," Vedrò said as he changed into his clothes. "We do owe Esmeralda. Without her, I would've died. I know so. I had a vision of my death."

Truman's gaze drifted to Style, who was fixing his hair in the mirror. The three of them left the cabin and stepped out into a sky bright with solar dragons.

"Where's the Aurora Mercurialis?" said Vedrò.

Truman shrugged. "Angenciel said shadow season just started, so it should be here."

Though he'd loved the Aurora Mercurialis, Truman was thrilled to see the Leonian dragons back in the sky.

At the breakfast table, the boys gorged themselves on bubur ayam, a warm mixture of shredded chicken and rice porridge. Across the table sat Esmeralda and Halle. Halle waved. Esmeralda looked away.

The boys shifted awkwardly. Neither of them knew how to thank Esmeralda for taking the blame *and* saving their lives. A simple "thank you" didn't feel sufficient.

When their watches struck eleven, Angenciel stood.

"I know you lot *loved* the Aurora Mercurialis," she said, "but earlier this morning, Cherry flew us to the Beethoven Basin on Mercury's other hemisphere. Today, Ereus will begin teaching you about vortexes and the act of warping. After that, our guest speaker, Dr. Nayelo Noxthomas, will introduce you to musical omnihealing. Now, has everyone finished breakfast? Good. Follow me."

They dismounted Cherry in a small town with a single main street. Quaint manors lined either side, each with a well-tended garden. Among every garden were jagged, glassy flowers that looked more like blown crystal than plants.

"These are called pierre plants," said Reuel. "They're a fathom—living, growing rocks!"

Truman clutched his necklace and wondered how Esmeralda had ever turned one of those glassy flowers into a chain.

"This here," Ereus said, gesturing to a black four-columned portico, "is a vortex. It's how most aliens travel through space. The process is called *warping*. Warping takes focus. Lose is and you might end up transporting yourself to someplace other than where you initially intended to go.

"It's easiest to warp to vortexes you've already visited. That's what you'll practice in your first trimester. Later, when you become more proficient at warping, you'll be able to warp to vortexes where you have never been. That won't be until the second trimester. And during your final trimester, when you become experts, you'll be able to warp anywhere without the aid of a second vortex.

"But for now, don't worry. We'll start easy, with three beginner-friendly vortexes inside this house."

He led them into a neighboring manor. Inside stood three porticoes arranged in a triangle. One was red, another yellow, and the last blue.

"Are we in a *Doctor Who* episode?" Vedrò whispered to Truman, staring at the Tardis-like box before him.

"Doctor what?"

"Never mind."

"The Savvies Station," continued Ereus, "has modified these vortexes for beginners. Don't get discouraged when I say this, but most of you will fail the first several times. That's okay. Most voyagers do. Here's how it works: start with the red vortex. While inside, focus on the yellow vortex. If you succeed at locating the destination in your mind's eye, you'll find yourself in the yellow vortex. If you fail, you'll automatically be warped to the blue one instead. Falsmira, would you like to help me demonstrate?"

She stepped through the saloon-style double doors of the red vortex, closed her eyes, and vanished in a swirl of stardust. It happened so quickly that Truman barely saw her body contorting into the starry whirlpool.

Moments later, Falsmira strutted out of the yellow vortex with a blasé look on her face.

Truman found himself disappointed. He had hoped she would stay gone.

"Thank you, Falsmira," said Ereus. "Everyone, form a line."

As Ereus had predicted, no one succeeded at first. Most stood awkwardly in the red portico without vanishing at all.

Though they stepped out disoriented, Style and Vedrò at least made it to the blue box. Style stumbled out and would've cracked his skull on the hard ground if it hadn't been for Schmidt who broke his fall.

Truman was last. When it was his turn, he stepped onto the red platform and closed his eyes. He concentrated hard on the yellow portico. In his mind, the red and yellow-scaled Leonian dragons soared behind his lids. His stomach dropped like a rollercoaster. The free-falling sensation made him feel dizzy.

When he opened his eyes, he was surrounded by yellow walls and applause.

"Well done, my *fratello*," Vedrò shouted excitedly, fist-bumping his friend.

"You, Mr. Howard," said Ereus, "have quite the focus!"

☆ ☆ ☆ ☆ ☆ ☆

The voyagers now stood in front of a mountainous glass pyramid. It looked out of place beside the old architecture of the manors.

In the Pyramid, saxophones, bagpipes, pianos, gongs, and violins floated in the air. Each panel of glass was tinted a different color. Sunlight filtered through the panels in varying wavelengths—some infrared, some ultraviolet, and some radio. The design made the Sun look like a Frankenstein of saturated colors.

At the Pyramid's center, beneath the garden of suspended instruments, stood an arbor overgrown with black and white wisteria. One of its sides was shaped like a treble clef, from which a five-line staff unraveled like sheet music to form an archway.

Under the archway stood a handsome Black man in funky boots and a red, woman's-cut jacket. Stars and ankhs were sewn onto his sleeves. His leather pants looked uncomfortably snug, and a leather baseball cap sat low on his head. A single brown curl peeked out the front. But it wasn't his outfit that caught everyone's attention—it was his voice. It echoed mellifluously off the walls.

The melody washed over Truman like a soothing balm. It eased something inside him—quieted a hunger he hadn't known he had.

The man paused and smiled warmly. In a flamboyant tone, he said, "Welcome, everyone, to the one and only Pyramid, supplier of medical instruments." His accent was American, and he spoke expressively with his hands. "My name is Dr. Nayelo Noxthomas, and I am a professional musical omnihealer. I work for the Venusian Hospitals, primarily making rounds at the Van Gogh Irisylum and moonlighting over at the Hive. Though I work on Venus, I live here on Mercury. I, of course, take a vortex to commute. If I'm not mistaken, you're coming from the practice vortexes, right? Any success?"

"Yes, actually! One voyager warped with flying colors—on his first go, too!" Ereus exclaimed. "Mr. Truman Howard!"

"Oh, is that so?" Nayelo grinned. "Just like your brother Kahlil!"

"You know my brother?!" Truman asked.

He nodded, came over, and gave Reuel a hug. "I know most of your family. Particularly Coelho."

He and Reuel exchanged a few words as the group wandered deeper into the Pyramid.

"Don't mind the invisible stairs," said Nayelo.

He stepped onto nothing. It looked like he was levitating. The voyagers dropped their jaws.

"It's an illusion," Ereus explained.

The four mentors and Humzah followed, leaving the voyagers hesitant.

Truman gently pressed his toes into the solid yet invisible steps and felt around for the transparent handrail.

"First things first," Nayelo said, confidently walking backward up the stairs, "there are many variations of omnihealing: general, musical, artistic, even photic. A.K.A. light therapy. You have a lightbearer in the group, don't you?"

"Yes, Miss Khoza."

Letsatsi smiled as she stumbled over a step.

"Maybe that's something you'll go into in the future," Nayelo said, helping her up. "Omnihealers have the will to heal the ill and injured."

On the first floor of the Pyramid, cellos, guitars, and violas hovered and strummed their own chords, as if played by ghosts.

"As an omnihealer myself," Nayelo continued, "I use music therapy to treat all sorts of physical wounds, diseases, and mental health disorders. For example, I can remedy minor cuts and burns by playing adagio for violin. Those are quite common. Astrobiologists singe themselves studying living lava and prick themselves growing pierre plants all the time. Reuel can attest to that!"

Reuel nodded. "It's true. That's how we first met."

Nayelo smiled at the memory.

"Fleferros are also loyal patients," he went on. "They tend to suffer from iron-deficiency anemia, which is generally easy to alleviate by reaching crescendo on a piano." He pointed upward at an invisible pianist playing his black-and-white keys.

"Uranians also tend to turn up in the emergency room from THun-deR-shOCK!" He jerked around as if he had been struck by lightning. "Actually, I shouldn't joke about that. It can be quite serious—manageable but serious. Not the worst thing, though. A few years back, we had a severe outbreak of Martiangitis. Complete mayhem! It was a devastating pandemic of solar-systematic proportions. A *solar-systemdemic* if you will. Anyway, it took months to discover the perfect vocal range to vaccinate the masses." Nayelo continued as the group paraded past a collection of self-playing lutes. "We call ourselves 'all-healing,' but the truth is, some illnesses still elude us, especially mental ones. The brain is just too complex."

After ascending a few more flights, Nayelo invited the voyagers to explore the rest of the Pyramid. "Feel free to play with the instruments. Strike a few chords. Go wild! All the best rockstars do!"

He walked backward as he spoke, his voice echoing. "The first floor is the string family. The second: the keyboard family. Third: brass, followed by the woodwind. At the top, you'll find percussion. Fair warning: the percussion level has the most surround sound. It'll rattle your eardrums."

Everyone dispersed around the room. Esmeralda and Angenciel floated to the golden harps and lyres. Halle blew into a bamboo flute called a xiao. Vedrò raced to the pipe organ, pressing keys with dramatic flair. Style took the stairs in strides toward the percussion floor. The others, trying to find their way up the staircases, fumbled around with outstretched arms like zombies.

Truman was about to strum a sleek purple guitar when a hand caught his arm.

"Tru," Reuel said, Nayelo at her elbow. "We have something to tell you."

"What's going on?" he asked, still eyeing the intricately designed fretboard.

Reuel glanced at Nayelo.

"It's best if Dr. Noxthomas explains."

Nayelo stepped forward.

"Empaths, Truman," he said with caring eyes and a serious tone, "can be vulnerable to a condition we call ESP: the Empathic Sickness of the Psyche."

Truman furrowed his brows. "What? Like telepathy?"

"No, not quite. ESP is when the omniscience of emotion becomes too overwhelming for a person's mind," Nayelo explained. "Though we are aliens, Truman, we are still very much human, and the weight of emotions can be constant, even unbearable."

Nayelo paused, letting the words settle.

"Emotions are, of course, normal," Nayelo continued. "But we mustn't let them consume us. With empaths, sensing others' emotions is based on proximity. For example, if someone far away from you got shot in the heart, you would most likely not feel their pain. But, if that person is near you, you'll feel every bit of it."

Truman's eyes widened with fear.

"We're not telling you this to scare you, Tru," Reuel said, comfortingly. "We're telling you this so you understand the gravity of your situation."

Truman touched his necklace, petrified.

"That's why you must keep your necklace near you at all times," Nayelo said, pointing to Reuel's creation. "Never *ever* go anywhere without it—it's your shield."

Then, with a faint smile, he added, "But hey, look on the bright side—some people can be completely heartless!"

Chapter 10

Esmeralda's Secret

For the following week, Nayelo's words hung over Truman like the scorching heat. Thankfully, the busy days kept him distracted.

The group traveled to Vivaldi Valley to see derelict temples from their primitive years as a society. Falsmira taught them about the terraformation of Mercury. On Picasso's Peak, they learned about artistic omnihealing. Back in Beethoven Basin, Ereus taught the voyagers the properties of vortexes and had them warp small objects using miniaturized red, blue, and yellow vortexes. Vedrò, Truman, and Yari were the only ones who had successfully teleported their Pinocchio doll, hacky sack, and Tamagotchi.

After that lesson, they revisited the life-size vortexes. Truman was still the only one who could warp flawlessly. Vedrò got close. He made it to the yellow but only in his boxers. The rest of his clothes went to the blue.

"That was a close one," Vedrò said, jumping into his pants.

The girls giggled. The boys bantered.

Esmeralda wasn't amused. In fact, she was fuming after the lesson. "How is he doing better than I am?" she muttered to herself.

Over Argentinian empanadas and beef stew in roasted pumpkins, Truman said to Vedrò, "We still need to thank Esmeralda. It's been a week…"

"Yes! *Carbonada en zapallo!*" Vedrò said distractedly, pointing to his pumpkin. "My mamma makes it for the holidays. She's from Buenos Aires. Did you know I'm half Argentinian?"

"That's cool, but did you hear anything I just said?"

"Yes, Truman," Vedrò sighed. "It's just weird. How do we even bring it up? 'Hey, thanks for saving us from our stupidity. Sorry I called you a know-it-all.'"

"Let's not remind her of that. Let's just thank her."

Esmeralda and Halle got up from the other end of the table and left for the Dragon's Back Trail.

"Come on," Truman said, tugging at Vedrò's arm.

The two girls sat by the lake, sharing notes from the day's lessons.

"Esmeralda," Truman began, "Vedrò and I have been meaning to talk to you."

"About?" she said without looking up.

"We wanted to… Well, we wanted to thank you for saving us. And Halle, thank you for following us. We wouldn't be alive if, you know, neither of you—"

"Don't mention it." Esmeralda returned to her notes.

"Really, Esmeralda," Vedrò added, feeling he needed to say something too. "You saved our lives! You took the blame. We obviously misjudged you and acted like idiots. We're sorry. I'm… sorry."

Esmeralda peered up at him and smiled. "I accept your apology, Vedrò."

Halle beamed.

"Would you two like to sit with us?" Esmeralda asked.

The boys sat. And like Rainbow Row, a conversation unraveled.

"Are you feeling any better?" Truman asked. "You know, since you passed out?"

"I am," she said. "It took a lot of energy to control the Arachnoid like that. I'm just as new to my will as you guys are. Even though my maman is upset with me for breaking the rules, I think she's proud of me too for mastering my will so early. Well, master might be too strong of a word. I shouldn't be fainting, but—still! I controlled a wonder!"

"Did you get grounded?" asked Vedrò.

"No. Maman says Falsmira's punishment will suffice. I wonder what and when that will be."

The force field began and quickly finished its sunset feature, leaving an orangey-red glow across Cherry's horizon.

"It's so beautiful here," Halle mused dreamily. "I can't believe we wake up to this every day."

"I have a feeling this is just the surface of what we'll get to see," said Vedrò.

Suddenly, every tree hollow in the forest of cherry blossoms began to glow red and blue and orange and green.

"What's happening?" Truman asked, looking around.

"It couldn't be…" Esmeralda said under her breath.

Just then, streams of lightning bugs poured from the cherry blossoms, moving in clusters. Their bright bulbs dappled the dark lake with a riot of color.

One landed beside Truman. It was the size of a hand and resembled an Egyptian scarab, with wide, colorful wings and a beetle-like body.

"Beautiful, aren't they?" Esmeralda said breathlessly. "They're called blossom bugs! I read about them in *The Wonders and Fathoms of Aether*. I'm shocked we're seeing them. They rarely come out—they hibernate for sixty years and only appear for a single night!"

Halle ran after one, trying to catch it. Vedrò ran away from one, trying not to be touched.

Esmeralda watched and laughed.

Truman turned to her and noticed her beautiful smile. He was reminded of Reuel.

"Esmeralda," Truman began, "this is a bit random, but do you know anything about my family?"

"Not much." She shrugged. "Why?"

"What do you know?"

Esmeralda paused. "Do you know what *Mercury's Message* is?"

"*Mercury's Message?*"

"It's a popular newspaper here on Mercury. My maman had a bunch of old copies back in France. I skimmed most of them. One was about your brother, Saint. It read like a gossip column—not exactly factual."

"What did it say?"

"That your family is 'suspicious.' That it's too coincidental for all your siblings to be aliens. I bet the printing presses are buzzing now that your powers have triggered."

He looked at his feet, unsure what to make of this.

"Don't lose sleep over it, though," Esmeralda said kindly. "*Mercury's Message* isn't a credible source anyway. Anyone who trusts it probably doesn't know how to think for themselves. Besides, according to *Famous Among the Stars*—a book I read in my maman's library—there have been plenty of alien siblings before. Granted, most of them were twins or triplets. Still, it must be genetic, right?"

"Do you say that because of your own family?"

Vedrò and Halle stopped chasing bugs to listen.

For a moment, Esmeralda went quiet.

"My mother and I are unique because we're not *just* aliens."

"What do you mean?"

She exhaled. "We're what are called *sirens*."

"Sirens? I thought you were enchantresses?"

"That was a lie. A lie I asked my maman to tell." She looked down at her feet. "You know, lying is an interesting game. When the truth comes out, the lie ends up sounding silly, doesn't it?"

"Why'd you lie?"

"In Greek mythology, sirens are evil creatures who use their enchanting voices to lure sailors to their deaths. But really, we just have the will to control minds."

"That's how you controlled the Arachnoid," said Truman. "We knew that, though. That's what an enchantress is, is it not? So, why hide being a siren?"

Esmeralda picked at the bark of a tree. "Speaking of the Arachnoid," she said, quickly changing the subject, "I've been meaning to ask you guys, what'd you think the Arachnoid meant when it said, 'You'll never know when your beloveds are slaughtered by the hands of imperialistic, bloodthirsty blah blah.' It didn't finish its sentence—it *was* rather long-winded. But I heard most of it. I can't help but think it means something."

"I still can't believe I dropped my phone!" muttered Vedrò. Truman shushed him.

"Esmeralda, why are you hiding that you're a siren?" Truman asked again. "If you don't feel comfortable, that's okay. I don't want to pry. I just hope you know you can talk to us."

"I do feel comfortable. It's just—" she sighed. "Sirens and enchantresses are not the same thing. We have the same will as they do, but we're not treated the same. In Aether, people see sirens as mean and evil. We're treated as less than. People fear us."

Halle put a hand on Esmeralda's shoulder. "I don't think that lie is silly at all."

Esmeralda gave a faint smile. "It's not just the prejudice," she continued, clearing her throat. "They say sirens are cursed. When sirens fall in love, our partners... end up dying. In tragic, horrific accidents. My papa died before I was born. So did my grandpapa." She looked away. "Perhaps that's why it's hard for me to connect with people."

Vedrò wrapped an arm around her and said, "Halle's right. It's not silly at all."

The four sat in silence, watching as bugs flickered in trees, lighting them up like Christmas.

Across the lake, Truman spotted his fellow voyagers chasing after flutters of purple and yellow. He saw Reuel giving Falsmira, who looked irritated, an unsolicited lecture. He assumed it was about the bugs.

Truman turned back to Esmeralda.

"I'm confused about one thing, Esmeralda," said Truman. "How do you know so much about this—the Assembly, aliens, wills, the bugs?"

Esmeralda straightened, her eyes lit up, clearly grateful for the change of subject.

"My will triggered months before our journey started. I had plenty of time to read. I couldn't stay at my boarding school—Maman was afraid my will would act out again. So, she sent me to her place in Reims. She was gone most days, but whenever she came back, she brought me books. It started with old bedtime stories she used to read to me, like *The Fickle, Felonious Four* and *La Tragédie d'Ondine*. But I wanted to learn more about Aether. So, she brought me *The Triggery of Magical Instincts: A Jupitarian Study* and *The Wonders and Fathoms of Aether*. When I finished those, I snooped around her library and found *Famous Among the Stars*, old news articles from *Mercury's Message*, and a draft manuscript called *Sirens and Dead Seas*."

A thoughtful expression stretched across her face. "That last one was interesting. It answered a lot of my questions about being a siren, like why I could suddenly play the harp and lyre, why I naturally have silver hair, why I don't have a father."

A blossom bug landed on her shoulder. She shooed it away absently.

"How did your will trigger?" Vedrò asked, straightening his pantleg.

Esmeralda tucked a wisp of hair behind her ear. "A couple boys in my high school were making fun of me. So, I, uh… made them eat dog food."

"You what?!" Vedrò gaped at her.

"No, you didn't," Halle said incredulously.

"I did," she admitted, smirking. "They totally deserved it too!"

The four of them broke into laughter.

Something unspoken passed between them. From that moment on, Truman, Vedrò, Halle, and Esmeralda were all friends.

Chapter 11

PSA: the Protection & Secrecy of Aliens

Today is our last day on Mercury," Angenciel said the following morning. "We'll be spending it in the Carnegie Rupes! The Carnegie Rupes are cliffs in Mercury's northern hemisphere that are roughly two hundred miles long and rise more than a mile high. Inside are several important departments: the PSA Proctors, the Mercurial World Court, and *Mercury's Message*. Our first stop is the PSA Proctors. They're in charge of upholding the Protection and Secrecy of Aliens. They investigate, prevent, and cover up PSA breaches. The president of the PSA Proctors, Ms. Elmory Moss, will explain more."

"Try the French toast," Vedrò whispered to Truman, his mouth stuffed with syrup and soggy bread. "It's—" He kissed his fingers and thumb dramatically.

Truman slopped some French toast onto his plate and inhaled a forkful. "Man, I love cinnamon!"

"Me too," Vedrò said, licking his plate clean. "And bread!"

"Shh!" Esmeralda hissed from across the table and returned to her notes.

Angenciel pursed her lips disapprovingly at the boys and checked her watch. "If everyone's done, let's head out! Be sure to bring your notebooks and undivided attention." She shot Vedrò and Truman a stern look.

"The apple doesn't fall far from the tree, does it?" Vedrò muttered to Truman, suppressing a laugh.

Everyone gathered their things and went to climb off Cherry, leaving Truman to wolf down his toast.

At the edge of Cherry, the voyagers glimpsed the Carnegie Rupes in the Mercurial distance. The cliffs gleamed with polished, cloudy gray granite. They towered high into the heavens, kissed by hints of the Aurora Mercurialis.

Mighty winds sang a powerful ballad. Angenciel said something, but Truman couldn't catch it. Once stepped beyond Cherry's force field, everyone's hair blew in every which way. For a split second, Truman caught a glimpse of something moving in the wind. He looked around to see what it was, but it had disappeared.

Halle grabbed his hand, screaming something and pointing at figures springing toward the Rupes. She tugged at him and burst into a sprint. Truman followed.

Falsmira—recognizable by her jet-black bob and flowing robes—was the first to disappear into the cliffs. Esmeralda and Angenciel dissolved next. Then, Ereus and Style. Vedrò, Reuel, Humzah—all of them disappeared, one by one.

"SHE SAID TO RUN THROUGH IT!" Halle shrieked.

"WHAT'D YOU SAY?!"

The wind was relentless.

Halle charged at the cliff and vanished. Truman's eyes stung, but he understood. He ran through the mirage.

It felt icy, prickling his skin. Before he knew it, he landed on his knees, panting.

"The Carnegie Rupes... often experience... heavy solar winds," Angenciel said, short of breath.

Clearly, Truman thought, rubbing his eyes and peering back at the Mercurial surface. The illusion of the wall acted like a one-way mirror, keeping the wind out.

"Will Cherry be okay?" Halle asked, gasping for air.

"Absolutely!" said Reuel. "The force field will protect her. Plus, she's strong, more powerful than the wind. Not to mention, she's been through a lot worse. Just wait 'til we go through the Asteroid Belt! Normally, she glides right through it, but, one time, she lost a cherry blossom to the major asteroid Hygiea. She was in a lot of pain then. It took her weeks on Jupiter to recover."

Truman got to his feet.

"Welcome to the Carnegie Rupes, everyone!" exclaimed Angenciel.

A colossal hall stretched before them in all directions. The ceiling soared high above their heads. Hundreds of granite staircases spiraled upward to countless floors. The walls were made of newspapers, papier-mâchéed into a billowing tapestry of current events. Floating in and out of every wall were thousands of melting clocks, their hands frozen in time. Icicles blanketed them. The word *DEADLINE* sat atop every clock. Some clocks rang and flashed *DEADLINE* in red. In the center of the foyer was a fountain. Instead of spurting streams of water, it gushed globs of fire.

"This is the Fountain of Flames!" Reuel gestured. "It was created to display some of Mercury's living lava!"

"That's living lava?" Truman queried. It looked like regular lava, or at least the lava he had seen in Earthling textbooks.

"Indeed, it is!"

To the voyagers' horror, the blobs of fiery fathoms began to clump together. Black and red infernos morphed into jagged armors of scales. Out of the embers emerged a bony carcass and ruby tendrils. The clump had grown into a giant, fearsome Leonian dragon. The serpent roared and circled the fountain. Everyone, except the mentors and Humzah, ducked for cover.

"AHHH!" Halle cried out, falling to her feet.

"Take it easy, y'all," said a voice with a Southern American accent. "It's just the security system. I must've forgotten to shut it off. My bad."

The voice belonged to a fair-skinned woman with curly brown hair. She wore denim jeans and boots and looked older than she was. She had dark circles under her hazy gray eyes.

"My name is Elmory Moss," said the woman. "I'm the president of the PSA Proctors. Like Mr. Eklöf here," she gestured to Ereus, "I'm an illusionist."

With a wave of her hand, the Leonian dragon subsided and melted back into the lumpy forms of living lava.

Halle rocked back and forth.

Esmeralda consolingly helped her to her feet. "You okay?"

Halle nodded, still trembling.

"I'm also an *oblivy*," Elmory continued, unfazed by Halle's fright. "Oblivies have the will to erase memories."

Truman looked down at his necklace and noticed a kink in the chain. As he tried to untangle it, something about Elmory unsettled him. Perhaps it was her vacant, unblinking eyes or how her gaze never quite met his, but he sensed a great emptiness in her, as if she wasn't all there. It was a foreign feeling. He didn't like it and threw the necklace back on, leaving the knot.

"There are three PSA Proctors," Elmory went on, her voice humdrum. "Each has different duties, but they all share one goal: to uphold the Protection and Secrecy of Aliens. The first Proctor is the Espionage Unit. The second is the Illusory Fleet. And the third, the Office of Oblivies." She pointed to three engraved signs above separate staircases.

Esmeralda scribbled down the names. Her peers opened their notebooks and followed her lead.

"We'll begin with the Espionage Unit. They infiltrate Earthling space agencies, like NASA and ESA, and track their upcoming space ventures."

She led them up a spiral staircase. The steps moved like a circular escalator.

"For example, if NASA launches a spacecraft to capture images of Mercury's surface, our *mimes*—aliens who have the will to change their appearances and manipulate their voices to impersonate others—learn everything they can about the craft. They learn the mission's goal, the launch date, and trajectory coordinates."

At the top of the stairs, a voice-activated door opened.

"Normally, only mimes are allowed to enter. They do so by mimicking my voice," she explained.

Inside, spies eavesdropped on phone calls and scrolled through mindboggling software. In one cubicle, a small woman spoke over the phone in Hindi with a deep, masculine voice. In the cubicle next to hers, a tall man spoke Portuguese with a high-pitched, womanly voice. They were impersonating astrophysicists and rocket scientists.

Truman heard a cacophony of languages. It reminded him of Lonely's Academy.

The back wall was a giant mirror. Mimes stood before it, staring at their reflections and practicing their morphing skills. Once bald men combed their luscious blonde hair. Women examined and felt their Adam's apples.

A young man with ginger hair accidentally transformed into a hairy beast—Bigfoot. He was the apprentice to the old woman next to him, who disapprovingly thumped the back of his head and demonstrated the proper technique for sprouting a mustache.

Elmory led them back to the downstairs lobby, taking the same staircase as before. It seemed to have a mind of its own. The stairs easily changed direction, from upward to downward, and only moved when the group stood on it.

"When our mimes obtain all necessary information about the spacecraft," Elmory continued, "they contact the IF, the Illusory Fleet."

They stepped onto another staircase.

"Illusionists then install invisibility illusions along the spacecraft's trajectory. They also double-check the invisibility features within our force fields to make sure all is up to code."

While the door to the EU was voice-activated, the door to the IF was illusion-activated.

"May I?" Ereus offered with excitement.

"By all means," said Elmory.

Ereus stepped forward, cracked his knuckles, cocked his head, and flicked his wrist. And from his neck a boil grew. It grew and grew until it became a second head. It looked like Ereus, only with more feminine features, longer hair, and stronger cheekbones.

A scanner confirmed the illusion and opened the door.

Ereus' second head popped and fizzled like a balloon.

"Wicked!" Vedrò exclaimed.

Inside the IF, illusionists sat at their workstations and stared up at large screens. Truman saw images of a rover on a red planet and a space probe floating in starry darkness. The illusionists glued their eyes to the monitors. They kept flicking their wrists back and forth.

Truman found the job tedious, especially after seeing Ereus' magic trick.

Elmory lingered before leading them to the third PSA Proctor.

"Once the illusionists veil the trajectory of the spacecraft," said Elmory, "our mimes keep an eye on the Earthlings. If the Fleet misses a spot, that's when oblivies step in to remove memories from people. The Office of Oblivies acts as quality assurance. Let's say the spacecraft captures an image of the Leonian dragons. The EU would contact the OO to erase everyone's memory and destroy the evidence."

The door to the OO was memory-activated.

"You feed the door a memory for it to open," she explained. "What memory do I not need? Let's see… My breakfast sandwich was awful. Let's give it that!" She tapped her temple with her fingertips.

Truman thought the gesture looked like the ASL sign for *to know.*

Dragging her fingers outward, she siphoned a yolky-colored vapor from her temple and flicked it toward the door. The door absorbed it and opened.

Her stomach growled. "My heavens, I'm starving! I don't think I've eaten anything today."

Inside, the OO was chaos. Paperwork was strewn all over the floor. The ceiling was billowing with memory vapor of every color. Oblivies ran around, scatterbrained. One oblivy scratched his head and muttered to himself, "Where are the keys to my spaceship?!" Another oblivy who entered the room said airily to herself, "I forgot what I came in here for…"

Elmory frowned at the disorder. "I swear to the Universe we're more on top of things than it appears."

They returned to the lobby.

"Those are the three PSA Proctors. Can someone summarize their roles for the class?" asked Elmory.

Esmeralda looked up from her well-constructed Venn diagram and raised her hand. "First, mimes learn what Earthlings plan to do. Illusionists then block their perceptions. And oblivies erase what they see, if applicable. *Et voilà!*"

"Perfect summation," Elmory said. "Thank you. Now, before I go, I have one last thing to say… The Protection and Secrecy of Aliens *is not optional.*"

Elmory looked at them sternly. "What I mean is anyone who is human—despite the relationship y'all have with the person—must never *ever* know about the Assemble of Aether."

The voyagers were disappointed to hear this. Most of them still had family and friends on Earth and thought they might one day share their space adventures with them.

"We have eyes everywhere," said Elmory. "If you're caught sharing information with a human, the Assembly of Aether will punish you on a 'three strikes, you're out' basis." She raised a finger and said, "First-timers will receive a warning. Second-timers will have the offense permanently on their record, which could prevent you from getting certain jobs. For third-timers, the Assembly of Aether will have no choice but to revoke your right to warp to Earth. You can file an appeal, but the chances of that passing are slim to none.

"This doesn't mean you can't visit your families or whoever. You just can't tell them about any of this. When you return to Earth, you must refrain from sharing with your family about where you've been. To ensure you haven't breached PSA, your whereabouts on Earth will be monitored at all times." She checked her wristwatch and gasped. "My Chiron, I gotta go. I have business to attend to. It was nice meeting y'all. Have fun exploring the rest of the Rupes."

They waved goodbye as she strode through the illusion of the cliff wall and onto the Mercurial surface toward Cherry.

Chatter broke out among the voyagers. They disliked the idea of lying to their families.

"What if I'm not a good liar?!" said Sweta.

"It's not fair!" whined Schmidt.

"I wish I could tell my yéyé," Halle grumbled.

"Ahem!" Angenciel coughed aloud. "Our day is yet to be over. We still have the Mercurial World Court and *Mercury's Message!* Please follow me!"

They headed up another flight of stairs.

"The Mercurial World Court," Angenciel continued, "is a fraction of Aether's judicial system. Every world from Mercury to Pluto has a world court, just like the PSA Proctors. Elmory forgot to mention that. She was in a bit of a rush. Anyway, there's a trial currently going on in the courtroom. When we enter, we must be quiet."

At the top of the staircase was a waiting room crowded with people. As they jostled through the masses, Truman could've sworn he saw six hairy arms holding up a large newspaper. *Was that a statue?* As he looked back, he bumped into a man with glasses and a camera. The camera fell and shattered.

"I am so sorry," Truman said, kneeling to help salvage the camera.

The man angrily picked up the broken pieces and said, "You really ought to watch where you're—" He looked up at Truman with widened eyes, gasped, and darted away.

That was odd. Truman turned to catch up with the group.

Angenciel pushed through the courtroom doors and held a finger to her lips.

The courtroom was a silver chamber, empty and tapered to a point like a teardrop.

Truman felt dizzy, his insides lopsided. Blood rushed to his head.

Faint murmurs came from above.

Everyone's hair lifted as if from static. Reuel and Esmeralda looked like they were standing upside down.

Truman's necklace caught on his chin as it, too, floated. He held it down and looked up.

Above his head, witnesses and jurors sat in pews. Judges in purple robes towered on high chairs. Gold medallions were pinned to their chests, reflecting the lights of the courtroom.

Perched on a low stool in the corner of the teardrop-shaped room was a young, pretty man awaiting his verdict. He had wavy blond hair that contrasted with his dark brown eyebrows, and wore fitted pants, a turtleneck, and a ruby earring. He filed his nails and looked unbothered.

Perhaps it was his androgynous look or nonchalant attitude, but something about the man intrigued Truman.

"Now I want a blessedbe," Vedrò muttered to Truman.

"What do you mean?"

"His earring is the Italian horn—a red chili pepper. It's said to ward off evil."

Falsmira hushed him.

The man with the earring peered up and met Truman's gaze. He looked at him like he knew who he was. A smile crept across his face.

With her scarred arm, Angenciel beckoned the voyagers out of the courtroom.

"How do you get to the other side?" Vedrò asked.

"You walk up the walls of the courtroom," said Ereus. "Illusionists and savvies created the design together. Neat, isn't it?"

"What's the purpose of its design?" asked Esmeralda.

"No real purpose. Sometimes you design things simply to design them."

"And that man?" asked Truman. "Who is he? What did he do?"

"Not sure what he has done this time, but his name is Krimmiel. He's a notorious lawbreaker—usually for breaching PSA."

Angenciel led them to their final staircase.

Krimmiel was still on Truman's mind. *Why'd he look at me like that?* he thought.

"Our last stop is *Mercury's Message*," Angenciel announced. "*Mercury's Message* is an Assembly-renowned publication. Aliens who work for the publication are called messengers. Alien slang for reporters."

"Truman, you have a knot in your necklace," Vedrò whispered.

Truman looked down and saw it was even more jumbled. "I tried getting it out earlier."

"Pass it to me. I have nimble fingers."

Truman handed him the chain. "Thanks."

They reached the top of the stairs.

"This is the headquarters to *Mercury's Message*," Angenciel said, opening the doors.

Suddenly, a swarm of messengers engulfed them. They jostled through the voyagers until they found Truman. They circled him.

"What do you have to say for your family?!" one messenger shouted at Truman.

"You're the fifth Howard to be alien!" yelled another. "Is that a coincidence or foul play?!"

"What're you hiding?!"

Camera flashes assaulted Truman's eyes.

One of the cameramen was the man with the glasses. He held a new camera.

Truman felt lightheaded. Someone elbowed his ribs. Without his necklace, he felt the messengers' excitement and his peers' overstimulation on top of his own.

Reuel pushed through and wrapped her arm around her brother. She hastily guided him down the stairs.

Halle, Style, and the rest of the mentors formed a wall to fend off the messengers.

Esmeralda whacked a man with her notebook.

"Leave my *fratello* alone!" Vedrò pushed one.

Falsmira, a torcron, squinted at the pride of messengers. They instantly went from savage to sloth.

Ereus flicked his wrist. Scorpions appeared to crawl all over their skin. They swatted at the creatures in fearful slow motion.

"That should hold them. Now run!" Ereus hollered.

They dashed through the mirage wall and toward Cherry.

Truman was so overwhelmed, he couldn't even think.

His vision blurred. He dropped to his knees, and his forehead smacked the ground with a thud.

Reuel rolled up her sleeve. Her bracelet of ivy grew long vines that wrapped around Truman and lifted him up. She ran with him over her head like an umbrella—a strange, plant-like umbrella.

They made it to Cherry. A branch curled down and scooped Truman up.

Once everyone climbed aboard, Cherry flapped her great wings and flew far, far away from Mercury.

Chapter 12

The Vivabees & the Honey Thief

Truman woke up to Vedrò and Reuel at his bedside. They both looked worried and somber.

"What happened?" Truman groaned, rubbing a tender bump on his forehead.

"You fainted," Reuel said. "You've been out for hours. I spoke with Nayelo. He said that without your necklace, your nerves were shot. Overstimulated."

"It's my fault," said Vedrò. "I had you take off your necklace."

"No, you were just trying to help," said Truman. "It was the messengers. What were they doing?"

"What hack reporters do best," Reuel muttered. "Harassing you. Trying to get a scoop. I expected something like this would happen. It happened to Saint during his journey but on a smaller scale. Instead of full-on bombardment, it was one messenger. He stalked Saint until he got him alone. You're the most vulnerable now. You don't fully know how to warp or use your wills. That's why they're targeting you instead of me, Kahlil, or Coelho who are more developed aliens. Not to say you're underdeveloped just—"

"I know what you mean," said Truman. "But if you knew this could happen, why'd we even bother going to *Mercury's Message?*"

"We're required to. It's mandatory teaching. Curriculum approved by the Assembly of Aether. I have a friend who works in the editing department at *Mercury's Message*. She told me most of the messengers were off covering a story on Pluto. Clearly, not all of them had gone."

"I did bump into a man outside the Mercurial World Court. He was one of the cameramen."

"He must've been covering Krimmiel's court case." Reuel sighed. "Ugh, we were doing so well!"

"What do you mean?"

"Well, the mentors and I rearranged the journey schedule and kept it hidden from the public. We knew we couldn't keep it up for too long. We are flying around on a big pink dragon, after all! Still, this shouldn't be necessary. You're newly alienated *and* an empath. The Assembly should forbid such behavior if they truly cared about their citizens!"

Truman rubbed his temple.

"You must be starving," Reuel said. "Let me check on your food." She kissed his forehead and left the treehouse.

"I'm so sorry, Truman," Vedrò said again.

"You don't need to apologize."

"Yes, I do. I should've seen it coming."

"No one could have seen that coming."

"I could have! That's my will!"

"Don't beat yourself up, Vedrò. We're all rooks here."

"He's right, you know," said Esmeralda, striding into the room. "It won't be until we are paired with an assigned mentor that we'll achieve power proficiency. And that won't be until after our journey."

"Easy for you to say," Vedrò grumbled. "*You* controlled the Arachnoid."

Esmeralda turned to Truman. "Are you feeling better?"

Just then, Style entered the treehouse, carrying a breakfast tray stacked with gourmet eggs and sizzling bacon in his muscular arms.

"I am now!" Truman perked up.

Style placed the tray onto Truman's lap and smiled. *"Eat,"* he signed.

Truman bit into some bruschetta. "So, did I miss anything?"

"Not much," said Esmeralda. "Because of what happened, my maman had to talk about *Mercury's Message* here instead of in the Rupes. Reuel covered the Arachnoid. And Falsmira taught about the Webbed War of '44. That's about it. Don't worry—I took notes for you." She handed him a stack of papers.

"Great," he said unenthusiastically. "Thanks, Esmeralda."

"Je t'en prie!"

"Speaking of Falsmira," said Vedrò, "she was annoyed with what happened yesterday."

"Falsmira? Are you sure? I thought she would've gotten a kick out of what happened."

"On the contrary," said Esmeralda. "She was as livid as the rest of the mentors. But that's because she had our detention planned for last night. She postponed it."

"Well, I guess one good thing came out of last night," he laughed. "Anything else I missed?"

"Not really. Our next stop is Venus! We should be arriving soon."

"Angenciel told me to tell you to wear something breezy for the day," signed Style. *"Apparently, Venus is much hotter than Mercury."*

After breakfast, Truman threw on shorts and a tank top. His head still throbbed.

"Good morning, voyagers!" Angenciel greeted them outside. "Today, we'll explore mine and Reuel's ruling planet—the second Rocky Realm, ruled by the strong-willed Taurus and balanced Libra. The planet of love and beauty, Venus!"

Truman shot a furtive glance at Style, who was focused on Angenciel's lips and Humzah's interpretations.

"Venus is the second innermost planet of the Solar System. It is, on average, sixty-seven million miles away from the Sun. A year on Venus lasts around two hundred and twenty-five Earth days. A Venusian day, however, lasts around two hundred and forty Earth days." She saw their eyes glaze over. "In other words, the Venusian day is longer than the Venusian year. There are about 5,832 hours in one Venusian day. When we land, update your watch settings.

"Venus, much like its namesake goddess, is known for its beguiling allure. Though the planet is stunning and jewel-like in appearance, without the proper protective technology, you would never survive the deadly clouds that swathe the Venusian atmosphere." The chilling words leapt off Angenciel's lips, capturing everyone's attention.

"Lethal clouds packed with sulfuric acid and carbon dioxide trap the Sun's heat, making it the hottest planet in the Solar System. The planet's temperature remains the same all year long. So, really, there's only one season on Venus. We call it *blister*. It's not really a 'season' because there's no change in the weather or in the amount of daylight."

"But Angenciel, how on Venus will Cherry get through the toxic clouds?!" Ereus asked dramatically.

"Thank you for humoring me, Ereus. To answer that question, follow me!" She led the voyagers to the orchard.

Ereus hopped onto his piano and began playing.

"Look there!" Angenciel said, thrilled. "That's my Venus!"

The voyagers crowded over the dip in the wing. As Cherry advanced, a creamy-white orb grew and grew. Truman thought it looked like a giant matte pearl.

Pale-yellow winds whirled inward, creating a cyclone. The cinnamon-colored surface of the planet could be seen through the eye of the storm. Cherry then plunged into the eye and plumped down onto a Venusian mountaintop coated with metallic snowflakes.

The voyagers watched in awe as the spiraling clouds settled into their regular Venusian pattern. The sky looked like an eternal sunset—a deep orange. Though the Leonian dragons were obscured, the Sun still glowed as a brilliant patch in the eastern heavens.

Scattered across the mountain range were marvelous amber castles.

"What we just passed through is called the cyclone—another ingenious contraption by the savvies," Ereus explained, getting up from his piano. "Cherry's force field could not survive the atmosphere. Cherry would, but we would not. The cyclone gives us safe passage through the atmosphere and into the bounds of the Venusian force field."

Ereus rambled on about the cyclone as they disembarked.

Truman fiddled with his watch and updated the time. *One more planet*, he thought. *One more planet until we're on the Moon. Until I can reunite with my family.*

"Fun fact," Angenciel interjected. "Venus rotates in the opposite direction of Earth, causing the Sun to rise in the West and set in the East. We're in the North right now among a mountain range called the Venusian Elps. We're headed inland. Down there!"

Truman trained his eyes down the hill and spotted a castle. Its gilding gave the castle an opulent façade. A jar, a dipper, and the words *The Hospital of the Inland Venusian Elps* were etched into the castle's drawbridge. Towers were buried in clouds. The windows were hexagonal in shape. Truman could hear violins and pianos and voices of angels. He thought he even heard a faint buzzing sound.

"Let's get moving!" called Angenciel.

The group wound down the mountainside.

Behind them, Cherry curled up and dozed off.

"How are there snowflakes if it's so hot?" asked Vedrò.

"It's not real snow," said Angenciel. "They're reflective minerals that were once vaporized by the intense weather and then frozen when they reached higher elevations."

They reached a plateau in the mountainside. The drawbridge reeled open.

"Everyone, grab a sled!"

Truman gave Angenciel a confused look. "A what?"

"A sled. Here, take one."

It was a large, flat honeycomb. The underside oozed honey.

"What are these for?" Vedrò asked, biting into his sled.

Angenciel swatted at him to stop. "Falsmira, would you do the honors?"

"Sure," she said indifferently. "See you numbskulls in the hospital!" She hopped onto her honeycomb and flew down the mountainside, right into the castle.

"W-w-we're sledding down?!" Halle said in fear.

Ereus, Reuel, Humzah, and Schmidt had already tucked their legs onto their sleds and launched down the hill.

Without hesitation, Yari leapt onto her honeycomb. "Cowabunga!" she shouted, standing upright the whole way down.

Sweta went next, her sari billowing behind her. She shared a sled with Letsatsi, who screamed bloody murder and grasped the sides for dear life.

Halle was peeking through her fingers, gliding steadily between Esmeralda and Vedrò.

"Let's go at the same time!" Style signed to Truman.

Truman nodded and dove headfirst onto his honeycomb. A warm, floral scent rushed through his hair, and the mountains grew taller as he hurtled inland. Style stuck out his tongue and flashed a hang-loose sign like a surfer. Truman laughed.

The fortress engulfed them as they slowed to a stop under a frescoed hexagonal dome dripping with chandeliers. White light from curly bulbs touched every inch of the dome. The fresco shimmered and displayed bees dancing across a sea of stars.

Truman stared at the fresco, mouth gaping open. *How is the paint moving?*

Angenciel sleighed into the castle, and the drawbridge slammed shut.

"Bzeze, everyone!" greeted a voice.

Everyone turned and saw three black-and-yellow striped creatures flutter forward. Each was five feet long, with six black legs. Pollen covered their hind legs. Their furry thoraxes looked like glamorous capelets. Their small, veiny wings kept them afloat despite their heavy-looking bodies. Their cinched waists bloomed outward into voluminous evening gowns. Except, they weren't gowns. They weren't even clothes. The gown-like extremities were their lower halves. Their hoop skirts were made of honeycomb thicker than the sleds. Honey oozed from every cell, and a giant stinger protruded out of the innermost cell.

Despite their stingers and mandibles, the bees looked kind. Their oversized, bejeweled eyes sparkled with warmth.

"I'm Jelly," said the bee with emeralds for eyes. "Welcome to the Hospital of the Inland Venusian Elps, also known as the Hive!" Her voice was mellifluous. As she spoke, her eyes glowed green, as though lit from within.

"*Bzeze* is Vivabee for hello, goodbye, and welcome," said the bee with blush pink gems for eyes. "It's like aloha or ciao." Her eyes gleamed a rosy shade. "*Bzeze*, I'm Embar!"

"And I'm Sus," said the bee with moonstones for eyes. Her voice was deeper than the others', and her moonstones shone like gray Earthling clouds passing in front of the Sun.

"As I'm sure you lot remember," Reuel began, "Aether is home to seven wonders. The Aristotelian dragons are the first. The Arachnoid—which most of you were fortunate enough not to have met—is the second. And the Vivabees are the third. Jelly, Embar, and Sus are just three of hundreds of thousands of Vivabees across Aether. They work alongside our omnihealers as medical practitioners and nurses. Today, they are our guides through the Hive."

"Yes," added Sus. "We recently admitted a few interesting cases I suspect you all will want to see."

Buzzing and waggling, Jelly, Embar, and Sus led the voyagers out of the dome and down the in-patient wing of the hospital.

The hallway was hexagonal, lined with black and yellow tiles.

They passed several concerning patients along the way. One patient was covered in scorch marks and white blisters. A Vivabee, with ghostly amethysts for eyes, gently dabbed a pink solution onto the burns and wrapped them in bandages.

"That's Scured," Sus said, glancing over her wing. "She's my sister."

"What happened to that poor man?!" Halle asked, horrified.

"Third-degree burns. He's a pyraura. Happens a lot with them."

"What's a peer-oar-ah?"

"It's pronounced pi-roar-ah," Angenciel corrected. "Think *pyre* and *aura* together. A pyraura is an alien who has the will to manipulate fire. They can set things aflame, put fires out, generate electricity, and manipulate heat."

Music drifted down the hall. In one room, an omnihealer sang softly to a man with a stiff neck. Across the hall, another omnihealer played the piano for a pale, ailing woman. Another patient, oblivious to the group, paced around the piano in a hospital gown. Her eyes were wide, and her hair frayed, like she had recently been electrocuted. A Vivabee with sapphires for eyes fluttered after the woman. His name tag read *Tragique*.

Farther down the in-patient wing was an omnihealer playing the violin to a woman picking at her puss-oozing abrasions. The omnihealer handed the woman a glass of amber liquid, and the woman downed it.

"That woman there accidentally cut herself while pruning her pierre plants. Poor thing," Embar sighed. "Those fathoms require a delicate touch."

"What's she drinking?" asked Vedrò.

"It's the Vivabees' Aether-renowned honey elixir," said Reuel. "They make it themselves. It's essentially—"

"Medicine!" blurted Esmeralda.

"Esmeralda!" Angenciel said through gritted teeth. "Reuel is the mentor here. Let her speak."

Esmeralda looked abashed and returned to her notes.

"Yes, it is a medicinal syrup," Reuel continued. "Vivabees collect the nectar from pierre plants, break it down into simple sugars, and store it in their honeycombed bodies. Their bodies keep the elixir under the most ideal conditions. The density of their anatomy keeps the substance from oxidizing. Their bodies also keep the elixir at a controlled temperature and perpetual suspension and protect it from light and humidity. Not all Vivabees can store elixir, though. Older Vivabees tend to have difficulty maintaining those conditions."

"Thanks for reminding us," Sus said bitterly.

"I'm sorry," Reuel said, scratching her head and smiling. "Where was I? Ah, the elixir—the elixir must be stored for over a decade to reach full potency. Century-old honey elixir is the most effective and, therefore, the most valued. Think of it as a medicinal wine. Vivabees often prescribe it to patients primarily as a painkiller, though it has other properties as well!"

"Honey elixir is actually the most effective painkiller in existence," Jelly added with pride. "It relieves our patients of their physical aches and pains instantly!"

Truman moved closer to the threshold of a room where a patient was crying out in pain.

"I wouldn't go in there," cautioned Sus.

"Why not?"

"You're the empath, aren't you? If you go in there, you'll be in excruciating pain. Ereus might explain it better, but the savvies developed a state-of-the-art system that contains the emotions of our patients within the walls of their rooms. It's like soundproofing but for feelings."

"It's called the empathproof framework," added Ereus. "Just stay clear of the rooms, and you'll be fine. You've got your necklace on, right?"

Truman nodded.

"Necklace?" asked Sus.

"My sister made it for me. It's made from pierre plants. It helps suppress my empathic will."

"May I?" Sus reached forward.

Truman's instinct was to pull away from the giant bee, but he stopped himself and let the Vivabee lift the necklace with one of her forelegs.

"Wow, this is beautiful! Reuel, you made this?! You must be a highly skilled ivy!"

"Aster. I prefer aster. But thank you so much!"

"My apologies," said Sus. "But seriously, you should consider selling these. I bet every Vivabee would line up for one of these bad bees! We need something practical like this. The empathproof framework allows us to focus on one patient at a time, but it only goes so far."

"Why would Vivabees need necklaces?" asked Truman. "Are you also empaths?"

"Indeed, we are. All Vivabees are." Sus turned back to Reuel. "Let me get your info later. I truly do want one."

"Okay!" Reuel laughed, a little flustered.

The group continued exploring the hospital.

Omnihealers in the out-patient wing kept sneaking glances at Truman. Truman caught two whispering over a newspaper.

What's that about?

The group stopped in a courtyard overflowing with a rainbow of pierre plants and Vivabees collecting nectar and pollen.

"Let's head to the cafeteria, shall we?" said Jelly. "Before we do, anyone need to use the restroom? The closest one is down this stairwell."

"I do!" Vedrò and Truman said simultaneously.

"Sus, will you make sure the boys don't get lost?"

Sus nodded and led the boys down the dimly lit basement.

"I'll wait out here," Sus said, polishing her eyes with one of her legs.

The bathroom was clean and sleek, with black tiles and yellow bulbs. It smelled like rose water.

"Even the restroom is a work of art!" Vedrò exclaimed, flushing the toilet.

As Truman washed his hands, a newspaper left on the counter caught his attention—the latest issue of *Mercury's Message*. Its logo was a man with winged feet.

On the cover of the issue was a picture of Truman in Violetteville. It read:

TRUMAN HOWARD: THE LEAST INTUITIVE EMPATH TO DATE

The fifth Howard child—Mr. Truman Howard, age eighteen—has found himself overwhelmed by the basic emotion of surprise. For a feeling that even a baby empath could handle, Mr. Howard has proven himself to be the least intuitive empath in alien history. Not only did the calming atmosphere of the Carnegie Rupes steamroll his senses, but his will failed him entirely when confronting Aether's heinous second wonder, the Arachnoid. His questionable choice of a companion—Miss Esmeralda Mortimer, siren daughter of Ms. Angenciel Mortimer—had to rescue him… cont'd on pg 6, written by Cava Lore.

Truman blinked at the page and laughed. "You've got to be kidding me," he sighed.

"What?" Vedrò asked, fixing his hair in the mirror.

Truman tossed him the newspaper.

"Yikes," Vedrò said, scanning the article. "How come you and Esmeralda got mentioned, but Halle and I didn't? I mean, Halle helped save us. She deserves credit too." He noticed

Truman angrily drying his hands. "Don't let it get to you, Tru. It's just gossip."

"I know. It's because I'm a 'Howard,'" Truman said, rolling his eyes. "It's crazy. Only a few weeks ago, I was just Truman Howard, the poor, lonely kid at the Academy. Now, I'm 'the fifth Howard child,' rare alien specimen. I feel a bit whiplash—"

Suddenly, a loud BUZZ pierced the air. Lights flashed overhead. An alarm system triggered.

The boys cupped their ears.

"Is that a fire alarm?" Vedrò shouted, his voice absorbed by the noise.

Truman flung the door open and saw Sus on the move.

"THIEF!" Sus screeched. "THIEF!"

Truman ran after her and caught sight of the figure she was chasing. It was a young man dressed in all black. He was clutching a jar of amber liquid. Through the blinding lights, Truman glimpsed the blond man and—his ruby earring.

Krimmiel.

Chapter 13

She Loves Me Not

V edrò and Truman bolted up the stairwell.

Out of nowhere, a dozen Vivabees with ruby eyes shoved the boys aside and swarmed after Krimmiel.

The boys burst into the cafeteria, panting.

Red-eyed Vivabees scanned the room. The crowd became still. The lights stopped flashing, and the alarm went silent.

"Did you two do something?!" Falsmira growled at the boys.

"No," said Sus, before they could respond. "Someone in black with blond hair stole from the honey elixir reserves!"

Truman backed out of the cafeteria and into the courtyard, gulping for fresh air. In his periphery, something moved down the adjacent hallway—a shadow shrinking along the floor. He followed it. At the end of the corridor, a door stood ajar. He opened it and found a bright sea of mountains.

The Venusian Elps. Must be an exit, he thought.

As his eyes adjusted, he spotted Krimmiel in the distance. In one hand, the man gripped the jar of honey. With his other hand, he snapped his fingers at something.

What's he doing?

Out of thin air, he conjured a black vortex and pushed open the double doors. Before stepping onto the platform, he paused and slowly turned his head. His earring flickered. He smiled and stared enigmatically at Truman.

A cool breeze brushed his skin and stole his breath. Truman shuddered.

In a flash, the honey thief warped away, bringing the vortex with him.

☆ ☆ ☆ ☆ ☆ ☆

"We've searched every floor, and the honey thief is nowhere to be found!" Embar said as Truman returned to the cafeteria, unnoticed. "Salty, Scured, and Delulu are double-checking, but we were thorough the first time. I'm afraid he got away."

"Jelly's checking the security footage, right?" asked Sus.

"Yes."

While the Vivabees continued debriefing, Angenciel ushered the voyagers to the buffet.

Truman looked around to see if anyone else noticed what he had noticed.

Everyone was normal, piling food onto their plates and sitting down at the cafeteria tables.

"—And then a bunch of Vivabees *trampled* us! I almost fell down the stairs!" Vedrò recounted to Halle and Esmeralda. "I wish I had seen who the thief was."

"Oh my!" Halle moaned. "You must try this bee bread! It's so good!"

"The what?" said Truman.

"The bee bread! It's like a moist shortbread stuffed with raw pollen and crystallized honey! Try some!"

"Honey—as in honey elixir?"

"Non, ce n'est pas la même chose," Esmeralda said, shaking her head. "Honey elixir has medicinal properties, remember? Crystallized honey is for eating. I read about it in *The Wonders and Fathoms—"*

"—*of Aezer.*" Vedrò said, mocking her. "We get it. You read!" He stabbed his fork at Halle's slice.

She rolled her eyes. "What's under your arm?"

"Oh, here! It's the latest edition of *Mercury's Message*. You're in it."

"I am? What do you mean?" She snatched the newspaper and read.

"Spread some royal jelly on the bee bread," suggested Halle.

"J'y crois pas!" Esmeralda gasped, slamming the newspaper down. "Me?! 'Questionable?!' A friend who saves your life is not a *questionable* friend! And how dare they call you the 'least intuitive empath to date.'" Her voice took on a protective tone. "They don't know you like that!" She angrily bit into her slice of bee bread. "Cava Lore… where do I know that name?"

"What I don't get," said Truman, "is how this Cava person knows about the Spider Cavity. I understand the Carnegie Rupes bit, but the Arachnoid?" he wondered.

"Probably from the Assembly. My maman told me that all voyager-related incidents must be reported to the Assembly for documentation. Maybe Cava knows someone who works there?"

Jelly suddenly zoomed into the cafeteria and shouted, "The cameras have been tampered with!"

"What do you mean?" spat Sus.

"The ones in the substructure and stairwells were burnt to a crisp! And the ones by the courtyard have pierre plants growing over them!"

Sus rubbed her furry forehead, exasperated. "We need to scope out the reserves and see how much we lost."

Embar nodded and turned to the mentors. "We'll have to cut this short, you guys. We're so sorry!"

"No worries," replied Reuel. "We understand."

"Thank you."

And with that, the Vivabees swarmed away.

Truman felt a pang of guilt. He considered calling after them to tell them it was Krimmiel, or at least that he thought it was Krimmiel. But something told him not to. Something was holding him back.

After the Hive, the group spent the next few days on Cherry. Reuel taught the voyagers about the Vivabees and their culture, anatomy, habitat, and behaviors. Ereus bored them with lectures on the mechanics of the cyclone. Falsmira covered the history of the terraformation of Venus. Angenciel taught Venusian culture, cuisine, art, and law. They traveled across the Elps, toured the Venusian World Court, and visited the other Venusian hospitals.

Truman told no one about what he had seen, not even Vedrò.

"Today, we're visiting the Van Gogh Irisylum!" announced Angenciel. "It's a psychiatric hospital. It's also my place of employment when I'm not with you lot."

To reach the Irisylum, the group hiked a winding trail through the Venusian heat.

The Irisylum was a much smaller château than the Hive but somehow more beautiful. They crossed the drawbridge into a painting of distortion and a symphony of colors. The walls were made of canvas. Irises unfurled in a midnight blue. Sunflowers wilted in a broken yellow. They grew on the walls. A starlit sky swirled on the ceiling. Sweeping brush strokes painted a battle between dream and reality.

"At the Irisylum, we practice art therapy," said Angenciel. "While we're here, please do not wander. We must not disturb the patients. But feel free to enjoy the art."

The voyagers dispersed among the many landscapes and still lifes and took in the smell of rain and fresh paint.

Truman gravitated toward the portraits. Below a portrait of a despondent man was an engraving that read, *"For my part, I know nothing with any certainty, but the sight of the stars makes me dream."* The man held a stalk of lifeless flowers. His complexion paled in comparison to the blue world that teetered in his eyes.

"This one is my favorite," Reuel said, appearing beside Truman. "I've never much cared for the title, though. In my book, I find words to be as artistic as art itself. *Dr. Paul Gachet* just doesn't do it justice, does it? That's why I call it by a different name… *She Loves Me Not.*"

A lonely smile stretched across her face. Her gaze moved from the man in the painting to Angenciel, who was standing before a painting of a woman hunched in sorrow.

Truman wondered what Reuel had meant, but did not ask.

Down the corridor, Ereus guided the group through the in-patient wing. A sign overhead read *Dalí Hall*. They passed a moving mural of an African oasis where swans swam, and elegant elephants strode on stilts.

A corridor labeled *Frida Way* ran perpendicular to Dalí Hall.

While Ereus babbled about the empathproof framework, Vedrò surreptitiously pulled Truman down Frida Way.

"As much as I love Spanish surrealism, let's check out some Mexican magic," said Vedrò.

"Angenciel said not to wander."

"She also said to enjoy the art. Come on, Tru."

"When did you start calling me Tru?"

"I don't know. But I like it!"

Something moved under the corridor's flickering lights.

"What was that?!"

A dozen Frida Kahlo paintings lined the walls. They moved like the fresco in the Hive. One Kahlo wore a necklace of thorns. Another wore a red velveteen dress. There was a wounded deer with the head of the Mexican artist. Apart from the iconic unibrow, the Kahlos bore one unmistakable resemblance: they looked like they were in pain.

Truman stepped up to a Frida with a broken column for a spine and rusty nails piercing her skin. He gazed into her blinking eyes, then placed his palm against the canvas. Her painted fingers met his as if trying, with all her might, to break free from the two-dimensional world in which she had been trapped.

"Something's wrong with them," said Truman. "They look so sad."

"Ém Path?" Vedrò read aloud. "What do you suppose is in there?"

A lone door stood closed before the boys. The words *Ém Path* were chiseled into the door's gilded façade. A Frida next to a monkey jumping madly up and down shook her head violently, as if warning them not to go in.

Vedrò stepped away. "W-we should go back."

Truman ignored him and creaked open the door. He heard voices and saw blue paintings on the wall.

"People are in there," he said.

Suddenly, a pair of wide, haunted eyes appeared. They belonged to a pale, emaciated man.

Vedrò recoiled.

Truman moved closer. "A-are you an empath?" he asked hesitantly.

"Emotions enslave the empathic ear," the man replied, eyes unblinking. He reached through the gap and seized Truman by the necklace. His hands were cold. "You'll be with us soon." His laughter turned manic.

Truman struggled, but his grip wouldn't budge.

At once, a sense of calm permeated the air.

The man stopped laughing, released Truman, and inhaled deeply. The many Kahlos slumped down in their frames and, for a moment, looked liberated from their pain.

Truman felt his heart return to its regular beat.

"Where have you guys been?!" Halle said, coming down the hallway. "The mentors are looking for you. Who's that man?"

The door swung open. The mad man was no longer there. Instead, Nayelo stood before them.

"Dr. Noxthomas?"

"Truman, what are you doing down here? And please, call me Nayelo."

"We just wanted to see Frida's artwork," said Vedrò.

"And your name is?"

"Vedrò Azzurro."

"Ahh, yes. Reuel told me about you. Said you and Truman are attached to the hip. Are you a serena? I could feel the calm from my office!"

"No, she's the serena."

Nayelo looked at Halle. "And your name?"

"Halle Xióng."

"Halle Xióng? What an interesting name! What does it mean?"

"I'm not sure. My yéyé named me."

"Well, Halle, that's quite a talent you have! Being a serena, that is. Have you ever considered becoming an omnihealer?"

Halle rouged. "I don't have the will of an omnihealer, sir."

"No need! With a will like that, you could help a lot of patients here at the Irisylum, especially in there." He gestured to Ém Path. "That's where empaths go when they need psychiatric care." He glanced around. "You know, you three really shouldn't be down here. It's not part of your tour."

"Right, we should head back," said Truman. "It was nice seeing you."

"Likewise! Oh and, I'm glad to see you're feeling better! Sorry for what happened in the Carnegie Rupes. Messengers can be brutal."

They returned to the group.

"Here come a few stragglers now," said Angenciel, flagging them down. "Halle, Vedrò, Truman, I have someone important for you to meet! This is Shiloh, one of my colleagues here at the Irisylum."

A small Vivabee peeked from behind her. Their large black gemstoned eyes sparkled. "Bzeze," Shiloh said timidly. "It's a pleasure to meet you."

"Hello," the boys harmonized.

"Bzeze," Halle echoed softly.

"Shiloh will be joining us for the rest of our journey," announced Angenciel, "in case someone needs urgent medical care. Think of Shiloh as a school nurse."

"Too bad Shiloh wasn't there when you fainted," Vedrò muttered to Truman.

Truman's cheeks flushed. *Shiloh's probably joining us because of me*, he thought to himself.

"I very much look forward to traveling with you all." Shiloh checked the time. "I should go finish packing, so I'll be ready to join you tomorrow!" They waved goodbye.

Angenciel resumed the tour through the Irisylum.

"Thank you for retrieving the boys," Falsmira said to Halle.

She then pulled Truman and Vedrò aside and spat in a hushed voice, "INSUBORDINATION: the refusal to follow a reasonable request!" Her voice rose, drawing the attention of other voyagers. "Angenciel *clearly* said, *NO WANDERING!* You are both receiving a second detention."

"A second detention?!" Vedrò sputtered.

"Yes! You haven't forgotten about the shenanigans you pulled in the Spider Cavity, have you, Mr. Azzurro?"

"No, but… we were just looking at art!"

"And yet you still wandered off, did you not?!"

The boys said nothing.

"That's what I thought," Falsmira snarled. "Tomorrow evening, you two, Miss Mortimer, and Miss Xióng will have your first detention. I have something *special* planned for you four. Let's hope you can swim." Her smirk turned a shade of wicked.

Chapter 14

Wishes, Stars, & Fates

T he following morning, Cherry flew the voyagers up the Venusian Elps, near a towering, active volcano. A column of smoke and ash billowed into the stratosphere.

"That," Angenciel pointed out, "is the largest and most active volcano on Venus, Mount Ma'at—named after the Egyptian goddess of balance and harmony. It is said that when the volcano becomes inactive, a time of disorder is near," she said with dramatic flair.

"Good thing it's always erupting then," Reuel said, laughing.

As they descended, the volcano roared, spewing lumps of lava.

"Due to its constant, inhospitable, Plinian eruptions," Angenciel continued, "not many Venusians live around these parts. Some do, but they legally must get their residential force fields checked every week, which can be quite costly."

Once they disembarked, Cherry flew to the top of Mount Ma'at and began munching on the blood-clot-shaped blobs that spurted from the conical opening.

"What's she doing?!" Halle asked worriedly. "She's going to get burned!"

"She's just having lunch," said Reuel. "She loves her living lava!"

"She's eating lava?!" Halle's voice quivered.

"Living lava, yes. Seriously, Halle, there's nothing to worry about. Remember what I said in the Carnegie Rupes? Cherry is beyond powerful. I haven't proven it yet, but I have this theory that the living lava acts as a fathomous antacid and soothes her stomach."

"Fathomous?" asked Truman.

"Yes, it's an alien synonym for 'wondrous' and 'marvelous' but relating to fathoms," Reuel defined.

Esmeralda jotted the word down. "Where are we headed?" she asked without looking up.

"There!" Angenciel pointed to the eastern flank of Mount Ma'at where a grand library towered above the landscape. "That is Writers' Incorporated—Writers' Ink for short. It's a famous library, bookstore, publishing house, and printing press. It even prints *Mercury's Message*. Writers' Ink is obviously a play on words referencing the ink of a writer. But it's also named after Irma Writer, a famous Venusian plume known for her detective novels. *Plume* is an alien word for *writer*."

She set off down the mountainside. *"Allons-y!* Let's go!"

The voyagers followed.

Reuel caught up to Truman and nudged him with an elbow. "Our namesakes were plumes, you know."

"I'm sorry?"

"Mum loves to read," Reuel explained. "She named you after Truman Capote. *Breakfast at Tiffany's* and *In Cold Blood* are two of her favorites."

"I didn't know that. We read *In Cold Blood* in school. I liked it a lot. Made me question what is just. I've never read *Breakfast at Tiffany's*, but I've seen the movie."

"The book's completely different—more of a character study," said Reuel. "The movie's just a love story. Blah."

"I take it you don't like love stories?"

"I see their value. They're just difficult to get through."

"I see," said Truman. "Well, what about you? What plume are you named after?"

"John Ronald Reuel Tolkien, also known as J.R.R. Tolkien. Mum's a huge *Strider* fan." She smiled. "I'm not sure if Tolkien pronounced his middle name as *Rule* or *Ru-elle*, but I'm happy Mum chose *Ru-elle*. *Rule* just sounds like gruel or drool. *Ru-elle* is prettier and more feminine, and I like that."

After an hour of hiking, the group arrived at the library, drenched in sweat. Up close, it was even taller and more impressive, resembling a cathedral. The arched door was inscribed with the cursive, jet-black words *Writers' Ink*.

As Angenciel opened the door, a frigid air that smelled of aged paper blew outward.

The silence inside was overwhelming.

"*Oh la*," Esmeralda said breathlessly. Prose prickled her nose, and poetry picked at her brain.

The library spanned six stories, each lined with rows upon rows of books, each book bound in a different color. The ceiling was vaulted, and the stained-glass windows warmed the room. A rich, black ink floated in the air, unraveling around the room and scribbling out iconic literature like Ray Bradbury, Maya Angelou, and Kahlil Gibran.

Librarians, publishers, and booksellers sat on high stools behind carved desks. They dipped quill pens into the floating liquid. Each time they did, Truman half expected the magical ink to crash and splash onto all their books.

"May I help you?" a librarian asked, looking over their half-moon spectacles.

"We're here to purchase textbooks," replied Angenciel.

While Esmeralda perked up at the words, discontent broke out among the other voyagers.

"Textbooks?!" repeated Vedrò. "What do you mean 'textbooks?!'"

The librarian shushed him.

"Sorry!"

Angenciel waved for the group to follow and ducked under the floating ink as she ascended a flight of stairs. They passed aisles of science fiction, suspense novels, and historical satires.

In the speculative fiction aisle, a red book caught Truman's eye. He picked it up. On the cover was an abstract suit and a deconstructed American flag.

"Truman," Angenciel called before he could read its title.

He returned the book to its shelf and caught up with the group.

They stopped in the education aisle.

"So far, we've learned experientially," Angenciel said softly. "Now, it is time for textual learning. The texts you are required to buy are listed on here." She passed out slips of paper and read aloud, "For Aetherly History with Falsmira, you'll need *From Chiron to Now* by Blyly O'Bygone. For Interplanetary Technologies with Ereus, you'll buy *Vortexes and More* by Marjorie Moore. For Astrobiology with Reuel, you'll buy *The Wonders and Fathoms of Aether* by Marvelo S. Grandeur. And lastly, for Worlds Cultures, you'll read *Heavenly Bodies and the Cultures Within* by yours truly!"

"Wait, what?" Esmeralda sputtered, confused, doing a double take at the list. "What do you mean 'by yours truly?' *You* wrote a book?!"

"What, like it's hard?" Angenciel shrugged.

"That's not what I'm saying. It's just... I'm a little surprised. I *am* your daughter, after all." She frowned, looking slighted. "How did I not know this? You let me read *The Wonders and Fathoms of Aether*. Why didn't you let me read this one?"

"It's her Mars Virgo," Reuel blurted. "Her passions are strong but kept under tight reign. Too humble. And her Venus Scorpio... secretive much?"

Angenciel rolled her eyes at Reuel, smiling.

"I wish you had told me," Esmeralda grumbled.

"I'm sorry, my dear. You're right. I should've told you."

Vedrò raised his hand.

"Yes, Vedrò?"

"I only have six euros. Does that mean I don't have to get the books?" His face brightened.

"The Assembly will cover the expenses for you," said Angenciel. "Besides, euros aren't our form of currency. We use *wishes*, *stars*, and *fates*. One fate is equivalent to six stars, and one star makes thirty-three wishes. You might want to write that down." She produced a black drawstring pouch from her pocket. It clanked as she opened it. "Each of you will be given two fates. That should be plenty to cover the four books. Alright, everyone, take your fates!"

One by one, the voyagers reached into the bag and pulled out two heavy yellow coins, shaped like thin lines that branched into two like a wishbone.

"I've done the math," said Angenciel. "After purchasing your textbooks, you'll have a couple of stars remaining. You're welcome to buy a fifth book or a souvenir if you'd like." She ran her fingers across a bin of spiral horns.

The sight of the horns made Reuel scowl.

"Textbooks are down that way," Angenciel pointed. "If you need help, we'll be at the Plume Café downstairs. Once you've checked out, meet us there!"

The mentors turned and left.

"Let's go find our textbooks!" Esmeralda exclaimed, her voice quivering with excitement. She darted ahead.

Truman, Vedrò, and Halle followed. The others meandered through the knick-knack section.

"O'Bygone, Moore, Grandeur, and Mortimer," Esmeralda read off the paper, climbing a ladder. "I'm a little hurt she didn't tell me she wrote a book. Who keeps that a secret? And how did I not find it in her library?"

"Maybe she doesn't like to brag," Vedrò said halfheartedly, letting Esmeralda scour the shelves herself.

"But I'm her daughter—she should feel comfortable to tell me things." Esmeralda found and held the book in her hands, and her eyes lit up. "I can't wait to read it!"

"That makes one of us," Vedrò said dryly, exhausted just watching her stack the textbooks. "If you've already read *The*

Wonders and Fathoms of Aether, why are you buying another copy?"

"Because I want my own copy." She passed them their books.

Truman examined the covers, mesmerized by their magic.

From Chiron to Now was the thickest of the four books, and the binding was made of glass. Trapped behind the glass was fog. The fog stirred and settled to reveal brief moments in time. He saw a moving image of people signing a treaty with quill pens. The image disappeared behind the fog. He then saw an image of limbless Arachnoids towering over bleeding soldiers. It, too, disappeared.

Vortexes and More was the sleekest of the texts. Its cover resembled a circuit board. When Truman touched certain spots, his thumb passed through miniaturized vortexes and emerged elsewhere on the cover. It looked like his thumb had been cut in half.

"*Cavolo!*" Vedrò exclaimed, mouth gaping. "That's so cool!"

"Right!" Truman agreed, grabbing the next book.

Heavenly Bodies and the Cultures Within was the most cosmic. Its cover displayed every major heavenly body between the Sun and the Kuiper Belt. The Sun was on the spine, and every planet rotated and orbited around the cover. It was as if the book were calculating every planet's current position.

The Wonders and Fathoms of Aether was the most beautiful, Truman thought. When he held it, it felt alive and glowed with marvelous creatures. He recognized Cherry, the Vivabees, pierre plants, and living lava. But he didn't know what to make of the other creatures. One marvel looked like wind. It moved so quickly it was hard to see. He thumbed through its pages and came across a chapter on Leonian dragons. The chapter was entirely made of fire, not paper. At first, Truman thought the book was on fire. He dropped it, expecting it to burn. But when the cover closed, the fire was extinguished.

"Wicked!" Vedrò murmured in awe. "Maybe I *will* have fun reading."

Truman picked it back up and noticed Halle flipping through a different book.

"Whatcha looking at?" he asked.

"A book on omnihealing. I think I'm gonna buy it with my extra coin."

Esmeralda descended the ladder with her pile of books. "I'm buying an extra book too!" She held up a hardcover that read *Arachnoids: Their Tangled Web of a History*. The cover had been woven out of a thick, sticky cobweb. The violet lettering glistened as if the pigmentation came from Arachnoid venom. She tried stacking the book onto her pile, but the cover kept sticking to her hand.

Truman used two of his textbooks to pry the book off Esmerald's hand.

"Merci," she said when Truman finally freed her hand from the sticky cover. "So, what're you boys buying with your extra change?"

"I'm saving mine," said Truman.

They headed to the checkout counter.

"I'm getting this!" Vedrò said, laying a spiral horn onto the counter.

"Do you even know what that is?" asked Esmeralda.

"No, but it looks cool!"

"It's a narwhal tusk, my dear boy," said the old woman sitting behind the counter. She had a husky voice and fiery hair. "They're extraordinary tools. Sharp but extraordinary. Savvies tinkered with the tusks so that they could purify poisoned waters and remove venom from infected areas of the body. Neat, huh?!" She took his books and placed them into one side of a balance. "Would you like a coin pouch to store your change? It's charmed to hold an infinite amount of cash without ever getting heavier. It's only a couple of wishes!"

"Sure! So, how do I use the tusk?"

"Here are the instructions." She handed him a pamphlet and plopped the tusk and velvet pouch onto his books. "Alright, that'll be one fate and five stars, please."

Vedrò handed her his two fates. She placed them into the other side of the balance. As the two sides balanced out, a brassy coin that looked like a juvenile drawing of the Sun came rolling out on a little ramp connected to the scales. It was the star coin.

"When will you ever need to use a narwhal tusk?" Esmeralda asked as she weighed her books and handed the woman her fates. "I'll take a pouch too. Thank you, *Madame*."

"You never know," replied Vedrò.

Halle and Truman paid for their things as well. Truman stored his remaining stars and wishes in his pouch, which felt like a deep pocket. The wish coin was shaped like a shooting comet.

"Where's the Plume Café?" asked Esmeralda.

"Head down one of those aisles there, and you'll see it," said the woman.

They thanked her and left. The aisle they took was long and serpentine like a Leonian dragon.

"Geez, how long is this aisle?!" Vedrò said, already tired of lugging around textbooks.

Between the fantasy and detective sections came a masculine voice. "Lost in the library, are we?" A man with a gold pen behind his ear looked down on them. He was handsome despite his wicked eyes. He smirked and said coolly, "Name's Cava… Cava Lore."

Esmeralda glared at him instantly.

"I take it you've read my work?"

"What work?" asked Truman.

"He's the one who wrote the article about you and me."

"Ah, so you have read my work." Arrogance rolled off the man's shoulders. "I quite enjoyed writing that article."

"You don't know us," spat Esmeralda.

"That may be true. But I definitely know more about your families than you two do. I see it in your tragic eyes."

"Don't you get tired of spreading rumors like some high school girl?" Esmeralda said, scowling. "You should try reporting actual news for once. Just a thought."

"Cheeky. I like that. But let me tell you this, missy: a pen that writes fiction is merely a needle of truth. I'm just sewing the dress."

Esmeralda snorted. "Ha! You come up with that yourself? What a stupid metaphor!"

Cava put his tongue to his cheek. "I can't wait 'til you read my next article." He smirked again.

Esmeralda clenched her books.

"There you are!" Angenciel said, coming around the corner. "Everyone's at the café—" She saw Cava.

"G'day, Angenciel."

"It was. What are you doing here, Cava?"

"Printing press."

"I see," she said stiffly. "Speaking of, has—"

"It's been rejected… again."

"But Cava, people *need* to be educated on—"

"The Writers' Ink Publishing House has already told you, Angenciel. We will not publish your text due to the subject matter. We do not wish to associate ourselves with you and your 'ideologies.'"

Angenciel bit her tongue. "Come on, kids. Let's not keep the others waiting."

As they wheeled around, Cava laid his hand on Truman's shoulder and hissed in his ear, "I'm a véritist, you know. And I know there's something up with your family. You may not know what it is, and I can tell you do not, but I will get to the bottom of it if it's the last thing I do." His words hung in the air.

Angenciel stepped in between them. "If you ever, *ever*, lay a finger on him again, you'll be answering to me. Do you understand?"

Cava backed off. "My apologies." He turned and left, bringing his smirk with him.

Chapter 15

The Great Cheryl Reef

"What text are you trying to publish, Maman?" Esmeralda asked as they headed toward the Plume Café.

"Oh, I just wrote another book, that's all," she said nonchalantly. "It's titled *Sirens and—*" She caught herself saying the word.

"It's okay, Maman. They already know."

Angenciel raised a brow. "When did you tell them?"

"The night the blossom bugs came out."

"I see." Angenciel paused. "That's good."

"So, the book?"

"Yes. It's titled *Sirens and Dead Seas*. It's a text all about sirens and siren culture, wills, history, and sociopolitics. In it, I break down the truths and falsehoods of being a siren. I believe you read my first draft back home, right? I saw it had been moved."

Esmeralda reddened.

"It's okay. I was hoping you'd read it. I want everyone to read it." She sighed. "Ugh, it's infuriating. Our voices deserve to be heard, not shamed into hiding." She shook her head. "Prejudice is a plague. People like Cava never change, or at least never try to. I know from personal experience how tough the worlds can be on people like us. It's why I'm dreading the end of your journey when you'll be on your own."

Esmeralda looked down and reached for her mother's hand. "W—we should tell the others about us."

"The other voyagers?" asked Angenciel. "Are you sure?"

Esmeralda squeezed her hand and smiled warmly. "Absolutely."

"Yeah!" added Truman. "What better way is there to fight prejudice than by informing others?"

"Truman's right," said Esmeralda. "I'm sorry I asked to keep our will a secret, Maman. But we should enlighten the others about sirens."

Vedrò and Halle nodded in agreement.

Angenciel smiled at them. "Alright, we'll do it tonight!" She hugged Esmeralda. "I'm so happy to see my daughter embrace her sirenhood! You've become such a beautiful and intelligent woman, Esmeralda. And to have found friends who encourage you to be yourself, I could not have asked for more!"

Truman, Halle, and Vedrò blushed.

"I am pretty great, aren't I?" Vedrò said playfully.

"Shut up," Esmeralda laughed.

They reached *The Plume Café*. The sign was in cursive, and the logo was a hand holding an inky quill pen.

Vedrò ordered an espresso and watched the old-fashioned, copper-and-brass machine work its magic.

Every voyager asked Angenciel to sign their copy of *Heavenly Bodies and the Cultures Within*, including Esmeralda. It put a smile on the author's face.

"How are the planets moving on the cover?" asked Style.

Humzah interpreted.

"The cover uses similar technology to the Wylaways' Worldswide Wristwatches," she said, signing his copy. "I worked with Ereus and my friend who's a savvy to design the cover."

"What about *The Wonders and Fathoms of Aether?* How can the chapter on Leonian dragons be made of fire?" asked Truman.

"That design is also an illusionist-savvy collaboration," said Ereus. "The magical technology merely gives the illusion that the chapter is on fire. It's not actually."

Once Vedrò finished his coffee, the group, laden with textbooks, headed back to Cherry, who looked merry from all the living lava she had eaten.

"You four, here, now," Falsmira said to Truman, Halle, Esmeralda, and Vedrò.

The others went inside the cabin.

"After dinner, meet me in front of Newton's Cradle. Eight o'clock on the dot. Cherry-time. A minute later, and you'll earn yourself another round of detention. Do I make myself clear?"

"Crystal," said Truman.

"Good. See you in the lavender fields." She turned and left.

In the lavender fields, the cohort ate an extravagant meal of French cuisine until the force field dimmed to a subtle glow. The long table was weighed down with escargot, ratatouille, raclette, warm baguettes, bœuf bourguignonne, and croquembouche.

Over dessert, Angenciel confessed to the group that she and Esmeralda were, in fact, sirens, not enchantresses. She debunked the myths of sirens and explained the daily prejudices sirens face. It was much of the same information Esmeralda had shared with Truman, Vedrò, and Halle the night of the blossom bugs.

After dinner, Truman, Vedrò, Halle, and Esmeralda found themselves in the cabin awaiting their detention.

"Ah, sugar!" Shiloh, the nursing Vivabee, came fluttering into the cabin, fumbling over their honeycomb-shaped luggage.

Esmeralda rushed over to help pick up toiletries that had fallen from a tote bag—wooden dippers, eye polish, and stinger cleaner.

"Oh, thank you. That's very kind," said Shiloh. "Your name is Esmeralda, right? Your mother has told me much about you! All great things!"

Esmeralda smiled. "These are my friends, Vedrò, Truman, and Halle."

"Good evening," Vedrò said, hoisting Shiloh's duffel bag over his shoulder.

"It's nice to meet you again," Truman said, grabbing a bag.

"Likewise!"

"So, where are these headed?" Halle asked, struggling to lift a backpack stuffed with medical books.

"To the nurse's room there." Shiloh pointed to the door near the fireplace. A honey dipper was engraved on the door.

The voyagers carried—or in Halle's case, dragged—the bags into the room which was long and lofty.

"Thank you again!" Shiloh said, fluttering to the queen-sized bed with seaweed and stingrays in it. A room divider was next to the bed, and three hospital beds were behind it. "This place is far too big! My siblings and I usually sleep in the same beehive together. I'm not accustomed to this much space."

"Must be nice to have so many siblings. I'm an only child," said Halle.

"It is nice," said Shiloh. "But compared to them, I'm the loner of the hive."

Vedrò checked his watch. "Guys, it's time." He returned to the lobby.

"Thanks again!" Shiloh said, seeing them out. "Bzeze!"

Just as she had instructed, Falsmira burst into the lobby at eight o'clock on the dot, her robes whisking behind her. "Follow me!" she ordered. "Put these on!" She opened a closet door across from Shiloh's room and pulled out neoprene body suits.

"What're these for?" Esmeralda asked, eyes narrowed.

"For your punishment," replied Falsmira. "You'll be collecting oysters from the bottom of the sea. I hope you all can swim!" She smirked.

"Collecting oysters?" Halle echoed, confused.

"What're you talking about? What sea?" Vedrò asked, taking a wetsuit.

Falsmira walked over to the fish tank and removed its lid. Pink water splashed onto the hardwood floor.

"Every waterbed, couch, and aquarium on Cherry is connected to the Cheryl Sea," said Falsmira. "The sea reflects the color pink due to the red-colored algae."

"Wait, wait, wait. Cherry has an ocean on her back?" Vedrò said incredulously. "And it's pink?!"

"Don't be surprised," Esmeralda said, putting on her bubbled headpiece. "Reuel *did* say, 'Cherry is beyond powerful,' remember? Besides, there is a lake just outside."

Once fastened, the headpiece became invisible, and once zipped, the wetsuit as well. All that was seen were their clothes underneath.

"Cool!" Truman murmured, bringing the wetsuit closer. He stretched the fabric and gave it a curious look.

"You knew about this 'Cheryl Sea?'" Vedrò asked, slipping the wetsuit over his shorts.

"Yes," said Esmeralda. "Now that you have a copy of *The Wonders and Fathoms of Aether*, you should read it sometime. You should read anything sometime."

Truman and Halle exchanged glances and laughed.

"Enough!" Falsmira snapped. She flung tin buckets and picks at their feet. "Now listen. You won't need headlamps while you're down there. The Cheryl Sea has a natural glow. Collect as many oysters as you can." She spoke quickly, leaving no room for questions. "The scuba suits will allow you to breathe underwater without an oxygen tank. They'll also provide you some physical protection against electric eels or giant squids or…" Her lips curled into a grin.

"I don't know—killer sharks that may attack!" She scoffed at the thought, making Halle whimper. "But since audiovisual technology is embedded in the headpieces, I'll keep an eye on you with this monitor." She held up a small screen. "If I see any approaching threats, I'll alert you. As quickly as I can, of course. Your headpieces will allow you to speak to each other, but only if you see something approaching. No chitchatting or dillydallying. Understood? Now off you go!"

With their fins on and buckets in hand, the four shuffled onto a footstool. One by one, they hesitantly leapt into the fish tank. At the bottom of the tank was a hole in a rock that led into the ocean. As their eyes adjusted to the lambent ocean floor, an expansive and colorful coral reef unfolded beneath them. From top to bottom, the ocean had a baby-pink-to-fuchsia gradient. Truman felt like he was wearing rose-tinted glasses.

Then, it hit him. *This is the first time I've ever swam in an ocean,* he thought. *And it's on the back of a dragon!*

The others were in awe as well. They paddled upwards and broke through the surface.

A pink, scaly sky stretched over the endless Cheryl Sea, resembling dragon hide. Esmeralda removed her headpiece and inhaled deeply, savoring the wind.

Truman followed suit, finding the breeze sweet and salty.

"Smells so good—what is that?" Halle asked, nose upturned.

"It's Cherry's aromatherapy," said Esmeralda. "In *The Wonders and Fathoms of Aether,* it says that—" She paused, shaking her head as if out of a trance. "—that the aromatherapy has the… the ability to… ensnare the senses if exposed for… for too long…" Her voice trailed off.

They buoyed in the water, their minds afloat. All that was heard was the lapping of waves.

Suddenly, a faint yet angry voice spoke out of nowhere. It drew them back to reality.

"*Dio?*" Vedrò addressed the heavens. "Is that you?"

"No, it's me! Falsmira! Put your headpieces back on and start picking, or you'll face another detention!"

The four hurried to obey. They swam down to the ocean floor and spent hours chipping away at clusters of oysters, gradually filling their buckets. As they worked, they encountered sea turtles the size of islands, clownfish of all colors, a whale as tiny as a thumb, and oddly, their waterbeds. The beds looked like bubbled portals into another world. They stuck to the reef like sea anemones.

"How do you suppose these work, Esmeralda?" Truman asked, stopping in front of a waterbed surrounded by blue sea dragons.

"They're called seabed anemones. Savvies developed them to display parts of the Cheryl Sea. Ingenious technology."

"How can technology do this?" Truman asked, bewildered.

"I'm not entirely sure. All I know is that the savvies don't just develop technology. They develop *magical* technology, whatever that means."

In one of the seabed anemones, Truman saw a handsome boy in boxers crawl under a comforter. His chest was toned and a bit hairy. It was Style.

Truman blushed and turned away.

Vedrò swam up to them. "Guys, I was collecting oysters near Sweta's bed, and she saw me! Now she probably thinks I'm spying on her!"

"NO TALKING!" Falsmira's voice crackled through their speakers.

"Um, Falsmira, how much longer?" Halle asked, wringing her pruney hands. "Everyone else is going to bed."

"And you will, too, once you finish filling your buckets!"

"But what are these for?" Vedrò whined.

"I want oysters tomorrow. That's what they're for! The quicker you finish, the quicker you can go to bed."

They all grumbled and returned to work.

Vedrò began hacking at a colony of oysters near a pile of spiky, red-and-white striped stones. The stones formed a wall over a hole in the ocean floor.

"STOP!" Esmeralda shouted.

Vedrò recoiled. "What?!"

"Those are lionfish!" She pointed at the stones. "They're highly venomous creatures. One sting is so painful it'll make you wish you were dead."

"Yikes. Thanks, Esmeralda." Vedrò leaned in, his eyes widening as he noticed the fins and eyes hidden in the stones. The creatures' color scheme was a trick of the eye.

Esmeralda stared unblinkingly at something behind Vedrò. Her body turned rigid. Vedrò followed her gaze and, too, froze in spot.

A grotesque shark was swimming toward them. Its teeth were everywhere. It looked like a dental experiment gone wrong—a mutation of selachian body horror. Its jaws and fins spiraled like a buzzsaw made of teeth. Serrated incisors protruded out of the most random places—its skin, gills, even eyes.

Truman clenched his pick.

"Get back to the fish tank!" Falsmira yelled. "NOW!"

Halle was already swimming away, her face pale.

The other three followed as fast as they could toward the hole in the rock. Fish jetted past them. Oysters rained from their buckets.

The shark thrashed through a smack of jellyfish, its jaws and fins grinding like a buzzsaw.

Halle was the first to escape. She leapt out of the fish tank like a dolphin bursting through waves.

Esmeralda was next, landing on the cabin floor with a thud.

Truman made it to the hole but glanced back just as the shark closed in on Vedrò. Its lower jaw snapped and clamped around Vedrò's leg. The shark's teeth sank into his wetsuit, but no blood came. Instead, the wetsuit began to malfunction. His pant leg was now visible, and cracks spread like a screen breaking. The shark kept biting. More cracks appeared. First, the pant leg, then the waistband, and, finally, his sleeves.

Truman's heart pounded.

"HELP!" Vedrò cried.

The shark pulled him into its gaping mouth until his entire body was consumed.

Chapter 16

Ivies, Oaks, & Asters

A whirlpool appeared behind the shark.

Falsmira dove into the water and narrowed her eyes. The whirlpool slowed to a near halt. The shark froze in place. She swam down, reached into the shark's open jaws, and pulled Vedrò out by the hand. Cracks spidered across every inch of his wetsuit. Water was leaking into his headpiece. He frantically swam toward the hole.

Truman and Vedrò flopped onto the cabin floor. Vedrò trembled as he yanked off his headpiece and gasped for air.

Falsmira lingered in the water, watching as the whirlpool and shark resumed their natural pace. The whirlpool sucked the shark into its vortex. It thrashed, fighting to break free, but the current was too strong—it vanished into the whirlpool's depths.

"I thought I was a goner," Vedrò spat.

Falsmira climbed out of the tank, her hair and robes completely drenched.

"Will he be okay?!" cried Esmeralda.

"Wh-what was that *thing*?" Halle blurted, voice quivering.

"What is all the racket?" Shiloh peeked out of their bedroom, a sleeping mask pushed above their bejeweled eyes.

"Miss Mortimer, please go find Reuel and your mother. They should be at the end of the Dragon's Back Trail," instructed Falsmira.

Esmeralda dashed out the cabin doors.

"Shiloh, can you please check on Mr. Azzurro here? He was attacked by a buzzsaw shark in the Cheryl Sea." Falsmira wrung out her hair.

"Oh my Queen Bee, of course!" Shiloh rummaged through their room and reemerged with a honeycomb-shaped emergency kit. "You poor thing, you're in pain. I feel it. Here, take this. It'll help." The Vivabee pulled out a wooden dipper and dunked it into the golden honey that oozed from their gown. "It's well-aged honey elixir. You'll like it, trust me."

The honey-covered dipper looked like a melting lollipop.

Vedrò popped it in his mouth and, at once, slouched in relief.

"I thought you said these suits were invincible," Vedrò muttered, wincing as Shiloh peeled off his scuba suit. There was no blood. But there were bite marks.

"No," said Falsmira coolly. "I said they would provide you *some* physical protection. You're not bleeding, are you? Clearly, it did its job." She turned to Truman. "Good job with the whirlpool. Next time, be quicker."

"I'm sorry?"

"You willed that whirlpool. Smart thinking—but too last minute. If I hadn't jumped in and slowed it down, both your friend and the shark would've been sucked into it."

"I… didn't know I did that," Truman said to himself.

Shiloh examined Vedrò's skin. "There appears to be no surface damage. Only indentations that should lift any second now. You may have some internal bruising tomorrow. So, take it easy, okay?"

Vedrò nodded.

Just then, Angenciel and Reuel burst into the room with Esmeralda close behind.

Reuel rushed to Truman, wide-eyed. "What happened?! Are you okay?!"

"I'm fine. It's Vedrò. A buzzsaw shark ate him."

"Ate him?!" spat Angenciel.

"The suit protected him, of course," Falsmira said, checking her nails.

"I gave him elixir for the pain," said Shiloh. "Possible internal bruising. But he'll be fine!"

"Thank you, Shiloh." Angenciel took a deep breath and locked eyes with her fellow mentor. "Falsmira, this is my daughter we're talking about. Reuel's brother. Our students! I understand they had detention. But this, Falsmira? This was a fool's errand!"

"You're telling me," sighed Falsmira. "They didn't even bring back my oysters! I was looking forward to those!"

"This is no joke, Falsmira!"

"Oh please, it's not like they died!" She rolled her eyes. "I wouldn't have let them either—no matter how much they annoy me. Besides, hopefully they've learned their lesson now!" She flung her soaked robes dramatically, flicking water onto them all, and swept out of the room without another word.

Reuel, Angenciel, and Shiloh helped the four voyagers up the stairs. When they reached their rooms, they shuddered at the sight of their waterbeds.

☆ ☆ ☆ ☆ ☆

For the next few days, Vedrò was the talk of the dragon. Everyone wanted to know what it was like inside the buzzsaw shark.

"It was dark inside," he said on the first day.

Despite Shiloh's prognosis, Vedrò had no internal bruising.

"I saw my life flash before my very eyes!" he said on the second day, grimacing and rubbing his leg as if it were in pain.

"I felt its teeth sink right into my liver!" he said on the third day. "But I didn't let that stop me! I pried its jaws wide open with my bare hands!" He flexed his arms and chomped his teeth.

The girls squealed and swooned. Vedrò playfully winked at Esmeralda, who remained thoroughly unamused.

The others were subjected to questions as well.

"What was the Cheryl Sea like?"

"Oh, it was beautiful!" said Halle. "The water was like a pink glittery bath bomb! Oh, you should've seen it, Shiloh!"

"Oh no, I don't swim. It's not good for my wings."

"Cherry's aromatherapy was my favorite," said Esmeralda. "Intoxicating!"

"How did you create the whirlpool?"

"I don't know," said Truman. "I was scared for Vedrò, and then it just appeared."

"Was the shark really that scary?"

"Horrifying! And ugly too," Halle said with a shudder.

Due to the incident, Reuel taught the voyagers about the Cheryl Sea and all its marine creatures and qualities. They used the chapter on Cherry in *The Wonders and Fathoms of Aether* for reference. The pages in that chapter were made of stone. The text had been etched into the slabs instead of printed.

"Buzzsaw sharks can be quite peaceful creatures," explained Reuel. "They're highly intelligent too. They can recognize a person by scent, even if the person is wearing a wetsuit. They're known as protectors of coral reefs. It likely attacked Vedrò and the others because they were hacking away at oysters, which it saw as a threat."

"I don't think *eating me alive* makes the shark a 'peaceful creature,'" Vedrò quipped, soaking up the sympathy.

At that point, everyone had grown tired of Vedrò, especially Esmeralda, who saw through every embellishment and blatant lie.

Truman was also fed up but for a different reason. In fact, he didn't mind that Vedrò was playing up the details—it drew the attention off him. What bothered him was the memory of the shark every day and the nightmares that followed every night.

"The elixir might be my new blessedbe flavor," Vedrò mused, realizing he had to pivot.

"I wish I could taste the elixir." Halle crossed her arms and pouted.

"I'm sorry," Shiloh said gently. "I'm only allowed to prescribe it to patients."

Still in eyeshot, Mount Ma'at continued to erupt in all its volcanic glory.

"Today is our last day on Venus," Ereus announced one morning. "Tomorrow, we're off to the last world of our first trimester: the Moon!"

"Already? I feel like we haven't seen much of Venus," said Esmeralda.

"That's the problem with traveling. You can't see it all."

"After the Moon, we return to Earth, right?" Halle asked excitedly.

"Yes. You'll have a short break on Earth," said Ereus. "But today, we warp! Let's begin!"

Unfortunately, the warping lesson was a disaster. No one had improved. Even Truman struggled, drained from his sleepless nights.

Ereus sighed. "We're nearing the end of our first trimester. By now, you should be warping to the yellow vortex with ease," he said, tapping his foot. "Concentration is key!"

The voyagers grew increasingly impatient. Esmeralda clenched her fists every time she failed.

"You must focus," Ereus said calmly.

"If I focus any harder, my eyeballs will pop out of my head!" Esmeralda muttered through gritted teeth.

She practiced until Ereus made her step aside so the others could practice too.

Vedrò failed but shrugged it off.

When Halle failed, she whispered kind affirmations to herself. "I will do better next time. I believe in myself. Be patient."

Only Style managed to warp to the yellow vortex. Esmeralda shot him a jealous glare.

"Let's stop here for today," Ereus said, leading the voyagers out of the vortex hall.

They hiked up a hill along the Venusian Elps.

"While we walk, I want to discuss *wanderlust*," Ereus continued. "Wanderlust is the renewable energy source that fuels vortexes. While Earthlings primarily use fossil fuels to generate energy, we use wanderlust. Unlike fossil fuels, wanderlust does not pollute our worlds."

"If we have a renewable energy source that could save Earth, why are we gatekeeping?" asked Halle. "I understand we can't breach PSA. But it feels wrong to gatekeep something so lifesaving."

Esmeralda looked up, intrigued. "She poses a good question."

"I agree," said Ereus. "It is good of you to ask those questions. You're demonstrating critical thinking skills and a moral obligation to others. Still, we cannot share wanderlust with Earthlings. If we did, then they'd know about Aether. And you know very well it's against our law to reveal Aether to non-alien Earthlings." He crossed his arms. "Besides, they have renewable energy sources: solar, wind, water, geothermal. They have the means, but they still choose fossil fuels because that's where the business is—a lucrative one too. Earthlings are greedy beings. If you haven't learned that yet, you will."

Truman and Vedrò exchanged ashamed glances. They risked their lives in the Spider Cavity because of greed.

"Okay, but what about omnihealing?" volleyed Halle. "Why are we gatekeeping that too? Omnihealers could be saving thousands of Earthling lives every day!"

"For the same reason, Halle. PSA." Ereus frowned, disappointed in his own answer.

Halle looked upset but didn't press the matter.

"So, what exactly is wanderlust?" asked Schmidt. "And where does it come from?"

Ereus looked to Reuel.

"Guess that's my cue," Reuel said, taking the lead on the hike. "Before I answer your question, Schmidt—an excellent one by the way—I need to introduce you to a place called Ivies and Oaks."

They were now standing at the northern flank of Mount Ma'at.

"Ivies and Oaks is where I work when I'm not mentoring. It's one of Aether's largest air filters, supplying us air-breathers with quality recycled oxygen through a connected network embedded in our force fields. Ivies and Oaks is also our Solar System's leading plant research and conservation facility." She gestured forward. "And there she is!"

The voyagers looked upon a cluster of greenhouses. They were colorful, vitreous, and scintillating. They towered so high they pierced Venus' hellish clouds.

"The greenhouses are grown from giant pierre plants," Reuel explained. "Astrobiologists have become so skilled at tending to the fathoms we've managed to build greenhouses out of them! More precisely, inside them."

Bird baths and lemon trees lined a pathway to the entrance. Inside, it smelled of flowers and fresh rain. Truman felt like he had wandered into the science-fiction version of a botanical garden.

The first greenhouse glowed red. A sea of plants lapped their eyes. Bamboo surged behind bushels of begonias. The greenhouse grasses whistled in the wind. Tricolored mosses grew on stone cairns levitating near a poetry of wildflowers and tiny waterfalls.

The waterfalls were quite peculiar. Some listened to gravity, while others defied it and cascaded upward.

The ivies and oak trees were the most abundant. Vines of ivy spiraled up the tall and mighty oak trees with purple daisy-looking flowers scattered at their roots.

The greenery stood out against the red plant-cell walls.

"Are those plant cells?!" Esmeralda gasped, racing to the wall. "I recognize the central vacuole! And the Golgi apparatus!"

"Nerd," Vedrò teased.

She stared blankly at him.

"Yes, the walls are indeed plant cells discernible to the naked eye," said Reuel. "This is a blown-up pierre plant, after all. Don't touch the walls—they're very sharp. As you can see, there's the rigid cell wall, the nucleus, and the mitochondria. The ribosomes are the little black dots."

She pointed to each part of the cell. "And those are the chloroplasts. Most chloroplasts store a pigment called *chlorophyll*, which gives plants their green color. All pierre plants have chlorophyll, but it may be masked by a different pigment. In this case, the red hue comes from *cocinophyll*, which masks the chlorophyll."

She turned to face the group. "Despite the abundance of ivies and oak trees, the name of this place has another meaning. 'Ivies' and 'oaks' are gender binary terms for aliens who have the will to manipulate plant life. Most women go by the term *ivy*. Most men go by *oak*. *Aster* is the inclusive gender-neutral option, usually adopted by anyone who is genderfluid, non-binary, or two-spirited—but anyone can use it. While my pronouns are she/her, I'm more comfortable being called an aster. I know—it's a unique case. But get into it." She winked.

Schmidt scoffed.

Esmeralda shot him a hateful glare.

"I've been pushing for the institution to change its name for quite some time," Reuel pressed on. "Ivies, Oaks, and Asters! It flows well, I think! Most ivies and oaks prefer the name as is. I just don't want anyone to feel excluded.

"On a different note, I've been promoted to the junior executive board here at Ivies and Oaks'. That means I'll be working closely with top leadership. I intend to take full advantage of that opportunity and make my voice heard!" Reuel beamed.

Truman smiled proudly at her.

Leaving the red greenhouse, they entered a pink one, where astrobiologists in winter jackets collected sap samples from snow-clad maple trees.

"Fun fact," said Reuel, "while Earthling greenhouses protect plants from cold weather, Ivies and Oaks' greenhouses do the exact opposite due to Venus' blistering heat. When scientists discovered that pierre plants can offer symbiotic relationships with other plants, the famous astrobiologist and *maximalist* Maxine Machado enlarged the first greenhouse," she paused to let the image sink in.

"A maximalist is an alien who has the will to enlarge objects. While pierre plants have natural properties that allow other plants to grow inside them, not all plants can thrive in the same environment. So, to control certain areas in our greenhouses, the savvies developed individual force fields for plants that require special attention. Some plants thrive in colder temperatures, like coniferous trees, while other plants require higher temperatures, like the oddlies."

They passed through the pink greenhouse and into a purple one. The temperature difference was stark—it went from shadow to shine the moment they crossed the threshold.

"What're the oddlies?" Halle asked, fanning herself with a large leaf she found on the ground.

"Their scientific name is *Medusagyne jellifolia*. No one calls them that besides us botany geeks," said Reuel. "Kids usually call them jellyfish trees. Around this time of year, they'll be in full bloom!"

The voyagers pushed through a curtain of ivy and stepped into a forest of odd-looking trees. Some trees were red, others were yellow. And some were blue. Every tree had dense filaments dangling from a bell-shaped crown like jellyfish tentacles.

"We've encountered many fathoms thus far along our journey," said Reuel. "Living lava, pierre plants, blossom bugs, buzzsaw sharks… But none of them hold a candle to the oddlies for the oddlies are why we have wanderlust. Wanderlust is a fine powder found in the roots of an oddly. It was accidentally discovered by Guillermo del Goro when he was digging a grave for his pet toad at the foot of an oddly. When his gardening trowel struck a root, he was warped to the Earthling pet store where he first adopted the toad. He's considered the first alien to ever warp—all thanks to a toad!"

The voyagers laughed.

"When the savvies began the mass-production of vortexes," Reuel continued, "oddlies nearly became extinct. To extract the wanderlust, they had to uproot the entire oddly, thus killing it. The Assembly was at fault. They ordered savvies to mass-produce the vortexes, but the oddlies were getting killed faster than we could regrow them."

"That's horrible!" exclaimed Sweta.

"Indeed. But before it was too late, astrobiologists went on strike. In response, the Assembly regulated production and saved the oddlies from complete deforestation. After further research, we found cleaner and safer ways of extracting wanderlust without needing to uproot the trees."

A gentle wind rustled through the thread-like branches. Truman inhaled the subtle sweetness of the oddlies and relaxed his shoulders. He then brushed a branch and felt a *zap*.

"Ow!" He recoiled.

"I should mention," Reuel added quickly, "the tendrils of the oddlies may sting a bit. But it's nothing to worry about."

A table with chairs and a pitcher of lemonade sat under a yellow oddly.

"Anyone care for lemonade?" asked Reuel.

A variety of yeses rang from the voyagers from *ja* and *sì* to *yeah* and *oui*.

She began filling glasses. "Could someone fetch a few lemons from the front entrance?"

"Why make lemonade when we could make limoncello?" joked Vedrò.

"Clever, but the lemonade's already made. The Nut should be warping in our lunch any moment now. I just want lemons for garnish."

"We'll go get 'em," Truman volunteered, dragging Vedrò along.

The two found their way back to the red greenhouse.

"If we dig up some wanderlust, do you think we could sell it on the black market? With all the regulations, I bet it's worth thousands!"

As they exited, they nearly collided with Elmory Moss. Her hair was disheveled, her eyes weary.

"Hi, Elmory," Truman greeted.

"I'm sorry. Do I know you?"

"We're voyagers. You showed us around the Carnegie Rupes."

"Right!" She shook her head dazedly. "Sorry—I'm actually on my way to check on Cherry's invisibility feature. Could you point me in her direction?"

"She's up that trail there."

"Thank you so much!" She waved goodbye with a bandaged hand and hurried up the hill.

"She seemed out of it, didn't she?" Truman said, plucking lemons from a tree. "And did you see her hand?"

"Yeah, weird. She was scattered last time too. Probably from being an oblivy. She's also the president of the PSA Proctors. Must be tiring work." He picked a lemon.

"That should be enough," said Truman.

With the lemons in hand, they returned inside, the trees whispering behind their backs.

Out of the corner of his eye, Truman spotted a gold newsstand.

It was the latest issue of *Mercury's Message*, authored by none other than Cava Lore. The cover was split into three columns. One column showed a picture of Truman with the headline:

TRUMAN HOWARD: FUTURE VAN GOGH PATIENT

Dr. Nayelo Noxthomas, an expert musical omnihealer, has expressed concern for the well-being of the fifth Howard child, Mr. Truman Howard. As an empath with little to no control over his will, Dr. Noxthomas expects Mr. Truman Howard to develop the Empathic Sickness of the Psyche, ESP for short. The mental illness is notorious for consuming most, if not all, weak empaths.

Just last week, Mr. Howard underwent a mental evaluation at the Van Gogh Irisylum. He was admitted to the Ém Path psychiatric ward shortly after being overwhelmed with the basic emotion of sadness... cont'd on pg 6, written by Cava Lore.

Truman reread the article and chuckled. "I know I should be mad, but honestly, my old roommate has spread far worse lies."

"That's a horrible picture of me!" Vedrò blurted, seizing the paper.

His column read:

VEDRÒ AZZURRO: OUR FALSE PROPHET

Mr. Vedrò Azzurro, voyager and friend of Mr. Truman Howard, has been identified as our new prophet. But our late, great Jupitarian wizard and prophet, Chiron, would no doubt be disappointed in his so-called heir. How could Mr. Azzurro fail to foresee the breathtaking grandeur of Aether? Or the Aurora Mercurialis? Or Cherry the Blossom Dragon?!

Even under threatening conditions, our so-called prophet can barely make a prediction. When he and Mr. Howard were in the Spider Cavity, he didn't foresee the killer Arachnoid chasing them. In the Carnegie Rupes, he failed to foresee Mr. Howard fainting. While he swam in the Cheryl Sea, he didn't anticipate the buzzsaw shark that bit off his leg. And he's supposed to be our new prophet? … cont'd on pg 1, written by Cava Lore.

Vedrò scoffed. "This man is *pathetic*."
"He really is," Truman agreed, sneering at the paper.
They scanned the third column.
"Beautiful picture of her, but she's not gonna like this," Vedrò murmured.
The final headline read:

ESMERALDA MORTIMER: LIKE MOTHER LIKE SIREN

Miss Esmeralda Mortimer is the daughter of Ms. Angenciel Mortimer, the Van Gogh wellfarer and author of Heavenly Bodies & the Cultures Within. During a visit at Writers' Incorporated, Miss Mortimer showed her true colors as an evil siren and flat-out liar.

I, Cava Lore, Assembly-renowned messenger and recipient of the Sincerity & Honesty Award for Messaging, personally witnessed Miss Mortimer harassing an idle bystander. The siren had to be restrained from attacking the individual with a large textbook.

According to Earthling psychologist John B. Watson, behavior is learned. About eighteen years ago, my esteemed colleague, Mr. Gus Sype, documented a scandal outside a Martian delivery room. In his piece, SIRENS: A DANGER TO ALL, he wrote, "[Ms.] Angenciel Mortimer disrupted busing omnihealers and disturbed slumbering newborns. The birthing center ultimately had no choice but to remove the siren from the premises."

In addition to their malevolent nature, the Mortimers have proven themselves to be pathological liars. Rather than disclose their identities as sirens, they have repeatedly claimed to be enchantresses. For the safety of our new citizens, the Assembly should reconsider Ms. Mortimer's position as mentor. She may be a danger to them. The rule of thumb should always be: if you are a siren, you must make yourself known… *cont'd on pg 3,* *written by Cava Lore.*

Chapter 17

Oddlietti Dolci Oddlietti

T hank you for picking these!" Reuel said, taking the handful of lemons from Truman. With her will, the aster split a lemon and squeezed the juice into her cup. It looked like a nonexistent knife had cut the fruit down the center, and an invisible hand had crushed the pulp.

"The lemonade's never tart enough for me—always too sweet," Reuel explained. "Take a seat! I saved you two spots."

Everyone was gathered around the table, chatting. A branch of the yellow oddly canopied the table like a flowering umbrella.

Truman handed the newspaper to his sister.

She glanced at it. "Don't read that hogwash." She pushed it back.

"You read it?"

She nodded.

"Why is Cava doing this?"

"You'd have to ask Coelho," she answered. "He and Cava used to date. Since Coelho dumped Cava, Cava has had a vendetta against all of us Howards and anyone connected to us. He's the one who stalked Saint during his journey. He's taking advantage of the societal perception of the Howard bloodline to get even."

"A bitter ex? How lame," Vedrò said, rolling his eyes.

"Okay, but how does he *know* all of this?" Truman held up the newspaper. "Yeah, it's mostly fictitious, but some of it *is* true."

"He has friends in high places," said Reuel. "But don't worry about it, Tru. No one in their right mind takes Cava seriously."

Esmeralda joined, pointed to the paper, and asked, "What's that? Is that *Mercury's Message?*"

Truman hesitated but handed it over.

Her eyes scanned the paper. Without saying a word, she stood up and went to Angenciel at the far end of the table.

As the two spoke in passionate French, placemats appeared on the table—a heads-up from the Nut.

"Food's coming!" Reuel said, excitedly.

Truman examined his placemat. Sailboats cut through linen waves.

A memory flickered—a child's face, familiar and laughing as someone bellyflopped off a boat.

"Reuel," Truman said, still thinking, "we went tubing as kids, didn't we?"

"Every so often, yes. Ages ago. Why do you ask?"

"I think I just remembered Minli's face."

"Really?"

"I think so. I'm not sure. She looked like you."

Reuel smiled. "Mum has pictures at her place. You'll see them when we visit. We're almost to the Moon!"

"Can't come quick enough."

"Hey Reuel," Ereus chimed in. "Could you squeeze some lemon into my glass? It's too sweet."

"That's what I said! They must add extra sugar for the kids. That's how you know we're getting old."

"Right? I used to love milk chocolate. Now I can only eat dark. The more bitter, the better."

As Reuel squeezed another lemon with her will, Truman looked up at Ereus.

"What's up with Cherry's invisibility feature?" he asked.

"What do you mean?" replied Ereus.

"When we went to get lemons, we ran into Elmory Moss. She was headed to check on Cherry's feature."

"That's odd. She usually asks me to run those checks. Must be something outside my scope of knowledge." He shrugged.

A pop sounded from the other end of the table where a steaming stockpot appeared.

"Lunch!" Ereus hollered, dashing for a plate. "I've been waiting weeks for this. Mmm, oddlietti! My favorite!"

"It's everyone's favorite," Falsmira said dryly, snatching a plate.

Truman jumped in line. Vedrò nearly trampled Halle.

The pot held thick, spiced spaghetti noodles topped with pancetta and freshly grated Parmigiano Reggiano. Like the oddlies, the noodles were red, yellow, and blue.

"We saw this pasta on Mercury, right?" said Vedrò. "In Violetteville?"

Truman nodded and slapped a pile onto his plate.

"We can talk about this later, Esmeralda," Angenciel whispered. "Now go get food."

She turned her attention to the group. "Alright, everyone! It's going to be a hearty lunch today. We're venturing into something new. This dish is called *oddlietti*. It is Venus' planetary dish and is made from none other than the oddlies! Once the branches or filaments or whatever you want to call them—"

"They're called tendrils," Reuel corrected.

"Right," continued Angenciel. "Once the *tendrils* fall to the ground, they are raked up and served as a lovely high-fiber meal! Venusians eat this at least once a week. We call it Oddlietti Wednesday. OW for short." She purposely touched a tendril. It zapped her. "OW!" She smirked. "Get it? Ow."

"We get it," said Reuel. "Dad jokes… man, we *are* getting old." She went around the table and, with her will, curled a lemon rind atop every plate.

Vedrò sat down and, without waiting for his garnish, began gorging himself on his mountain of oddlietti.

Truman thought the dish looked more like candy than a proper meal. When a noodle touched his tongue, the sensation was unlike anything he had ever experienced. Instead of zapping his tongue, it prickled it. His lips tingled. The subtle sweetness of the noodle paired beautifully with the savory and spicy sauce.

"As you may notice," said Angenciel, "when oddlietti is boiled, the natural sting of the tendrils cooks down to a mere prickle. It's a highly unique experience, isn't it?!"

"Man, I love food!" Vedrò said, slurping up a noodle.

As everyone raved about the oddlietti, Truman noticed Esmeralda playing with her food.

"Are you okay?" he whispered. "Is it the article?"

"I'm fine," she said, twirling a noodle with her fork. "I'm just worried. An article like that could put my maman at risk of losing her jobs. I don't really care what Cava has to say about me, but I am protective of the people I love. I feel like he's putting a target on our backs. It's unscrupulous of him. And all for what? Fame and fortune?"

"I don't think it's about either." Truman filled her in on Cava's vendetta.

"A bitter ex? How reprehensible," said Esmeralda.

Truman laughed. "That's what Vedrò said. Close to it anyway."

"Oh wait!" It dawned on Esmeralda. "That's how I knew Cava's name! Cava wrote that article about your brother Saint. The one I found in my maman's library."

Across the table, Vedrò moaned with every bite. Shiloh tried talking to him, but he was too mesmerized by the oddlietti to hear.

"So, how did you and Vedrò feel about the article?" Esmeralda asked Truman.

"Fine, I guess. Vedrò didn't seem to care. I don't either, really. Cava doesn't know me, so—" He shrugged.

"I know what you mean," said Esmeralda. "Maman always says that the more secure you are with yourself, the less you care about others' opinions. I wish I were more like you and Vedrò in that way, especially Vedrò. He really doesn't care what other people think about him. It's admirable."

They watched Vedrò lick his plate clean with sauce on his chin. He burped, rubbed his stomach, and went up for seconds.

They smiled and laughed.

"Coelho must've *really* hurt Cava," said Truman. "That, or Cava's just incredibly jealous. And narcissistic."

"I could see him having NPD," said Esmeralda. "True narcissists lack empathy. They don't care about the effect their actions have on others."

"I wish I could lack some empathy myself," Truman muttered, clutching his necklace.

"No, Truman, you don't," Esmeralda said softly. "That, is your superpower."

"I thought it was called a will." He smirked.

She smiled back and took a bite of her oddlietti.

☆ ☆ ☆ ☆ ☆ ☆

"Oddlietti dolci oddlietti. Oddlietti, dormirò bene," Vedrò sang to himself to the melody of *Alouette*. He held his belly as if to prevent it from bursting. *"Basta,"* he told himself after his third serving. "Enough."

Everyone was in a food coma.

"I'm so full," grumbled Ereus.

"If everyone's finished, we can head to the next greenhouse," said Reuel. "My colleagues kindled a fire for us. If you have room, there's stuff to make s'mores."

The voyagers groaned at the mention of more food and dragged themselves toward the lime green greenhouse.

As Truman followed, he heard another popping noise. He turned and saw the mentors tossing dishes across the table. Instead of shattering, the dishes vanished with a pop.

Inside the next greenhouse, rows and rows of tulips stretched before them.

Truman took a seat by the fire and basked in its warmth. Vedrò and Schmidt roasted marshmallows on sticks. Humzah told ghost stories to Shiloh. Halle and Letsatsi chatted away. Style sat on the ground and taught Esmeralda and Yari a few signs in ASL. Sweta walked up to Vedrò and asked for a piece of his chocolate bar.

Vedrò broke off a chunk and awkwardly handed it to her. His cheeks flushed. "I wasn't spying on you in your bed, you know!" he blurted. His marshmallow caught on fire and fell into the pit. He didn't notice. "I was in detention."

"Okay," she said simply.

"Ask Truman if you don't believe me! He was there!"

"I don't know what you're talking about," Truman said, suppressing a laugh.

Sweta smiled and turned to the field of tulips.

"I'm not a peeping Tom, I swear!" Vedrò hollered after her. "Wait, where are you going?"

"I'm going to talk to the tulips," Sweta replied, her mouth full of melting chocolate.

"To talk to the tulips?" He looked over at Truman. "She's bonkers."

"I'm not crazy. I'm a flutterby, remember? I have the will to talk to plants. Reuel told me that many flutterbies work here at Ivies and Oaks. I see why. The tulips are so kind."

"What about the oddlies?" said Truman. "Can you talk to them too?"

"I could've but didn't want to. I heard the things they were saying." She looked around to make sure no trees were listening. "I found them rather superficial."

"Really? How so?"

"Well, when we were eating, all they talked about was how 'slender' their tendrils were and how 'gnarly' the roots of other trees looked and how the plates of oddlietti were making their 'roots water' and were a 'perfect reflection of their beauty.' It's not a bad thing to care about your appearance, but they just seemed really into themselves."

"Sounds like someone," Truman said, watching Vedrò fix his hair in the reflection of his necklace.

"I'm curious," Sweta said to Truman. "Since you're an empath, can you sense how plants feel?"

"I don't know. I've never tried. I didn't even know plants had emotions."

"Not like us, they don't. They merely react to different stimuli, which, in their way, is how they feel. Try it!"

He removed his necklace. "I don't sense anything. Not even from you guys, for that matter."

"It's because we're in a giant pierre plant, remember?" Esmeralda interjected. "You know, pierre plants—as in what your necklace is made of. Pierre plant cells have an enzyme in their cytoplasm called *sensase*. When used in chemical reactions, sensase breaks down human emotions into energy. Sensase is what gives pierre plants their empathproof characteristic. When you wear that necklace, it blocks others' emotions because the enzymes break them down for you."

"What happens to the energy it creates?" asked Truman.

"It's released into the air like how plants release oxygen."

"Wait, so my necklace is alive right now? I knew it was made from a pierre plant, but I thought it was dead or preserved or something."

"Reuel may have preserved the plant cells in some type of contained cryoprotectant to keep the cells in a viable state. That's my guess anyway. Otherwise, I don't see how else the cells would still function. Maybe it's fathom-related?" she mused. "But even if the plant is dead, the enzymes aren't. Enzymes technically don't die because they're never alive to begin with. They might become denatured over time, though. If that happens, the necklace may eventually stop working, and Reuel would have to make you a new one."

Truman threw his necklace back on. *Sensase. Denatured. Cryoprotectant. Maybe I should crack open a textbook*, he thought.

A breeze whistled through the tulips.

Sweta laughed.

"What is it? Did the tulips say something?" asked Vedrò.

"They're giggling at us. They find the way we talk humorous."

"Well, tell them the way Esmeralda talks is not the way we all talk," said Vedrò. "No one in their bloody right mind wants to talk like that."

Esmeralda glared at him.

Sweta leaned down and blew a gentle breath toward their closed petals.

"You didn't tell them that, did you?!" said Esmeralda.

"No, of course not," laughed Sweta. "I asked them to open. They're afraid we might trample them like we did the grass. They may need a little encouragement." She gazed back at the bonfire. "I have an idea. Letsatsi, come here!"

Letsatsi left the conversation she was having with Halle.

"What's up?" she asked.

"Could you use your will to help the tulips open? They're being shy."

"I'll try. I'm a little exhausted from eating that giant plate of oddlietti. But I should have enough energy to bear some light." She approached a tree covered in dark green leaves and woody vines.

As she went to sit down to roll up her pant, Sweta gasped, "Don't sit there!"

"Why not?!" Letsatsi recoiled.

"Leaves of three, leave them be!"

"What?"

"*Leaves of three, leave them be,*" she repeated. "That's poison ivy! You touch that, and you'll be itching for days. When we were in Writers' Ink, Reuel recommended a book called *Ivies and Oaks and Their Oaks and Ivies.* I bought a copy. The plume of the book, Fiona Cynn Theseus, wrote about all the different plants at Ivies and Oaks—poison ivy being one of them."

"I bet they're nasty to talk to, aren't they?" asked Vedrò.

"The poison ivy? No, actually…" She looked sad. "I feel bad for them. They're lonely creatures. All they want is to feel a human's touch."

Letsatsi moved away from the tree and sat between two rows of tulips. She rolled up her pant leg and concentrated on her will. Her skin began to twinkle. The twinkle grew to a glow. Then, a full flash flooded the tulip field. Light kissed every petal and bud. And in that instant, the tulips began to bloom.

"*Cavolo,*" Vedrò murmured, eyes widening in awe.

"I knew all they needed was a little encouragement," Sweta said, tickling a tulip with the tip of her finger.

Darkness fell around the voyagers. The s'mores were gone, and the bonfire was dwindling.

"I hope you've had an enjoyable evening," Angenciel said to the group. "Since it's our last night on Venus, we thought to take it easy. Tomorrow is a travel day. You should spend it studying. As a reminder, at the end of the trimester, you'll be tested on everything you've learned so far."

The voyagers groaned.

"Ereus, Reuel, Falsmira, and I," she pressed on, "took the liberty of putting together a review guide." She passed around slips of paper. "You won't know all the bullet points, but you will after our Lunar visit."

The paper read:

FROM CHIRON TO NOW
by Blyly O'Bygone

    Ch. 1: Cherry Meets Chiron
    Ch. 2: The Assembly of Aether & the Aetherly Agreement
        Sec. A: The Ascension
        Sec. B: Governing the Solar System
    Ch. 3: PSA (the Protection & Secrecy of Aliens)
    Ch. 4: The Deforestation of the Oddlies
        Sec. A: The Extraction of Wanderlust
    Ch. 5: The Terraformations
        Sec. A: Mercury
        Sec. B: Venus
        Sec. C: Luna
    Ch. 9: The Webbed War of '44 & the Meteorite
    Ch. 10: The Arrival of the Vivabees
    Ch. 11: The Great Scare of Apollo Eleven

VORTEXES & MORE
by Marjorie Moore

THE WONDERS & FATHOMS OF AETHER
by Marvelo S. Grandeur

HEAVENLY BODIES & THE CULTURES WITHIN
by Angenciel Mortimer

"I know it seems like a lot, but—"

"A lot?!" Vedrò interrupted. "There're like, a million sections!"

"Oh, drop the theatrics," said Angenciel. "What I was going to say: I know it seems like a lot, *but* you have from now until the end of our Lunar visit to prepare for your exams!" She checked her watch. "We have about an hour before bedtime. Could someone please gather more firewood? Might as well relax a bit more."

Halle volunteered.

Conversations broke out among the voyagers.

"How am I supposed to relax now?" grumbled Vedrò.

"These tests are going to be brutal," said Yari.

"From the looks of the study guide, I think the tests will be fairly easy," said Esmeralda.

"That's easy for you to say, Miss 'I-Read-About-It-in-*The-Wonders-and-Fathoms-of-Aether*.'" Vedrò teased.

"He he, very funny." She rolled her eyes.

Halle returned to the group with a pile of sticks, twigs, and dark green vines. She swung the pile toward the fire.

"HALLE, NO!" Sweta hollered.

It was too late.

Halle had already let go of the poison ivy.

☆ ☆ ☆ ☆ ☆ ☆

"If inhaled, the fumes of burning poison ivy can cause painful and, in extreme cases, fatal respiratory failure," Angenciel repeated the following morning. "Poison ivy burns very quickly and releases urushiol oil into the air. Miss Xióng inhaled the smoke, and her lungs had a severe allergic reaction. Thankfully, we have Shiloh, who is taking great care of Miss Xióng. I'm surprised no one else was affected."

"She'll be okay, though, right?" Esmeralda asked, her eyes puffy from a sleepless night.

"Yes," said Angenciel. "Shiloh believes Miss Xióng will recover in less than a full Moon's time. But she may miss our first Lunar visit."

"When can we see her?" asked Truman.

"Let's let her rest for now. Perhaps in the afternoon. Since you have today to yourselves, be sure to spend your time wisely and study!"

The voyagers branched off. Vedrò, Truman, and Esmeralda found themselves by the lake. Esmeralda threw herself into her studies more than usual. Truman bounced in and out of focus, slowly but steadily grinding away. Vedrò twiddled his pencil, hardly studying at all.

"I have read and reread every chapter listed on the review guide," said Esmeralda. "I need a break."

"Me too," Vedrò said, sounding exhausted.

"You've done nothing."

"Not true!" he snapped back. "I've doodled! *Guarda!* Look!"

Esmeralda glanced at the drawing of her picking her nose. *"Charmant,"* she said dryly. "Charming."

He chuckled. "Oo, I have an idea! Why don't we pick some flowers for Halle?"

"That's not a bad idea." She eyed him. "Okay, let's do it."

They left their books behind and found a bush of blue hydrangeas.

"Esmeralda!" Sweta called, approaching them with a book in hand. "Do you know where the properties of wanderlust are listed? Letsatsi and I checked the section on wanderlust in *The Wonders and Fathoms of Aether* but couldn't find them."

"They're in *From Chiron to Now* under the section 'The Extraction of Wanderlust,'" replied Esmeralda. "Read both sections to get the full picture."

"Thanks. You're an angel." A snap of a stem caught her ear. "Hey! Why're you tormenting those beautiful flowers?! Poor things are crying!"

"We were gonna give 'em to Halle," explained Truman. "Wanna join?"

"Oh, in that case, don't worry about the flowers! They *live* to brighten the sick. They'd give their lives for it. And sure, I could use the break. Let me get the others. Maybe they'll join too."

As Esmeralda and Truman plucked some white daisies, Sweta returned with Letsatsi, Style, and Yari. They were carrying a basket of peaches and blessedbes.

"In case Halle's hungry," said Sweta.

"You guys head in. I'll be right there!" Vedrò said, turning toward the Dragon's Back Trail.

Inside the cabin, they knocked on Shiloh's door.

Shiloh opened. "Bzeze," they whispered. "Shouldn't you all be studying?"

"We came bearing gifts," Truman said, looking over Shiloh's wings to see Halle lying in bed.

"Shh! Halle's sleeping. She needs all the rest she can get if she wants to join tomorrow's visit."

"Oh, sorry." Truman said, lowering his voice. "Could you pass these along to her then?" He held out the basket. "We wanted Halle to know we're thinking of her."

"How sweet. Of course! It's a good thing I have six legs." The Vivabee outstretched their pollen-covered limbs and took hold of all the flowers and fruits.

"Take these too!" Vedrò arrived, holding a cluster of dead skull-like flowers.

Everyone except Truman stared questionably at him.

"What? They're dragon flowers. The first time Tru and I met Halle, she said these were her favorite!"

Esmeralda eyed him again.

"You should put those in the window," Sweta instructed Shiloh. "They like the wind."

A groan came from behind Shiloh. "Aw, you guys shouldn't have," Halle croaked, her eyes half-open.

"Go back to sleep, Halle," Shiloh said sternly. "You need to rest those delicate lungs. Perhaps you guys should go. I'm sorry."

"We understand," said Truman. "Thank you so much for looking after her. Bye, Halle! Get well soon!'

Everyone waved.

"Bzeze, Shiloh!" said Vedrò.

As they left, Esmeralda looked back at Halle and saw the girl reach for the dragon flowers, her eyes welling with tears.

Chapter 18

Earthrise, Moonquake

R euel!" Truman said excitedly. "Now that we'll be on the Moon, is that family party happening soon?!"

All night, Truman had stayed up thinking about his family. *What do they look like? What are their wills? Who do I take after? Have they missed me?*

"I told you," Reuel said, laughing. "Mum's throwing you the party at the end of our Lunar visit. We have a lot to learn about the Moon before then."

Truman frowned.

"I *know* you're excited," she continued, smiling sympathetically, "and I know how you feel. But it's required by law that the journey takes precedence, Tru."

Truman sighed. "Well, at least tell me what they look like. Don't you have any photos? I'm getting impatient."

"All my photos are at home." She looked away. "Ah, Halle!"

Halle exited the cabin alongside Shiloh.

"She's alive! SHE'S ALIVE!" joked Vedrò.

"Yes, Halle has made quite the recovery, if I say so myself," Shiloh said, proudly polishing their eyes. "It's amazing what honey elixir and a little bee dance can do for a respiratory allergic reaction!"

Esmeralda ran to hug her.

"I don't know how Shiloh did it," said Halle. "I once got poison ivy when I was a kid. It took forever to heal! What Shiloh did was magic! Thanks again, Shiloh."

"Of course! It's my job!"

"I'm happy you're feeling better, Miss Xióng," said Angenciel. "Perfect timing too! Are you able to take notes?"

Halle nodded and flipped open her notebook.

"Excellent!" Angenciel stood and turned to the group. "Now, my lesson. The Moon, also called Luna, is the third Rocky Realm and the astrological ruler of the home-loving Cancer. The Moon is also Earth's lone natural satellite and is situated near what's called *the Goldilocks Zone*. Can anyone tell me what that is? It was in your reading for today," she hinted.

Esmeralda shot her hand into the air, and to her surprise, so did Vedrò.

"Yes, Mr. Azzurro?" said Angenciel.

"The Goldilocks Zone is the range in which there is liquid water, a livable atmosphere, and sunlight levels suitable for life," he said, counting on his fingers. "Mercury and Venus are too hot to be in the Goldilocks Zone. Mars and beyond are too cold. Earth is just right!"

"Exactly!" Angenciel beamed. *"Bravo!"*

"How did you know that?!" Esmeralda hissed in his ear.

He smirked and said nothing.

"In other words, Earth—and only Earth—*is* in the Goldilocks Zone," added Ereus. "It is the only world where humans can live without an alien-made force field. Since the Moon has a very weak atmosphere—really, an exosphere—a force field is crucial." He checked his watch. "While you continue your lesson, Angenciel, I'll see how far we are from the Moon." He left for Cherry's orchard.

"Thank you, Ereus," said Angenciel. "Some facts about the Moon: it has two seasons on its surface—shine and shadow. These seasons are like Mercury's but not nearly as brutal or long-lasting. Within the Moon, also known as Middle Moon—
"

"Middle Moon?" Halle echoed, looking up.

"Yes. Middle Moon has no seasonal change because it's insulated. The temperature is regulated. Like blister on Venus, we've given this 'season' a name. We call it *igloo.*

"Another fun fact: a day on the Moon lasts about 656 Earth-hours. When we land, don't forget to update your watches. Oh! The most interesting fact: eons ago, the Moon began its life as a giant meteorite that collided with Earth and rebounded into its gravitational field. Since then, it's been roughly 239,000 miles away from Earth. That's closer than it sounds. So close, in fact, the Lunar surface can be seen from

Earth with bare eyes. This is why the Assembly of Aether—once aliens began spreading across the Solar System—required Lunars to dwell solely inside the Moon. It wasn't until illusionists learnt how to produce and sustain invisibility illusions that the Assembly allowed Lunars to terraform the surface. Falsmira will discuss that later."

Truman glanced at Falsmira. As usual, her arms were crossed and her lips curled.

"Angenciel!" Ereus hollered. "Cherry is approaching the brim of the Mare Imbrium! Hurry over!"

"You heard the man!"

The voyagers ran to the dip in Cherry's wing and jostled one another for the best view. Sunlight reflected off the Moon, briefly blinding them. As their eyes adjusted, the Moon grew larger. The various shades of gray across the Lunar plains and craters became more discernible. Something red, white, and blue rippled in space—it was planted in the Lunar soil.

"That there is the Mare Tranquillitatis," said Angenciel. "The site of the Apollo Eleven Lunar Landing. It's designated with the flag of the United States."

Cherry flew past the site and nestled in the depths of a shadowy basin.

"Everyone, remove your trainers," Angenciel instructed, slipping off her shoes. "Keep your socks on, though."

The other mentors complied without blinking. The voyagers looked at each other, confused.

"Come on now!" said Angenciel.

One by one, they climbed off Cherry barefoot.

Down the hill, a Vivabee awaited their arrival. He had tarnished rubies for eyes and a gown much larger than Shiloh's. His wings had yellowed with age. The honey dripping from his body had hardened and crystalized. He fluttered beside a pile of headlamps and boots. The boots were all funky-looking and had ten-inch platforms. Each pair was a different solid color. Aligned, they assembled a rainbow. Truman remembered seeing similar boots on Mercury. While those were new and shiny, these were worn and scuffed.

"By Orion!" Shiloh mumbled in awe. "That's… That's Sin, that is! I've read about him. He's a legend—one of the oldest Vivabees alive! He used to work with the late, great Jupitarian wizard and prophet, Chiron! I, myself, have only a few decades on me, but I've heard Sin is over 333 years old! After retiring from omnihealing, he's been guiding travelers through Middle Moon, or so I've heard. I didn't know it was true. I've never taken the traditional route to Middle Moon. Normally, I just warp in."

"What's that odor?" Esmeralda asked, scrunching her nose in disgust.

It smelled like spent gunpowder.

"Moondust," said Angenciel. "You get used to it after a while. Now everyone, as we exit Cherry's force field, take it step by step. Or should I say, hop by hop."

"What do you mean?" Truman asked. As he strode outside Cherry's force field, he felt his stomach lift. His next step sent him bouncing toward the shadowed Vivabee, who grew with every spring.

The whole group was soon bouncing. Yari fell to her hands. Schmidt tripped and scraped his knees. Vedrò twirled in the air. Halle, fearing she'd spiral into space, was taking little hops at a time. Truman held his stomach, feeling queasy. Eventually, they found their groove, albeit clumsily, and made it to the old Vivabee.

"Well, it's about time," the old Vivabee said, his voice deep and raspy. "Bzeze. My name is Sinful, but you may call me Sin. I'll be guiding you through Luna's Well today. Now, please, put on a headlamp and a set of boots. We have everyone's size. The Assembly made sure of it."

The voyagers butted heads bouncing toward the gear.

Truman found a size twelve and slipped them on. Despite standing a foot taller, he found the boots made it easier to balance and leap.

"These are called *luney boots*," said Ereus, "also known as Lunar boots and astronaut boots. They're equipped with special technology that absorbs tectonic shock and prevents the wearer from falling while leaping. Savvies and threaders— alien term for designer—fabricated the boots to counteract the lack or abundance of a gravitational pull. The Moon's gravitational pull is roughly one-sixth of Earth's. These boots create suction on landing and release on takeoff. Ingenious, really.

"Dr. Nayelo Noxthomas was wearing the latest model of these in the Beethoven Basin, if you recall. Those have jetpack technology that lets you hover between places. They're tricker to use, so we'll be using an older version.

"Like all great fashion trends, luney boots have gone in and out of style. In fact, before savvies installed the gravity-stabilizing feature in every force field, citizens across every world wore luney boots daily. Lunars, however, enjoyed the sentimental value of the boots so much that the force field on the Moon remains the only one without the gravity stabilizer. All other features, like the atmospheric pressure and air supply, are still present, of course."

With their headlamps on, the voyagers looked like spelunkers ready to descend into a cave.

"What are the headlamps for?" asked Halle.

"You'll see," Sin said, leading them up the hill.

Vedrò caught up to the wonder. "A little bee told me you used to work with Chiron. What was he like?"

"A good man. A bit misunderstood but very kind. But I'd prefer not to talk about him, if you don't mind."

Before Vedrò could ask more, Sin stopped at the peak of the hill. His ruby eyes swirled with grassy greens and sky blues. "Do you guys miss home yet?" he asked.

As Truman took another leap, Earth rose over the Lunar horizon. Leonian light engulfed the planet, crowning it with golden locks. White clouds swathed across oceans. Truman recognized continents and felt that if he leapt high enough upward, he'd plummet toward what was once his home. The memory of his old roommate, Ash, made Truman press his toes deeper into his boots as if to root himself to the Moon's surface.

"I love a good earthrise," Sin said, cocking his head to one side.

A wishing well made of moonstones stood before them. Each stone held an intricate pattern, with a Trinacria carved into the center.

"This is Luna's Well," said Sin. "And down it lies Middle Moon."

"Who's Luna?" asked Halle.

"'Luna' is Italian for the 'Moon,'" said Vedrò. "Also, Spanish."

"That is correct," said Angenciel. "You have all the right answers today, don't you, Mr. Azzurro?"

"I mean, those are my first two languages. I sure hope I'd know." He scratched his head, smiling.

"I wouldn't put it past ya," Esmeralda teased.

Vedrò stuck his tongue to his cheek, feigning offense.

"The name," Angenciel pressed on, "also comes from the Sicilian-Neptunial painter and sculptor Luna Lisandra Cavallo, who built the wellhead and engraved all the moonstones."

The voyagers looked into the well and found nothing but darkness.

"And in we go!" Sin declared, buzzing into the hole.

What?! Truman thought, exchanging fearful glances with Halle.

One by one, they hopped down like rabbits.

Truman anticipated to freefall into Middle Moon. But when it was his turn, his boots touched the ground nearly seconds after jumping.

The inside of the well was a staircase. The steps were sporadic and made of stone.

The group bounced gently from one step to the next, trying hard not to slam into the stone wall. At times, they landed on floating boulders.

"While Luna Lisandra Cavallo created the wellhead, the well itself is a natural geological formation," explained Sin. "No one sculpted it. It was here when aliens terraformed. I help maintain it."

As they deepened their descent, darkness thickened around them.

Letsatsi reached down to roll up her pantleg, but Angenciel held up her hand. "It's okay, Miss Khoza. You want to save your energy. It's a long descent."

Truman heard a clicking noise above his head. He looked up and saw something moving on the underside of a step. It was a rock formation that tapered like a large icicle. He adjusted his headlamp and saw it was a mound of tiny neon crabs, their claws snapping as they crawled over one another. He froze, goosebumps prickling his arms.

Halle stood beside him, terrified. "Wh-what are those?" she stammered, inching closer to Truman. "Are those cr-crabs?"

Everyone stared at the stalactites of crabs writhing above their heads.

"Finally," said Reuel. "I've been waiting for someone to notice. They're called *stalacrabs*. They are a fathom native to the Moon and Neptune. If you don't bother them, they won't bother you."

She extended her hand and let a crab crawl onto her palm. "While their pinches are painful, they're usually sweet. Empathetic creatures, they are. Loyal to their kind. Very family-oriented. That's why they're all piled togeth—"

Suddenly, the ground began to quake.

The step beneath Yari cracked and broke off. She slammed into the wall.

Pebbles struck Shiloh's wings.

Stalacrabs tumbled off the mounds, their tiny limbs flailing in the air.

A loud noise reverberated up the well. It was like the toll of a giant bell.

BANG! GOUDOU! BOOM!

Chapter 19

One Brief Retreat for Alienkind

The rumbling died down.

"Is everyone okay?" Sin asked, extending a limb out to Yari.

She found her footing. "Yeah, I'm fine," said Yari. "Just a blow to my shoulder. Good thing I'm an immortal."

"And you, Shiloh? Can you still fly?"

"Yes. Just a tear in my chitin. I'll be fine."

"What *was* that?!" Truman asked, his heart thumping in his throat.

"It was a moonquake," answered Sin. "They're fairly common down here."

"What was that ringing?" asked Halle. "It sounded like a bell."

"Moonquakes reverberate through the interior of the Moon, hence the loud bell-like sound," Sin said, patting moondust off his wing. "When aliens first terraformed the Moon, the quakes used to last for *hours*. Thankfully, savvies have reduced their duration and magnitude substantially, but they have yet to figure out how to eliminate them entirely. Perhaps one day."

A boulder floated past them in midair.

Angenciel pointed to it. "This is another reason the gravity-stabilizing feature wasn't installed in the Lunar force field—so that boulders like these won't crush anyone inside the Moon. Oh, dear." She pulled a neon-yellow stalacrab from her hair and gently lifted it toward its mound.

Other stalacrabs suspended in the air hooked their claws to one another to form a mass. Those still on the stalactites caught hold and reeled them in.

"Reminds me of Barrel of Monkeys," Halle said curiously. "A toy I had when I was a kid."

Reuel pointed to the stalacrabs. "*This* is what I mean when I say stalacrabs are family-oriented," she said. "They catch each other when they fall. This behavior is likely an evolutionary trait. Since moonquakes occur often, they've learnt to work in tandem to survive." She, too, pulled a stalacrab from her hair and lifted it toward the cluster.

The group continued their descent.

Everyone trained their eyes on where to bounce next. The deeper they plunged, the more weightless they felt and the more difficult it became for their feet to find solid ground.

"The closer we get to the core of the Moon, the weaker the gravity becomes," said Angenciel. "As long as you leap toward ground, your luney boots will detect a surface to create suction, thus preventing you from floating away." She held out a hand to Halle who was dogpaddling midair. "You might also begin to feel queasy or sleepy. Don't worry. It is normal. Just give your body time to adjust to the weightlessness."

Truman clutched his necklace.

"Question," Esmeralda said, raising a hand. "Why is it getting cooler and not warmer? Aren't cores supposed to be warmer than the surface?"

"Excellent observation," said Angenciel. "This is due to the Lunar season igloo. Again, it's not really a season. It's air conditioning. Technically, geothermal cooling. Middle Moon is set at a constant sixty-nine degrees." She landed in a puddle. "We've arrived! Wow, that was quicker than last year's trek. Last year's cohort was much larger, I suppose."

Truman reached the bottom. His boots were submerged in a foot of well water. When he moved, he splashed, causing raindrops to trickle upward.

"Ah, sugar!" Shiloh uttered. "The water is dampening my wings!"

"Here, take this." Sin passed them a glove with Velcro on the palm.

Shiloh slipped the glove onto one of their limbs and gently patted their wings. The Velcro drew the moisture out like a needle pulling thread. "Thank you! I forgot mine."

"What is that?" asked Halle.

"It's Vivabee Velcro," said Sin. "It's made of a specific fiber that dries our wings when they get damp. If our wings get too wet, it can be difficult to fly."

Sin guided the group through a tunnel.

"Make sure you don't step on any stalacrabs," said Reuel.

Halle held her breath, forcing herself not to look down at the creatures scuttling under the surface.

The group emerged from the tunnel and entered a bright new world. Cool air, tinged with the scent of metal and moondust, embraced them. Houses hung upside-down. Walkways veered right-side-up. People floated through the space, leaping from errand to errand.

"This is the main reason why the gravity-stabilizing feature was not installed," said Angenciel. "If it had been, Lunars would have no way of returning home!" She laughed and spun in the air. "Well, everyone—welcome to Middle Moon!"

☆ ☆ ☆ ☆ ☆ ☆

"This is where I leave you," said Sin.

"You can't join us for the day?" replied Angenciel.

"Can't. A group of spelunkers is coming to explore the Lunar caves. I'm leading the expedition. You guys have a busy day anyway. You don't need an old bee slowing you down."

Shiloh removed the Vivabee Velcro and handed it back to Sin.

"Keep it. I have an extra," Sin said, smiling. He turned and left.

"Oh my Queen Bee..." mumbled Shiloh. "I have Sin's glove... *the* Sin." Their eyes widened with admiration.

The group bounced onward as the mentors began their lessons.

First was Interplanetary Technologies. The group met with Lunar threaders, who explained the mechanics behind luney boots. They learned how the fashionable technology absorbs the vibrations of moonquakes and adjusts to varying degrees of gravity. Ereus lectured about the specifics of the Lunar force field, particularly its invisibility feature.

"It is the strongest invisibility illusion in all of Aether," he said. "It gets checked thrice a day! It must be since the Moon is so close to Earth."

In the afternoon, the group occupied themselves with Worlds Cultures. Angenciel brought them into a mosque-like structure and taught them about Lunar magic, a branch of witchcraft that aligns with the phases of the Moon.

"Lunars find that when the Moon wanes, their wills are at their weakest," Angenciel said, circling a stalacrab pond at the center of the mosque. "When the Moon waxes, their wills are at their strongest."

The group spoke with Lunars in the mosque, who expressed their devotion to Luna, the Moon goddess. They referred to her as "the High Priestess." Nearly all of them mentioned how the dearth of sunlight inside the Moon could feel "depressing at times" and how the moonquakes are "not so bad." Most of the aliens barely glanced their way. They seemed shy and withdrawn, like stalacrabs tucked in their shells.

Middle Moon was not like the Mercurial World Court. Whether the voyagers were upside-down or sideways, they always felt right-side-up. Blood never rushed to their heads. Their hair never stood on end. It was the most convincing illusion Truman had experienced so far on the journey.

At the end of the day, the group concluded with Aetherly History.

"This place is called the Eraers Embassy," Falsmira said, shepherding the group into a torchlit cave. "More commonly known as the Memory Bank."

Truman recognized the name from their study guide.

"For those of you who chose not to get ahead of your studies," Falsmira continued, "*eraers* are historians. They work here at the Memory Bank."

"*Errors?*" Vedrò furrowed his brows at the word.

"Not errors," said Esmeralda. "Eraers."

"For a bank, this place doesn't seem rich." Vedrò scratched at the cave's brittle wall.

"Will you two quit yapping?" Falsmira snapped. "As I was saying, eraers usually have the will of either a *mnemonic* or *memoir*. They're often mistaken for each other, so be sure to memorize them as they *will* be on your test."

Several voyagers groaned.

"Mnemonics," Falsmira continued loudly, "are aliens who have the will to remember everything. Their memories have an infinite storage capacity. Anything they experience, see, do, hear, taste, smell—they can recall it in extensive detail. Think photographic memory, but stronger. In comparison to memoirs, mnemonics are a bit limited."

"What are memoirs?" asked Halle.

"I was getting to that, Miss Xióng!" Falsmira hissed. "You know, patience is a virtue. If you're so eager to know, you could've looked at your study guide like you were supposed to do yesterday."

"B-but I was ill yesterday…"

"Being bedridden is a perfect opportunity to read," she snapped, giving her no chance to reply.

"Memoirs," Falsmira pressed on, "are aliens who have the will of a mnemonic *and* the will to extract memories from themselves—or others—and store them elsewhere, like in another person or here at the Memory Bank."

"Oh, so like an oblivy?" said Vedrò.

"No, not like an oblivy!" she snarled at Vedrò. "Oblivies make people *forget* memories. Those memories still exist somewhere in their mind, just buried. Memoirs extract memories entirely. Together, eraers and savvies designed the Memory Bank to preserve our history and to serve as both an educational and governmental resource. The famous plume and eraer, Mr. Blyly O'Bygone, used the Memory Bank as a primary source for his work *From Chiron to Now*. Most eraers consider this place the crème de la crème of primary sources. There are memories stored here that date back to the Era of Chiron."

The voyagers yawned, their hops becoming sluggish. Halle massaged her throbbing temple. Truman rubbed his upset belly.

"Space sickness," Shiloh said, noticing their behavior. "It's starting. Here, everyone, take a mint." Shiloh opened the kit around their waist and passed out yellow honeycomb-shaped candies. "The candy is made from a special mint grown at Ivies and Oaks. It'll alleviate some of the symptoms of space sickness. Don't bite. Let it melt on your tongue. If you need another, just let me know."

Truman unwrapped the candy and placed it in his mouth. The intense flavor pierced and cooled his tongue, soothing his stomach almost instantly.

"My headache's gone!" Halle said, the candy tucked in her cheek. "Wow! Thanks, Shiloh."

"You'll still feel tired, but the other symptoms should be palliated for the day," said Shiloh.

The group plunged deeper into the cave.

Falsmira stopped beside a plaque embedded in the cave wall. It read: *The Sojourner Rover.*

"You'll learn about this memory when we head to Mars," she said, pointing to the blank wall.

Truman was confused about what she was pointing at—that was until the cave wall chipped away, revealing a misty image of a rover on a red planet. Slowly, it became more and more visible. The cave was a museum. Instead of paintings, the exhibition held memories—memories so realistic that Truman felt like he could jump into the wall and immerse himself in that world.

Falsmira moved to another portion of the cave wall. Its plaque read: *The Great Scare of Apollo Eleven.* The wall chipped away and revealed an astronaut climbing out of a spacecraft wrapped in what looked like gold foil. The flag of the United States was on the man's shoulder.

"The Great Scare of Apollo Eleven," said Falsmira. "Also acknowledged as the Lunar Landing. One of the largest PSA scares in all of Aetherly history happened on July 20th, 1969. Neil Armstrong and Edwin 'Buzz' Aldrin landed in the Mare Tranquillitatis, making them the first two non-alien humans to walk on the Moon. The landing was broadcast live to all of Earth. You can imagine how on edge the Assembly was.

"There were a lot of moving parts that day," Falsmira continued. "The Espionage Unit had already infiltrated NASA. Oblivies and torcrons were on standby. The Illusory Fleet shrouded the trajectory of the spacecraft in illusions as a precaution. Savvies temporarily deactivated the force field around the Mare Tranquillitatis so that NASA couldn't pick up on features of the force field like its air supply feature or moonquake suppressor feature.

"The Assembly warned all aliens to stay away from the area—no one wanted to risk exposure or step outside the bounds of our force field and die from the vacuum of space and ebullism."

Truman was taken aback by her bluntness.

"Fortunately," Falsmira went on, "none of that happened. Armstrong and Aldrin bounced around, planted a flag, collected some rocks, and returned home."

"If nothing bad happened, why is it considered one of the largest PSA scares?" asked Esmeralda. "Just because it was the first time Earthlings ever stepped on the Moon?"

"Precisely," said Falsmira. "It took all three of the PSA Proctors and then some to come together and protect our people. Since then, Earthlings have returned several times. With each visit, the process of monitoring their actions became progressively easier to control."

"You said the Espionage Unit had already infiltrated NASA," Esmeralda said, referring to her notes. "If the Assembly knew Earthlings would step foot on the Moon and pose a threat to PSA, why wouldn't they shut down the Apollo missions from the get-go? Or any Lunar landing since then? Couldn't mimes have impersonated NASA scientists and urged them to abort the mission?"

"Because we understand how insatiable Earthling curiosity can be, Miss Mortimer," Falsmira answered, her patience wearing thin. "Had we shut down those missions, Earthlings would've persisted as they always do. The Assembly finds it best to let Earthlings satisfy their curiosity but to monitor them closely. This applies to all Earthling space ventures."

Esmeralda raised her hand again. "And did—"

"Perhaps we should let others ask questions," Falsmira sighed, tapping her foot.

Everyone looked sheepish. Truman felt like he *should* have questions, but he was too overwhelmed with information to know what to ask.

"Fine," Falsmira caved. "What's your question?"

"Did mimes convince NASA to land in the Mare Tranquillitatis?" asked Esmeralda. "I remember reading that the area still hasn't been populated."

"That is correct."

Before Esmeralda could ask another question, Falsmira turned and bounced farther down the cave. Truman figured they must be walking backward on a timeline—the deeper they plunged, the grainier the memories became.

They passed other PSA scares, the deforestation of the oddlies, and a memory of a kingdom cloaked in clouds. He didn't see much of it, but what he did see was dazzling. The clouds were so dense that the castle looked like it was floating.

They continued until they reached a memory labeled *The Arrival of the Vivabees.*

The wall broke away.

A flood of Vivabees swarmed through space, trailing snail-like ribbons of honey behind them. Their eyes gleamed in the dark.

"Oh, we've gone too far," Falsmira said, looking back. "Well, anyway, this was the day the Vivabees migrated to the Venusian Elps. It was the first time our kinds ever met. It was a peaceful meeting."

"When Reuel and I were voyagers, we used to come here to watch this memory on replay," interjected Angenciel. "Didn't we, Reuel?"

Reuel nodded but averted her gaze. Truman noticed.

"OH!" A thought popped into Angenciel's mind. "Do any of you remember the fresco in the Hive? It was on the dome and showed the arrival of the Vivabees."

"Where did the Vivabees come from?" asked Vedrò.

"From the South of Venus," Shiloh answered. "I wasn't hatched then, but that's what I've been told."

"Wait, I'm confused," said Vedrò. "Was there a force field around the South of Venus? If not, how did Vivabees survive without one?"

"Vivabees are a wonder, remember?" said Reuel. "Wonders do not depend on atmospheric pressure to survive. Just like Cherry and the Leonian dragons, Vivabees can fly out into space and not die."

"Right. Sorry, I forgot."

"I will add, though, that living within a force field is easier on our wings," said Shiloh. "At least for me anyway. I find I get tired quicker whenever I leave the bounds of a force field. That might just be because I rarely leave. My body's not used to it."

"When did the Vivabees migrate?" asked Halle.

"Around the time of the War," said Shiloh. "That War back there."

The voyagers followed Shiloh's limb. The plaque read: *The Webbed War of '44.*

The wall chipped away and revealed aliens and arachnoids engaged in battle. Giant spiders chewed off flesh and bone. Venom and blood dripped from their fangs. Aliens dragged themselves out from under burning, hairy legs. Fireballs flew in every direction. Baby arachnoids were caged under ropes of ice. Limbs trashed like trees in a storm.

Though the voyagers heard nothing, the memory screamed bloody murder. Truman felt queasy again but not from space sickness. He turned away and leaned on his knees.

"You alright?" Reuel asked.

"Yeah. Just… graphic."

Falsmira moved on to a neighboring memory of miners covered in moondust. "This is where we'll end for today: the terraformation of Middle Moon. The Moon was the last heavenly body to be added to the Assembly. During construction in the Earthling year of 1849, we discovered that the Moon was naturally partially hollow."

As Falsmira talked, Truman stared at the miners using their wills to dig out bedrock.

"Weird," Vedrò whispered in his ear. "I feel like I've seen this image before, like in a dream."

Truman looked closer at the memory and noticed a reliclike stone sitting among the bedrock. Words were chiseled into it. As he squinted to read what was carved, the memory sealed back up, and the torches dimmed to a subtle glow.

"It's closing," said Falsmira, "the Memory Bank. Best be off, then."

Chapter 20

Once Upon a Timeline

For the following days, the voyagers had back-to-back lessons. On the surface of the Moon in the Mare Nubium, Reuel taught the group about stalacrabs and their anatomy and ecosystem.

"Stalacrabs only pinch those who are untrustworthy. That's the superstition anyway," said Reuel. "If you ask me, I think stalacrabs only pinch those who grip them too tightly. They don't like to be boxed in."

She pulled out a fishbowl of stalacrabs.

"When you reach into the bowl, do not clench them. Simply let one crawl onto you. Who wants to hold one first?"

No one raised their hand.

"Oh, come on! No one? ... Tru?" She looked at him desperately.

Truman felt Style's gaze.

"Sure," he responded.

He held his breath, reached into the bowl, and fished out a neon-orange stalacrab. It crawled up his arm and sat on his shoulder. He froze.

"Excellent! Who's next?"

One by one, the voyagers reached into the bowl. To everyone's surprise, no one was pinched.

"I suppose that means everyone here is trustworthy!" Reuel said, feeding a dried sardine to a neon-pink stalacrab.

It wasn't until Falsmira held one with total ease that the voyagers realized it truly was a superstition.

The next day was dedicated to Interplanetary Technologies and started with a lecture on the Memory Bank.

"The savvies," Ereus began, "developed what they call a 'faux brain.' Eraers store Aether-related memories in the faux brain. Think of it as a hard drive."

Afterward, he brought the voyagers to the Lunar Vortexes where they continued to practice warping.

"Remember to think long and hard about where you want to warp," he said sharply. "Correction: you can't just *want* to warp to the yellow vortex. You must *desire* it. I know that sounds dramatic, but when it comes to travel—and most things in life, I might add—wanting is never enough."

Ereus hoped he had inspired some of the voyagers.

It was a mixed bag. Truman returned to his flawless warping. Style warped. Vedrò warped. Yari warped. The rest failed. Esmeralda at least warped her boot to the yellow vortex.

"Don't worry. That's an improvement!" Ereus took an encouraging tone. "A couple more tries, and I'm sure everyone will get the hang of it!"

Falsmira and Angenciel split the third day.

The torcron gave a lecture on the terraformation of the Moon's surface, while the siren brought the voyagers on a tour around the Lunar Espionage Unit.

"Lunars call it the Spyatory," said Angenciel.

The Spyatory was a domed structure strewn with optical telescopes, astronomy books, and star charts. As the cohort walked around the observatory, they crossed paths with mimes. Some spoke into transceivers with altered voices, while others morphed into Earthling diplomats.

In the evenings, the voyagers spent most of their time preparing for their exams. One night in Cherry's orchard, they huddled and quizzed each other on different chapters. When vortexes came up, they asked Truman for advice.

"I just think of something yellow," he said. "Like the yellow vortex or the scales on a Leonian back."

During their breaks, the group plucked blessedbes and talked about their favorite flavors. As Sweta raved about dark chocolate, Halle cupped something in her hands and held it to her lips like a blade of grass. She blew. An eerie, wistful melody chilled the air. The others fell silent.

She stopped and blushed when she saw them staring. "Sorry, I didn't mean to interrupt."

"Don't apologize. That was beautiful," said Vedrò. "It made the hair on my neck stand up!"

"What was that?" asked Esmeralda.

She held out a dragon flower. "When I had poison ivy, Shiloh showed me you can make music with them by blowing into one of the holes." She passed around the withered, skull-like flower.

"Creepy," said Yari. "I like it. Play some more." She handed the flower back to Halle.

As she played her melancholic tune, Truman let his gaze wander toward the Lunar horizon. It pulsed with the greens and blues of Earth. It felt like a lifetime ago since he was last there, alone on a mountaintop, letting the days trudge by. While the Rocky Mountains were no doubt beautiful, they paled in comparison to the days he'd captured since.

☆ ☆ ☆ ☆ ☆ ☆

"Today is your last lesson of the trimester," Falsmira said the following morning as they returned to the Memory Bank. "Tomorrow, you'll have your exams."

"Why did our last lesson have to be with Falsmira?" Vedrò grumbled to Truman.

"You two!" Falsmira snapped at the boys. "Tonight, you'll have your second detention. Newton's Cradle. Nine o'clock sharp. It'll feed into your study time. But hey, if you can't do the time, don't do the crime." She smiled wryly.

Truman had completely forgotten about their second detention. "Good thing we've been studying," he whispered to Vedrò.

"I just thought she had forgotten," Vedrò whispered back. "She's real sadistic for saving it until now."

"Psst!" Reuel nudged Truman. "Don't let her get to you. Mum's throwing you that party tomorrow after your exams. She told me you can bring a mate if you'd like. Knowing Mum and Father, there'll be loads of guests."

"I'm excited to meet everyone!" he replied. "Well, nervous excited. Are you bringing anyone?"

She shook her head. "And you?"

Truman turned to Vedrò. "Hey, Vedrò, wanna go to a party with me tomorrow?"

"Will there be food?"

"Plenty," said Reuel.

"I'm in!"

Falsmira coughed. "Excuse me, Reuel. I don't talk to the voyagers during your lessons, do I?"

"You're right. My apologies, Falsmira. Please, carry on."

Falsmira continued down the Memory Bank. The memories were getting grainier by the bounce.

"At the beginning of our journey, I briefly discussed the formation of the Assembly of Aether," said Falsmira. "Tonight, we cover it in full, starting with the first-ever memory in the Bank. We'll take a shortcut through the timeline. Otherwise, we'd be walking for years."

Halle raised her hand. "What year are we going back to?"

"Must be the beginning of the Era of Chiron," Esmeralda blurted.

Falsmira glared at her. "Miss Mortimer, while you are indeed knowledgeable, you clearly lack the understanding of the most basic classroom function: *speak only when called upon!*" She veered into a new tunnel that curved up, around, and back again. Her black robes whisked behind her.

They reached the end of the cave.

"This memory marks the beginning of the Assembly of Aether."

The wall chipped away. They stood on a vibrant, earthy bluff. A great shadow grew in the sunlit sky and plopped down onto the bluff. A colorful ribbon unraveled around the beast—it was Cherry and Rainbow Row.

Though it was a mere memory, Truman could've sworn he smelled honeysuckle and felt the wind brush his face.

As Cherry settled her enormous wings, the memoir from whom the memory came approached the Aristotelian dragon. A group of characters waved from the top of Cherry, beckoning the memoir aboard.

Truman saw a powdered wig, an embroidered gown, a silk kimono, a bald head, a Korean gat, and an elaborate turban. He reckoned the group must've come from all over Earth.

The memoir scrambled up onto Cherry, passing a construction mess of a log cabin.

"As you can see, the aliens whom Cherry collected had already started making a home of the great dragon," said Falsmira. "A few savvies built a makeshift stabilizer, which would eventually evolve into the force field you all know of today. It prevented them from flying off as Cherry flew around. It also stabilized the log cabin and anything else that wasn't growing out of her back."

The memoir joined the group at a round table in Cherry's burgeoning orchard.

"We call this moment *the Ascension*," said Falsmira. "This was the day aliens left Earth to terraform the other planets. At first, the savvy in the powdered wig, Sir Warren Woe, proposed using their wills to prevail over normal humans. *Normans,* they called them. It wasn't until we adopted the title *aliens* that we started to call them *humans*."

While Vedrò stared unblinkingly at the memory, Esmeralda scribbled in her notebook to keep up with Falsmira.

"Being the leader *and* a pacifist, Chiron rejected Sir Warren's idea," Falsmira continued. "He knew that if they used their wills on normans, it would lead to war and bloodshed. Their numbers were small. They stood no chance despite their wills. Worse, it'd propel them into the public eye. Chiron knew better. He preferred living a more inconspicuous life. He's the bald man in the red robes."

"Was he a monk?" Vedrò asked, pressing his nose into the wall of the memory.

"During this time, yes," she answered. "Valentina Vivera, the woman in the opulent green gown, was a polyglot. She suggested going to the recently colonized New World. Chiron rejected that idea as well. He had a vision of how densely populated the New World would become. Then, one night, an idea came to him in a dream: the idea of inhabiting the heavens—space. Being the great wizard he was, Chiron conjured the first-ever spacesuits and oxygen tanks. And off they went. Cherry continued her search for aliens on Earth, and their numbers increased. For the next couple of years, Cherry helped them explore the Solar System and spread across it."

"Why did they choose to live on every planet in the Solar System and not just one? Like Mars or something?" asked Truman.

"Well, Mars *was* the first planet to be terraformed," Falsmira replied. "But as they explored more of the Solar System, people had affinities with other worlds."

Falsmira moved to a neighboring memory, ignoring Halle's raised hand. "In the Earthling year of 1787, our founding leaders signed what's called *the Aetherly Agreement*. It established the Assembly of Aether as the government of our Solar System."

The second memory showed the same characters as the first but with a few new faces. They passed around a scroll and a quill pen. Chiron's signature was the last to be added.

Aloud, Falsmira recited the Agreement by heart:

> *"We the Aliens of the Assembly of Aether,*
> *In order to form a more perfect System,*
> *Establish the unity of all heavenly bodies,*
> *Ensure the protection and secrecy against all humans,*
> *Promote the general welfare of all Aliens,*
> *And permit the exploration of space,*
> *Do hereby ratify this Aetherly Agreement for the Assembly of*
> *Aether."*

"As a reminder," Falsmira carried on, "while the Agreement mentions 'a more perfect System' and 'the unity of all heavenly bodies,' this excludes Earth. While Earth *is* part of the Solar System, the planet *is not* part of the Assembly of Aether."

☆ ☆ ☆ ☆ ☆ ☆

"Supper's on Cherry tonight," Angenciel said after Falsmira's lesson. "Until then, you're welcome to explore the Memory Bank. It might help with your exams." She winked. "For those who wish to return to the surface with us mentors, we're popping by the Fountain of Tears on our way out. It's stunning. There's an old wives' tale that says if you throw a wish into the fountain, the waters will 'bring you as much joy as you have sorrow.'" She shrugged. "If you don't want to join, we're trusting you to return to Cherry before curfew. Don't stay out too late—you don't want to skive off your studies the night before your exams!"

"Remember," Falsmira directed at Truman and Vedrò, "nine o'clock, sharp."

The mentors left with Shiloh, Humzah, and a few voyagers. Halle joined them to see the fountain. Those who stayed behind broke apart. Truman, Vedrò, and Esmeralda clung together.

"Hey guys, do you mind if I join you?" Style asked Truman. *"Humzah's been interpreting all week, and he's exhausted. I told him not to worry about me. Normally, I'd wander alone, but since you sign, Truman, I thought I'd ask."*

"Yeah, join us!" Truman spoke and signed simultaneously. "Oh, um, Esmeralda, Vedrò, would you mind if Style came with us?"

"Of course not!" Esmeralda said, smiling. "Where do you guys want to go?"

"I wanna revisit the memory of the terraformation of Middle Moon," said Truman. "I saw an engraved relic in it the other night. I'm curious what it said."

"Lead the way!"

The four bounced forward in time down the torchlit cave, took the shortcut, and passed many inexplicable memories on the way. One memory chipped away to reveal Earth.

"Is anyone else nervous about going back to Earth?" Vedrò asked, passing the memory.

"I am," Style signed, reading Vedrò's lips. *"I don't know how I'll lie to my family about all this. I'm a bad liar."*

Truman interpreted.

"How does that will work?" asked Esmeralda. "Do you just sense when someone lies?"

"A big red sign that says LIAR appears on top of your head." Truman laughed as he interpreted.

"I'm kidding. Like you said, I sense it," Style signed then frowned. *"I wish I had a cooler will like you guys."*

"Véritist sounds pretty cool to me," said Esmeralda. "It's like an everlasting truth spell, but only you know the truth. That's power. But who knows! Wills can deepen and evolve. You might get a whole second will like Truman."

"There it is!" Truman leapt toward the memory. The wall chipped away, and the memory stirred to life. "Can anyone read that?" He pointed to the relic. "My vision's not that good."

"Better than mine," said Esmeralda. "I wouldn't have noticed that if you hadn't pointed it out."

Vedrò read the inscription aloud,

"A sacrifice must first be paid
By touch of hand upon a blade.
Then two snakes will hiss and bite
If not played their song of fright.

A riddle here, a riddle there,
Be nothing short of smart and fair.
Now trace the archer's nightly chart
To find the love of broken heart.

At last, you stand alone yet true,
O' save her soul by being you!"

"Huh?" Vedrò said, squinting at the poem, thinking he had misread.

"Save whose soul?" Truman asked confusedly.

"A sacrifice?" Style signed. *"Sounds… morbid."*

"I bet the snake is Falsmira," Vedrò added, laughing under his breath.

"Snakes. Plural," Esmeralda corrected. "Mhm, interesting. Why did you want to return to this memory, Truman?"

"I don't know," said Truman. "I felt drawn to it, I guess. I wanted to see what was engraved. Vedrò also said he had seen this image before. Maybe it means something?"

"Is that true?"

"Yeah, I know," Vedrò said, rolling his eyes. "Of all things I could've predicted, it *had* to be Falsmira's boring lesson!"

A shadow grew on the cave floor, spooking Vedrò.

"W-what's that?" Vedrò stammered.

They turned around and saw a large Vivabee with ruby eyes emerging from another tunnel.

"What're you voyagers doing down here?" asked Sin.

"Sin, where're you—" said another voice from the tunnel. A blond man came bouncing out of the shadows. He wore a ruby earring and a snakeskin turtleneck.

"—Oh, hi there," Krimmiel greeted, smiling and looking from Truman to the relic.

From behind Sin and Krimmiel appeared a third man—a soldier. He was more handsome than pretty, with a strong build and a buzz cut. He wore red camo pants and a red wool jacket. His fingers were covered in gold rings. Each ring was a different shape: one was a panther, another a spider, and another a Leonian dragon.

Truman looked into the soldier's familiar brown eyes.

"Hey, Tru," said Vedrò, "he kind of looks like you!"

J.Q. Gagliastro

"Hey, Tru," said Vedrò, "he kind of looks like you!"

Chapter 21

Baby Air Dragons

T ruman stared at the soldier.

What Vedrò said was true—he looked just like Truman, only broader and more muscular. He had the same eyes, same jawline, and same hair color as Truman and Reuel.

"Aren't you Krimmiel? The notorious lawbreaker?" Esmeralda asked the blond man.

"Is that what they're calling me nowadays? 'A notorious lawbreaker?'" Krimmiel smirked, his voice buttery. "I suppose that's better than 'menace to alienkind.'"

"I told you," said the soldier, "you gotta stop going to Earth whenever you please."

"Why are you with him, Sin?" Esmeralda asked, her tone sharp.

"He's a good man," said Sin. "Just likes to travel without permission, eh?"

"You got it," Krimmiel replied, winking.

Truman tried to listen, but his gaze kept drifting back to the soldier. And the soldier stared right back.

A wall chipped away. It was the boat memory again. This time, the soldier was next to Reuel, only younger.

"And who are you?" shot Esmeralda.

"I'm Kahlil," said the soldier. "Truman's brother." He paused and smiled at Truman. "Don't remember me, do ya?"

"I'm—I'm not sure," Truman admitted, feeling conflicted. Kahlil was with Krimmiel. The honey thief. A lawbreaker. A bad guy. But he knew it had to be Kahlil—when he looked at his face, all he saw was Reuel.

"Are you a thief too?" Truman queried, furrowing his brows.

"Kahlil, a thief?" Krimmiel scoffed. "He's in the Martian Militia, kiddo. He *lives* by the rule book."

"Not true." Kahlil crossed his arms. "I didn't rat you out when you stole the elixir, did I?"

"Touché," said Krimmiel. "Guess it's in your blood to protect me. Your brother didn't rat me out either. And he *saw* me leave the Hive with the elixir."

Truman's face reddened.

"Is that true, Truman?" asked Esmeralda. "You saw it was Krimmiel and didn't say anything?"

"I wasn't sure if it was him or not," he answered, shrugging. "He *was* far away from me."

Esmeralda turned back to Krimmiel. "So, why did you need the honey elixir? You know there are patients out there who need it, right?"

"Krimmiel stole the elixir to save someone's life," Kahlil said firmly.

"Who did you save?" signed Style.

Fraught with emotion, Truman had forgotten to interpret for Style, who kept up by reading lips.

"I haven't saved them yet," Krimmiel said while signing.

"You know ASL?"

"Yeah," Krimmiel replied, bobbing his fist back and forth. "I'm a bit of a Renaissance man, you can say."

"Subtle," Kahlil mumbled.

"So, who will *you save?"* asked Style.

"To be determined."

"And we're supposed to just trust you on that and not turn you in, right?" said Esmeralda.

"Silver hair, strong-willed, French… You must be Angenciel's daughter," said Kahlil.

"And what if I am?"

Amused by her sharp tongue, Kahlil laughed. "Well, Esmeralda, if you don't believe us, which is understandable, just ask your friend Style here. He's a véritist, no? I'm sure he'll know if we're lying."

Style stared at Kahlil's lips. *"How do you know I'm a véritist?"*

Truman interpreted the question aloud.

"The Martian Militia is given a roster of all new voyagers and their wills every year. So, Style, were we lying?"

Style hesitated. *"They're telling the truth, I think. I'm not an expert véritist."*

The response appeased everyone except Esmeralda.

"Why are you down here?" she asked suspiciously.

"Just checking out some old memories," Sin replied casually. "And you?"

Truman felt a cold breeze on the back of his ankle. Strange, considering they were deep inside a Lunar cave.

"Studying for our exams," Esmeralda said shortly.

The breeze shivered up Truman's spine.

"Well, I'll be," Sin said, squatting. "You've brought some friends with you, I see. What adorable little air dragons!"

"Pardon?"

Out of the corner of his eye, Truman saw something move. Three little wisps of wind dissipated in a blink.

Esmeralda looked but saw nothing. Vedrò and Style too.

"Ah yes, I forget," said Sin. "You voyagers can't see them yet. They must have followed you through Luna's Well." He scooped up empty air and cooed at it as if it were an infant. "Did you get stuck down here? Yes, you did! Yes, you did!"

The voyagers thought he looked crazy—as crazy as a giant bee could look.

"Sin, we have to go," Krimmiel said, checking his watch.

"But what about the uh-h… the air dragons?" asked Truman.

"I'll take care of them." Sin carefully gathered the wisps of wind into his six limbs.

"Here, I'll help." Kahlil took one.

"I think I just saw something!" exclaimed Vedrò. "It was quick."

"Probably," said Krimmiel. "Your vision will develop over time."

"Since you can't see them yet, want to pet one before we go? It's a unique feeling," said Shiloh.

The voyagers exchanged glances and reached out a hand. A gentle gust prickled their palms and tickled their wrists.

"Wow!" signed Style.

"It's like… petting bottled wind," Vedrò said in awe.

"Told you."

"Best be off now," Krimmiel said, leaving without the others.

"Geez, so impatient." Shiloh fluttered after him.

"You're coming to the dinner tomorrow, right?" Kahlil asked, giving his brother an awkward half-hug.

Truman nodded.

"See you tomorrow then. Kill those exams!"

And just like that, he was gone.

When they were out of sight, Style turned to Truman. *"While they weren't lying, I did pick something else up. It's hard to explain. But something about Krimmiel and his presence felt… I don't know, fake."*

"Fake?"

"I'm not sure. We haven't exactly mastered our wills yet. I wish we could start practicing them. Why haven't we? That's why we're here, isn't it? Our wills."

"The Assembly doesn't want to overwhelm us," said Truman. *"We're traveling and learning so much, I don't think I'd have the energy for all that. But fake, you say? Mhm, I wonder what that means?"*

Ahead of them, Esmeralda and Vedrò bounced in sync, lost in a talk about air dragons.

Chapter 22

A Family Feast

We're not collecting oysters again, are we?" Vedrò asked begrudgingly, standing in the cabin with Truman and Falsmira.

"No, Mr. Azzurro," Falsmira answered, leading them outside and handing them gardening gloves and trowels. "You'll be weeding the Dragon's Back Trail instead." She grinned. "Manual labor. It's the best kind of punishment."

Unlike last time, Falsmira did not watch their every move. Instead, she sat against a tree and revised her test outline, glancing up intermittently.

While the other voyagers were off studying, Truman and Vedrò were hunched over the trail, smelling like dirt and sweat. The weeds were stubborn, abundant, and tall. The trail looked like it hadn't been weeded in years, if ever.

The force field had completely dimmed. The only light came from the cabin and the stars.

"Is this a weed? Ah, whatever," Vedrò said, tugging at a shrub. "So, are you excited to see your family tomorrow?"

"Honestly—" Truman paused, biting the inside of his lip. "I don't know. I mean, I am. Yes, I definitely am. It's just— I've been waiting so long to meet them, the anticipation is… unbearable. And I'm not just talking about since my will triggered. I'm talking about since I was a kid at Lonely's Academy." He stopped digging and stared unblinkingly at the ground.

"When I was younger, I used to dream my parents would come back for me. As years went by, I outgrew my clothes, got a job, and learned to live on my own. Ultimately, I realized they weren't coming back. I cried a lot over them. It was difficult to accept, but, eventually, I got there. I let that dream go. But the one dream I didn't—or couldn't—let go of was my siblings. I dreamed they would come back for me too. That maybe they'd be different… But they didn't. In ways, I felt— or feel, I don't know—abandoned by them too?" He shrugged, sighing.

"Now, I feel like I have to forgive them, knowing why they couldn't come back for me. Feels weird to say that because if it wasn't their fault, is there really anything to forgive?"

Vedrò nodded compassionately while pretending to garden.

"And as the anticipation builds," Truman pressed on, "I'm thinking about all these things, like what if I don't like them or what if they don't like me?" His eyes widened.

"I've been in Aether for three months now. I'd imagine once my will triggered, they'd try to meet me somewhere, anywhere, like the Dragon's Belly on Mercury or at Writers' Ink. Reuel said I couldn't meet them during the trimester because our schedule was 'too busy.' And yes, that's true. We have been busy, but we could've made the time. That's what family's supposed to do, right? Make the time for each other?" He peered up at the stars.

"And this party—why does it have to be a party? It's my first time meeting them. Why can't it just be us? I don't wanna meet random people. I just wanna meet *them*. And then, there's the whole Kahlil thing. How am I supposed to feel about him hanging with Krimmiel? Is that worsening the suspicion around my family? It can't be helping—"

"SHHH!" Falsmira hissed over her papers.

The boys put their heads back down and continued weeding.

"If they don't like you, Tru," Vedrò whispered, "there's something seriously wrong with them."

Truman smiled. "Thanks, Vedrò."

"It's true, though. You're a great friend. And Reuel is so kind and loving. I'm sure your other siblings are too. So what if Kahlil is friends with Krimmiel? Kahlil could still be a good person. Heck, *Krimmiel* could still be a good person. He could be experiencing the same things we've been experiencing with Cava. We don't know the whole story. So, let's just go to the party tomorrow, keep an open mind, and enjoy ourselves. I'll be there by your side. If we don't have a good time, at least the food will be free!"

Truman laughed, causing Falsmira to shush them again.

As they continued stuffing bags with weeds, the boys took turns quizzing each other for their exams.

Before they knew it, detention was over. Though they were sweaty and gross, they both crawled into bed and passed out.

With a narwhal tusk in hand, Truman was sucked into his waterbed. The buzzsaw shark dragged him to an abyss deep below the Cheryl Sea. Stalacrabs crawled over his skin. The shark gnawed at his throat, and buckets of saltwater poured into his singing lungs.

"Vedrò!" the shark yelled. "Truman! Wake up!" The shark whacked him with a flatfish.

Truman jolted awake from his nightmare and saw Esmeralda thumping him and Vedrò with a pillow.

"Get up! And take a shower! You reek." Esmeralda hopped out of the treehouse. "Our first exam is Aetherly History. It's in twenty minutes!"

"Twenty minutes?!" Truman bolted to the shower.

"I had another nightmare about the buzzsaw shark," Vedrò said, rubbing his forehead.

"I did too," Truman replied, drying himself quickly. He threw on clean clothes and his necklace as Vedrò jumped in the shower.

Once dressed, they ran down the rope bridge into the lobby. Rows of desks replaced the usual water couches.

"I was hoping you two would sleep through the exam," Falsmira said, perched on a stool, glaring at Esmeralda. "Would've saved me the hassle of reading whatever nonsense you're about to write."

She handed them their exams as they found the last two empty seats.

Chocolate muffins and coffee sat at the corners of their desks.

"I grabbed you guys breakfast since you didn't make it," Halle whispered. "Good luck."

Truman and Vedrò thanked her and scarfed down the muffins and coffee.

"Sorry I didn't wake you," Style signed to Truman. *"I didn't think you'd oversleep."*

"No signing during the test," Falsmira said sternly. "Alright, everyone, you'll have forty-five minutes to complete each exam. You'll have a fifteen-minute break in between each subject. First is Aetherly History. Pencils up, and—your time starts now!"

Before any of them had the chance to write their names on the test, Falsmira briskly pulled out her pocket watch and started the timer.

Truman staggered through the exam. He didn't know if it was because the questions were exceedingly complex or because he had just woken up. Halfway through the exam, he slipped off his necklace just to sense how everyone was feeling.

They were all struggling. He sensed Sweta getting frustrated. He sensed Schmidt getting angry. And he sensed Halle being overwhelmed. He tried homing in on Esmeralda to feed off her confidence, but she sat too far away.

He threw his necklace back on and distractedly gazed at the sunlight fiddling through the stained-glass skylight. He caught himself, refocused, and powered through the seemingly endless booklet.

After Aetherly History came their Interplanetary Technologies and Astrobiology exams. While they were both extensive, they were not as grueling as Falsmira's. Truman found Ereus' questions easy and Reuel's fun.

Once they finished the written portion of their IT exam, Ereus tested the voyagers on warping. Vortexes had been brought into Shiloh's room for the occasion.

During the break between IT and Astrobio, the voyagers brewed a fresh pot of coffee and chatted in the cabin's kitchen. It was a cute space with a rustic light fixture over a marbled island.

Esmeralda sat in the corner, feverishly rereading her study guide, cramming in whatever she could.

"Your trick to warping helped me get to the yellow vortex," Sweta said to Truman, blowing on her mug. "Thanks for the tip!"

"Of course!" Truman beamed.

"It helped me too!" Letsatsi added. "I was worried I was gonna fail."

"My wrists hurt," Vedrò interjected, groaning and cracking his knuckles.

After the break, Reuel started the exam with a practical. With a fishbowl in hand, she asked them to demonstrate how to properly handle a stalacrab without getting nipped. Her multiple choice asked questions about marvels, like *Which wonder inhabits the Sun?* and *On Venus, which fathom is found inside another fathom?* The most laborious part of her exam: an illustration of the Arachnoid. Truman tried drawing all one hundred legs, but it was more difficult than he had imagined. He gave up after the twenty-fourth leg.

"What kind of question was that?" Esmeralda muttered, washing graphite off her palm.

Reuel had left, and the voyagers were waiting for Angenciel.

"I liked it," replied Halle. "I liked the change of pace. I drew mine with big googly eyes!"

Angenciel arrived, and to everyone's dismay, the Worlds Cultures exam was nearly as difficult as Falsmira's.

When time ran out, Truman and the others gladly passed in their work, thankful to be done.

"Just a couple more minutes, please," Esmeralda asked, without looking up.

"No, Esmeralda. I'm sorry," her mother replied. "Time's up. Now drop the pen!"

Esmeralda did not listen, and Angenciel had to rip the booklet from her grip.

Esmeralda recoiled in shame.

"Alright, you lot," Angenciel said aloud, shuffling the tests together. "That's it for today. You're free to do as you wish. Don't leave Cherry. If you need us, the other mentors and I will be in our cabin, grading your exams."

The siren glided out of the cabin, her silver hair bouncing in the wind.

The moment Angenciel was out of earshot, chatter broke out among the voyagers.

"What did you guys write for the function of Ivies and Oaks?!" Halle asked aloud. "I think I misinterpreted the question."

"Yeah? Well, I forgot what the Firm of Fleferros does," said Schmidt. "And I'm a fleferro!" When everyone laughed, he gave a glimmer of a smile.

"I'm still thinking about Ereus' exam—I don't think I did well on the warping practical," Esmeralda said, flipping through her copy of *Vortexes and More* as though this would correct her mistake. "I managed to warp to the yellow vortex, but I left my cardigan in the red one!"

The voyagers who hadn't warped at all rolled their eyes at her.

Afterward, out in the lavender fields, the group shared stories and laughed until their jaws became sore. Shiloh came bearing tea and honey. The honey was not elixified but delicious, nevertheless. They ate fajitas for lunch and napped in the afternoon. While the others returned to the log cabin, Truman and Vedrò went for a walk along the Dragon's Back Trail and ran into Reuel.

"Ah, just the gentlemen I came for," she said with a smile. "For tonight, be ready by six o'clock Cherry-time!" She looked them up and down and scrutinized their sweats and untidy hair. "You should also change into something more… formal. Father is a bit picky when it comes to attire."

"I don't know what to wear," Vedrò said back in the treehouse. "I didn't bring much formal attire."

Truman wore pink flared pants and a matching button-up, both from Goodall's.

"Wear your green corduroy pants and borrow my suede dress shirt," said Truman. "Green looks good against your olive skin. Brings out your eyes."

"Oh, stop it! Stop it! I blush." Vedrò said, playfully tucking an imaginary hair behind his ear.

With their luney boots tied and shirts tucked in, the boys met Reuel outside the cabin. She stood by the tree of bleeding hearts, her hair in an elegant updo. She modeled a long satin dress that masked her pair of boots.

"Don't you two look dapper," she said approvingly. "Very handsome, both of you!"

"Thanks, Reuel. You look gorgeous! And different."

"Different?"

"Yeah. Normally, you wear tougher clothes like leathers and blacks. But the satin looks nice too. Softer."

"Thank you, I think. While I do love leather, I can be girlie sometimes too."

"Me too," Truman said, grinning. "So, how'd the grading go? Did we do well?"

"I haven't gotten to yours yet. I will tomorrow. We should get going, though. You are the guest of honor, after all! Best not be late. Since we're so well-dressed, I'll use my will to get us down. Ready?"

"For wh—"

Before Truman could finish his sentence, he felt something gently wrap around his waist and lift him into the air. His stomach flipped. He looked at Vedrò and saw a cherry blossom branch twisted below his rib cage. The bough elongated and rocked the boys in its clutch like babies in a cradle. Once their luney boots touched ground, the branch gingerly released them.

"I wish I could be an aster," grumbled Vedrò.

Reuel slipped off her branch and patted it before it shot one hundred feet back into the air.

"This way, boys!"

They bounced away from Cherry.

In the distance, Truman discerned a directional signpost. Each sign was blue and shaped like a teardrop. Each teardrop pointed in a different direction. The topmost teardrop read *Mare Nubium.* Its tapered tip pointed downward, labeling where they stood. Other teardrops read *Luna's Well*, *the Spyatory*, *Lunar Vortexes*, and *the Nubium Neighborhood*. *Fountain of Tears* was etched into the bottommost teardrop and pointed in a forward direction.

They headed toward the Nubium Neighborhood.

"There it is," Reuel said, nodding toward the end of a poorly lit lane where a Victorian house towered over the rest of the neighborhood. Its brickwork was a deep and haunting purple. The gate around the house was cast iron and razor sharp. Rocking chairs creaked on the front porch. Figures moved behind the windows.

A wave of foreboding swept over Truman and so did a sense of remembrance.

Above the front door hung a sign and a flag. The sign read *the Howard Household*. The flag was blue and had a mound of stalacrabs in its corner like the stars on the Star-Spangled Banner. As the fabric rippled in the Lunar wind, it gave the illusion that the stalacrabs were crawling all over each other.

"Nervous?" Reuel asked, bouncing up the porch.

"Excited-nervous," Truman said, peering through the glass door. He glimpsed fur coats, tailored suits, and a hologram of a singer.

Reuel reached for the crystal knob.

"Is that a diamond doorknob?!" Vedrò asked wildly.

"I believe so." She opened the door, and a cacophony of voices and music poured out.

"Here I am sewing up socks, and my own family has diamonds for doorknobs," Truman muttered to himself.

As they stepped inside, everyone stared at Truman. The hologram froze. The music screeched to a halt.

Truman felt his cheeks flush. He and Vedrò exchanged stunned looks.

"To Truman!" everyone shouted, clinking their glasses together.

"What am I, chopped liver?" Reuel said sarcastically, sitting on a bench near the door and removing her boots.

"You can leave your luney boots here," she told the boys. "They're not necessary inside most Lunar houses. Most families install a home gravity-stabilizing feature. Besides, Mum's a bit picky about wearing shoes in the house."

Truman and Vedrò kicked their boots next to Reuel's.

The crowd was larger than Truman had expected. While some guests returned to their previous conversations, others continued to gawk at him. He forced a sheepish smile.

The hologram unfroze and proceeded to sing a jazzy tune.

The house's interior was a feast for the eyes—decorations were hung everywhere. Art was in every corner, like a ghostly El Greco and an unsettling Caravaggio. Their gilded frames flowed together like streams of melted gold. The place was rich and flashy—things that made Truman uncomfortable back at the Academy.

"My Tru…"

A woman in a fur coat emerged from the crowd. She was pretty with graying-brown hair. Her eyes were brown like his, but one was darker than the other.

"Look at you!" she said, eyes brimming with tears. "You're all grown up."

Truman looked uncertain at her. "Mom?" The word felt cumbersome in his mouth.

She nodded and pulled him into a rib-cracking hug. "Welcome home, my beautiful baby boy!"

He patted her back awkwardly. Her embrace was warm, but perhaps it was just the fur coat.

The hug lasted a little too long—too long for two strangers. *Is this performative?* Truman thought skeptically. *No, Truman, keep an open mind.*

Once she released him, she spotted Vedrò.

"Hi there!" she greeted. "Are you Truman's friend?"

He nodded. "Hi, I'm Vedrò. Thank you for having me tonight, Mrs. Howard."

"Please, call me Lavenza." She turned to Truman. "Polite and handsome? Are you two going steady?"

"Ew no," Truman replied.

"What's going steady mean?" asked Vedrò. He got distracted by a shrimp platter and drifted toward it.

"Sorry for asking," said Lavenza. "And sorry for the glitter." She dusted glitter off Truman's chest.

The glitter returned a memory to Truman. He was five, maybe. They were in a library. Glitter fell into the spine of a book.

Vedrò came back with a handful of shrimp. "These are amazing."

"Look who it is," said a man in a diaphanous button-up and a silver tailcoat.

"Hey, Nayelo," said Truman. "How's the Pyramid?"

"Hanging in there!" He winked.

"Love the outfit," Vedrò said, his mouth full.

Reuel gave Nayelo and Lavenza kisses on the cheeks. "That better be fake fur, Mother."

Lavenza ignored her. "Nayelo, dear, do you mind ushering the boys to the back?"

"Of course."

"And Reuel, can you help me in the kitchen, please?"

They parted ways, Nayelo leading Vedrò and Truman through the masses.

"Mr. Truman Howard!" said a Greek man modeling a flashy belt. He vigorously shook Truman's hand. "Name's Orion Sybelle. Such a pleasure!"

"Congratulations on the triggery of your will, Mr. Howard!" said a fair woman wearing an alligator pin. "My name is Allie! Allie Geyne!"

"Good job not passing out for once," said a twangy voice. It was Elmory Moss in a denim dress. While her hair was straightened for the occasion, her eyes were hazy and tired like usual.

Truman shook many hands as he threaded his way through the crowd. He forgot names as quickly as he learned them.

The living room was less occupied. Two individuals sat on a crimson couch. A third leaned against a wall. All three had his jawline, his light brown hair, and his eyes.

Kahlil sat on the couch. The soldier's buzz cut was clean, and his uniform untouched from the day before. He had one leg over the other and a paperback of poetry in his beringed hand. He closed the book and rose from the couch. "Good to see you again, Tru!" He clasped his brother's shoulder and smiled.

The young man seated next to Kahlil looked only a couple of years older than Truman. He wore a crisp black suit and sat cross-legged on the couch. His necktie was red and was tied into an Eldredge knot. It resembled a blooming rose.

"Tru, meet Saint, your other brother," said Kahlil.

"Hi, Truman," said the young man. *"Enchanté… encore.* Nice to meet you… again."

"You speak French?"

"Mom and Father sent me to *L'École des Petits Princes* on Earth," Saint explained. "I picked it up there. And I know you've been taking classes at the Academy. Anyway—who's your friend?"

As Saint and Vedrò exchanged pleasantries, Truman watched Nayelo take the wallflower's hand into his own.

"Coelho?" said Truman.

"Hi, Tru," Coelho said brightly. "Am I the only one you remember?!"

"He only recognized you because you look like me," Kahlil said dryly.

This was not exactly true. While their faces looked identical, Kahlil and Coelho had little in common physically. Kahlil was bulky and clean-cut, whereas Coelho was lanky and artsy. His eyes were smudged with eyeliner. His hair was in a bun. And his pants were stained with paint and charcoal.

"Also," Kahlil added, "haven't you ever heard of the process of elimination?"

Truman was reminded of Esmeralda.

Coelho replied with a glare. "So, Tru, do you?" he asked.

"Do I what?"

"Remember any of us. Any lingering memories?"

"Uh, well, I already told Reuel how I remember playing dress-up with her. I have a memory of Mom in the library. And I have a vague memory of us on a boat. Reuel was there. Kahlil was there. And I can now see Coelho bellyflopping off the boat. But the girl… I think it's Minli. I don't know what, but something unique about her is shining through the memory."

"Perhaps this will help." Coelho reached for a picture frame next to a lighthouse figurine and passed it to Truman.

It was a moving photograph of five little children on a boat—Reuel, Kahlil, Coelho, Truman, and a girl with short, wet hair. She had blue-and-pink striped floaties on her arms. They all looked happy.

"She knew she was a girl at a very young age," Lavenza said, coming into the room with a tray of flute glasses. Reuel was behind her with a bottle of champagne. "We all knew."

"What do you mean?" asked Truman.

"She's trans," she answered. "That might be what you mean by 'something unique.' I'm only guessing. Maybe it's something else. She's doing very well."

"You keep an eye on her?" Truman asked, furrowing his brows.

"Every day! I did with each of you when you were on Earth."

Truman glanced from his thrifted clothes to the rich artwork on the walls.

"How do you keep an eye on us?"

"I have my ways."

"I didn't know PSA allowed that," replied Vedrò.

"I only watch from afar," said Lavenza. "It's all I can do."

Reuel pointed to the picture Truman was clutching. "That was a very special day," she said. "It was your sixth birthday— the mandatory age when all Aether-born kids must be sent to Earth with their memories wiped clean. It was the last time you were with us. Saint wasn't with us because he was on Earth by then."

"What do you mean Aether-born? My birth certificate says Massachusetts."

"It's fake," Lavenza said, waving her hand. "You were born in Aether and were given a Massachusetts birth certificate when you were sent to Kahlil's alma mater. But the school closed a few months after you enrolled. You probably don't remember that since you were so young. That's when I found Lonely's Academy and sent you there. They accepted your documents, no questions asked. That's why we didn't get you new Canadian ones."

"Sounds convoluted."

"Lying has that effect," said Reuel.

"Wait. So, how were you three there on my sixth birthday? You're, what, a decade or so older than me? Wouldn't you have been on Earth by then too?"

"Our wills triggered before you turned six," said Reuel. "It was nice to spend those six years with you. An adorable little tyke you were!"

Truman smiled, looking down at the picture. "She's in the U.K., right? Minli?"

"Yes," Reuel answered. "She's studying at my alma mater, Swotting's School for Sisterhood—S.S.S. for short."

Truman returned the picture to the mantel.

"So, Tru, any other memories of us?" asked Coelho. "Of me? Of this house?"

He shook his head, frowning. "Not really… I'm sorry."

Vedrò gave him a sympathetic smile. "Feels surreal meeting everyone, doesn't it?" he whispered to Truman.

Truman nodded, stealing a shrimp from his hand.

Reuel uncorked the bottle of champagne and poured a stream into each glass.

As Lavenza passed out the glasses, Truman heard someone walk into the room. Their footsteps were harsh though steady.

Truman noticed his siblings exchange glances. He wheeled around and saw a man looming over him.

The man wore a deep violet suit. The tail of his coat resembled droplets of Arachnoid venom. His belt was shaped like a snake eating its own tail. He was bald and had a permanent cut through one of his brows. The cuffs of his sleeves were rolled up. Like Angenciel, burn marks coursed down his forearms. He was handsome—not traditionally, but in a gaunt way. He had sunken cheeks and a tall, slim build.

"Well, I'll be damned," the man said coolly. "Look who it is." He smirked at Truman and flicked his gaze toward Coelho.

Coelho dropped Nayelo's hand.

The man's face became cold. "Coelho, what is this?" He gestured to his outfit. "You're covered in paint."

Truman looked around and saw that Coelho was not the only one cowering. Nayelo crossed his arms. Reuel steeled herself. Saint was gone. And Kahlil returned to his book.

Who is this man? Truman thought, looking confusedly at Vedrò.

"This is not your art studio," the man said, his tone biting. "This is your mother's house. As long as you're under it, you'll do as I say. Now go upstairs and put on a suit from my closet. While you're at it, wash that dirt off your eyes."

Coelho left without replying.

The man reached for a glass of champagne and smiled.

"Was that necessary, Kvell?" Lavenza said, frowning. "It's just a party. It doesn't need to be *that* formal."

"My son," Kvell said, flashing his teeth toward Truman, "deserves a proper soirée."

"*You're* our dad?" Truman blurted.

Reuel choked on a sip of bubbly. Kahlil widened his eyes.

No one spoke. It felt as if air dragons had flown out of the room, taking all the air with them.

Kvell stiffened. "It's alright. Truman, since this is our first time officially meeting, I'll excuse you for now. For future reference, never call me *Dad*. It is *Father* to you. Understood?"

Truman's face reddened. He had forgotten about this little idiosyncrasy that Reuel had told him long ago. He was so taken aback by how cold their father was it simply slipped his mind.

Considering who Reuel was, Truman hoped their father would be a bit warmer. He was disappointed to learn he was wrong.

"Yes, Father," Truman said stiffly. "Understood. Sorry."

"Do not apologize. Reuel clearly did not tell you."

"Well, she did. I just... forgot."

"I told him a while ago, though," said Reuel. "I should've reminded him."

"I see." Kvell's gaze fell onto Vedrò. "You must be Vedrò, Truman's guest."

Vedrò nodded.

"You may call me Mr. Howard."

Vedrò shook Kvell's hand and shifted uncomfortably without saying anything.

Kvell looked up at Lavenza. "Is dinner almost done, my love?"

"Oh, yes, let me check on that!" She bustled off, dabbing champagne off her fur coat.

"Why don't you check on dinner yourself?" Reuel said irritably.

"Reuel," Kvell said calmly, cocking his head to one side. "Where's my hug? Where's my 'Hello, Father! How have you been?' No? You're my firstborn!"

Reuel exhaled and reluctantly hugged him. "I'm sorry, Father. You're right. How have you been?"

"I'm good, I'm good. Better now that my fifth child is here! Just waiting on Minli."

"But her will may never trigger," Kahlil said over the top of his book.

"True. But at this rate, it must happen. Five out of six kids? Who are we kidding?!"

A muscle twitched in Kahlil's jaw. "Certainly not the Assembly," he mumbled.

"And what's that supposed to mean?"

"A lot of people think we're devious, Father," Kahlil answered, closing his book. "Honestly, I've been thinking maybe we should make a public announcement to clear the air or something."

"That would just draw more attention and suspicion." Kvell waved away the idea.

"Well, not saying anything is more suspicious," Kahlil countered. "We must say something, Father, especially since it concerns us, your children. I mean, come on! Truman was practically suffocated in the Carnegie Rupes. Those savage messengers never quit! They haven't with Saint, and they haven't with Truman. Reuel, Coelho, and I are skilled enough to evade the messengers, but for how long? Seriously, have you read the latest *Mercury's Message?* It's defamation. Not to mention, if Minli's will does trigger, we must protect—"

"Enough!" Kvell spat through gritted teeth. "I'm the head of this household—*I'll say what goes.*"

Kahlil bit his tongue.

Voices from the other rooms trickled in, replacing the silence.

"I'll see if your mother needs help," Kvell said finally, and left.

Truman and Vedrò exchanged looks.

"Can't believe you stood up to Father like that," Saint said to Kahlil, reappearing. "You too, Reuel. Pointless but impressive."

"It's not pointless," said Kahlil. "At least the idea is in his head, if it wasn't already."

"Where'd you go?" Truman asked Saint.

"He always does that," Kahlil said, rolling his eyes.

"Does what?"

"Vanish."

"I don't vanish," replied Saint. "I'm an illusionist. I just bend what people see—or not see. It works wonders for avoiding him."

"Why do you do that?" asked Truman.

"Did you not just meet him? He's dreadful."

"I wish I could've done that," Vedrò muttered. He pulled out an ivory horn from his pocket and stirred his glass of champagne with it, making it fizz more.

"What'd you bring that for?"

"People have been saying your family is up to something. After meeting Kvell, I understand why they think that. *Scusami* for not wanting to be poisoned."

"You know what that is, right?" Reuel said, shooting the horn a disapproving look.

"It's a narwhal tusk."

"Yeah, well, do you know how they're extracted? Aliens detusk the narwhals by chopping it right off their heads, while they're alive too! It's disgusting and barbaric."

Vedrò looked down at what he was holding, horrified at what he heard, and guiltily put the tusk back into his pocket.

"So, ehh, how did Kvell burn his arms?" Vedrò asked, aiming to change the subject.

Truman elbowed him.

"What?! I noticed they were a bit scabby. I'm just curious."

Coelho returned to the room in an oversized suit, his eyeliner removed.

"Did you guys hear about the Leonian dragon that escaped the Sun a few months back?" asked Kahlil. "Well, our father was helping the Assembly tame the beast when it burnt him. A similar situation happened to him on Uranus too. An air dragon gave him severe windburn and a permanent slash through his eyebrow. It almost cracked his skull open."

"What's his will?" asked Truman.

"He's a wizard," replied Kahlil. "Don't be impressed, though. He can barely cast a curse."

"Wow. Like, flying on a broomstick and all?" Vedrò asked, chuckling at the image.

"No. Think spells and potions."

"And Mom?" Truman asked. "What's her will?"

"She's a *miroir*," answered Kahlil. "A miroir has the will to copy another will. She doesn't steal them or keep them indefinitely, but she can mimic them until she touches another alien. She's skilled enough to remember two wills. Once she touches a third alien, the first will she mirrored is lost. But since she doesn't know how to control every will, sometimes she can't use the will if it's too powerful, like mine and Coelho's. She tried once but couldn't handle it." He cocked his head arrogantly.

"What're your wills?" asked Vedrò.

"I'm a pyraura and a *riaura*. Coelho's a *terraura*."

"A pyraura has the will to set things on fire, right?" said Truman. "I remember Angenciel telling us back in the Hive."

Kahlil held out his hands, and fiery wisps shot out and danced above his fingertips like a candelabra.

"Wicked!" Vedrò exclaimed, eyes widened.

"We can do more than just setting things on fire, though," said Kahlil. "Pyrauras can also generate electricity and heat." He extinguished the flames and held out his palms. A thin bolt of electricity shot from one palm to the other.

"Wooh!" Vedrò's mouth gaped open. "Man, my will is so lame," he muttered to himself, looking away.

Truman turned to Coelho. "And I assume from its prefix, a terraura can, what, manipulate rocks?"

Coelho chuckled, clenched his fists, and made pebbles appear out of nowhere. They revolved around his knuckles like mini Solar Systems. "Terrauras can control and reshape earth. Many terrauras work with the savvies to manipulate planetary cores and tectonic plates. All that gets very technical, which is why I'm just an artist."

"What type of art?" Vedrò asked, intrigued.

"I sculpt for a living. But I like to dabble in other mediums too: watercolor, acrylics, oils, charcoal, digital. I'm currently working on a commission piece for Union Square on Uranus. It might be my biggest sculpture yet!"

Nayelo squeezed his hand and smiled at him proudly.

"So, a pyraura manipulates fire. A terraura manipulates earth. An aquaura—that's me—manipulates water. What's a riaura? Air?"

"Bingo," said Kahlil. He flicked his wrist, and a tiny tornado blew across the mantel, bringing the lighthouse figurine with it.

"Why do all those words end in *ora*?" asked Vedrò.

"Aura. A-U-R-A," said Kahlil. "According to Aetherly witchcraft, our auras reflect our wills. A pyraura has reds and yellows in their aura. A riaura has whites and grays. Aquaura blues. And a terraura greens and browns. I don't know if I believe in all that, though."

"I do," said Coelho.

"Can you see auras?" Vedrò asked, producing more shrimp from his pockets and stuffing them into his mouth.

"Not literally. I just see them in our personalities. While Kahlil is fierier and more capricious, I'm more grounded and headstrong, I'd like to think."

"It's good you can think," said Kahlil.

Vedrò chuckled. Coelho rolled his eyes.

"But you're one of us now, Tru," continued Kahlil. "Together, we make one *elomni*—an alien who can fashion all four elements. That will is very rare, though."

"Are you and I the only ones with two wills?" asked Truman.

"No, Saint's also a flutterby, if you want to call that a will."

"Hey!" Saint protested.

"I mean, really, what's the purpose of talking to roses and ferns?" Kahlil gestured to the plant in the corner of the room.

"He didn't mean that, Fern!" Saint said sympathetically to the plant.

Reuel laughed and topped off their flutes with champagne. "Let's do a toast, shall we? To Truman and Vedrò?"

"To Truman and Vedrò!"

Truman smiled. He had waited so long to be with his siblings. It hadn't quite hit him that just months ago, he was alone in Canada, sewing up socks, with a hateful roommate. Now, he stood beside his loving, bantering siblings and a best friend, surrounded by music and magic.

Through the dense crowd, Truman saw two individuals enter the house. One wore a gold dress, while the other a silver slip. They looked beautiful.

"I told Mum not to invite her," Reuel muttered.

"Is that Esmeralda?" Vedrò asked.

"And Angenciel," Truman said, glancing back at Reuel and seeing her sneak out the back exit.

It then dawned on him.

Chapter 23

The Fountain of Tears

Truman pulled on a random pair of boots and followed his sister out the door. He spotted Reuel in the distance and bounced after her. She was a mere shadow.

He passed houses, lampposts, and mounds of moonrock that mounted into space. An imposing fountain grew and grew on the Lunar horizon—the Fountain of Tears.

He arrived sweating.

Her face was in her hands. Her back was hunched in sorrow. She sat on the marble brim of the fountain.

He sank beside her and noticed the once-perfect hem of her satin dress was now ripped from being dragged on the rocks.

She looked up. Her eyes reflected the fountain.

"You love Angenciel, don't you?" he asked.

She looked away. "It's complicated."

"Do you want to talk about it?"

She picked at her hem, not speaking for a moment.

"We met when we were voyagers," she said finally. "I was the youngest of my cohort. But that didn't stop her from taking me under her wing. For a good while, we were best mates, like you and Vedrò. Stuck to the hip and all. After our journey, we started new lives on Venus together. Our friendship flourished. We shared the same passions and strove for the same things, like becoming mentors!" Her voice rose and dipped.

"But the closer we got, the more we realized that the love we had for one another was… more intense than friendship. We kissed." She paused to breathe.

"It confused us. But I knew I wanted her. And I wanted her to want me." She furrowed her brows. "I think she did. But she was afraid and shut me out. We went years without speaking after that *one kiss*. And that's when… when she met him…" Her voice trailed off.

"Esmeralda's dad?"

"Yes." Her voice cracked. "But when she was pregnant, he passed away. Angenciel was still very young then. I felt terrible she was going through pregnancy, motherhood, *and* the loss of a loved—all alone. I wanted to say something but didn't have the courage. I feared being rejected again. So, I stayed silent.

"Then, you and Esmeralda were born. I found myself running into her outside the delivery room at Midwives of Mars. I took it as fate… Stupid, stupid," she sighed, shaking her head.

"I professed my love to her right there. I even offered to help raise Esmeralda! So embarrassing. 'We could never be together,' she told me. 'Being with a siren is like waiting for the ship to crash.' I'll never forget those words." She stared blankly at the ground.

Truman gently placed his hand onto hers and looked at her with kind eyes.

"She blamed herself for his death, of course," Reuel pressed on. "She didn't want the same to happen to me. She said sirens are not given the same opportunities as 'normal aliens,' and that sirens aren't allowed to live as happily as others. But I wanted to prove her wrong. Prove that it wasn't her fault, only an accident. She disagreed. And we started fighting.

"I said she was being stubborn. And she said she was trying to protect me. We ended up causing a scene in the hospital. The authorities got involved and threw *her* out. They even considered taking Esmeralda away. I stepped up and said it was all my fault, not hers, which *was* true. But they didn't listen. They never do. All they saw was her will."

She turned away angrily and sighed.

"Thankfully, Mum forced Father—who has a lot of friends in high places—to vouch for her in court. Institutional prejudice against sirens, that's what it is." She rolled her eyes.

"She got to keep custody of Esmeralda until, you know, she had to be sent to Earth like all other alien children. Angenciel and I didn't exchange one word during those years. We buried ourselves in our work and families. While she was busy raising Esmeralda, she began writing *Heavenly Bodies and the Cultures Within*. She also started an internship at the Van Gogh Irisylum and was asked to become a mentor. I, on the other hand, spent a lot of time with you guys, trying to be there for you and Minli as much as possible before you were sent to Earth. I also began working at Ivies and Oaks and became a full-time student of Astrobiology. I was in the middle of researching the wonders and fathoms when I was offered *my* mentor position."

Truman noticed a glimmer of a smile.

"That was when we started talking again," said Reuel. "You know, because we had to. We're civil now. But obviously, those feelings still… linger. At least for me…"

She stopped.

"I'm so sorry, Reuel," Truman said, squeezing her hand. "I did sense something back in the Van Gogh Irisylum and the Memory Bank, but I had no idea it was all this."

"I'm sorry I didn't tell you sooner. I'm just embarrassed by everything."

"You shouldn't be," he replied, smiling at her warmly. "You can always tell me anything, Reuel. I'll never judge."

She smiled weakly back at him.

"So, why now?" he asked.

"Why now what?"

"Why did this spill out tonight?"

"Good question." She paused to think. "Maybe it's the alcohol, I don't know. That, or I suppose I find it difficult to see Angenciel—someone I once loved—around people I do love."

She stared into the depths of the fountain, reached into its waters, and pulled out a stalacrab.

It looked at her with sorrowful eyes, as sorrowful as a crab could be.

"Empathetic creatures," she mused. "It's fascinating how others' emotions become theirs. Kind but unhealthy. I think that's why their family-oriented behavior is what it is. They can sense when each other is in pain."

She let the stalacrab writhe in her grip before returning the critter to its family.

"I have a question for you, Tru. It's a bit random."

"Let's have it."

"When we walked into Mum's place earlier, I heard you mutter to yourself something about 'sewing up socks.' What did you mean by that?"

"Uh, well… exactly how it sounds, I guess. I didn't have much money at Lonely's Academy. I rarely ever bought new socks—or new clothes, for that matter. I just couldn't. I either bought used ones from the thrift store or sewed up the holes." He pulled off a boot and showed her his ratty sock. "Before I got a job at the mountain, I got kicked out of class several times because my clothing often never met the dress code. My pants were either too short, or my shirts had too many holes."

Reuel looked concerned.

"I'm happy I had a job, don't get me wrong. I learned how to take care of myself and learned self-discipline and responsibility—all that stuff."

"But you never received money from Father?"

"How would I?"

"Father regularly sent cash to my school. I know Kahlil, Coelho, and Saint received deposits as well because we've talked about it. But why didn't you? I'm sorry, Tru. I didn't know. If I had, I would've spoken to Mum and Father about it or sent you money myself. There must be a reason."

Truman didn't know what to say. It was hurtful to hear that their parents supported his older siblings but not him. What did he do to deserve that?

Reuel wiped the shine from her cheeks. "I'll find out why, Tru. I promise. We should head back home, though. Mum's probably worried sick."

"That's strange to hear," said Truman. "*Home.*"

"I know what you mean." She stood.

"I'll catch up to you," he said. "I'm gonna make a wish. By myself, if you don't mind."

"Don't be long." She smiled thankfully at him and left.

He crisscrossed his legs and faced the lugubrious fountain. Water spouted like teardrops and cascaded around sculptures of woeful mermaids. Though the mermaids sat together, they could not have looked more alone.

Through blurry vision, Truman stared into the moving waters and daydreamed about a lost childhood—one free of stress and burden. A childhood with his siblings. Sadness, anger, and frustration washed over him. Sadness for what would have been. Anger for what should have been. And frustration for what could never be.

He heard footsteps. "Reuel?"

A man in an oversized suit stepped out from behind a mermaid.

"Sorry for sneaking up on you, Tru," said Coelho. "I saw you head after Reuel. Where is she?"

"She went back to the house." He wiped a tear from his chin.

"Are you okay?"

"Yeah, just thinking."

"About?"

Truman looked into his hands. "What life would've been like if the Assembly never separated us. We could've spent our childhoods together, Coelho. I could've known what you guys were like back then. I could've seen what you've all been through. How you've changed. But I've been robbed of that. The Assembly—they took it all away, and it's not fair!"

Coelho frowned compassionately. "It is unfair. It is wrong to separate children from their parents. Immoral and deplorable. Nothing excuses that behavior. Not even PSA."

He shook his head.

"As for us, Tru, your siblings… do not waste time and energy dwelling in a world of what-could've-beens. Those feelings are natural, but they're not worth holding on to. Trust me, I felt the same way when I became an alien. All of us did and still do! But take it from me: things of the past are just that. It's best to live in the moment and to bridge-water."

"Bridge-water?"

"Yeah, I read it in a book once. Build yourself a mental bridge, allow the water to flow underneath, and get over it. I know it sounds blunt, but what's important is that we're together now. You can still get to know us. Let's start now! Ask me anything."

"Okay," Truman said, smiling. "How about something easy like… what's your favorite color?"

"That's not easy at all! I'm a painter, for Sepulcreul's sake!"

"For what?"

"Ah, just a Plutonian saying," said Coelho. "I suppose I've been into blues lately. My favorite alien painter, Ém, had one of the most prolific blue periods. Her full name's Émilie Péril, but she always signed her paintings *Ém*. She was an empath like you."

Truman thought back to the Irisylum.

"What about you?" asked Coelho. "What's your favorite color?"

"Mmm, probably red. A blood red, though."

"That's not creepy at all," Coelho chuckled.

"Like a deep crimson or something."

"If you like red, just wait 'til you see the Northern Rose on Saturn. You're gonna love it. Anyway, what else would you like to know?"

"Mm." Truman thought. "Are you and Nayelo dating?"

Coelho grinned. "You could say that. We've been friends for quite a while now. It evolved rather recently. We haven't made it official or anything because, well, once we do, I'll have to talk to Father. Mom already knows. I feel Father knows too. But he didn't react well when Reuel came out. I'm not in any rush to go through that myself."

Truman nodded. "Does he make you happy? Nayelo, I mean."

"Very much so."

"That's all that matters. Forget what Father thinks."

Coelho hugged Truman. "Thank you for that."

"Of course," said Truman. "Another question. What happened between you and Kahlil?"

"What makes you think something happened?"

"You two banter *a lot.*"

"We do, don't we?" Coelho smirked. "It's nothing, trust me. Like your favorite color, we're blood. We love each other no matter what. It's just, sometimes, Kahlil gets on my nerves. That's all."

"How so?"

"Well, he's condescending, if you haven't noticed."

"I have. He reminds me a bit of my friend Esmeralda. She can be condescending at times too. But she always means well."

"I like to think Kahlil does too. It's still irritating. What's more irritating is when he tries to one-up me. It happened more when we were kids, traveling together. For example, he used to hold his second will over my head all the time. Said he was cooler because he had two. He also once said his American accent was better than my Brazilian. But you can't compare those."

"You have a Brazilian accent?"

"It sneaks out now and then, but I've shed it mostly."

"Do you speak Portuguese?"

"It's my first language! While Kahlil grew up in the States, I attended a boarding school in Brazil."

"Why would he make fun of your accent? Everyone has one. My old roommate used to mock kids with accents different from his, but he was a bully."

"Well, Kahlil was a bully. *My* bully. Don't get me wrong. He has changed a lot since then. And I wasn't perfect either. I just don't think he knew much better. He had to learn."

"Wait, wait, wait. You said you guys traveled together? As in, the journey through Aether?"

Coelho nodded.

"That means your wills triggered the same year."

"Mine and Kahlil's wills triggered the same day."

"No way?!"

"Way. And when we found out we were twins, it was quite the shocker!"

"What do you mean? You guys forgot you were twins?"

"Well, we were forced to forget. But there was always something itching in the back of our minds. Twin sense or whatever you want to call it. I always felt like a part of me was missing. When we met, it all clicked. And though he was a bully from time to time, it was still nice having a sibling during that chapter in my life."

"Yeah, I know what you mean," Truman said, thinking of Reuel.

"The reason why Kahlil and I still banter, I think, is because it's easy to slip back into those dynamics." He pulled back his baggy sleeve and checked his paint-splashed watch. "We should go back. Before we go, have you thrown a wish into the fountain? It's a rite of passage for voyagers. You ought to." He dug into his pocket and pulled out a coin pouch. "I assume you've heard of the old wives' tale?"

Truman shook his head.

"You know, throw a wish into the fountain, and the waters will bring you 'just as much joy as you have sorrow.'" Coelho shook the bag, and it rattled with wishes. "To be honest, I don't know why the tale isn't *more* joy than you have sorrow, but whatever."

Truman reached into the pouch and felt around for a coin. "So, all I wish for is 'just as much joy as I have sorrow?' That's all?"

"That's all." Coelho grabbed a coin himself.

And together, they tossed the gold into the fountain.

"Now, let's head back before you cry again."

"Oh, shut up!" Truman laughed.

As they turned around, they bumped into a tower of a man in a violet suit.

Chapter 24

Nightly Whispers

K vell looked down at Truman.

"Your mother and I spent weeks prepping for this party, and instead of being with your family and meeting our friends, you're out here crying?" He shot Truman a sharp, reproachful look. "Did it ever occur to you that no one wanted to start supper without you? It is rude to have people wait, Truman. Very rude indeed."

While his eyes were ablaze, his tone was collected. "Coelho, go back to the house and tell your mother we'll be there shortly. I must have a word with your brother."

Coelho gave Truman a sympathetic glance before leaving.

"I'd first like to say, Truman, I am happy your will has triggered," said Kvell. "Truly, I am. But since you've been gone, I've noticed you've become—how shall I say?—soft around the edges."

Truman shifted uncomfortably.

"I was expecting it," Kvell pressed on. "Without me, your father, in your life, how else were you going to learn how to be a real man?"

Truman held back his laughter, stuck his tongue to his bottom jaw, and nodded, narrowing his eyes at Kvell.

"The same thing happened to Coelho and Reuel," Kvell continued. "Reuel, without her mother, never learned how to be a real woman. Coelho, like you, became soft. And don't even get me started on Minli. Not everyone was as lucky as Kahlil. Nevertheless, you are a part of this family. And now that you're with us again, I'm here to teach you what you should've learned years ago."

How is this man my father? Truman thought, tapping his foot. He knew at that moment he did not want Kvell in his life. He despised him.

"With Reuel and all this Angenciel garbage, of course, she'll be emotional," added Kvell. "She's a woman. It's inevitable. But you, Truman, you are a man. And as a man, emotion is a weakness. It will be difficult since you're an empath, but you will learn to hide those emotions. You must. And I know you know so. You've seen how people think of you. *Mercury's Message* called you weak. Prove them wrong, Truman. Be a real man."

Truman wanted to tell him off.

But instead, he thought of his siblings and mother. He loved Reuel. And he could sense Coelho, Saint, and Lavenza were good people. Kahlil too. He wanted them in his life, no question. Then it struck him: *As long as Kvell is in their lives, he'll unfortunately have to be in mine as well.*

☆ ☆ ☆ ☆ ☆ ☆

Kvell and Truman returned to the house in silence.

Inside, Truman slipped away from his father and stepped into a room buzzing with strangers. He spotted his siblings scattered around the room.

"Truman!" Lavenza called across the room. "Come get your plate!"

As he pushed through the crowd, Truman saw Esmeralda and Kahlil sitting on the couch. They were deep in conversation about Kahlil's book.

Vedrò sat next to them, looking bored and hungry. Truman made eye contact and gestured to him to follow. Vedrò sprang up and made a beeline for the table laden with platters of sushi, sashimi, maki, nigiri, and uramaki. Bowls of edamame and soups were piled on one end.

Lavenza carefully set the table with fine china and sterling chopsticks.

"This one is stalacrab uramaki." Lavenza pointed. "It is the dish of the Moon."

"You made all of this?!"

"My Queen Bee, no. All the girls in the neighborhood helped me. Rolling sushi is a Lunar pastime." She gestured toward the other women setting the table. They waved and smiled at the boys.

"Poor things," Lavenza whispered to Truman. "Most of them are grieving mothers who had to send their children to Earth. They're helping because we're friends, of course. But I just know it gives them hope—hope that one day their children might return. Like you."

She cupped Truman's face and smiled.

"Poor, Alessia, though," she said, letting him go. "She sent her son Giovanni to Earth just last week. She couldn't come tonight. She's been bedridden since. It has that effect. You never truly heal. The girls and I have been taking turns checking on her, bringing her food, making sure she eats. But nothing truly helps. Nothing but time. Maybe a distraction or two, but mostly time."

The last platter of sushi was placed on the table.

"You boys dig in!" Lavenza walked over to a wall and rang a bell. "Dinner is served!" she announced.

As guests shuffled into line behind them, Truman and Vedrò grabbed chopsticks and piled mounds of sushi onto their plates. They slumped into the nearest chairs, gorging themselves with rainbow rolls, dragon rolls, yellowtail sashimi, and pickled ginger. They washed it down with kinoko soup, which was warm and smelled of broth.

Truman loved the stalacrab uramaki. The crab meat was so fresh it tasted like the stalacrabs were caught just hours ago. The stalacrab in his roll must've been neon-green because the meat had a faint lime color to it. It didn't look appetizing, but he had to contain himself from devouring the whole platter.

"I could guzzle that soup," Vedrò said, his mouth full.

"You are guzzling it."

Coelho and Nayelo joined the boys with four wine glasses and a bottle of Riesling.

"What's the legal drinking age in Aether?" Truman asked, wiping spicy mayo off his lip.

"Every celestial body is different," said Nayelo. "It's seventeen on the Moon. Sixteen inside the Moon."

Vedrò sipped the dry wine and smacked his lips.

Truman was grateful he was wearing his necklace. Everyone was getting drunk. He felt tipsy after one glass. Like Vedrò, he fell into a giddy, outgoing mood.

Saint inhaled his sushi and began dozing off with his hand on his belly.

Esmeralda and Kahlil bonded over more poetry.

Tipsy herself, Esmeralda became more passionate about the lyricism. "He is utterly brilliant! 'The righteous is not innocent of the deeds of the wicked!' That one sentence could reform a whole justice system!" she gushed.

Nayelo broke into song with the hologram and nudged Coelho to join.

Coelho smirked and gave him a peck on the cheek. "You're beautiful," he said to Nayelo.

Reuel sentimentally flipped through old photo albums. "That's when Saint was sent to Earth," she said. "And that's when you caught stalacrabs for the first time. And that there is your first time in Middle Moon!"

"Why do non-Aether-related memories return to me more than Aether-related ones?" asked Truman. "It doesn't make sense. I should remember neon crabs, no? And the inside of the Moon?!"

"Oblivies blur over Aether-related memories more than non-Aether-related memories," said Reuel.

Drunk on Pinot Grigio, several of Lavenza's girlfriends cried about how much they missed their children.

"Your mother is just so lucky to have you back, my dear," one woman said, teary-eyed as she squeezed Vedrò's cheeks.

"Yes," Vedrò replied, playing along. "She *is* lucky."

Truman elbowed him.

While everyone was relaxing, Lavenza never stopped moving. She darted from room to room, making sure everyone was content. Truman noticed how she doted on Kvell—waiting on him hand and foot—while all he did was smoke hookah and entertain some guys in the foyer.

Surrounded by his siblings, Truman basked in every moment he shared with them. He gathered that Coelho, who had been talkative at the Fountain of Tears, was more introverted in group settings.

He discovered that Kahlil also spoke French when he recited a Rimbaud poem to Esmeralda and asked for her thoughts.

He heard Saint, energized by a shot of espresso, tell Vedrò stories from his days journeying across Aether. While Vedrò oohed and gasped in all the right places, Reuel kept pulling Truman's attention back to the photo album.

"Minli's fourth birthday," she said, pointing to a photo of Kahlil shoving Minli's face into a chocolate cake and laughing. "You on a beach." The picture was of Truman buried under a heap of seaweed. "Mum and Father used to take us to the ocean all the time—"

"Does anyone know where Elmory went off to?" interrupted one of Lavenza's neighbors. "I wanted to get her opinion on my fried butterfly spanakopita."

Reuel shook her head and returned to the photo album.

The lady left without noticing Vedrò snagging one of the flaky pastries off her plate.

Truman laughed, returning his attention to Reuel.

She flipped the page to a photo of Truman dolled up as the tooth fairy and Minli as a pearly-white tooth.

"You two won best duo for that year's Halloween contest," Lavenza said proudly, peering over their shoulders, smiling fondly at the memory.

"Come with me, Tru. I have something to show you." Lavenza held out her hand.

He stood without taking it.

She frowned, brushed it off, and led him up a flight of stairs and into a vacant room.

"You and Minli shared this room," she said, flicking on the light.

Twin beds faced each other—one bed resembled Cherry, the other a Leonian dragon.

"We bought the Leonian dragon bed for you, and Cherry for Minli. But she loved how fierce the Leonian dragon looked. You let her have it." On the Leonian bed sat a stuffed animal with a plush horn and four white legs. "This was your favorite toy as a child." She handed him the unicorn. "I kept it in case it'd restore any memories."

He stroked its fur and shook his head. He laid it down and felt the scaly comforter. The Leonian dragon looked down at the head of the bed. Its ruby tendrils dangled like a mobile. He brushed the felt tendrils, and a memory came to him.

"She used to braid these before bed," he said, smiling. He turned to Cherry and pressed down onto the soft blossom-shaped pillow.

A rocking chair and table stood in the corner. A box of red candies sat on the table. He recognized them. They were Hot Tamales. He picked up the box, rattling the cinnamon candies inside.

"Those were your favorite when you were a kid," said Lavenza.

"They still are," he replied softly, looking up at her. "Blessedbes taste like these to me."

"Really?" She smiled. "You and I were the only ones who liked them." She rocked the chair with her hand. "Sometimes, I sit here, eat Tamales, and think of you and your sister." Tears filled her eyes. She wiped them away before Truman saw. "I should check on our guests. Take your time in here." She left.

Truman saw a toy chest at the foot of the bed. Inside, he found stuffed Arachnoids, Vivabees, spaceships, dolls with witchy costumes, and a silver journal with a reflective binding. The handwriting inside was cursive and too difficult to read.

He returned everything to the chest and crawled onto the Cherry bed. His legs hung off the edge.

"Looks like you've outgrown that," Esmeralda said, standing in the doorway next to Vedrò. "Is this your old room?"

He nodded.

"Does it bring back memories?"

"Some, but not many."

She frowned. "Maybe seeing more of the house will help?"

"Probably. Wanna look around?"

"Sure."

The three of them meandered around the second and third floors. Downstairs, the guests' voices were faint, muffled beneath the floorboards. Music hummed softly in the background.

Truman peeped his head into each room and had a good sense of whose room was whose. The first room was overgrown with pierre plants. *Reuel's.* Another room had bunk beds on one side and an art easel and toy guns on the other. *Easy,* he thought. *Coelho and Kahlil's.* The third was a simple room painted with clouds. Plush air dragons were organized in a corner. *Saint's, I guess.*

"So that's what they look like," Vedrò said, picking up the stuffed wonder.

"Any memories so far?" Esmeralda asked.

"Not really. I slightly remember playing hide-and-seek here." He opened a bathroom cabinet and nodded in remembrance. "This was one of my go-to hiding spots."

As they wandered, Truman noticed that every door had a diamond knob. Every bed frame was gilded. And every vanity was polished chrome. He couldn't help but wonder why Lavenza decorated every blank wall with something beautiful and shiny.

They reached the topmost part of the house. The stairs creaked with every step. Truman ran his hands along the violet walls to find a light switch, but to no avail. They were shrouded in darkness. Their shadows stretched before them, long and thin.

"Why's it so cold up here?" Vedrò said, rubbing his arms for warmth.

Twilight poured in through a window at the top of the stairs.

A door was cracked open at the end of the hall.

From behind it, two hushed voices whispered.

"Did you reflect her will?" asked a deep voice.

"I did," said the other. "So, what do you want me to do to her now?"

Truman, Vedrò, and Esmeralda quietly stacked their heads in the gap of the doorway. It was the master bedroom with a velvet king bed and two shadows inside.

"You must alter her memory," said the deep voice.

"Again?"

"Yes."

"But how will she remember to find Cherry's heart?"

"Do not worry about that," said the deep voice. "I am the greatest wizard since Chiron. All we need is this potion here."

Truman saw a hand go for a vial of glowing purple liquid.

"It's my strongest brew yet. I admit the last two times were not my best work. This time, she'll be under my complete control."

Truman gingerly cracked the door open. A woman in a denim dress lay unconscious on the bedroom floor. Lavenza and Kvell stood over her.

"When will she do it?" asked Lavenza.

"Tonight," said Kvell. "Tonight will be the best time for Elmory to sneak in and poison Cherry."

Chapter 25

The Heart of Cherry

K vell pried Elmory's jaw open, uncorked the vial, and poured the purple liquid down her throat.

Lavenza laid a hand on Elmory's temple.

Elmory jolted awake, coughing.

"Are you alright, my dear?" Lavenza asked with a kind smile.

"Where am I?" she asked, bewildered.

"You had a bit too much to drink, I think. You must've stumbled into our bedroom."

"That's weird. I don't remember drinking that much," she said, rubbing her forehead. "I don't feel drunk either."

"Perhaps you need rest. You think you can manage to warp home?"

"I think so."

As Kvell helped her to her feet, he hissed in her ear, *"Yrrehc Nosiop!"*

Elmory's eyes glazed over.

Kvell smirked and handed Elmory a vial of red liquid. She took it without question and made for the door.

Truman, Esmeralda, and Vedrò rushed to the stairs. Vedrò accidentally bumped into a console table, sending a crystal ball tumbling to the floor. It shattered.

"What was that?!" roared Kvell.

Before the door swung open, the three flew down the stairs and blended into the throng.

"Do you think Kvell saw us?" Vedrò asked, panting.

"I don't know."

Truman scanned the room and saw Elmory in the foyer. She pulled on a pair of luney boots and left the house.

"She looks like she's in some sort of trance," said Truman.

Esmeralda pulled the boys into a corner. "Truman, is your dad a wizard?"

Truman nodded.

"And your mom?"

"She's a miroir, which means—"

"I know what a miroir is. She must've reflected Elmory's will and used it against her. Altered her memory or something."

Truman shook his head.

"Something's off about your father, Tru," said Vedrò. "I don't like him."

"I know. I don't either. But why would he and my mother want to poison Cherry? Why would she do that?"

"I don't know," said Esmeralda, "but we can't let it happen. We must stop Elmory."

"We should tell my siblings. Maybe they can help!"

Vedrò and Esmeralda exchanged uncertain glances.

"What? What is it?"

"How do we know we can trust them?" said Vedrò. "What if they're in on it and try to stop us? I mean, I thought Lavenza was nice. Clearly, I was wrong."

"You're right," Truman swallowed, looking away. "I thought Lavenza was nice too. And I just met Coelho and Saint. Not to mention, Kahlil hangs out with Krimmiel," he sighed. "But what about Reuel and Angenciel? We've been traveling with them for, what, three Earth months now? Surely, we can trust them!"

He thought about earlier when Reuel opened up to him.

"I trust Reuel," he said firmly, eyes shut. "I do."

Vedrò and Esmeralda looked at each other and nodded in agreement.

They split up and searched the crowd for their mentors.

"Have you seen Reuel? Have you seen Angenciel?" Truman asked stranger after stranger.

Most of the guests shook their heads. Others were too inebriated to listen.

"Did you find them?"

"No," said Vedrò. "You?"

"No."

"Then, we'll have to save Cherry ourselves, won't we?" Esmeralda said fiercely. "Let's hurry!"

They grabbed their luney boots and slipped out the front door.

On Mercury, the Leonian dragons took up most of the sky. When they didn't, the Aurora Mercurialis painted the sky instead. On Venus, the Sun hid behind treacherous clouds as one blurry blob. On the Moon, however, the Sun resembled a bright flashlight in a dark room.

The three bounded after Elmory and climbed aboard Cherry. She entered the cabin. They kicked off their boots and followed. As they burst through the doors, they glimpsed Elmory plunge into the Cheryl Sea. They ran to the tank and saw her swimming downward.

"You're back sooner than we thought," Halle said behind them. Shiloh fluttered beside her. "We thought you'd be out all night!"

"Halle!" Esmeralda said urgently. "No time for chitchat! That woman who just jumped into the Cheryl Sea—"

"You mean Elmory? I was curious why she's here."

"Yes, Elmory," Esmeralda pressed on. "She's going to poison Cherry!"

"What? Wh-What do you mean?"

"No time to explain. We need your help! You too, Shiloh!"

"Anything!" Halle and Shiloh said together.

"Tell us if the buzzsaw shark is approaching." Esmeralda flung open the closet door and handed Halle Falsmira's monitor.

"Wait, what?" Halle said, stunned.

Esmeralda ignored her. "Truman, Vedrò, we need to swim after her!"

The boys gulped and nodded.

"Let's do it!" Vedrò said, reaching for a suit.

Esmeralda fastened her headpiece and dove into the tank. The boys exchanged looks and followed. When their eyes adjusted to the glow of the ocean, the three saw Elmory on the ocean floor. She was placing her hand on a wall of red-and-white spiky stones.

The lionfish? Truman remembered.

At her touch, the lionfish broke apart, revealing an opening. Once Elmory entered, the fish swam back into formation.

"Didn't you say those fish are venomous?" Truman asked Esmeralda.

"They're supposed to be, yes."

"Everyone," Halle's calm voice came through their transceivers, "stop where you are."

"W-why?" said Vedrò.

"The shark is ahead of you, watching."

The three lifted their gazes and saw the beast.

Their hearts raced.

"What do we do?" Esmeralda said, trying hard not to move her lips.

"Keep eye contact and do not panic," answered Shiloh. "Wait 'til it passes."

They froze and stared deeply into the shark's empty eyes. The clams lining the ocean floor sealed themselves shut. Schools of fish blended into the coral reef.

A current caught hold of Truman. And the shark thrashed toward them.

"SWIM!" Halle shouted.

Truman hurled himself under a stone slab. The shark banged its snout on the rim of the rock. Its lower jaw whorled and lashed at Truman, shredding bits of coral. The shark was inches from his feet. Truman kicked its nose. Vedrò and Esmeralda hid under another slab. Truman spotted a serrated coral polyp. He seized it and turned to face the beast. Its teeth hovered just above his head. He plunged the tip of the coral into the shark's eye. The shark recoiled violently and swam away with the coral sticking out of its torn socket.

Truman slipped out from under the rock and found the shark heading for Vedrò and Esmeralda. It wouldn't quit. He scanned the ocean floor for something. He grabbed a rock and looked up to see the shark suddenly switch direction and fly up and out of the ocean's surface.

"What just happened?! Where'd it go?"

"Never mind that," said Esmeralda. She swam over to the lionfish and stared at them. "How did Elmory get in?!"

"I have an idea!" Vedrò unzipped his lower suit and pulled out the narwhal tusk. He handed it to Esmeralda and pressed his hand into the spikes of the fish. He winced.

The wall of fish opened.

Truman and Esmeralda grabbed Vedrò's arms and swam in. Their heads burst through a surface. Inside was a dark cave lit with torches—an air pocket under the sea.

Truman hauled Vedrò onto the cave floor.

He was shaking.

"Why did you do that, Vedrò?!" spat Esmeralda. "I told you their venom is painful!"

"The narwhal tusk!"

"Oh!"

Esmeralda unzipped her suit, tore the hem of her dress, and used the hem to pluck the spines from his palm.

"I have to remove these first."

He winced.

"Sorry." She shakily held the tusk above his hand. "So, how does this work?"

"Just stab me with it!"

"Stab you?!"

"Just do it!"

Flustered, she closed her eyes and brought down the tusk. His hand crumpled, but his skin began to effervesce.

He exhaled. "Much better."

Esmeralda wrapped his hand in another piece of fabric and leaned him against the wall.

Truman was looking around the cave for signs of Elmory.

"Are you guys alright?" Halle asked through the transceivers.

"We're alive."

Esmeralda looked down and found another narwhal tusk and a crushed dragon flower.

A hissing sound came from the tunnel. She glanced at the lionfish, then toward the hissing sound, and then to the dragon flower.

"The poem," she mumbled, furrowing her brows, thinking. "'A sacrifice must first be paid by touch of hand upon a blade. Then two snakes will hiss and bite if not played their song of fright!'"

"What?" said Truman.

"The poem on that relic! It's not a poem. It's a prophecy! The sacrifice upon a blade was what Vedrò did with the lionfish! And that hissing down there? Yeah, those are snakes."

The boys looked at each other.

"How do you even remember that poem?" asked Truman.

"I have an excellent memory. I also wrote it down. It had a nice flow. Anyway, the song of fright—" She bent down and picked up the crushed flower.

"Halle," she said into the transceiver, "you may not like this. But we need you to swim down here and bring that flower you play music with. Right away!"

"You mean the dried dragon flower?"

"Yes!"

"Why?"

"No time! Just hurry!"

"How will she get through the wall of lionfish?" Truman asked, looking down at his friend's bloody palm. "And what if the buzzsaw shark returns?! We barely escaped it ourselves! Actually, how did we escape it?! How did it go flying—"

"Got 'em!" Halle said through the transceiver. "I'm jumping in now!"

"I'll be back." Esmeralda rezipped her suit and hastily plunged back into the water.

Truman turned and kept a lookout for the snakes. "Do you know what happened to the shark, Vedrò? Why did it go flying out of the water?"

"I have no clue," Vedrò said, getting to his feet. "When Esmeralda and I were under the rock, I was praying for the shark to just disappear."

He gasped.

"Truman, do you think I did it? Am I developing another will?!"

"Possibly."

Vedrò winced again.

"You okay?"

"Yeah, just stings."

Truman heard clicking noises coming from the corner of the cave. He edged toward it and noticed stalacrabs crawling under rocks.

Halle and Esmeralda then burst through the surface, scaring Truman.

"That was quick. No shar—?"

"Someone stab me with the tusk now!" Esmeralda shouted, dragging herself onto the cave floor.

With the fabric Esmeralda used on him, Vedrò extracted the spines from her hand. He seized the tusk and stabbed her palm. He ripped off the cuff of his pants and, with it, gently staunched her foaming wound. "Better?"

"Much. Thank you."

"Shiloh told me to give you these elixir dippers," Halle said, extracting two medicine bottles from her suit. "They said the tusk will only extract the venom. The elixir will help with the cuts and pain. Also, here's the dragon flower. I didn't want it to get squashed, so I stored it in a third bottle. What's it for? You mentioned something about snakes in a poem?"

Soft hissing echoed off the walls.

"W-wait, are those actual sn-snakes down there?!" Halle stuttered.

"Yes, and you need to play that tune for them. Now let's go!" Without waiting, Esmeralda led the way down the torchlit cave.

"Thanks for the honey, Shiloh," Vedrò said into his transceiver.

Shiloh did not respond.

"Shiloh?"

"Our headpieces must've lost connection," said Truman. "We must be too deep."

They stopped at the sixth torch and removed their headpieces. A large fissure stretched out before them.

"Do we have to jump?!" Halle asked, peeking over the ledge. "I don't know if I could make that. My legs aren't long enough."

The hissing started up again. But it did not come from down the tunnel. It came from below.

Truman quickly pulled Halle away from the ledge. They fell onto their backs and stared up at two snakes uncurling their giant heads out of the fissure.

They were the size of a building. Their scales were violet, black, and white. Their tongues were forked. And their heads… Their heads were conjoined at the tail.

The tail slithered up and out of the fissure and circled the voyagers.

"Halle, the flower!" shouted Esmeralda.

Halle fumbled for the medicine bottle and, with trembling hands, fought the lid open. She dumped the flower into her hand, placed it on her lips, and began to play the eerie tune—the snakes' song of fright.

Upon the first melancholic note, the double-headed snakes stopped hissing. They stared at Halle and swayed side to side.

Halle gestured for the others to go.

"We're not leaving you?!" Truman whispered.

Halle gestured again more aggressively.

Truman and Esmeralda exchanged looks.

"She's got this," Vedrò said confidently, watching her charm the snakes. "We'll come back for her!"

Hesitantly, the three leapt across the fissure and pressed deeper into the cave. While Halle's flute playing began to muffle, they could still hear her.

"You really think she'll be okay?" asked Esmeralda.

"As long as she doesn't stop playing, she'll be fine," said Vedrò. "So, what comes next in the poem? Wasn't it something about riddles?"

"'A riddle here, a riddle there. Be nothing short of smart and fair,'" Esmeralda recited.

"Riddles. Thank goodness that's all," said Truman.

They rounded the corner and found themselves in a large circular chamber. A stone door fell shut behind them, blocking their path back completely. They could no longer hear Halle's flute playing.

Another door sealed shut at the other end of the chamber. Vedrò tried pushing it open, but it wouldn't budge.

"Does it feel hotter in here, you guys?" Truman unzipped his suit and fanned his shirt.

"Look." Esmeralda pointed to the cave floor. The ground was split into wedges like a pie. The cracks between the wedges ran up the walls and led to the center of the chamber where a stone tablet stood. They approached it and tilted their heads to read the topmost inscription.

Hands make me, ears love me, but eyes never catch me.

Esmeralda followed the direction of the riddle and walked over to the wall adjacent to that wedge. On the ground was a handful of letters that looked like Scrabble tiles made of stone. A rack protruded out of the wall.

"I think our answers go here." She picked up the letters and found *s, c, u, i,* and *m.*

"Hands make me, ears love me, but eyes never catch me," she repeated, arranging the letters onto the rack.

"Wait, what're you doing?!" asked Truman.

"I'm answering the riddle."

"You know what it is?"

"Isn't it obvious? It's music."

She put the last letter into its place, and the tiles shimmered. The door ahead lowered a third of itself into the ground—still too high to reach.

"Climb onto my back," said Vedrò.

"It's too high. If we answer maybe two or three more, I think we'll be able to reach it and climb through."

"What happens if we're wrong?" asked Vedrò.

"Let's hope we never find out." Esmeralda returned to the tablet and read the second riddle.

I adapt to all tongues, but I am always the same.

Vedrò gasped. "I've got it! Oh, wait, no. Can't be… Wait, yes! No…"

"Shh!" Esmeralda reread the riddle over and over.

"I've got it!" said Vedrò.

Truman and Esmeralda stare at him irritably.

"Polyglot. The answer is polyglot!"

"That… might be right," said Truman.

Esmeralda considered it. "I despise riddles," she said. "I feel like there're always multiple answers." She shook her head. "Fine, let's try it."

Vedrò ran to the wall and arranged the letters on the rack.

As he added the final letter, Esmeralda shouted, "NO, WAIT!"

It was too late.

The letter blazed red. A *t* shape seared itself into Vedrò's thumb.

He yelped.

The wedge beneath his feet began to quake and crumble. Heat rose from the cracks. Chunks of ground fell and splashed into a seething pit of living lava.

The chamber was now scorching.

Vedrò ran to the adjacent wedge and felt the ground give way. He jumped.

The entire wedge was now gone.

Vedrò was clinging onto the neighboring wedge, his legs dangling over lava.

He was slipping.

Truman ran to him, lifting him over the ledge. "I got you."

"You saved me, Tru!" Vedrò sobbed, pulling Truman into a bear hug. "Thank you so much! I almost died!" He panted. "Why is there a bloody volcano inside Cherry?!" He smacked the wall.

"Can either of you still reach the rack?" Esmeralda said, grabbing letters from another wedge. "I know the correct answer."

Vedrò steadied Truman as Truman extended his arm over the lava and touched the rack. "Yeah. Hand me the letters one at a time. In reverse. What's the word?"

"Blessedbe."

Vedrò groaned. "Ugh, duh."

Truman put the last letter into place, and the door slid further into the ground.

"Still too high," said Truman, wiping sweat from his brow. He joined Esmeralda at the tablet.

You hang on my edge while I prey on your darkness.

Esmeralda rubbed her temple and mouthed the sentence over and over. "Edge… Darkness… Prey…"

"I have nothing," said Truman.

"Nor I," said Vedrò. "Let's try a different wedge."

Though no hands I possess, I pull you down.

"Quicksand?" said Vedrò.

"I know what it is!" said Esmeralda. "It's shadow!"

"Shadow pulls you down?"

"No, the other riddle. You hang on my edge while I prey on your darkness. That's a shadow." She ran to the riddle's corresponding wall and spelled it out.

The door ahead vanished into the ground.

"You did it, Esmeralda!" exclaimed Vedrò.

The entrance door also reopened. The missing wedge restored itself, covering the lava below.

"Do you guys hear Halle's music?" Esmeralda asked, straining her ears toward the tunnel of snakes. "I don't. We should be able to hear her. We did before the door closed. Something must be wrong. I'm gonna check on her! You two go forward without me, okay?"

"But we need you, Esmeralda," Vedrò said, grabbing her good hand.

"No, you don't," she said, smiling. "You two are more capable than you know. Brave, smart, and true. Vedrò, you're the next prophet. A soul like that comes once a century—so I've read. And Truman, you're an unexplainable Howard. You can scale oceans!" She dropped his hand and made for the door. "I believe in you. Both of you." She looked from Truman to Vedrò. "Just, uh, take a beat before making any rash decisions, okay?" She left.

"That was almost a compliment," Vedrò said, blushing.

"Wait, the poem—" Truman said, heading after Esmeralda.

Vedrò stopped him. "It's okay. I remember it. It was the part that intrigued me the most. 'Now trace the archer's nightly chart to find the love of broken heart. At last, you stand alone yet true, O' save her soul by being you.'"

The boys entered the cave beyond the chamber. The door sealed shut and left them in darkness. There were no torches. As their eyes adjusted, they realized they could see. Specks of white light were scattered on the cave walls, ceiling, and floor. It was like they were standing in a sphere of stars.

"Stay there." Truman took a step—and floated.

"Wicked!" Vedrò mumbled. "How is all this inside Cherry?!"

"What do you suppose we do for this obstacle?" asked Truman. "The poem mentioned tracing something. What was it again? The archer's nightly chart? What does that mean?"

Vedrò spotted a ladle in the stars. "That's the Big Dipper! And that's the Scorpius constellation!" He pointed to a scorpion's tail.

"Is there an archer constellation?"

"Not really," replied Vedrò. "But there is Sagittarius. It's a centaur with a bow and arrow. That must be it."

"Do you know where it is? Or what it looks like?"

"It's shaped like a teapot or a crown." Vedrò's gaze moved around the sphere, darting across constellations. "Let me think. If Sagittarius season follows Scorpio season, then the constellations must be next to one another." He tilted his head, and his eyes lit up. "There it is!"

He leapt eagerly into the sea of stars and paddled to the top of the sphere, southwest of the Scorpius constellation. He laid his hands on the stars and felt the cold cave wall beneath his palms.

Nothing happened.

"I could've sworn this was it."

He retraced the constellation, outlining the stars that resembled a teapot. Then, as his finger passed over the brightest one, a soft *pop* echoed in the chamber. Two hidden doors slid open—one leading back to the chamber of riddles, the other deeper into the cave.

"I knew it!" he said triumphantly.

Then came a scream—sharp, distant, unmistakably Esmeralda.

"Was that—?!"

"Esmeralda? Definitely!" Vedrò said, hastily swimming back to the chamber. "You go onward, Tru! I'll see what's wrong!"

"Why don't we both go back—"

"If we both go back, we might have to redo the chamber of riddles!" barked Vedrò. "There's no time. You must save Cherry, Truman. You can do this. Just freeze her with your will or something."

Vedrò dropped from the starlit sky and disappeared through the returning door.

Truman gulped.

"Okay, Tru," he said to himself. "Be brave."

He swam through the other door, and as he crossed its threshold, gravity brought him back to earth.

He stood in another tunnel.

Vibrant colors flickered at its end. A sweet breeze called his name. He emerged from the tunnel and entered a forest of oddlies. Like in the Cheryl Sea, a dome of glowing pink scales stretched high above his head. Grass whistled as Cherry breathed. A million creeks of pink water weaved around the trees. At the center of the forest stood a magnificent cherry blossom larger than any on her back. The gargantuan roots were Cherry's arteries. And the creeks were her veins. Cherry's heart was still beating.

He stared in awe at the blossom tree. The place seemed so pure. He felt like he shouldn't be there, nor the black vortex in front of the tree, swirling and dark.

Sweat beaded across his brow.

He peered around the tree and saw Elmory pour the vial of glowing red liquid into a creek. The red curled like smoke, spilling into every stream.

The water turned red—blood red. The grass blackened, fading to ash. The breeze stopped, and the blossoms became still. The forest of oddlies, vibrant just minutes before, began to wilt.

Alone in the dark, upon the surface of the Moon, Cherry roared out in pain and slowly, incomprehensibly, began to die.

Chapter 26

The Battle of Honey
& Memory

Truman rushed at Elmory and smacked the vial out of her hand. "Why would you do that?!" he screamed, tears in his ferocious eyes.

Elmory said nothing. She just stood there with a glazed look about her.

Branches began crashing down around them.

"I hope one day you feel the pain you caused Cherry!" Truman slammed his eyelids shut, his chest heaving. All he wanted was for Elmory to suffer.

Suddenly, Elmory shrieked. She dropped to her knees and clutched at her heart, as though it were about to burst.

Truman took a step back, confused. *Why is* she *screaming?*

Elmory staggered to her feet and flicked her wrist toward Truman.

Brown hairy legs began to form and writhe into shape before him. Beady eyes and clicking fangs popped into place. It was grotesque.

"Th-the Arachnoid," Truman faltered, backing into a tree.

The Arachnoid scurried toward him, venom dripping from its fangs. It smelled of decay.

A whooshing sound erupted from the vortex, and a man appeared. He had wavy blond hair, dark eyebrows, and a chili pepper earring. An emerald pouch was tied to his waistband, and in his hand was a staff crowned with a hefty, shiny ruby.

"Flesou!" Krimmiel shouted, pounding the staff into the ground. Sparks burst from its base. Truman felt tremors beneath his feet. The ruby glowed like Vivabee eyes, and a strong wind shot from its tip.

Within the gale, Truman glimpsed wisps of wind with wings and scaly tails—air dragons. They sent the Arachnoid sprawling into a blue oddly, which crumpled under its weight.

"Otmen!" Krimmiel muttered through gritted teeth.

The tendrils of the dying oddlies wove around the spider's one hundred legs and restrained it.

But the Arachnoid broke free, splitting the tendrils like fraying rope, and charged.

Krimmiel, quick with his staff, pointed the ruby at the creeks and streams.

"Ondin," he hissed softly, whisking his staff in a circular motion.

The reddening pink waters levitated into a whirlpool and spiraled toward the beast, dragging it into its currents.

Stray droplets struck Truman's skin like pellets.

Krimmiel stomped his staff again.

"Feren!" The strange French word erupted from his lips.

The whirlpool burst into a fiery tornado. Severed burnt legs thudded to the ground. The smell of roasted flesh permeated the air.

Krimmiel directed his staff at Elmory.

But even in her somnambulant state, she was quick. In one swift robotic movement, she snapped her fingers and summoned red-eyed Vivabees with protruding stingers.

They swarmed toward Krimmiel.

"Vivabees? Is that all you got?" he sighed, rolling his eyes. *"Flesou."*

He tapped an oddly with his staff. Its tendrils began to whorl like a turbine, blowing a gust so strong it tore off their wings.

A Vivabee slammed into Krimmiel, knocking the staff from his grip. It struck a tree, showering it in sparks. Another soared toward him with its stinger aimed at his back.

Truman snatched the staff and bludgeoned its stinger into two.

"Whew—thank you, Truman!"

The wingless Vivabees got to their limbs and scurried toward them.

"Cherro," Krimmiel said, trilling his *r.*

He jerked his head, and his earring flickered.

The ground beneath the Vivabees folded inward like flytraps, slowly crushing them. Pierre plants shot upward, skewering their thoraxes and gowns.

Elmory, unfazed, began hallucinating something purple with a thorny tail.

But Krimmiel was quick too. He reached into his pouch and blew a puff of green powder into her face.

She collapsed.

The purple illusion vanished before it materialized. The severed legs of the Arachnoid and the burial mounds of the squashed Vivabees also disappeared.

"Is she—?"

"No, just unconscious," Krimmiel said, looking down at her with pity.

Another branch fell. It was blackened and shriveled.

Krimmiel extracted a vial of amber liquid from his pocket and flicked it with a finger. He uncorked it, emptied the thick liquid into a stream, and consolingly patted the soil. He spoke soothing words under his breath as though talking to Cherry.

"An antidote," he said over his shoulder. "It'll undo Elmory's poison."

It worked rapidly. Truman began seeing the antidote's effects. The grass was reverting to green. The oddlies stiffened. The water cleared. And the air moved again.

"Is that the elixir you stole?" asked Truman.

"It's a potion I brewed with the honey elixir as the main ingredient, yes."

Truman handed him his staff. "You're a wizard then?"

"I am."

"What did you blow into Elmory's face?"

"Sleeping powder."

"And your earring?"

"*Ah sì, il mio peperoncino!*" he said with an Italian accent. "One of my more useful designs. It's bewitched as a wand, which I have here as well!" He lifted his pant leg and revealed a ruby-encrusted wand stashed behind a spotted sock. "I brought all three just in case."

"The rubies are beautiful."

"They're my favorite. I just love a deep red color."

Truman dusted a tendril off his shoulder. "How did you know Elmory would be here?"

"Most wizards specialize in particular fields of magic," replied Krimmiel. "Recently, I've had a real knack for distortion."

"Distortion? Is that like, shapeshifting?"

"Precisely. But before distortion, I started with prophecies. Sometimes, I see things moments before they happen. Other times, I see things that take years to unfold, like tonight. The most vivid visions I've ever had came to me long, long ago, around the time when my will triggered."

Truman took in his youthful features. *It couldn't have been that long ago*, he thought.

"I'm surprised I even remember them," Krimmiel continued. "I guess some visions just never leave you." He peered up at the blossom tree with a dreamy look.

"Wild teeth. An eerie song. An empty brain. And a guarded heart... You were in those visions too," he said, turning his gaze to Truman. "You and your friends. When I saw you in the Mercurial World Court and the Memory Bank, I knew those visions were about to come true. You guys are clever for decoding my prophecy."

"Prophecy?" Truman echoed confusedly. "You mean the engraved poem?"

Krimmiel nodded. "Prophecies... they come at strange times and in unusual ways," he said airily. "I've written them on paper before, carved them into rocks, and painted them on walls. Heck, they've come to me in dreams, even. Depends on what I'm doing at the time, I suppose. When that Leonian dragon escaped the Sun and terrorized Violetteville a few months back, I saw *you* in the dragon's scales. Your will was moments from triggering."

"You saw that?" Truman asked, his face flushing.

Krimmiel nodded again.

"Wait, that doesn't make sense," said Truman. "My friend Vedrò is said to be the first prophet to exist since Chiron. If that is true, how can you predict the future?"

"Technically, anyone who is clairvoyant can make predictions with the help of mediums like astrology and tarot. But predictions and prophecies are different. Prophecies reveal significant societal events and major turning points in history. Predictions reveal life events and everyday matters of an individual. In other words, prophecies deal with the big picture, while predictions deal with the little things." He smirked. "There are witches on Pluto who are highly skilled fortune tellers."

"Okay, but you said you had *prophecies*, not predictions. How is that possible if Vedrò is the first *prophet* since Chiron?"

"I think you know the answer."

"I really don't."

"Think about it."

Truman squinted at him, pausing to think.

"There's no way," said Truman.

"If there's a will," Krimmiel said with a smile, "there's a way."

"So, you're telling me you're, what, a thousand years old? What are you, an immortal too?"

"I'm 346 years old, I think. I lose track. And no, I'm not an immortal. I'm just an old wise wizard who knows how to brew immortality!"

"But how doesn't everyone know?"

"Like I've said, I have a real knack for distortion." He winked.

"I don't believe you. Angenciel said Chiron died long ago. You can't be him!"

"What you hear, Truman, may not always be the truth." He flashed his staff before his face. His hair disappeared, and his youthful features aged into the monk Truman had seen in the memory of the Ascension.

Truman jumped. "Y-you are Chiron! B-But why did you fake your death?!"

"I didn't fake it, really." He waved his staff again and became Krimmiel. "During the Webbed War of '44, I stepped onto the battlefield to call for a ceasefire. Instead, I was struck down. A part of me truly did die that day."

Grief briefly crossed his face. "Everyone thought I had perished. But my friend, Sin, revived me. I woke up to the news of my death. I won't lie. I quite liked the idea of starting fresh. To live a life of my own, without the responsibilities of being 'the great Jupitarian wizard and prophet, Chiron.'" He sighed.

"So, I altered my features, made my wrinkles disappear, and changed my name. From then on, I lived how I wanted—on Earth. I traveled wherever my heart desired. I caught up on modern Italian vernacular in Naples, studied Egyptian hieroglyphics in Giza, and ate *a lot* of Thai food in Bangkok. That was a good time." He smiled wistfully. "You know, there are so many wonders right there on Earth, even Earthlings overlook their grandeur." He shook his head, smirking at his own words.

"But because I chose a path of freedom," he continued, gazing unblinkingly at the blossom tree, "far from the eyes of the Assembly, I knew I could never return to those who mattered most to me, like Cherry."

"The Assembly knew that I, Chiron, was very close with Cherry. If they detected even an ounce of our old friendship, my cover would've been blown. Then, one day, when the asteroid Hygiea tore a blossom right off Cherry's back, Sin, who kept my existence hidden all those years, wrote and informed me of the accident. I whipped out my crystal ball, saw she was on Jupiter, and went to check on her. Upon my arrival, members of the Assembly caught me snooping. They questioned who I was and where I came from. I played dumb like I had no clue how I got there. And because I was so convincing as a young, good-looking blond," he flicked his hair dramatically, "the Assembly assumed I was an Earthling whose will just triggered. That I'd somehow managed to warp to Jupiter," he said, rolling his eyes.

"They classified me as a warper and stuck me into a cohort. Kahlil and Coelho's cohort, to be exact. During our journey, I pretended to know absolutely nothing about Aether—even though I am one of the founding leaders." He chuckled.

"Wait, how did the Assembly not detect you on Earth?" asked Truman. "They found me not a second after my will triggered."

"When wills trigger, you have a stench about you that's easy to detect."

Truman smelled himself.

"No, no. Aliens can't smell the stench. Only air dragons can. Since my will triggered forever ago, that stench has long dissipated. I also covered my warping trail with spells, just in case. I've been slacking at that lately."

"I see. So, if you wanted to live so badly on your own, why didn't you just alter your looks again?"

"I can't say I haven't thought about it. I just really like the body I created. Isn't it snazzy?!" He looked over his shoulder with flair, smirking. "I also didn't want to have to say goodbye to Cherry *again*. That was difficult enough the first time. But above all, Kahlil and Coelho reminded me of *you*, Truman. I saw your face in theirs the moment I met them. And I couldn't ignore the visions I had of people trying to take advantage of Cherry."

"People? You know it was more than one person?"

"I do. And I know who they are—and that Elmory wasn't the one at fault here. Do *you* know who they are?"

Truman hesitated.

"Yes. My father and mother. They brainwashed Elmory into poisoning Cherry."

Krimmiel nodded knowingly. "I've been watching Kvell for quite a while now. He's had Elmory come here a couple of times to test my obstacles. It wasn't until tonight that he finally learned how to get past the sphere of stars, which your friend Vedrò cracked in barely a minute." He smirked.

Truman felt proud of his friend.

"Wait—*your* obstacles?"

Krimmiel nodded. "Well, the lionfish, the double-headed viper, the riddles, and the sphere of stars were all my doing. The buzzsaw shark and the pit of living lava were Cherry's. I implemented obstacles long ago as a preventative measure.

But I haven't visited in a while—suppose Cherry felt the need to guard her heart a bit more."

He picked his nails. "I didn't mean to hurt her. I just couldn't visit her as often as I would've liked. She's an amazing wonder who dedicates her life to finding lost souls and bringing them to Aether, where they can find themselves and become part of a community. How could I take her away from that? Besides, she doesn't belong to me. She's her own being, making her own decisions, powerful and independent. That's probably why your father was so set on poisoning her. He fears anything that lies outside his control and challenges his power.

"Your mother knows that all too well. What she doesn't know is that your father is a flawed wizard—powerful but flawed. He has never understood the strength of vulnerability. It's what keeps him from understanding not only his children but also the many mysteries of magic." He caught Truman's gaze. "I apologize. I should not be bashing your parents like this."

Truman turned away. He wanted to believe he came from goodness, but he couldn't ignore what he had seen tonight.

"They tried poisoning Cherry," Truman said firmly, gazing back at Krimmiel. "I get it. What I don't get is, why would my parents want to poison Cherry? Because they fear her strength? That doesn't make much sense to me."

"It's only your father who wants Cherry poisoned," Krimmiel corrected. "Your mother is acting on his behalf. She must be under his spell or something. Maybe he has something over her that's preventing her from challenging him. I'm unsure about that one."

"Under a spell?" Truman echoed. "I met Lavenza earlier tonight. She didn't seem like she was under a spell, at least not like Elmory." He gestured to Elmory, who was now snoring.

"You make a fair point," said Krimmiel. "Lavenza is conscious of her actions. Perhaps she has a more complex reason for working with Kvell."

He noticed Truman's frown and clasped his shoulder gently.

"I'm sorry they're not everything you'd hoped them to be," Krimmiel said, furrowing his brows.

Truman looked up at him.

"And I'm sorry I don't know why they're doing what they're doing," Krimmiel continued. "I know *Chiron* is placed on a pedestal and all, but I don't know everything. I, too, make mistakes. What I do know is: tonight was a trial run for Kvell, a test to see if his potion would work. Your father has a larger scheme going on. I'm not sure what it is. He's placed a spell over him and Lavenza to prevent anyone from reading their minds. Whatever he's planning, I'll be on his tail."

"What makes you think he's scheming?"

"Like I've said, I've been watching Kvell—as much as I can, given his slyness."

"You said wizards specialize in particular fields of magic," said Truman. "Which field does Kvell specialize in?"

"Conjuring, mostly. And from the looks of Elmory, he's not bad at potions and spell work either."

"Do you know how to conjure?"

"Yes. You saw me conjure a vortex outside the Hive, remember?"

"Right. Well, if you know how to conjure, why didn't you conjure the elixir from the Hive rather than break into their reserves?"

"That's a good question. Simply put, Vivabees have complex magic. They don't possess magic the way I do. They're not wizards or anything. Their magic comes from their wondrous genetic makeup. The cells of their body and Hive contain a protective antibody. This antibody is how Vivabees live for so long. It's how they can live outside a force field. And it's how their vaults are so infallible. Warpers cannot teleport in. Conjuring wouldn't work. And no spell can override that magic.

"Even at a fundamental level, the antibody is so peculiar. Most antibodies are found in the bloodstream. Yet, this antibody exists in their cells *and* Hive. Over time, the antibody weakens and seeps into their honey elixir, which is why the elixir is what it is."

Truman felt like Esmeralda was talking at him. "So, if you didn't magically break in, how *did* you?"

"The old-fashioned way. I walked in." He smirked. "Sin also helped."

"Why didn't you just create your own elixir?"

Krimmiel laughed shortly. "If only it were that easy. Only Vivabees can produce honey elixir."

"Couldn't you have used the elixir from Sin's body?"

"Unfortunately, once Vivabees reach a certain age, they can't produce honey elixir the way they used to." He shrugged.

Truman nodded, narrowing his eyes.

"Did you hex me or something that day?"

"What day?"

"The day you stole the elixir. Because something told me not to rat you out."

Krimmiel paused. "No, I didn't. It may have been your empathic will. Perhaps you intuited I was doing good, not harm."

"But I was wearing my necklace then. It's made from pierre plants and blocks my empathic will."

Krimmiel scrutinized the accessory. "Perhaps it was your intuition, then. That necklace might block your empathic will, but not your intuition. And you do seem highly intuitive."

"I'm not too sure about that," Truman said sheepishly.

He thought of Lavenza and the cinnamon candies. He thought of her running around the house, checking on guests, making sure everyone was fed. He thought of how she embraced Minli and welcomed Vedrò. Truman felt conflicted. He wanted to like her—love her, even—but her actions infuriated him. Mostly, he was disappointed—disappointed to learn that he may never belong to one big, happy family.

"What do you mean?" Krimmiel asked.

"I didn't think my mother would be evil," he said, avoiding his gaze.

"*Evil* would be an inaccurate description. She's complicit, yes, but I suspect she has her children's interests at heart. Your father takes advantage of that. Your mother lacks bravery, a quality most people overlook.

"In any case, you *are* intuitive, Truman. Believe me when I say you are a powerful empath. A very powerful one indeed."

Truman shook his head.

"It's true. You know how I know? Every night since I recognized your face in the Mercurial World Court, I've been looking into my crystal ball to see if Elmory was on her way to poison Cherry. After I finished my court-ordered community service earlier tonight, I looked into my crystal and saw you use your empathic will on Elmory. You inflicted pain on her. Not physically, but emotionally. That's why she screamed and attacked back."

"Wait, what?!" Truman blurted, blinking. "What're you saying?!"

"I'm saying you can make people feel what you want them to feel."

Truman gaped at him.

"Is that possible?! Can Sin or Shiloh do that?"

"I don't know about this Shiloh, but Sin cannot. It is a rare will to have. Only a handful of empaths have ever possessed that ability."

Truman stared at his hands, wide-eyed and disbelieving.

"I should warn you," Krimmiel pressed on, "forcing anyone to feel an emotion against their will is literal manipulation and honestly inappropriate. Use that part of your will *only* when necessary, like tonight."

"Of course." Truman nodded, still in shock.

He looked down at Elmory. "What should we do about her?"

"You needn't worry. I'll undo your father's hex and cast a protection spell over her. She'll no longer be under his control. I'll take her to the Hive and let the Vivabees look after her from there."

Krimmiel adjusted Elmory's arms into a more comfortable position.

"So, Krim—I mean, Chir—I mean… What should I call you?"

"Krimmiel."

"Right. So, Krimmiel, why did you use your will on Elmory's illusions? It's not like they were real, right?"

"On the contrary, Truman, illusions can be very real, especially if you let them be. Fear wills us to believe that what we see is true. Sometimes it is. Sometimes it isn't. And though I knew her visions were mere illusions, fear gets the best of all of us, myself included."

"You didn't seem scared. You seemed brave."

"You can be afraid and brave at the same time. That's the definition of courage, is it not? To overcome fear?" Krimmiel smiled and noticed Truman picking his nails.

"You've been through a lot tonight," Krimmiel added. "Would you like a change of scenery?"

"What do you mean?"

"I can take you someplace. Anywhere you want—in the entire Solar System. You tell me where, and I'll warp us, if you want."

Truman eyed him suspiciously. "How do I know you're not gonna take me someplace where you'll harm me?"

Krimmiel tilted his head. "I did just save you, you know. And Cherry. I could harm you right here if I wanted. Besides, what does your intuition tell you?"

Truman smirked at him, then frowned. "Curfew is soon. I think Falsmira's on duty tonight too. I don't want another detention, especially the night before break."

Panic rushed to his mind.

"Also, my friends! They might be in danger!"

"Don't worry. They're not. I promise."

"But we heard Halle scream—"

"They're fine. Trust me. They're all together and safe. Let me take you someplace as a thank you for protecting Cherry.

We'll be gone for a few minutes and bring you right back. Come on. There must be someplace you're dying to see. I love a good spontaneous, if brief, adventure."

Truman thought for a minute. "Okay, but not for too long. Can we bring my friends?"

Krimmiel pulled out a crystal ball from one of his many pockets and peered into it. "They're actually having the ride of their lives right now."

"What does that mean?" Truman leaned in to look into the crystal but saw nothing.

"They'll tell you when we get back." Krimmiel put the crystal away. "So, where would you like to go? The Northern Rose on Saturn? The Serengeti in Tanzania? The Bell Towers of the Uranian Skies? Ooh! Ooh! Or how about a Ben & Jerry's?! I love ice cream."

"I want to visit the Swotting's School for Sisterhood," Truman said firmly.

"Swot-ah-what-what?"

"Swotting's School for Sisterhood."

"And where may that be?"

Truman shrugged. "Somewhere in the United Kingdom."

"Somewhere in the United Kingdom? Okay, I think I can manage that." He stepped into the black vortex and held out his hand. "I know you haven't mastered warping yet, so I'll bring you as a passenger."

Truman excitedly grabbed his hand and felt the familiar dropping sensation. When he opened his eyes, they were standing on a dune overgrown with beachgrass. A glistening ocean extended before them. A gated school towered over the dune. A coat of arms was on the iron gate and displayed two reflected snakes and the sinuous letters *S.S.S.*

The wind was strong and smelled of saltwater.

A group of girls jogged along the shoreline. Two stretched by the tide. One had a freckled face and ginger hair. The other had light brown hair and a strong Howard jaw.

Truman smiled. His eyes lit up.

"Why'd you choose this place?" Krimmiel asked as a seagull landed on his shoulder and tried to nip his pepper-shaped earring. "SHOO! SHOO! … If a beach is what you wanted, I could've taken you to Fiji or the Maldives!"

"I didn't come for the beach. I came to see her." Truman nodded toward the second girl. "That's my sister, Minli."

"Ah yes, the sixth and final Howard. You know, I quite like that name. It sounds like, 'How weird?!' And I love weird!"

Truman walked toward the girls.

Krimmiel grabbed his arm. "You can't meet her."

"I know. I just want a closer look."

Krimmiel let go and followed.

They were now close enough to hear the girls.

"That bampot Casey put me in the four-by-four, but I'm a long-distance runner," the ginger said with a Scottish brogue. "I dinnae ken what to dae. Should I say something to coach? What dae ye think, Minli?"

"Oh, just do it," Minli snapped, her accent British.

"In the name of the wee man, Minli, there's no need to be ragin' at me. I was only asking a question."

"You're right, Su. I'm sorry. I'm just stressed about next month's field trip. I don't know where I'm going to get the money. I might have to miss it."

Only then did Truman notice his sister's tattered clothes and worn-out shoes.

He thought for a moment and turned to Krimmiel. "Could you do me a favor and conjure up some money? A few hundred dollars or so. Well, pounds, I guess, since we're in the U.K. I could maybe find her locker and slip the money into it."

Krimmiel sighed.

"You don't understand. Conjuring isn't that simple. I can't just snap my fingers and make money out of thin air. When I conjure something, I'm essentially calling it from someplace else. In other words, I'd be stealing. Yes, I stole the honey elixir. But I did that to save Cherry's life. I recognize you want to help your sister. I do. But I'm not comfortable stealing someone else's hard-earned money. I'm sorry."

"I understand," Truman said disappointedly. "Wait—what about converting alien currency to Earthling currency? I have a few wishes and stars here!" He pulled out his pouch and dumped its contents into his hand.

"I could do that! There's a bank on Saturn I could conjure from and exchange with." He counted the coins.

"How much is there?"

"Not much. It'll be like… forty-seven pounds, give or take."

Krimmiel whisked his staff over the wishes and stars. They transformed into sterling coins and colorful bills.

"Would you like me to teleport the money into her locker, assuming she has one? Might save us some time." He checked his crystal ball. "She does have one."

"Sure, do it!"

Krimmiel flicked his earring, and the money vanished from sight. *"Et voilà!"*

The two looked up and saw Minli and Su running through the gate.

"Dae ye see that man over there? Looks like a wizard with that staff," said Su.

"The boy looks familiar. Was he on the tele?" asked Minli.

Krimmiel and Truman exchanged glances.

As the gate closed, a security guard glanced at them suspiciously.

"We should go!" Krimmiel said.

Once the coast was clear, he reconjured the vortex and extended his arm.

Truman took it, and in a blink, they were back in Cherry's heart.

Elmory was still unconscious, snoring peacefully.

Krimmiel checked his watch. "You have fifteen minutes before curfew. I'll give you a master key—it'll let you pass the obstacles without redoing any of them." He pulled out his wand and drew a heart shape in the air. A glowing, bleeding heart appeared. "Next time you want to get down here, I recommend snatching one of these from the blood tree. You think you can manage your way back on time?"

"I'm cutting it close, but I think so." Truman turned.

"Oh, and Truman! I'm trusting you with my identity. If you don't think you can keep my secret, I could brew a forgetting potion. But it would mean altering your mind. I don't want that. It could be dangerous. Look at Elmory… But if Kahlil can keep my secret, I'm sure you can too."

"Kahlil knows your secret?"

"We got close during our journey," he said, smiling, a flicker of memory crossing his face.

He dragged Elmory's body onto the vortex platform.

"But what about my friends? They helped. Shouldn't they know what happened too?"

"I suppose that is only fair. They *did* help save Cherry. I guess I can trust them too. But no one else, okay?"

Truman nodded.

"See you later!" He winked.

Truman smiled and made for the tunnel, the bleeding heart lighting his way. When he turned to wave goodbye, Krimmiel was already gone.

Chapter 27

Earth to Truman

"WOOH! Slow down!" Halle hollered as she, Vedrò, and Esmeralda came barreling into Cherry's heart on top of the double-headed viper.

Truman toppled over.

"Is Cherry okay?!" said Esmeralda. "Where's Elmory?!"

"What is this place?" Vedrò asked, looking around.

"Cherry's fine. This is her heart. Elmory's gone. I'll tell you all about it later. It's a long story. But we should go! We have curfew!"

"Well, hop on," said Halle. "Truman, meet Purr and Vye." She pointed from head to head. "I was playing music for them, and they absolutely adored me!" She patted Vye's scales. Vye licked her face with its forked tongue. "Silly things pretend to be big and scary when they're just a couple of snuggle bugs! Cute, aren't they?"

"That's one word for it," muttered Truman.

"They're not an *it*—they're a *they*," Halle corrected. "There are two of them. Just conjoined."

"Yeah, anyway," interjected Esmeralda. "Sorry we didn't come sooner. I went back for Halle and thought the snakes were attacking her. That's why I screamed. Turned out they were just cuddling her."

"Then the snakes took us on a joyride through some underground tunnels!" exclaimed Vedrò. "It was like a rollercoaster! There are so many pierre plants inside Cherry, Truman. Crystal caves, subterranean rivers—it was beautiful—"

"That's great, Vedrò, but we gotta go! Curfew's in… eleven minutes!"

With the four voyagers on their backs and the bleeding heart guiding them, Vye and Purr slithered through the sphere of stars, out the room of riddles, into the Cheryl Sea, and back to the tank's opening.

Halle waved goodbye as they kicked off the snakes.

No longer needing the bleeding heart, Truman pushed the flower away and watched it wither in the waves, gracefully, petal by petal—a fitting end to a night that would stay with him for quite some time.

They burst into the log cabin, sopping wet.

"Oh my Queen Bee! Thank goodness you're alright!" said Shiloh. "What happened down there? Forget it. No time. Falsmira's snooping outside the cabin. Hurry to bed! I'll mop up."

The four sprinted up the rope bridge.

"But we don't know what happened tonight!" said Esmeralda. "How're we supposed to go to sleep?!"

"Just know that tomorrow, you're going to hear a fantastic story." Truman winked. "Good night, you two."

"Ugh, fine. Good night, boys."

As they leapt into their treehouses, the clocks struck midnight.

☆ ☆ ☆ ☆ ☆ ☆

"We're getting our grades today!" Esmeralda squealed at the crack of dawn. "They won't hand them out until everyone's downstairs! Come on! Wake up!" She darted around, rousing the others.

Truman, Vedrò, and Style groaned and rolled out of bed. They exchanged decisive looks and deliberately took their time to get ready.

As they sauntered down the bridge, Esmeralda scowled at them, tapping her foot with exasperation. The boys took one look at her and burst into laughter.

"It's not funny!" Esmeralda whined. "Maman told me I got only *two* gold stars. That means I might've failed the other exams!"

"I'm sure you didn't fail," Truman said warmly.

"What do you mean 'gold star?'" asked Vedrò.

Angenciel, Falsmira, Ereus, and Reuel began handing out graded booklets.

"Everyone, listen up!" Angenciel announced. "A gold star on your exam means you scored the best in the class. An emerald star means your score was exceptional. A sapphire star means you passed, but barely. And lastly, a ruby star means you failed."

"Horribly," Falsmira added. She clicked her tongue disapprovingly as she handed out exams. "I hate to admit it, but for Aetherly History, my gold star goes to Miss Esmeralda Mortimer."

"And for Astrobiology, my gold star also goes to the brilliant and hardworking Miss Esmeralda Mortimer," Reuel said, beaming at her.

Everyone clapped as Esmeralda looked bashful.

"For Interplanetary Technologies, three of you earned a gold star," said Ereus. "Mr. Style Leone, Mr. Truman Howard, and Miss Halle Xióng!"

Everyone applauded.

Truman smiled humbly and glanced at Halle, who was fidgeting with something in her pocket.

"I must say, Halle, you were without a doubt the most improved! The warping you pulled off in the lab practical— flawless! Keep it up!"

"Thank you, Ereus," she said, bowing her head.

"And for Worlds Cultures, the recipient of my gold star is Vedrò Azzurro. Great work, Mr. Azzurro!"

Esmeralda looked gobsmacked.

"Now, before you lot begin comparing grades," Angenciel went on, "each of you must meet with Falsmira and me. We'll be giving you your individual PSA cover story. It is the story you must commit to memory and share with your Earthling family and friends.

"Remember: PSA has eyes everywhere. Do not stray from your designated story. For those of you staying in Aether, we'll discuss accommodations instead." She referred to her clipboard. "First up: Anand, Sweta!"

As Sweta followed Angenciel and Falsmira into another room, everyone broke into conversations about their grades.

Esmeralda marched up to Vedrò. "How did *you* get my maman's gold star?!"

He smirked. "Envy looks good on you, you know."

Unamused, Esmeralda snatched his test and began comparing their answers.

"Where'd you guys go last night?" Reuel asked Truman. "You left the party without saying goodbye. Mum was upset. I hope you remembered to thank her. She put a lot of work into last night."

More than you know, he thought bitterly. "We were exhausted from the exams, so we came back early. We tried finding you and Angenciel."

"Ah, that must've been when she and I had a little conversation."

Truman raised a brow.

"It's nothing," she said, lowering her voice. "I told her how I felt about seeing her around our family. She understood."

"Anyway, I spoke with Mum. She said you could stay with her and Father during your two-week break if you'd like. But if you'd rather not, you're welcome to stay with me at my place. I could show you some of my favorite hiking spots in the Venusian Elps. I'll have a few things to take care of at Ivies and Oaks, but it'd be fun to have you! What do you think?"

"That sounds great. I'd love that."

She smiled. "Well then, perfect! When Angenciel and Falsmira call you in, just let them know."

Truman nodded.

"Hey, Reuel! Are you ready?" Ereus called.

"Be right out!" she replied and turned to Truman. "Gotta help Ereus get Cherry moving. Apparently, last night, Cherry was roaring and writhing around like she was in pain or something. Ereus and Falsmira said they had gone to see what was wrong, but she stopped before they could help. I bet it was a sharp moonrock stuck in her paw. Anyway, it shouldn't be long until we're back on Earth."

She headed for the doors. "Oh, and by the way, good job on your exams. Three emerald stars and one gold! Mighty impressive. I'm proper chuffed!" She beamed proudly at her brother and left.

"Azzurro, Vedrò," called Angenciel.

Sweta came out.

Everyone engulfed her, wanting to hear what her story would be.

"Come on, let's hear it!" said Yari.

"I've been at college for the past three months," said Sweta. "That would have been true if my will hadn't triggered. I really did have a scholarship to UCLA. An environmental engineering program—that's where my family thinks I've been. It should be an easy lie. I'm just not a good liar. Angenciel gave me brochures on the program so I could refresh my memory. I should get to it." She left the cabin.

"Khoza, Letsatsi," Angenciel summoned.

They skipped me, Truman thought.

"Apparently, I've been working for the *Aeronautica Militare*," Vedrò said, leaving the room. "The Italian Air Force."

After Letsatsi and Style received their assigned stories, Angenciel called for both Esmeralda and Truman.

Falsmira sat in the corner, arms crossed.

"You two are the only voyagers who have families here in Aether," said Angenciel. "Let's discuss accommodations. If you wish to return to Earth for any reason, I'd be happy to help organize your return. Esmeralda, would you like to stay with me or visit friends—?"

"I'll go where you go, maman."

"Let's go on holiday then. Girls trip."

Esmeralda laughed. "That would be lovely."

Angenciel smiled.

"And you, Truman? Any idea of what you wish to do?"

"I'll be staying with Reuel."

Angenciel wrote on her clipboard. "You'll just love it there. Her balcony overlooks the Venusian Elps—!" She cleared her throat. "Alright, easy enough." She led them out and called in Schmidt.

Yari soon followed. After everyone shared their cover stories, they left to study their brochures. Truman, Vedrò, and Esmeralda waited with Halle.

"What's that smell?" Vedrò said, sniffing the air.

Shiloh fluttered toward them in an apron with a tea set and a platter of green cookies.

"Bzeze!" they said, placing the tea and cookies onto the coffee table. "Where'd everyone go? I baked my famous pistachio cookies to celebrate the end of your first trimester. They're not actually famous. Everyone back home just loves them."

"You baked these?!" Vedrò said with his mouth full.

"They're so warm and gooey and sweet!" Esmeralda raved, her mouth also full.

"Delicious, Shiloh!" said Truman. "Might be my new blessedbe flavor!"

"Stop it, stop it!" Shiloh waved away their compliments. "But keep it coming, keep it coming!" They winked.

"What's in them?" asked Halle.

"Family recipe. Finely chopped pistachios, orange zest, lemon zest from the lemon trees of Venus, sugar, egg white, and a secret ingredient. Okay, twist my mandibles—it's a dollop of honey elixir! But that's between us, so shh! Just a little elixir, so it doesn't have any medicinal effect."

"Well, they're lovely. Thank you, Shiloh!" said Halle.

"My pleasure!" Shiloh sat on the couch and poured them all tea. "So, how'd you all do on your exams?"

"Halle and I got the same grades," said Vedrò. "One gold star, two emeralds, and one sapphire."

"Two gold and two emeralds," said Esmeralda.

"One gold, three emeralds," Truman said, noticing something writhing in Halle's pocket. "What's in your pocket, Halle?"

"Nothing!" She cupped it to stop it from moving.

A neon-green crab leg poked out between her fingers.

"Is that a stalacrab?! Halle!" Esmeralda said sternly.

Halle sighed and pulled out a baby crab. The fathom crawled around in her hands and looked up with bulging, adoring eyes.

"Her name's Scallion," said Halle. "When I was with Vye and Purr, I saw a whole mound of stalacrabs in the cave. This one," she leaned down and kissed the top of the crab's head, "had fallen on my shoulder. At first, I jumped. But when I tried returning Scallion to her family, the other crabs kept moving away from her as if she wasn't one of their own. And when I walked away, Scallion followed me. I would've felt bad if I had left her!"

"Wait, didn't Reuel say stalacrabs are only native to the Moon and Neptune?" asked Vedrò. "That was a question on our exam."

"It's true," said Esmeralda. "You should tell her, Halle. As an astrobiologist, I'm sure she'd want to know about a new colony. Also, it could be considered unethical to separate a stalacrab from their family. I don't think we're allowed pets either."

"Ugh," Halle groaned. "I can't tell Reuel. She might make me return Scallion! And I adore this little booger."

Before Esmeralda could reason with her, Yari came out of the room and tapped Halle on the shoulder. "You're up, hot stuff."

Halle handed Scallion to Truman. "Please, don't tell Reuel!" She gave Truman an imploring look before disappearing into the room.

Truman peered down at the delicate, adorable creature. It tickled as it crawled around in his hand.

"I didn't know we could have pets," Yari said, leaning over Truman's shoulder.

Vedrò joined them. "We should let Halle keep her!"

"It's not our decision to make," said Esmeralda.

"Buzzkill," Vedrò muttered. "So, Yari, what's your PSA story?"

"I'm a pilot for a mortician."

"A what?"

"Yep, that's supposedly what I've been doing for the past few months. Of all things," she laughed, rolling her eyes. "I fly corpses to their final resting places. What a lovely story."

She left the cabin as Halle, Falsmira, and Angenciel emerged from the room.

Truman quickly hid Scallion in his pocket.

"We'll see you guys out there," Angenciel said, snagging one of Shiloh's cookies as she and Falsmira headed out the door.

Halle sat back down.

"So?" asked Vedrò.

"It's not an elaborate story like everyone else's. I don't think I've told you guys, but my yéyé is the only family I have left on Earth. He doesn't have the strongest memory. All I have to do is tell his nurse how 'boarding school' has been. That's all. So, are you guys going to rat me out or what?"

"We can't tell Reuel where you found Scallion," Truman said decisively.

"But it's not our decision to make!" Esmeralda repeated.

"Yes, it is."

Truman went on to tell Vedrò, Halle, Esmeralda, Shiloh, and Scallion everything that happened the night before.

"Your parents brainwashed Elmory?!" Halle echoed, sipping her tea.

"Krimmiel is actually Chiron?!" Esmeralda whispered, eyes widened in shock.

"Krimmiel didn't take you to a Ben & Jerry's?!" Vedrò gasped.

Esmeralda glared at him.

"I mean, your will evolved?! That's so cool!"

Truman laughed.

"It's also scary," Esmeralda added without blinking.

Halle nodded in agreement.

When Truman finished, everyone was so stunned by the news, even Scallion gaped at Truman.

"You can tell Reuel you found Scallion in Luna's Well," said Truman. "But if you tell her the truth, she'll ask why we went into the Cheryl Sea. And if we tell her that, then I'd be breaking my promise to Krimmiel."

"And he's okay with you telling us?" asked Vedrò. "He doesn't even know us like that."

"He said because you helped save Cherry, he feels he can trust you."

"I still can't believe Krimmiel is actually Chiron," Esmeralda said, shaking her head in disbelief.

"I wonder what that'll mean for us in the future, knowing one of the most famous and powerful aliens ever," Halle thought aloud, a little worried and a little in awe.

"Your powers are evolving just like mine, Truman!" Vedrò interjected excitedly.

"What do you mean just like yours?" asked Esmeralda.

"You'll never believe it, Esmeralda! When you and I were hiding under that rock, I made the buzzsaw shark fly out of the water!"

"That wasn't you, Vedrò," Esmeralda said, laughing. "That was me. Earlier this morning, I asked my maman about it. Don't worry. I didn't tell her anything. I kept it vague. Anyway, she said it's a normal evolution for sirens. Apparently, she can do it too. Telekinesis. Mind control but for inanimate objects. I must've missed that chapter in her book."

Vedrò pouted and crossed his arms.

"Would've been nice to have a second will," he grumbled.

"But if you can move things with your mind," said Truman, "why didn't you move the lionfish from our path or lower the door instead of solving those riddles?"

"I tried to, but I think those obstacles were charmed." She shrugged. "That, or I can't control my will yet. Likely both."

"Well," Halle said at once, "now that that's all settled, I'm going to keep Scallion and not tell Reuel!" She scooped up the stalacrab and bolted out the front door before Esmeralda could say anything contrary.

"That girl, I swear—" Esmeralda shook her head, smiling.

"Oh, let her be," said Truman. "You just focus on your holiday."

"Holiday?" Vedrò echoed. "Where to?"

"Don't know yet." She shrugged.

"Well, I'll be in Italy and Argentina, getting kissed by the Sun! One week in Roma with my papà, and one week in Buenos Aires with my mamma. After Vega passed away," he paused, "my parents split up."

Truman placed a hand on Vedrò's shoulder.

"I'm sorry, Vedrò," Esmeralda said, tilting her head.

"It's okay. My mamma now lives with my abuela." He smiled. "It'll be nice to see her and the rest of that side of my family."

Falsmira burst through the doors, shrouded in robes, pocket watch ticking. "You three," she pointed, "outside. Angenciel wants a word with everyone before we arrive."

The three of them followed Falsmira into the orchard and joined the others around the dip in Cherry's wing.

Shiloh fluttered behind them, carrying the platter of cookies and tea.

While Earth grew before their eyes, the Moon shrank in the distance behind them.

Angenciel counted the heads of all nine voyagers. "Okay, you lot! Our first trimester has officially come to an end!

We've traveled from Mercury to the Moon, have beheld wonders and fathoms fantastic and grand, have learnt about ingenious technologies beyond anything any normal human could imagine, and, of course, have begun a marvelous journey that will last for the rest of your alien lives. The next time we'll see each other will be when we travel from Mars to Saturn!"

A gentle wind blew through her silver, starlit hair and carried with it a scent of lavender.

"Before we arrive on Earth, I must stress the importance of abiding by PSA regulations. *Please* stick to your assigned cover stories whenever an Earthling asks where you've been the past three months and where you will be after your break! Okay, enough mentor-talk. Let's just enjoy the last few moments we have, shall we?"

She looked at Ereus, who began playing the piano. He closed his eyes as the air filled with a classical tune.

Truman sat down on a cushion of grass and took in the view.

Butterflies fluttered over everyone's head as light dappled through the branches.

Sweta and Humzah took a cookie from Shiloh.

Vedrò and Yari plucked and sucked on blessedbes.

Halle and Esmeralda leaned over the dip in Cherry's wing and pointed at oceans blue and wide.

Truman could've sworn he saw the faintest of smiles across Falsmira's lips.

Style, handsome as ever, stretched out onto a bed of petals and caught Truman's gaze. He smiled at Truman, and Truman smiled back.

As Cherry soared through Earth's atmosphere, clouds of white and flames of red coated the edges of the swirly and never-ending Rainbow Row.

Reuel sat beside Truman and nudged him with an elbow.

Truman wrapped his arm around his sister, looked up at the stars, and knew, for the first time in his life, just where he belonged.

Acknowledgments

Thank you, Leon Ning, for the fabulous cover design and keeping the integrity of my original illustrations, all the while elevating my vision. Thank you, Jessica Raymond of Turned Pages Co., for the succinct editing. Thank you, Tram Bui, for your thorough edits. You broke down my sentences, gave fantastic feedback, and helped me polish a punchier tale. Thank you, Daniel Larson, my fellow gator, for the helpful, constructive critiques. Thank you to the Smithsonian for *The Planets: The Definitive Visual Guide to Our Solar System*—a book to which I clung, sewing facts into fantasy. And last but certainly not least, thank you to my mother, Tracy Lee, for being my biggest supporter and the first to hear the story of Truman.

- 343 -

About the Author

J.Q. Gagliastro is the author of *The Diary of a Sugarbaby* and *Mercury to the Moon. Mercury to the Moon* is a fantasy fiction adventure novel for all reading ages and was illustrated by Gagliastro. *The Los Angeles Book Review* hailed *Mercury to the Moon* as "an imaginative triumph!" *Readers' Favorite* called it "thrilling, witty, and suitably odd." *Mercury to the Moon* is a #1 bestseller in Young Adult Fiction, Magical Realism, and Alien Sci-Fi.

The Diary of a Sugarbaby is an adult fiction speculative sci-fi novel, a #1 bestseller in LGBTQ+ Coming-of-Age Fiction, a #2 bestseller in Dystopian Fiction, and a top seller in Epistolary Fiction and Political Fiction. NYC's Queer Book Club selected *The Diary of a Sugarbaby* for October 2024. The Queer Book Club of the Purple Couch Bookshop picked *The Diary of a Sugarbaby* for August 2025. An instructor at the University of Florida shortlisted *The Diary of a Sugarbaby* as required text for their queer studies program. *The Diary of a Sugarbaby* was a 2023 finalist in the Wishing Shelf Book Awards in Adult Fiction. In August 2024, Gagliastro appeared on Chicago's *WGN TV* with journalist Sean Lewis. *The Diary of a Sugarbaby* was featured in *The New York Review of Books*, both April and May 2024 issues.

Gagliastro's Sugarbaby Book Tour took them to NYC, D.C., Chicago, West Hartford, Glastonbury, Annapolis, Keene, and Philadelphia. Over 1,000 copies of *The Diary of a Sugarbaby* were sold within the first year of its publication. *The Manhattan Book Review* hailed *The Diary of a Sugarbaby* as "*The Handmaid's Tale* on steroids!" *Kirkus Reviews* called it "a frightening novel about an unthinkable future!" And according to *The BookLife Prize*, *The Diary of a Sugarbaby* is a "dark satirical work of sci-fi!" While *The Diary of a Sugarbaby* is fiction, Gagliastro ties in their experiences as a homeless youth and twists them into a dramatic political satire. Please visit *www.jqgagliastro.com* for merch, tour dates, signed copies, and more.

If you enjoy *Mercury to the Moon* by J.Q. Gagliastro, please
PLEASE leave it a 5-STAR review on the following platforms!
Reviews help A LOT! Thank you so, so much!

Amazon   Barnes & Noble   Goodreads

If you love the book, buy alien
merch! Oddlietti, Shiloh's cookies, signed copies,
school supplies, and more!

www.ingramcontent.com/pod-product-compliance
Lightning Source LLC
Chambersburg PA
CBHW020238010826
48973CB00006B/1563